ENDORSEMENTS

"Extremely creative! Who would think that the world of figure skating could be so dangerous. I found this book to be very engaging."

—*Rocky Marval,* two-time U.S. National Champion with partner, Calla Urbanski.

"Not only did I find *Cammie and Alex's adventures with the Skateland Monster* fascinating, my eleven-year-old daughter also truly enjoyed it. Olga was able to take the world of figure skating and turn it into a compelling read. I would recommend this book to all those who love figure skating."

—*Isabelle Brasseur,* two-time Olympic bronze medalist and five-time Canadian pairs champion with partner Lloyd Eisler. Isabelle and her husband, Rocky Marval, have one daughter, Gabriella Marvaldi, who was 2012 juvenile pairs champion with her partner, Kyle Hogeboom.

CAMMIE & ALEX'S
adventures with the

SKATELAND MONSTER

Cammie & Alex's
adventures with the
SKATELAND MONSTER

Olga Jaffae

TATE PUBLISHING
AND ENTERPRISES, LLC

Published by Tate Publishing & Enterprises, LLC
127 E. Trade Center Terrace | Mustang, Oklahoma 73064 USA
1.888.361.9473 | www.tatepublishing.com

Tate Publishing is committed to excellence in the publishing industry. The company reflects the philosophy established by the founders, based on Psalm 68:11,
"The Lord gave the word and great was the company of those who published it."

Book design copyright © 2012 by Tate Publishing, LLC. All rights reserved.
Cover design by Karla Durangparang
Interior design by Errol Villamante
Illustration by JZ Sagario

Published in the United States of America

ISBN: 978-1-62147-774-7
1. Juvenile Fiction / Fantasy & Magic
15.05.05

ACKNOWLEDGMENTS

I would like to thank my wonderful husband, Gary Jaffae, for his support and encouragement. This book is every bit as much your accomplishment as it is mine. My thanks and love go to my family: Mom, Dad, Ksyusha, and Kostya for always believing in me.

I would like to extend a very special thank you to my coaches, Maria Pocheykina and Oleg Petrov, who have turned me into a figure skater.

I also thank my first coach, Nancy Garber, for introducing me to the wonderful and magical world of figure skating.

And, of course, I deeply appreciate the wonderful work of Tate Publishing in helping me along the path of turning my manuscript into a book.

Table of Contents

PROLOGUE

"It's been a rough winter, Mother. The western wind is brutal, and I could barely skate through that snow." A pretty brunette unwrapped her scarf and threw it in the closet.

Her mother, whose name was Wilhelmina Van Uffeln, scowled from her wheelchair. "The western wind again, huh?"

"That's it. And the mailman says there have been huge avalanches in the mountains. It's the third time this month that mail hasn't been delivered from outside Skateland. People say mail trucks can't make it across the mountain range. Isn't it unusual?"

"Avalanches," Wilhelmina repeated. Her gray eyes lingered on the thick, shimmering curtain outside the window. The snowflakes seemed to be performing an intricate footwork.

"Unusual, yes," Wilhelmina said softly. "And interesting too. Very, very interesting."

CRAZY MORNING

Cammie woke up from a screech followed by a loud song.

> The night is gone, the weather's fine.
> Wake up, o skater; rise and shine!
> Get ready for a long new day,
> Your medal's just a skate away.

"A long day! That's for sure!" Cammie muttered. She knew the singer too well; it was the Kanga bag, Cammie's Most Charming Skater prize from last year. Designed by Mr. Reed, Skateland's most distinguished skate sharpener and inventor, the bag wasn't merely equipped for carrying people's stuff around. It had several other functions, and the talking alarm clock was only one of them.

> You can't slack off; get on your feet!
> Warm up your muscles, stretch, and eat.
> Have something light, oatmeal or rice.
> Then you'll be ready for the ice.

"I'm not even hungry!" Cammie groaned and turned to the other side.

Mornings always came too soon in Skateland. The first practice started at seven o'clock. But because everybody had to skate to the rink, you had to be out of bed at five.

Just another minute, Cammie thought. *I'll get up, of course, but maybe…* She closed her eyes again.

> Now don't you go back to sleep!
> Or I will pounce; then you'll weep.
> But don't get mad; when you're through,
> You'll be a champion; that's true!

"All right, all right!"

Cammie quickly sat up and lowered her feet on the carpet. She knew better than to ignore Kanga's third warning. Mr. Reed had been smart when he programmed the bag. If the skater wasn't out of bed by the end of the song, Kanga would leap forward and pull the covers off the victim. Cammie had felt the impact of the animal's sharp claws more than once, and she wasn't looking forward to another experience.

Flinching from the morning cold, Cammie glanced at the lantern outside the window. At least Kanga was right about one thing: the weather *was* fine. The tall trees outside the dorm were still, and not a snowflake swirled in the air. The trip to the rink was going to be easy.

Cammie turned away from the window. "Sonia! What's wrong?"

She had expected to find her roommate asleep in bed. Yet Sonia sat at the desk, dressed in her blue velvet robe and thick wool socks. The desk was cluttered with books and papers.

Sonia yawned. "That's what I want to ask you. Did you program Kanga to wake you up at three in the morning?"

"What?" Cammie reached for her wristwatch. Sonia was right; it was only five after three.

"I don't understand." Cammie looked outside again. It was pitch dark. "Kanga!"

The animal's eyes glinted yellow. Cammie could swear Kanga was laughing at her.

"I'm going back to sleep!" Cammie announced as she got under the covers again.

"Gr-gr-gr!" Immediately, Kanga was by her side, its claws sharp and pointed.

"Gosh. You're not leaving me any options, are you?" Cammie jumped off her bed.

Sonia grinned.

"It's not funny, you know. Did it wake you up too?"

Sonia rubbed her eyes. "No. Actually, I've been up for an hour. The essay, remember?" Sonia lifted a stack of papers from the desk.

Cammie stared at her friend, feeling bewildered. "Do you mean our history assignment?"

"Of course! *The Evolution of Dance Positions in Ice Dancing*. That's my topic." Sonia sighed and picked up *The Complete Manual of Ice Dance Patterns*. "It does tell you about different positions, but very briefly. There is more in the *Judging Manual for Ice Dance*, of course, but the teacher wants us to show how those different positions actually developed, so—"

"Now wait a minute!" Cammie shuffled through Sonia's notes. "When's the assignment due?"

"The day after tomorrow." Sonia's baby blue eyes darkened. "And I only remembered about it yesterday. Can you imagine? It's all that triple flip I've had trouble with for the last two weeks. I couldn't think about anything else."

"The day after tomorrow?" Cammie gasped. "But... but I haven't even started."

"Well, you'd better." Sonia pushed the stack of notes closer. "Now that you're awake anyway."

Cammie moaned. "But I don't have any books here."

"You can use mine."

Cammie scowled. "Especially considering that my topic is *Evolution of Lifts in Pairs Skating*. No. I'll have to go to the library. When?"

She did a mental run-through of her day's schedule: morning practice and then school and then afternoon practice 'til six o'clock. Not a minute to spare. Well, perhaps she would skip dinner, grab something at Sweet Blades, and head straight to the library. At least the library was close to Main Square.

Cammie shook her head and sank on her bed. She felt dizzy from lack of sleep. Kanga sat two feet away, eyeing Cammie closely.

"Something must be wrong with you, my dear," Cammie said slowly. "It looks like your inner clock is fast."

"Hey, you forgot your guards again!" Kanga said nastily.

"What?"

There was nothing wrong about being reminded about skate guards, but not now. Surely Cammie wasn't ready to leave for the rink.

Cammie approached the bag. The animal stuck out its claws.

"Look, Sonia. It's really going bonkers."

"Maybe you need to take the bag to Mr. Reed," Sonia said without looking up from her notes.

"I guess." Cammie tried to stroke Kanga, but the animal bared its teeth. "And right before morning practice. But there is no choice. I don't want a monster for a skating bag."

For nothing better to do, Cammie spent the next two hours working on her homework. By the time Mrs. Page rang the bell summoning the girls for breakfast downstairs, Cammie had finished her math homework and even had a head start on the Pythagorean theorem, the following topic.

"Well, perhaps you don't even have to get Kanga fixed." Sonia smiled as she watched Cammie put her schoolbooks into her old backpack.

Cammie shook her finger at Kanga. "No way. You're not waking me up at three in the morning anymore, Kanga."

The two girls headed for the dining room on the first floor. Cammie tagged behind as Sonia zipped up her yellow parka. Sonia was a junior skater, so she practiced at the Yellow Rink. Cammie, however, was still at the intermediate level, which meant that she had her freestyle practices at the Green Rink.

They joined Liz, a small Asian girl who wore her hair in a tight ponytail.

"Where's Dana?" Sonia asked.

Liz gave her a look of warning. "She's not hungry."

"Now, I'm not buying this!" Mrs. Page's round face registered disapproval. With a loud clang, she put bowls filled with hot oatmeal in front of Sonia and Cammie and shuffled up the steps to the third floor.

"What's going on?" Cammie added butter to her oatmeal.

Liz's lip twitched. "Dana's trying to lose weight, as simple as that."

Mrs. Page reappeared in the dining room, her short fingers clasped tightly around Dana's elbow. Dana, a tall, longhaired blonde, practiced at the Green Rink with Cammie and Liz. Coach Ferguson had always spoken of Dana as a promising skater. In fact, just a year ago, Dana had gone to the nationals.

Even though she had only come in seventeenth, it still wasn't bad for a first-timer. Everybody expected Dana to build on that experience, moving up a level and perhaps starting working on triple jumps. Yet, for some unknown reason, Dana started gaining weight. Now that she was almost twenty pounds heavier, triple jumps were out of the question. The most Dana could do was hang on to her doubles, and even that was a problem. Without consistent jumps, Dana seemed to be stuck in intermediates forever, just like Cammie.

Surreptitiously, Cammie flexed her right ankle. Last year, she had had a bad skating accident that resulted in a broken ankle. Cammie had even needed surgery. Her leg was perfectly fine now, but Cammie still didn't jump as easily as before. Perhaps it was because of the two-month layoff from training last year.

Dana took a seat next to Cammie, looking defiant. Cammie noticed that the girl wore a loose green sweater over her leggings to conceal her bulging thighs.

"What's our first class today?" Liz asked Sonia.

"We're starting music interpretation today. I wonder what it'll be like."

Cammie covered her mouth with her hand to conceal a yawn.

Mrs. Page ladled oatmeal on a bowl and put it in front of Dana. "Here! You aren't leaving the building until you polish off your oatmeal."

Dana pouted and folded her hands on her lap. The kettle whistled, making Mrs. Page run to the stove.

"This witch isn't going to keep me in size eight!" Dana whispered loudly.

"Have some toast with your tea at least," Sonia said.

Dana gave her a dirty look. "There are sixty calories in that toast, for your information."

"That many?" Reluctantly, Cammie put her toast away.

"Now, Cammie, *you* don't have to starve yourself!" Sonia said.

"This stuff tastes like chalk!" Liz got up abruptly and ran to the counter.

The girls watched her add butter to her oatmeal and then top it with slices of banana. With her compact, boyish figure, Liz didn't have to worry about her weight. No matter what she ate, she never gained an ounce. "You can probably have half a banana, Dana." Liz licked her spoon. "Now that's much better."

Dana's eyes filled up with tears. "That would be seventy calories. No way."

"How many calories are there in a cup of tea?" Cammie asked.

Dana's eyes brightened. "You know what? Zero. Thanks, Cammie. I can have that."

"I already told you, Dana. You aren't going anywhere until you finish your oatmeal." Mrs. Page hovered over Dana, her hands on her wide hips.

Dana ignored the woman and kept sipping her tea.

Mrs. Page sighed gravely and turned on the radio.

"Good morning, Skateland residents and visitors," a cheerful female voice announced. "It's Tuesday, December third, five fifteen a.m. Sunrise is at seven thirty-five. Current weather conditions: it's calm and partly cloudy. The temperature is seventeen degrees. Skaters should expect hard ice on sidewalks, so make sure your edges are nice and sharp…"

Cammie looked at her blades. She had only had them sharpened a week ago. Good.

"A vigorous upper-level snowstorm will roll in from the west tonight…"

Mrs. Page's hand, holding a towel, froze in midair.

"By ten o'clock p.m., we expect wind gusts, snow, and some avalanches in the mountains alongside

Skateland's limits. Snow accumulation is twelve to eighteen inches. For safety reasons, be in your homes before ten p.m. We wish you all a pleasant day and very successful skating."

"Did you all hear that?" Mrs. Page glared at the girls as though it was their fault that a snowstorm was heading toward Skateland.

Sonia squinted at the darkness outside. "It's still nice and calm."

"Well, you heard what they said. A strong wind is coming from the west, and it's by far the worst." Mrs. Page collected the empty bowls.

"What's so special about a western wind?" Cammie asked.

The dishes clanged angrily as Mrs. Page put them in the dishwasher. "Am I your science teacher? Anyway, I expect you all to be home before dinner."

Cammie pushed her tea away. "Hey, I need to go to the library."

Mrs. Page clicked her tongue. "Can't it wait?"

"No. Mr. Stevens wants the essay the day after tomorrow."

Mrs. Page looked annoyed. "Okay, Cammie. But you still have to be back by ten. Okay?"

Before Cammie could say a word, Mrs. Page positioned herself next to the front door, blocking Dana's way. "Dana, I'm not letting you out without breakfast."

Dana's hands shook as she pulled on her green knit hat. "You won't turn me into a fat loser like yourself. Okay?"

Mrs. Page turned pale. "Dana—"

"Just leave me the freaking alone!" Taking advantage of Mrs. Page's shock, Dana grabbed her backpack and rushed out of the dorm. There was a very uncomfortable pause. Mrs. Page was obviously trying to compose herself. "Well, that's it, then. You'd better go too, girls. And Liz and Cammie, just keep an eye on Dana. Okay? She doesn't look good."

"Sure."

With the corner of her eye, Cammie saw Liz roll her eyes. At that point, Dana wouldn't listen to anyone. If Dana's extra weight messed up her jumps, she had to get rid of it, as simple as that. With Mrs. Page's skating years long over, the woman didn't understand how damaging just a few extra pounds could be for an athlete. For example, nobody would ever call Cammie overweight. Yet she had grown during the last year, and those three extra inches were now playing havoc with her jumps.

But I'll be all right, Cammie thought as she followed the rest of the girls into the crisp, frosty morning. *All I need is more practice and my jumps will be back.*

The first thing Cammie did was take her rebellious Kanga bag to Mr. Reed. Taking a detour to the Icy Park meant coming late for her morning practice, but Cammie had to take that risk. There was no way she could endure Kanga's wake-up call at three in the morning again. The day had barely begun, and Cammie was already dead tired. She simply couldn't imagine how she would be able to last through two skating practices and a whole day at school.

It was only when Cammie reached Mr. Reed's cabin that the blackness around her began to thin out a little. The sky over Mr. Reed's Purple Rink was slowly turning ultramarine. Then one of the cabin's windows lit up. Encouraged, Cammie put on her skate guards and walked up the three steps to the porch. She gave the silver blade hanging on the front door a tentative pull and heard a bell ring inside.

The door swung open, and Mr. Reed's tall figure stepped from the dimly lit lobby. In spite of the early hour, the man looked fresh and clean shaven. He wore a long purple robe and black slippers.

"You don't have an appointment, Cammie Wester," Mr. Reed said, skipping the usual good-morning.

Cammie pushed her Kanga bag ahead. "I'm sorry to bother you, Mr. Reed. My Kanga bag is really acting up, and I don't know what to do."

"Hmm. Is that true?" Mr. Reed stepped back to take a better look at the bag. "I think you'd better come inside."

Cammie followed the man to the huge living room that was filled with all kinds of skating paraphernalia. There were old skates from different centuries, skating dresses and books, soakers and lifeguards, boot covers and protective gear. In the middle of the room was a miniature rink, where tiny skaters did complicated footwork and jumps. Shelves and glass cabinets lined the walls. Skating dolls and figurines—marble, glass, wood, and metal—took every inch of available space.

Cammie glanced at Mr. Reed's famous good-luck pins—bronze, silver, and gold—thinking of her own experience with one of them. Three years ago, a girl whom Cammie had trusted had slipped Cammie the gold good-luck pin. However, instead of making Cammie skate better, the pin had thrown off Cammie's performance completely. Cammie had ended up in last place, and all because the pin didn't belong to her. It could only reward Mr. Reed's previous achievements, and if another skater tried to use it, the pin had just the opposite effect.

"Would you mind proceeding to my work room?" Mr. Reed asked.

"Ah. Sure."

Cammie joined the man as he entered a smaller room, where he kept his grinding wheel and other sharpening tools. She cast a longing look at a pair of self-spinning boots sitting on one of the shelves. A skater who wore those magical boots could perform multi-revolution jumps with confidence and ease; no technique was necessary. Unfortunately, self-spinning boots were illegal in Skateland.

"Okay. I see the problem." Mr. Reed, who had been examining Kanga with a long instrument that looked like a metal detector at airports, straightened up. "Your Kanga bag has a virus."

"What?" That was the last thing Cammie expected to hear. Her bag was a mechanism, not a live animal.

"No surprises here; your bag is a computer in some way."

"But who gave Kanga the virus?"

Mr. Reed looked at her with his powder blue eyes. "Don't you have any ideas?"

"The witches?" Cammie couldn't think of how the evil women could possibly tamper with her skating bag.

"You've got your answer." Mr. Reed bent over Kanga again. "So what do you say has the bag been doing wrong?"

Briefly, Cammie described Kanga's weird behavior this morning.

"Definitely the witches." Mr. Reed lifted the bag and put it on one of the shelves. "I'll have to dissemble it, clean the system, and put the bag back together. Unfortunately, the whole process will take about three weeks."

Cammie lowered herself on a stool next to the shelf. "Three weeks? But—"

"At least. In the meantime, you'll have to learn to get around without Kanga, which reminds me. Aren't you supposed to be at practice now?"

Cammie glanced at the clock hanging on the wall. The clock looked like a rink, and the arrows were shaped like skaters in the lounge position. "It's ten after seven!"

"You'd better run." Mr. Reed walked Cammie to the foyer.

"Could you write me a note? It's not my fault Kanga got a virus." Cammie could only imagine what Coach Ferguson would say once Cammie showed up at the rink half an hour into practice.

"Well..."

"Please!" Cammie clasped her hands together in front of her face.

The man grimaced. "Spare me the excesses, young lady. I hate being manipulated. Yet Kanga's virus isn't your fault, indeed, so I'll give you a note."

With a sigh of relief, Cammie watched Mr. Reed scribble a few lines on a card with *Melvin Reed's Skate Sharpening Shop* logo.

"I'll let you know when Kanga is ready," he said as Cammie sat down on the step to take off her skate guards.

Cammie thanked Mr. Reed and skated away in the direction of the Green Rink.

A BUSY DAY IN SKATELAND

As tired as Cammie was, she made it to the Green Rink in twenty minutes, her record time. An unusual thing about Skateland was the fact that all residents skated to their destinations. The policy had been introduced by Wilhelmina Van Uffeln, Skateland president. Wilhelmina was originally from Holland, where she had grown up skating on long frozen canals. The woman insisted that hours of stroking on outdoor ice could give a skater extraordinary leg strength.

Some skaters and their parents were skeptical about the rule. Yet now, in her fourth year in Skateland, Cammie could surely feel the effect of skating everywhere instead of riding in her parents' SUV. Her thigh and calf muscles felt strong, and even after stroking fiercely for twenty minutes, she wasn't out of breath. Another good thing was that there would be no need for a warm-up.

Cammie pulled the heavy door leading to the ice arena and bent down to take off her skate guards. The rest of the skaters were practicing moves in the field to

Chopin's mazurka. Cammie stepped onto the ice and looked around furtively. If only Coach Ferguson could hold her rant 'til after the session. Yet, to Cammie's great surprise, she didn't see her coach. The skaters were doing multiple three turns on their own.

"Where were you?" Dana stepped out of her backward outside three to let Cammie catch up with her. Dana's face looked sweaty.

"I had sort of emergency," Cammie whispered. Surely it wasn't the best time to tell Dana about Kanga's weird behavior. "Hey, did Ferguson ask about me?"

"Nope." Dana's blades cut deep into the ice as the girl skated away from Cammie.

That was weird. Coach Ferguson wasn't the kind of coach who could merely walk out in the middle of a practice. Cammie joined the rest of the skaters, trying to keep her knees bent and her body in a perfect skater's posture.

"*Faster* doesn't mean *sloppy!*" the familiar voice said from the entrance. "And, George, don't lean forward so much. I can hear your toe pick." Coach Ferguson zipped up her green parka and skated to the middle of the rink. "George, didn't you hear me? Get on that edge *now!*"

"I am on the edge." Ten-year-old George Belgrave snorted. A juvenile-level skater, George was a powerful jumper, but he absolutely detested moves in the field. No wonder Coach Ferguson was always on his case.

The coach was now right next to Cammie. Cammie raised her chin and held her forward outside edge for as long as she could. She turned naturally and gracefully.

"Very nice, Cammie!" Coach Ferguson said without stopping.

From where she was, Cammie heard the woman criticizing George again. Cammie exhaled slowly. Instead of rebuking her for coming late to practice, Coach Ferguson had actually complimented her. Perhaps the day would turn out good after all.

"Excuse me, Coach Ferguson! Mr. Deelan is calling again!" a squeaky voice called.

Cammie looked at the boards. Kelly Hogan, the Green Rink receptionist, stood looking at the ice longingly. Kelly had graduated from Skateland School last summer but decided not to go to college yet. She was determined to make it at least to the junior level. Now she worked in the Green Rink office and practiced every spare minute.

"Hmm." Coach Ferguson's cheeks turned scarlet. "I'll be back in a minute!"

Angela, a pretty, dark-haired girl, put her hands on her hips. "Uh huh! It's the third time today."

"The fourth." Rita, a plump twelve-year-old, giggled.

Liz smirked. "Sure, but the first call was from Mrs. Van Uffeln. The mysterious Mr. Deelan only called three times."

"Do you mind keeping quiet, all of you? Someone is trying to work here!" Dana said. She hadn't even stopped moving.

She is right, Cammie thought. *Who cares who Mr. Deelan is, after all?*

They would find out sooner or later.

Cammie thought their new music interpretation class would be an extension of the skating music course that she had been taking for the last three years. Therefore, she was surprised when a short, muscular man appeared in the classroom right after the bell and instructed them all to go outside.

"Where to?" Jeff asked as he reached for his jacket.

"To the school rink," the teacher said.

"I hope he doesn't make us skate," Michael Somner said.

Michael was a new student in Cammie's class. A novice skater, he had just moved to Skateland. Though Cammie had never seen the boy skate, she remembered Alex's words about Michael's strong potential. But still, Cammie couldn't help feeling resentful when Michael voiced his opinions about the ways things were done in Skateland.

"I hope you're here to become a better skater," Cammie said.

Michael's dark eyes narrowed. "I am a good skater, honey. At least better than those who are still stuck at the Green Rink."

The comment surely hit home. Cammie felt as though air had been sucked out of her insides.

Sonia squeezed Cammie's hand. "Ignore him. He isn't that good. Believe me."

"Oh yeah?" Michael took a huge chocolate bar out of his pocket, unwrapped it noisily, and took a big bite. "Anyone want a piece? I know you girls like sweets."

Cammie couldn't help noticing that Michael was looking at Dana. Dana swallowed and looked away.

"Thank you. We're fine," Sonia said icily.

"Suit yourselves!" Michael pushed the heavy exit door and ran outside.

Cammie caught Dana's jealous look, and she knew why. Michael was almost too skinny. Everything about him was narrow as a blade: his face, his nose, even his black hair falling below his chin. The boy gobbled on something without stopping, yet he never gained a pound.

"You can take your seats on the bleachers," the teacher said as they approached the school rink.

Located right at the back of the building, the school rink was smaller than a regular Olympic-sized rink. It had no borders, and Cammie had never seen any skaters actually practice there. The rink was mostly used for math classes, where the teacher taught students about different geometrical figures. Ice geometry—that was the branch of math every Skateland student was required to take.

The students took their seats in the second and the third rows of the bleachers.

"I'll be right with you," the teacher said as he turned to a CD player positioned at the edge of the rink. Cammie also noticed four speakers around the perimeter of the arena.

"He doesn't look like a skater to me." Liz wrinkled her nose.

As Cammie studied the teacher's short, muscular figure, his red face, and his goatee, she couldn't agree more. The man would probably look better chopping wood in a forest than gliding around the rink. Yet she would give up skating before siding with Liz.

"His eyes are nice, though, brown with gold specks," Nikki Anderson, a novice-level pairs skater, said. Cammie wondered how Nikki could have possibly discerned the color of the teacher's eyes from a distance.

"All right, people. I want your attention now." The teacher had finally finished adjusting the CD player and was facing them.

"My name is Mr. Dulcimer, and I'm here to teach you how to interpret music properly. In case some of you are unsure about my credentials, I am a former competitive skater." The teacher shot a quick glance in Liz's direction.

"At the moment, however, I'm a choreographer and a composer."

There was a collective *oh* as the students pondered over the teacher's words. A choreographer. That was something every skater needed. And a composer was even cooler. Cammie wondered what kind of music he wrote.

"The purpose of this course is to help you convey the deep feelings and emotions embedded in the pieces of music you perform to. I've got to warn you, however, that in my class you will be doing something entirely different from what you are used to. Your final grade will be based on your ability to interpret music, not on your technical skills."

Out of the corner of her eye, Cammie saw Sonia shrug. Sure enough, each of them had competed in the so-called interpretative events at least once. Interpretation meant that a skater didn't perform a previously choreographed program. Instead, a skater skated to a piece that he had only heard twice before he stepped onto the ice. Though challenging, the assignment was also interesting, for it gave people a chance to explore their creativity. And yet even during interpretative events, good technique was an absolute must.

"During all of my years of watching figure skaters, I have seen few true performers," Mr. Dulcimer said. "While many skaters are good at jumping and spinning, only a select few manage to truly touch people's hearts. However, if there are no feelings involved, figure skating is no longer a beautiful sport. It's nothing but a set of gymnastic tricks, a mere jumping contest. Are you guys following me?"

Cammie looked back and around and watched a few skaters exchange smirks. She knew what they were thinking. Every skater had heard that stuff before. Grace, inner vibes, emotions; those things sounded good, except they weren't practical. All that mattered in competitions was skating technique. If you managed to nail all of your difficult jumps, the judges would also discover deep feelings in your performance. Yet it never worked the other way. Mess up your jumps, and you would end up right at the bottom of the pack, no matter how graceful you were.

"The idea may be difficult for you to embrace, but the best skater will be able to make his most difficult elements unnoticeable," Mr. Dulcimer said.

Michael snorted and took another bite of his chocolate. On Cammie's left, Liz bent over her history report.

"Judging from your stunned faces, we are not in agreement here. So let's move on to the practical part. I will ask each of you to skate to a famous piece of music, something you have heard many times and know really well. Each of you will receive a pair of earphones. Here. You can pass these around."

There was a lot of commotion as the students passed around multicolored earphones. Cammie grabbed a dark blue pair.

"Don't put them on yet. Listen to me. As I call your name, take your seat in the front row and listen to your piece. The music will be played twice. After that, I will instruct you to step onto the ice and do a program to the music. However"—Mr. Dulcimer raised his red-gloved hand—"I don't care about your big jumps or fast spins. At this point, I want you to focus on the meaning of the music. Let your audience understand what the composer wanted to say. Think of skating as a means of conveying a message. Am I making myself clear?"

Cammie watched her friends exchange confident looks and nodded.

"All right, then. Liz Tong, why don't you come down, please."

Liz hopped down to the edge of the rink and stopped next to the teacher. Mr. Dulcimer motioned for her to take a seat in the front row then pressed a button on the CD player. The only sound that reached Cammie's ear was the rustling of the wind in the trees.

The sun still stood high in the sky, though from time to time, a cloud would slide over it, dimming the light.

"I hope it won't start snowing now. I hate skating in the snow," Sonia said.

"The snowstorm isn't supposed to start 'til later. But it's coming from the west, so it's going to be rough," Jeff said.

Michael crunched on a potato chip. "What's all that fuss about the west wind?"

"You'll see," Jeff said.

"Okay, Liz. Show us what you can do!" Mr. Dulcimer called.

He took Liz's earphones away. "Now, before Liz starts her program, I want Sonia Harrison down here."

Looking uncertain, Sonia approached the teacher and put on her earphones. From the way Sonia stomped her foot and nodded, Cammie could tell that she was listening to her music intently.

"All right, skaters. Let's extend a warm welcome to Liz Tong!"

With a slight smile, Liz skated to the middle of the rink and took her opening posture, one knee on the ice, the other leg straight behind her, her arms arched over her head. When the music started playing, Cammie recognized a famous tune from Tchaikovsky's *Swan Lake*. That was an easy piece to interpret; Cammie wished she would get something similar.

Liz started with a beautiful double axel and then soared up in a flashy double lutz-double toe loop combination. She did a few steps and turns and finished with a fast combination spin. Liz's final posture was identical to the start of her program. The students clapped hard.

"Bravo!" Nikki squeaked.

"Not bad." Michael put another potato chip into his mouth.

"Okay." Mr. Dulcimer signaled Liz to return to her seat. "Michael Somner, I need you down here, please."

Liz squeezed into her seat between Dana and Cammie. She was slightly out of breath. "Well, how did I do?"

"That was great!" Cammie said. Oh how she wished her jumps were as good as Liz's.

"Attention, everybody!" Mr. Dulcimer's voice came. "Next on ice is Sonia Harrison."

Sonia did all of her triples perfectly. Aside from a slight mistake in her footwork, she was very good.

"You rocked!" Jeff gave Sonia a high-five.

"My rockers were fine, but that counter…" Sonia smiled, realizing Jeff hadn't been talking about her steps. "I don't think I have the twizzles down, though—"

"Oh, forget it—"

"Jeff Patterson!" Mr. Dulcimer announced.

As Jeff listened to his music, Cammie watched Michael skate. She couldn't suppress a deep sigh. Really, the boy had every reason to show off. His athletic skills were outstanding. Somehow, Michael managed to make triple jumps appear easy.

Michael shook his long hair and returned to his seat behind Cammie. Now he looked even more smug.

One after another, the students skated to famous pieces of music. Cammie thought that Mr. Dulcimer had deliberately selected the tunes all of them had known since their early childhood. There was *Carmen*, *The Nutcracker*, *Nessun Dorma*, *Pirates of the Caribbean*. In Cammie's opinion, everybody had done well, except Dana, who had fallen on every jump. Cammie cringed as she watched her friend repeatedly crash onto the ice. What if the same happened to her? Her jumps had been off lately. At some point, she even thought of excusing herself, faking a stomachache. But it was too late; Mr. Dulcimer had already called her name.

Cammie's hands trembled as she put on the earphones. Her ears buzzed. She didn't even recognize the piece right away, though it sounded familiar. Oh, okay. It was Rachmaninoff's second piano concerto. As much as Cammie liked the music, she wished she had gotten something different. Rachmaninoff's music called for strong, powerful jumps.

Cammie felt slightly dizzy as she glided to the middle of the arena. The sun reappeared from the clouds, blinding her for a couple of seconds. Cammie froze in the T-position, not quite sure what to do with her arms. She started moving along with the music, barely thinking of it. She would take those doubles one at a time. *Okay, why not start with her easiest jump, the double salchow? Yes.* She landed it. *Okay, Cammie. Keep going. Don't let your confidence falter! Double toe loop. Yes!* She picked up speed. The sun blinded her again. *Who cares? There!*

She landed her double loop, although her free foot brushed the ice. Well, it wasn't a competition. She glided backward on her left outside edge in preparation for her double lutz. Her leg shook under her. She hadn't landed a double lutz since her injury. Michael's derogatory smile popped in her mind. He would laugh her to scorn.

At the last split second, Cammie decided to do a single. No problem! Cammie did a beautiful camel spin and then performed a single flip. She finished with a blurry scratch spin. Overall, she was happy with her performance. As she went back to her seat, she felt herself smiling.

"Maybe you need to practice at the Pink Rink," Michael hissed from behind her.

She stiffened but forced herself to ignore the jerk. Instead, she watched Nikki, who, after complaining that she wasn't used to skating without her partner, finally pulled off a nice performance to a piece from the musical *Chicago*.

"Well, as much as I enjoyed your strong technical abilities, I'm going to tell you the truth. All of you did a very poor job," Mr. Dulcimer said in his deep voice.

Everything became very quiet. Even the wind seemed to have subsided. As much as they were used to constructive criticism, what the teacher had just said was totally unfair. The next thing Cammie heard was a loud, "Come on!" Then everybody started talking at the same time, interrupting one another.

"But this…this is unfair!"

"I skated my butt off out there!"

35

"I'm sure I did well! Come on!"

"What does he want, for crying out loud?"

The teacher stood at the edge of the rink, his legs slightly spread, a smile playing on his lips. Somehow, he seemed amused by the students' outrage. And finally, the wave of protests subsided and everybody became quiet.

"Okay. Let's see. Sonia, what were you thinking about as you performed your program?" Mr. Dulcimer folded his arms on his chest.

Sonia straightened up. "Well…hmm…I tried to take it one step at a time…I know my footwork still needs work—"

"Okay." Mr. Dulcimer didn't wait for her to finish. "How about you, Jeff?"

Jeff's mouth twisted. "The entrance edge of my triple lutz. But I didn't flutz, did I?"

"I told you: pick closer to your skating foot," Sonia said.

Mr. Dulcimer's eyes flicked in Cammie's direction. "You, Cammie? Be honest."

Cammie looked at the gray ice, feeling miserable. "I know I freaked out. I need to get my double flip and double lutz consistent."

"I see…" Mr. Dulcimer scratched his chin. He looked sad.

"Well, *I* was perfect," Michael said. "I didn't make a single mistake."

"Your triple lutz was underrotated," Liz said.

"What? I bet *you* don't try triples even in your sleep!" Michael barked.

"That's enough!" Mr. Dulcimer's voice boomed over the students' angry remarks. "This is exactly the point I wanted to make. None of you focused on the music. All of you were driven by a strong desire to outskate the next person in line. There was too much showing off and very little sincerity in your performance. Skating out of a desire to impress others is a true sign of mediocrity."

An indignant silence followed his words. Dana hid her hands in the sleeves of her parka and looked away.

"We skate in order to impress judges," Michael said.

"And there's nothing wrong in trying to be the best," Nikki added.

"That's what competitions are about," Cammie said.

Mr. Dulcimer nodded. "It's true. During competitions, one skater is judged against another. But this isn't what I meant at all."

He paused, looking at the tall fir tree at the edge of the rink. The snow glazing the branches made the bright green color of the needles stand out even more.

"Skaters come and go. Some win big competitions. Others never get recognized for their efforts. Yet throughout skating history, there have been individuals whom skating fans would never forget. And it had little to do with the height of their jumps or the number of revolutions they managed to pull off. The desire to win, to beat your competitors, often takes away the joy of skating. The performance becomes dull, almost robotic. Yet if you skate merely because you love your sport, if you think about the music and the beauty of movement, your audience will be captivated. They won't see the effort behind the difficult elements, but they will remember the magic."

Mr. Dulcimer looked at them intently. Nobody said a word.

"Have you ever thought why figure skating is done to the music? Because of all forms of expression, music has the most magic. I don't think you have heard of music of life and music of death. Have you?"

Cammie looked at Sonia and saw her friend shake her head.

"Music of life has strong restorative power. It will heal you of physical ailments and free you from inner turmoil. On the contrary, violent, destructive pieces might cause sickness, even death."

A few students cleared their throats.

Michael chuckled. "Is there really such a thing as music of life?"

Mr. Dulcimer's brown eyes flickered under his bushy eyebrows. "I did mention that I am a composer, right? I do believe music speaks louder than words. How about this piece? Watch me closely."

The teacher approached the CD player. Cammie watched him slide a bright golden CD into the slot and then skate to the middle of the rink.

There was a short pause, and when the music started, Cammie thought it was the most unusual piece she had ever heard. The beginning was soft and tender. For some reason, Cammie thought of a little child smiling as his mother picked him up. She recognized the delicate chirping of a flute, and as the tune flowed further, a violin took over.

Piano chords sustained the bright, airy theme, and a beat started somewhere in the distance. Cammie couldn't tell whether it was a drum, a cymbal, or just the sound of a human heart. Pleasant warmth swept through her body, and the next thing she realized was that the headache caused by the lack of sleep was gone. With each note, Cammie felt stronger and more joyful. She realized that she was smiling.

Mr. Dulcimer didn't take the ice immediately. He merely stood at the edge of the rink, looking deeply absorbed in the piece. Finally, he started moving, first slowly and then faster and faster. His blades flew across the arena, barely touching the surface, and Cammie realized that the man was, indeed, a great skater. Yet for some strange reason, she barely noticed what exactly he was doing on ice. All she could see was a seamless, fluid motion. A saxophone began to play, and in another moment, Mr. Dulcimer soared off the ice in a magnificent split jump. His landing was soft, as though the teacher had descended on a patch of snow.

The oboe seemed to be talking to the saxophone. Joy bubbled inside Cammie. She thought of herself as a bird. She could rise above the cares of the world; she was happy. She remembered she was a skater, and the thought made her excited. Mr. Dulcimer was spinning now, faster and faster. The music swirled around like snowflakes. Cammie closed her eyes. If only she could spend the rest of her life with the music carrying her away!

The cello sang, and then the final sound melted in the air. Cammie opened her eyes. The deep silence felt deafening, almost unnatural. She longed for more of the music. Someone clapped next to her, and another moment, all the students applauded loudly.

Mr. Dulcimer grinned at them from the middle of the arena. "That was the music of life, folks."

Sonia raised her hand. "Mr. Dulcimer, could we… could we skate to it?"

The teacher shook his head. "You can't. Only a person with pure motives can handle the music of life. A skater who thinks of beating others might take a terrible fall and hurt himself. Unfortunately, at this point, none of you are ready to skate to the music of life. It's too deep, too powerful. However, we're going to work on it. Okay. I think that's it for today. Homework: think of all we have done today, and next time you skate, try to focus on the message of the music. Class dismissed."

There was a clanging of skate guards against the wood and the cracking of the benches as the students started getting up.

"Mr. Dulcimer!" Jeff called.

The teacher turned around from the CD player. "Yes?"

"And what's the music of death like?"

Mr. Dulcimer looked Jeff up and down. "Believe me, young man. You don't want to know."

"But—"

"You'd better hurry if you don't want to miss your next class," Mr. Dulcimer said.

As Cammie followed Sonia to the school building, she heard Jeff and Michael talking loudly about the music of death.

When Cammie came to the rink for her afternoon practice, Coach Ferguson was already there, looking like her usual busy self.

"I liked your moves this morning, Cammie."

Cammie felt her weariness slip away immediately. "Oh thanks!"

"I believe you're ready for your moves-in-the-field novice test. However"—Coach Ferguson raised her index finger—"you need to really get those jumps straightened out for your freestyle test."

"I know." Cammie sighed.

Life was so unfair. Just a year ago, she had been able to do all double jumps and combinations easily. Of course, the double axel had given her some problems, but she had finally managed to get even that tricky two-and-a-half-revolution jump consistent. Last year, Cammie had even won Skateland Annual Competition. She had felt so confident back then believing that she would get her triples in no time, until she got injured; and from that time on, everything had gone downhill.

"Let's not waste time, then," Coach Ferguson said. "Why don't you warm up with singles and work up from there."

Cammie nodded and skated around the rink, picking up speed. She started with the easiest waltz jumps, trying to make them long and high. Then she moved up to salchows and toe loops. She knew her single jumps were good, and on her loop, flip, and lutz, she held the landing edge as long as she could.

41

"Okay. Are you ready to try an axel?" Coach Ferguson asked.

"Sure." Cammie did several backward crossovers and then turned forward and jumped as high as she could. *Yes!* She landed cleanly on her backward outside edge. Her double salchow was equally good.

It was when Cammie tried her double toe loop that her body started rebelling. For some unknown reason, she couldn't fully rotate the jump. Cammie made sure she reached back far enough with her toe pick. She swung her arms fast around her body. She pulled in tight. Still, she either ended up on both feet or only completed one revolution. Cammie kept trying, but her jump only seemed to be getting worse.

"That's enough!" Coach Ferguson finally said.

Breathing hard, Cammie skated up to her. "I've been doing everything right."

"You're pre-rotating the jump," the coach said. "Your upper body gets ahead of your feet."

Cammie brushed the snow off her tights. "I don't understand. I could do the double toe loop in my sleep last year."

"It happens," Coach Ferguson said. "You have grown three inches since last year. Is that right?"

Cammie moaned. "But—"

"Coach Ferguson, Mr. Deelan is on the phone. He says it's urgent." Kelly stood next to them, looking at Coach Ferguson eagerly.

"If you will excuse me, Cammie." The coach quickly skated away. Before stepping off the rink, she glanced back. "Practice single toe loops into backspins. I'll be right back."

Liz approached Cammie and Kelly. "I wonder who's calling Coach Ferguson all the time."

Kelly smiled slyly. "I think it's her *boyfriend*."

George looked from behind Liz. "But Coach Ferguson is old!"

"She's only twenty-nine, and that's not exactly old," Kelly said. "Now back to practice, everybody!"

Without waiting for any of the skaters to say another word, Kelly started stroking around the rink. She did a quick Mohawk into backward crossovers and a moment later, shot up in the air in a delayed axel. Cammie had to admit that the girl was good, even though her dark business suit looked out of place at the rink.

"Do you expect to get your jumps back by watching other skaters? And, Kelly, I think they pay you for your receptionist duties."

Cammie hadn't even noticed that Coach Ferguson was back.

Muttering something under her breath, Kelly stepped off the ice.

"Let's try a double loop now," Coach Ferguson said.

By the end of the practice, Cammie's doubles hadn't improved at all. After about the seventh fall from her double flip, Cammie found it hard to suppress tears. What was wrong with her? So she had grown, but hadn't everybody? Sonia was also fourteen, and she was about to take her senior tests. Cammie, however, couldn't even dream of passing her novice freestyle test without consistent doubles.

Coach Ferguson finished their private lesson after telling Cammie to practice jumps on the floor and work out in the gym more. Then the coach started working with Dana. At least Dana's jumps were even worse than hers, Cammie thought. The girl didn't seem to be getting any height at all.

At six o'clock, there was a sound of the gate opening, and the green-and-white Zamboni machine sailed unto the ice.

"Practice over, skaters!" Coach Ferguson said.

One by one, the kids stepped off the ice.

"Do you need a special invitation, Dana?" Coach Ferguson asked.

Cammie saw Dana's face contort into a grimace of pain. "I'm staying for the public session."

"Public session is cancelled. Storm warning," Coach Ferguson said.

"Ouch. We'd better get to the dorm fast," Rita said. "Come on, Angela!"

Laughing and talking, the skaters started leaving the building in groups of two and three.

"Coming, Cammie?" Liz called. She was zipping up her parka next to the skulking Dana.

Cammie shook her head. "I'm going to the library first. Gotta do that history essay."

"I only have two pages left," Liz said. "How about you, Dana?"

"I'm working on the conclusions, but I still have two nights." Dana adjusted the straps of her backpack.

"See, Cammie. You shouldn't have put off your homework 'til the last minute!" Liz said in perfect imitation of Mrs. Page's deep voice.

Cammie glared at her. "Spare me the lecture, okay? Anyway, I'll see you later."

She pushed the exit door and walked out into the cold. It was still quiet; the snow-covered limbs of the maple trees surrounding the rink didn't even move. Stars had already appeared in the sky.

Cammie shivered and tightened her scarf around her neck. After the grueling practice, her legs felt weak. She was also very hungry. She wished she was going to the dorm with the rest of the kids. Mrs. Page would be serving chicken with mashed potatoes and Brussels sprouts tonight. Did she *really* have to go to the library that late at night? Perhaps it would be better to head to the dorm, eat Mrs. Page's delicious dinner, and then watch a movie in the living room with the rest of the kids.

Cammie looked longingly at Axel Avenue stretching ahead of her. Her friends were already gone, but perhaps she could still catch up with them. Cammie thought for a moment then shook her head. She had already made a decision to write her essay tonight.

Cammie took a map of Skateland out of her backpack and spread it over her knee to locate Skateland library.

"Wow!" Cammie whistled.

The library appeared to be miles away, in the northern part of Skateland, in the western circle of Figure Eight Square. Cammie knew the place. Figure Eight Square included two equal circles. In the middle of the eastern circle stood the Skating Museum. The museum consisted of several halls featuring different periods of skating history. There were rinks with real ice in the building and wax figures of skaters of old. But the museum was not only known for its beautiful exhibits; it had magic powers. In fact, two years ago, Cammie and her friend, Alex, had taken a few trips to the past from the museum. The library, however, was even farther away, in the Western Circle.

"Well, it's no use wasting time," Cammie said out loud. She put the map into her backpack and headed north.

On her way to the library, Cammie stopped by Sweet Blades and bought a dark skate pastry, her favorite treat. As the wonderful taste of dark chocolate filled her mouth, she felt stronger right away. Suddenly, Cammie believed that everything would be fine. She picked up speed as she thought of Coach Ferguson's behavior during practices. Never before had Cammie's coach talked on the phone so much. *Who could that mysterious Mr. Deelan be? Surely not Coach Ferguson's boyfriend.* The woman was too serious for those sorts of things. Perhaps the man was a reporter or a promoter.

Half an hour later, Cammie did a hockey stop in front of a three-story stone building. A metal plaque saying "Skateland Public Library" hung over the entrance. Cammie put on her skate guards, walked up the steps to the porch, and pulled the polished wood door.

The spacious lobby was lit by half a dozen lamps suspended from the ceiling. Fire licked up heavy logs in the fireplace. An older lady sat at the counter in the middle of the lobby. As Cammie came closer, the woman raised her head and smiled. Cammie noticed that the librarian had bushy eyebrows and wore a beige felt hat over her shoulder-length, salt-and-pepper hair.

"Welcome to Skateland Library. My name is Jane Libris. How can I help you?"

Cammie smiled back. "I am Cammie Wester. I need some books about the evolution of lifts in pairs skating for my history essay."

"No problem. The pairs skating section is on the second floor." Mrs. Libris pointed to the steps leading upstairs. "Would you like me to help you find the books you need?"

By the quick look the lady cast at a cup of tea next to her, Cammie could tell that the librarian didn't feel like walking upstairs.

"I'll be fine. Thank you," Cammie said quickly.

"Here is the key to your locker. It's number eighteen." Mrs. Libris must have noticed Cammie's puzzled look. "Surely you want to take your skates off. You can find a pair of slippers in the locker."

"Hmm. Thanks."

The lockers were across from the counter. Cammie found the one with number eighteen scribbled on the door. Inside, there was a pair of green fluffy slippers. As Cammie took off her skating boots, she sighed with relief. She had a nice pair of custom-made Riedells, but after the whole day of skating, her feet felt stiff and cold. The slippers, however, were incredibly comfortable. As Cammie headed to the second floor, she felt as though she walked on cushions.

A huge sign, "Pairs Skating Section," greeted her at the entrance to the hall on the second floor. Cammie stared at long rows of books and picked up a thick volume from the closest shelf, *Figure Skating Championship Technique. Hmm. Not bad.* She glanced at another book, *Pairs Skating: A History.* Yes, that would work too.

She walked past two or three shelves, looking at the titles. She had never seen so many skating books in her life. There were dozens and dozens of volumes, thick and thin, old and new, big and small.

I'll definitely finish this essay tonight, Cammie thought.

She saw a few people sitting at small desks next to small, circular windows, although there was no one close to her age. Poring over thick volumes were mostly older people.

Cammie dropped about a dozen books on the nearest desk and looked outside. Random snowflakes whirled in the light of a street lamp. Cammie stretched her legs and opened the first book, *A Glossary of Skating Lifts.* She would start with a description of different types of lifts.

"The Star Lift is a lift in which the male raises his partner from his side, by her hip, into the air." Cammie wondered what floating over the partner's head felt like. It seemed kind of cool, but it had to be scary too. "Isabelle Brasseur and Lloyd Eisler made the no-hand star lift famous. In this lift, Lloyd lifted Isabelle into the star lift position, with one hand placed on her hip and no other point of contact." *Hmm.* Cammie rubbed her forehead, trying to picture the no-hand star lift.

She would probably have to include some pictures; otherwise, her essay would be hard to read.

Cammie got so caught up in her work that she completely lost track of time. She was vaguely conscious of other people leaving the hall. At some point, she glanced through the window, noticing that the snowfall was getting thicker. She didn't care. Her toes burned slightly in the warm slippers, as though she held them close to a fire. Her eyelids began to droop. She lowered her head on her folded hands just to take a short break.

The next thing Cammie heard was a loud bell. She moaned. *Not Kanga again! Is it morning already? If so, I'd better get up before Kanga leaps on me.*

Cammie opened her eyes. For a moment, she couldn't understand where she was. The light of a small, green lamp fell on a page called The Lasso Lift. Outside, snow hung like a thick, white shawl.

"Library is closed!" a voice came from downstairs.

"Closed," Cammie mumbled. She turned a page. Her essay wasn't even close to being finished.

A tall figure bent over her. Cammie recognized Mrs. Libris.

"Dear me. And I thought everybody was gone."

Cammie stood up. "I was just leaving. Uh…can I take these books with me?"

"Sure. Wait!" Mrs. Libris looked at the raging snow. "Will you be okay skating home in this weather? Perhaps I'd better call the police. They'll give you a ride in their icemobile."

Yes, and then Cammie would have to listen to the cops' diatribe about taking their precious time.

During her last encounter with Skateland police, she had almost got arrested. She doubted the cops would be more forgiving this time. She could almost hear Lieutenant Turner's words, "So you chose to neglect the storm warning, Cammie Wester? Too bad! Captain Greenfield, I don't think this sort of behavior should be left unpunished. I suggest expulsion and disqualification."

"I'll be fine. Thank you."

"Are you sure?" Mrs. Libris watched as Cammie changed into her skating boots. "Where do you live?"

"At the intermediate girls' dorm off Axel Avenue." Cammie picked up her heavy backpack. "Don't worry, Mrs. Libris. It's not that far."

Mrs. Libris still looked concerned. "The west wind is the worst, you know."

It was weird how everyone was scared of the west wind. Cammie gave the librarian her warmest smile and zipped up her parka.

BLIZZARD

The moment Cammie walked out into the porch, a strong gust of wind hit her in the face. She cringed and almost fell over. The snow was so dense that she could barely see two feet in front of her. Cammie clenched her teeth and skated forward. Another blast of wind struck from the right. She stopped and pulled her wool cap down tighter. It didn't help much; the wind was ice cold. Cammie's green-and-white gloves didn't provide much protection either; she could barely feel her fingers.

She opened her mouth to complain, but immediately a lump of snow flew in her mouth. She coughed and almost choked as the frosty wind made its way down her throat. She looked around frantically. Perhaps Mrs. Libris was right. What did Cammie have to prove? Perhaps it would be better to return to the library and ask the librarian to call the police. The icemobile would take Cammie to the dorm in no time.

Bending against the strong gusts, Cammie turned around and skated back. Now the wind lashed the left side of her face. She lowered her head and dashed forward. There it was, the library building. She ran up the steps and pulled the front door. It was locked. How could it be? Mrs. Libris had been there five minutes ago. Cammie looked at the tall windows of the first floor. They were dark. The lights in the lobby were off. Trying not to panic, Cammie pressed her forehead against the glass. There was no motion inside.

"Mrs. Libris!" she called.

The only sound Cammie could hear was the howling of the wind.

"So I have to get home on my own," Cammie said, "and I will."

She skated along the street called Spiral Footwork. With its unexpected twists and turns, the street was fun during the day. Yet now that Cammie could hardly see ahead of her, every change of course was a huge challenge.

"Ouch!" Cammie's right blade caught something, causing her to lose balance. She flailed her arms awkwardly, trying her best to stay upright. No luck. She fell hard on her side.

"Oh no!" Cammie made a weak attempt at getting up. Her backpack felt too heavy; it pulled her backward. Cammie loosened the straps and slid off her cumbersome load. Breathing hard, she rose on her knees and peered into the dark. She could discern absolutely nothing beyond a grayish swirling mass.

"Just great!" Cammie said out loud. She spat out the snow and rubbed her face. Her cheeks stung. "I have to get out of here!" Cammie forced herself to stand up and put her backpack back on.

Was she supposed to go left or right? Everything looked the same. She moved randomly to the left, grimacing as cold chunks hit her face. Thick snow made it impossible to glide.

Another gust of wind pushed her off her feet. It felt as though the rampant blizzard didn't want to let Cammie out of its tight grip. She gritted her teeth. The west wind was strong, but Cammie wasn't a weakling either. *I'm probably close to Toe Loop Avenue,* Cammie thought. *Now wait a minute! The west wind?* She sat up, trying to think hard. She had fallen on her right side, which meant the west wind blew from her left. Her dorm was south from the library. Oh no! She had been heading north all the time. Cammie groaned. How could she lose her way like that? She turned around and ploughed ahead.

She didn't know how long she had been skating. Breathing hard, Cammie strained her eyes, trying to discern houses. Perhaps she could ring some doorbell and ask the owners to call the police. Only, she couldn't see a single house. Even the streetlights were off. The heavy wind must have torn the wires. Or was Skateland completely buried under one of those avalanches the meteorologist had spoken of?

Cammie's right blade slid forward unexpectedly, causing her to fall on her knee.

"What happened?" She ran her gloved hand against hard smooth ice. How come the snow hadn't covered the sidewalk completely?

Something silvery-white glinted in front of her. As Cammie looked up, she saw a sliver of the moon between rushing clouds. Before everything plunged into darkness again, Cammie managed to notice that she wasn't in a residential area. Instead, she sat in the middle of a winding ice path, and tall trees grew on both sides of the road. She had skated into the Icy Park.

Completely exhausted, Cammie crawled off the path and leaned against a tree. She had to think before moving any farther.

The Icy Park was huge, and at some point, it merged into a forest. Nobody in Skateland knew the outlay of the park well enough. On top of everything else, the Icy Park was the place where skating witches lived.

Something both soft and prickly brushed against her knee. As she groped the thing with her hands, she realized it was a fallen fir tree. With a sigh of surrender, Cammie sank onto the spongy limbs and brought her knees to her chest. She wasn't going to make it to the dorm on her own. Once Mrs. Page found out that Cammie wasn't in the dorm, she would call the police. Sooner or later, the cops would come for Cammie in their icemobile. All she had to do was wait.

Then Cammie shivered. Skating in the Icy Park was against Skateland law. And Cammie had been disciplined several times for doing just that. Another confrontation with the police was the last thing Cammie needed. Unfortunately, she had no choice. Hopefully Mrs. Libris would explain to Mrs. Page that Cammie had not been practicing in the Icy Park; she merely stayed at the library late. There was nothing illegal about working on a history essay. After all, whose fault was it that Mr. Stevens had assigned the skaters such a humongous amount of homework? With all the skating practices, off-ice training, and ballet classes, there was hardly any time to complete the assignment.

"Everything will be all right!" Cammie assured herself.

A loose twig pricked her side, causing her to change position. Perhaps Skateland authorities would even be impressed with Cammie's diligence. Staying at the library late at night, wasn't that true dedication? Perhaps Cammie would even be awarded a special prize for enthusiasm and commitment. Last year, she had got the Charming Skater's prize, the Kanga bag.

Kanga... Cammie shook her head sadly.

If her faithful skating bag were with her now, she would have no problem getting to the dorm. Kanga had a built-in navigator, which made travelling around Skateland easy. Cammie wouldn't even have to bother skating to the dorm. It would be enough to hold on to Kanga's handle, and the bag would pull her forward. Really, the witches had chosen the worst time to plant a virus into Kanga's computer.

Cammie rubbed her hands and hid them on her chest under her parka. Her fingers stung as blood rushed through her capillaries. She wiggled her toes. They were slightly numb, but not too badly. At least Cammie was away from the wind. She would stay here, on the fallen fir tree, until the police found her. And when she came to the dorm, everybody would be impressed with Cammie for defeating the west wind.

There was a loud creak and then a few stomping sounds as though something huge and heavy was making its way through the forest. She turned around and looked back.

The next thing Cammie heard was herself screaming so loudly that her ears began to sting. Her legs collapsed under her. Looming over her was a monster. The beast stood on its hind legs, the long, sharp claws of its front paws pointed straight at Cammie. Its body was covered with brown fur like a bear's, and there were eight horns growing from the creature's head.

"No!" Cammie whispered, barely moving her lips. "No! Go away! Please go away!"

The beast came closer. His eyes were fiery red. They felt like burning coals. He opened his mouth. Hot saliva splattered Cammie's face. Then the creature began to growl like a bear deprived of her cubs. The roar just about burst Cammie's ear drums. The next thing she felt was hot steam coming out of the beast's nostrils, singeing her eyebrows and eyelashes.

He's going to kill me!

The evil predator would devour her, and nobody in the world would even know what had happened to Cammie Wester.

"Please!" she said again, the tears hot on her cold face. Her body shook uncontrollably.

The monster opened his mouth again. She saw two rows of long, spiky teeth.

That's it. I'm dying, she thought, and then fire shot out of the beast's mouth again. It burned her face. She couldn't stand it anymore. She drifted away.

She woke up feeling pressure on her chest. *The monster!* So he hadn't killed her yet. But he was beside her. His paws were on her chest. In another moment, she would feel the pain of her flesh being torn apart.

"Help!"

"Heed, Choctaw!" a male voice sounded from a distance.

Cammie felt as though a huge weight had been lifted off her chest. She could breathe again. She opened her eyes. Silhouetted against the dark trunk next to her stood a gigantic dog. The animal's piercing black eyes stared at Cammie out of a white mane of thick hair.

"Where...where's the monster?" Cammie thought she was speaking loudly, but the sounds that came out of her mouth were nothing but a whisper.

The dog sat down next to Cammie, his hair white and long. Though huge, the animal didn't appear unfriendly.

"Or was it you who scared me?" Cammie rose on her elbow, studying the dark silhouettes of trees around her. She wondered if the horrible beast she had seen before was this particular dog. Perhaps it was her imagination that had turned the husky into something much scarier. Or probably the horrible animal had been one of the Witch of Fear's tricks. Giving people horrible visions was exactly the thing that particular witch was famous for. At the thought of the Witch of Fear, Cammie gave a faint squeak.

The dog's pointed ears twittered slightly, as though it was trying to detect something in the howling wind.

"What do you want?" She looked around frantically. Her face stung, and as she ran her hand against her cheeks, she felt a thick crust of ice under her glove.

The dog sniffed her parka and then turned around and leapt away, wagging its bushy tail.

"What did you find there, Choctaw?"

That time, the male voice was closer to Cammie. The ice scraped under somebody's blades. The snow squeaked. There was a flash of light, and a face swam into Cammie's field of vision.

The man wasn't exactly young, perhaps in his thirties. Yet he was the most handsome person Cammie had ever seen. "What are you doing here, little girl?" the man asked in a pleasant baritone.

At fourteen, Cammie could hardly be considered a little girl, but she enjoyed the genuine concern in the stranger's voice.

"Just enjoying my dream," Cammie wanted to say. If she could only move her lips, that kind of answer would be the closest to the truth.

"Did you lose your way, honey?" The man bent over Cammie. A slight wrinkle appeared between his eyebrows.

Cammie tried to speak, but her lips felt like ice. All she could do was nod.

The dog materialized from behind a tree and sat down on the snow next to them.

"His name is Choctaw, and he is a husky," the man said. "He's a great dog. He even pulls a sled for me. Choctaw is the one who found you."

Found me? What does he mean? Surely I'm not lost.

"Where do you live?"

"In th''ntrm'diate dorm," Cammie managed to say.

"The intermediate dorm!" There was a flicker of recognition in the man's eyes. As he brought his face closer to Cammie's, she saw that they were blue, yet not the light baby blue like Sonia's. The man's eyes were darker, midnight blue, and they were tinted with deep sadness. "We'll take you home, little one. Now wait a minute. Choctaw, follow me!"

The light went off. Cammie heard the man and the dog move away. So Choctaw was the dog's name. It could only mean one thing; the stranger was a skater.

There was a familiar scraping of the ice under blades. The light came on again. Cammie felt strong arms pick her up.

"Put your hands around my neck. Good girl."

Cammie felt the park sway around her. Her face brushed the man's neck. She discerned a faint smell of cologne.

"Here you go!"

Cammie lay on something soft and leathery. A moment later, a thick quilt fell over her. "Wr 'my?"

Fortunately, the man didn't seem to have a problem with Cammie's garbled speech. "You're in my sled. We'll let Choctaw take you to your dorm. But first, drink this."

Cammie felt a cup next to her lips. She took a sip. "Ouch!"

It burned her tongue. Cammie coughed and tapped herself on the chest.

"Trust me. It's good for you."

59

Cammie swallowed the hot drink. It tasted wonderful, both sweet and sour, with some flowery scent. "What's it?"

"The drink? It's waltz whiskey."

"Whiskey?" Cammie couldn't believe her ears. She had never drunk anything stronger than skate shake in her whole life.

The man's full lips spread in a warm smile. Cammie noticed a dimple on his chin.

"Let not the word *whiskey* scare you. Waltz whiskey only has two percent alcohol. But it's perfect for someone who has been exposed to the cold for a long time."

It was at that moment that Cammie remembered the horrible beast. As she peered into the dark thicket, she couldn't suppress a shudder. "Is he gone?"

"Who?" The man brought the cup to her lips.

"The monster."

"What?"

"Or maybe there wasn't any monster. It's one of the Witch of Fear's tricks, right?"

"Shh shh! Drink it."

Cammie finished her drink, feeling a hot wave spread over her whole body. The tips of her fingers and toes began to prick. Her head spun. "Who are you?"

"A skater." He looked away. "Choctaw, move!"

The sled lurched forward, shaking slightly as it took a sharp corner. Cammie raised her head, watching the dog make his way through the blizzard with amazing ease.

"He's strong, Choctaw. And what's your name, sir?" The waltz whiskey had warmed Cammie up perfectly. Now she could finally talk.

The man turned to her. His eyes looked almost black. "You need to rest, little one. Tomorrow, you won't remember anything."

"I will," Cammie said passionately. "Because…"

Suddenly she felt happy, yes, really happy, and it didn't matter that she had gotten lost. She no longer cared about the Witch of Fear. She looked around. The charming stranger's presence had transformed Skateland into a magical place. The frozen limbs of fir trees looked like emeralds with threads of silver. Snow slithered down, enclosing Cammie and her rescuer in a tight cocoon. As the man turned on his flashlight, the snowflakes sparkled gold.

They rode along bumpy, snow-covered streets. Cammie's heart stung as she recognized Axel Avenue. She didn't want the magical ride to end.

"Here we are," the man said as Choctaw stopped in front of Cammie's dorm. The light on the first floor was on.

"Thank you!" Cammie studied the man's handsome face. Would she ever see her rescuer again?

"What's your name, little girl?"

"Cammie Wester."

"It's been a pleasure."

Did it mean he liked her?

The front door of the dorm opened wide, and Mrs. Page ran out, wearing a white cardigan over her blue robe. "There she is! Did you find her, sir? Oh, thank

God! The police are looking for her all over Skateland. Cammie, you just wait! I—"

The man lifted Cammie again and carried her inside easily, as though she were a feather. As Cammie leaned against her rescuer's shoulder, she could feel hard muscles on his arm. *What kind of lift is that?* A weird thought crossed her mind.

"Where do you want me to take her?" the man asked Mrs. Page.

Cammie noticed that his blond hair was now concealed by a black ski hat. A matching scarf covered his mouth, as though the man didn't want to be recognized.

"Do you think she needs a doctor? Is she hurt?"

"I don't think so."

As they walked up to the third floor, Cammie hid her face in the man's black-and-white ski jacket. As long as she was in his arms, she could pretend they were still alone in his magical sled.

"Cammie!" Sonia squeaked somewhere close.

The next thing Cammie felt was being lowered on her soft bed. "Have a good night, Cammie Wester."

"Wait! Will you…will I…?" Tears blurred Cammie's vision as she watched the man head for the door.

"But, sir, I don't know your name." Mrs. Page's brown eyes travelled from Cammie to her rescuer.

"Have a good night!" The man raised his hand in a farewell and walked out with Mrs. Page following him.

"Look, I really need to—" The dorm supervisor's voice sounded from the hallway.

The door shut.

Sonia sat up in bed, eyeing Cammie with a mixture of fright and amazement. "What happened?"

Cammie brushed the tears off her face and smiled brightly. "Oh, Sonia!"

She was sure she wouldn't be able to sleep, but the moment her head touched the pillow, the room swirled around her. Cammie felt herself rushing through thick darkness, with snow flying at her.

MAGIC ON ICE

It was eleven forty-five on Saturday morning, and Cammie had just woken up. She had spent the whole Friday in bed with a 103-degree fever. Now her fever was gone, and she was actually looking forward to the afternoon practice. Besides, Saturday was an easy day. Skaters only had a long public session at the Silver Rink at one o'clock. That gave them plenty of time to sleep in, to work out, or just to have fun.

As soon as Cammie began to feel better, she filled Sonia in on what that had happened to her the night of the storm.

Sonia's eyes sparkled blue on her freckled face. "Oh my gosh. Cammie, who could that scary creature be?"

"Well, I thought it was just a vision from the Witch of Fear—"

"Yes! She can do those things. When I was a captive in her castle, she did it to me all the time. She—"

Cammie shook her head. "But my face is all burned. See? It means the monster was real."

Mrs. Page had been putting generous amounts of Solarcane on Cammie's face, but the skin still looked red.

"Yes, I was wondering what happened to your face. I thought it was frostbite. Still…" Sonia frowned. "I was born in Skateland, but there've never been any monsters here. Perhaps the Witch of Fear can make people feel strange things."

Cammie waved her hand. "Oh well. Never mind."

The truth was, she didn't feel like talking about the beast. There was a more pressing issue on her mind.

"Sonia, did you see the face of the guy who brought me to the dorm?"

Sonia looked surprised. "I didn't even look him in the face."

"Oh my gosh. You should have. I wonder who he is."

"Why's that so important to you?" Sonia pulled her red, curly hair up and fastened it with a blue velvet band. "It was probably one of the security guards. Everybody looked for you, you know."

"No security guard looks that gorgeous!" Cammie stared dreamingly at the patch of blue sky outside the window.

"He was a terrific skater. I could tell," Cammie said. "Do you remember *Swan Lake* and Prince Siegfried? Remember how he danced? So that's what my rescuer looked, like a northern prince!"

Cammie surely knew what she was talking about. Last year, a Russian ballet company had visited Clarenceville, Cammie's hometown. Cammie's father had thought watching a dancing performance would help his talented daughter's skating. So he had bought two tickets, encouraging Cammie to bring a friend. Of course, it was Sonia whom Cammie had invited. That night, the company was showing *Swan Lake*.

"And how could you tell he was a good skater? Did you actually see him skate?" Sonia asked sharply.

"Well, I didn't have a chance to see him perform. He was there to rescue me. But he was so strong and graceful, and absolutely gorgeous."

Sonia rolled her eyes. "Cammie, you're such a baby! There's nothing extraordinary about that guy."

"How would you know?"

"I saw him too, remember?"

Oh. Right.

When the man had brought Cammie in, Sonia had been awake.

"And I assure you, he's quite ordinary, just a tall man in black clothes."

"But his eyes!" Cammie rose on her knees, feeling a rush of inspiration. "Blue, like…like the evening sky. And his hair is so fair and long. He's like…like Prince Siegfried from *Swan Lake*."

Sonia stood up and fluffed her pillow. "You're really acting strange, Cammie."

Cammie felt blood rush to her cheeks. She turned to the side so Sonia wouldn't see her face. For the last thirty hours, the image of her rescuer hadn't left her even for a minute. Again and again, Cammie felt the west wind pressing against the sled. She remembered strong arms carrying her through the night in a…what lift had it been? Okay. Let it be the star lift. As Cammie closed her eyes, she felt the smooth fabric of the man's parka against her cheek. She saw Choctaw's bushy tail wagging ahead of her as the dog pulled the sled. "His dog is cute too," Cammie said. "Do you know what his name is? Choctaw."

Sonia's eyes widened. "Choctaw? Hmm. Maybe the man *is* a skater."

"That's what I'm telling you." Cammie threw off her covers and sat up. The room spun a little, but she ignored the unpleasant feeling. "You know what, Sonia? I'm in love!" As soon as Cammie said those words, a warm, fuzzy ball began to grow in her chest, filling her with joy. She couldn't wait to get to the rink and dance her heart out. Perhaps...perhaps, she could ask Ryan, the sound man, to play the soundtrack from *Swan Lake*.

"Sonia, have you ever loved anybody?" Cammie lay down on her stomach and rested her chin on her folded hands.

"Uh, no. Not yet."

"I thought maybe Jeff. You know, he really likes you."

"Jeff...yeah, I know. He's nice. But Alex likes you too."

"Alex?"

Cammie couldn't believe Sonia had said that. She had known Alex for four years and always considered him her closest friend. Alex was smart, funny, and a talented skater. They had been through a lot together. But Cammie would never think of Alex as a boyfriend.

"Alex is just a...friend," Cammie said slowly. "But that man...he was different. Prince Siegfried. That's what I'll call him. There's something mysterious about him, like he's not from this world. And if he only asked me…" Cammie stared into space. "If he only wanted me to follow him…anywhere, I would."

Sonia shook her head. "Cammie, I don't think—"

There was a knock on the door. Cammie jerked backward and fell on her pillow. The door opened, and Mrs. Page walked in, a pale green scarf wrapped around her head. The dorm supervisor was carrying a tray.

"Here's your lunch, Cammie," Mrs. Page said. "How are you feeling today?"

"Fine. Thank you." Cammie sat up again and lowered her feet on the carpet. "Thank you, Mrs. Page, but I could eat downstairs."

"And where do you think you're going?" Mrs. Page barked.

That was a ridiculous question considering that Cammie was a competitive skater. "To the practice. It's after twelve already."

"Oh no you're not going. Here." Mrs. Page pushed a plate with a grilled chicken sandwich closer to Cammie.

"What?"

"Yes, and your medicine. Take it now, and then another pill at night. The doctor wants you to take this antibiotic today and tomorrow." Mrs. Page handed Cammie a white pill and a glass of water.

Not to make the dorm supervisor upset, Cammie swallowed the pill obediently. "Mrs. Page, honestly, I can skate. I—"

"Cammie, spare me the tantrums, all right?" With a grimace of pain, Mrs. Page rubbed her temples. "I have my hands full making Dana eat."

Cammie glanced at Sonia, who was lacing her skates.

"Dana passed out in the gym," Sonia said.

"A witch's attack?" Cammie asked.

She wouldn't be surprised if one of the Skateland witches had chosen Dana as a target. The witches hated all promising skaters. And even though Dana's technique had suffered lately, the girl was surely—

"Ha!" Mrs. Page put two spoons of sugar into Cammie's tea. "The witches aren't always the culprits. It was Dana's obsession with losing weight. You girls tell me, can a skater survive four hours of skating on two cups of tea and two carrot sticks? What do you think?"

Cammie and Sonia exchanged helpless glances.

"That's it, then," Mrs. Page said almost triumphantly. "And you, Cammie, how could you stay outside in a storm? What were you thinking?"

Cammie sighed. "But I had to finish my assignment. Hey, isn't it due today? I couldn't finish it yesterday, so—"

"Don't worry!" Sonia smiled at her. "Technically, the deadline is today, but because it's Saturday, you can hand in your essay on Monday. It's official."

Cammie chuckled. "I bet it's Mr. Stevens's way of getting us to finish the essay on time."

"Well, that settles it." Mrs. Page took the empty plate and cup away from Cammie. "You can work on your essay now."

"But, Mrs. Page, skating is more important!" Cammie pleaded. "I need to move up to novice, but my double jumps are still nowhere close."

The dorm supervisor gave her a skeptical look. "If you develop a serious illness, your doubles will be the last thing on your mind. So back to bed! Let's go downstairs, Sonia."

As Cammie watched her roommate follow Mrs. Page out of the room, she remembered one more thing. "Mrs. Page, do you know the man who brought me to the dorm Thursday night? Who is he?"

Mrs. Page froze in the doorframe. "Actually, I was going to ask you the same question. Where did you meet him?"

"Well, I accidentally skated into the Icy Park and—"

Mrs. Page spread her arms. "Accidentally? How come I'm not surprised?"

"But I didn't mean to. I lost my way!" Cammie cried out. When the dorm supervisor didn't say anything, Cammie went on. "Really, Mrs. Page, are you sure you never met that man? He also has a white husky who pulls his sled."

Mrs. Page raised her head abruptly. "A husky pulling a sled? I've lived in Skateland all my life, but I've never heard of anyone using dogs and sleds as a means of transportation. Cammie, I want you to promise me that you'll never set a foot in the Icy Park again. Do you hear me?"

"Not unless I absolutely have to," Cammie said sincerely.

Mrs. Page didn't seem to hear her. "My goodness, that man could have been a warlock. You know what? He did look suspicious dressed all in black."

Muttering under her breath, Mrs. Page walked out of the room with Sonia trailing her.

As the door closed behind the two of them, Cammie pulled the covers to her chin. Could Mrs. Page be right? Was her handsome prince Siegfried a warlock?

The next week turned out to be one of the most demanding in Cammie's life. With the history essay out of the way, she finally managed to concentrate on her jumps. She worked extra hard. Cammie couldn't wait to make it to the novice level, so she could practice at the Yellow Rink, where Sonia, Jeff, and Alex skated. At that point, the only other intermediate skaters from Cammie's class were Liz and Dana.

During her last practice session, Cammie realized that she couldn't even do a single loop. There was no way her coach would allow her to take her freestyle test unless she could land all of her doubles consistently.

"Coach Ferguson!" Cammie looked around, hoping her coach would give her some tips.

"She's on the phone. And it's that guy again," Kelly said.

Cammie watched Kelly complete a beautiful triple toe loop. "Who is that man?"

The older girl shrugged. "How would I know? Ferguson doesn't share the details of her private life with me."

Feeling lost, Cammie asked Kelly if she could help her with her jumps. Unfortunately, even though Kelly was a strong skater, she didn't seem to have any coaching abilities. Her advice about a proper weight shift and arm position left Cammie even more confused.

"All right, Cammie. Are you ready to skate your program for me?" Coach Ferguson's eyes were bright, and she looked as though she could barely conceal a smile.

What's she so happy about? Cammie thought as she took her starting position.

She somehow managed to land her first jump, the double flip, but the rest of the program was a disaster. When she finally skated up to Coach Ferguson, she had to bite her lower lip to keep tears from streaming down her cheeks. She watched the expression of joy leave the coach's face.

"Cammie, I'm sorry but you aren't ready for your test."

Cammie took a deep sigh. "But—"

"We'll just keep working on those jumps. Don't get discouraged, you'll move up to novice in no time."

Something was really going on with Coach Ferguson, Cammie had never seen her so happy. Yet she would prefer her coach to be more serious about Cammie's novice test. It was really time to move up. For example, Sonia, who was also fourteen, was about to take her senior test. And Cammie would have to keep practicing at the Green Rink with younger kids. Life was really unfair!

Cammie spent the morning of the test skating aimlessly around Skateland and didn't return to the dorm till four o'clock. She dragged her feet to the third floor of the dorm building, pausing at each floor, listening in. She didn't want Mrs. Page to walk out of her room just to tell Cammie for the umpteenth time that not being able to move up a level wasn't a disaster at all. Yeah, right! Fourteen-year-old girls who were serious about skating worked on their triples, not doubles.

She also hoped Sonia would be out with Jeff, celebrating her moving up to seniors, for Cammie had no doubt Sonia had passed both tests with flying colors. Sonia's skating life was perfect; the girl never messed up.

Yet when Cammie opened the door to her room, there was a surprise awaiting her. Seated in bed, on top of the covers, was Sonia. The girl still wore her skating clothes, a black skirt and a pink blouse, and her eyes were red and puffy. A man sat on one of the chairs across from Sonia, patting the girl's hand. Perched on the edge of Sonia's bed was a slender woman with blonde streaks in her dark brown hair. The woman's beige cashmere pants went well with a white wool turtleneck.

As Cammie froze in the doorframe, the woman fixed her coffee-colored eyes on her. "Oh, hi there! You must be Cammie. Sonia told us a lot about you."

I hope good things, Cammie thought, forcing a polite smile. She already realized the couple were Sonia's parents.

The man looked around and jumped to his feet. "Hello, beautiful skater. I'm Jarod, Sonia's father, and this is Leanne, Sonia's mother."

"Nice to meet you," Cammie said as she watched Jarod step forward to hug her. Judging from his perfect posture and the way he moved, the man could easily be identified as a skater. Cammie also saw that Sonia had inherited her father's blue eyes and freckles.

"Uh…you guys probably want to talk in private." Cammie shifted her eyes to Sonia's mother. "I'll go to the living room and—"

"Oh, of course, you should stay!" Jarod pushed his hands through his red curls. "We are going out for dinner. Would you like to join us, Cammie?"

"Uh…thank you, but I really can't."

"Except that we don't really have a reason to celebrate," Sonia's mother said, lifting her perfect eyebrows.

"I failed my moves test," Sonia said in a small voice.

"No!" Cammie couldn't even hide her shock.

Leanne slid off Sonia's bed and folded her arms on her chest. A whiff of French perfume reached Cammie's nostrils. "When will you learn the importance of work ethic, Sonia? You really let me and your father down."

What? How could anyone accuse Sonia of not working hard?

"Sonia is the most dedicated skater I know," Cammie said.

Leanne pressed her full lips together. "You probably don't know that many good skaters, then. How did you do, by the way?"

"I didn't test today."

Leanne's eyes darted back and forth between Cammie and Sonia. "So what level are you? Novice?"

"Intermediate." Cammie felt heat spread up her neck to her cheeks.

"Intermediate?" Leanne stared at her as though Cammie had just stepped onto the ice with her skate guards on. "I thought Sonia and you were the same age."

As much as Cammie wanted to stay calm, that was more than she could take. Tears rushed out of her eyes. "That's enough, Leanne." Jarod turned to Cammie. "Look, Cammie, it's all right. I only moved up to novice at fourteen. How about you, Leanne?"

"I was twelve, and my partner was thirteen. And you two..." Leanne glared at Cammie and Sonia. "If you want to be champion skaters, you need to become more serious."

"More serious than they already are? But it'll be scary to even be in the same room with them!" Jarod jumped to his feet, his freckled face twisted in an expression of sheer terror.

Cammie and Sonia chuckled.

"That's better!" Jarod said. "Anyway, girls, in case you don't remember, Leanne and I are here for the show."

Cammie glanced at Sonia.

"*Magic on Ice*, remember?" Sonia said.

"Ah!"

Of course, Cammie had heard about the famous show *Magic on Ice* performing in Skateland. She had always wanted to see a skating rendition of one of the famous fairy tales. However, with all of her practices, tests, and schoolwork, she hadn't realized the performance would take place that weekend. Now it was probably too late to get tickets.

"We gave Sonia three extra tickets," Jarod said.

"For you, Jeff, and Alex." Sonia smiled faintly.

"Not that you girls deserve it," Leanne said.

Behind her back, Jarod did an exaggerated gasp. Cammie and Sonia stifled grins.

Leanne sighed and took a tube of lipstick and a small mirror out of her black Gucci pocketbook. "You'd better get dressed, Sonia. We have a reservation at Skater's Finest Food."

Sonia headed for her closet.

"Mr. Harrison, who else will be in the show?" Cammie asked.

The man waved his hand. "Just call me Jarod. Okay. Let me see...Karen Ballack and Gaston Bouchard. They are our best friends."

"Oh, wow!" Cammie felt a rush of excitement. She had always dreamed of watching the two-time world champions perform live.

Leanne put away her lipstick and mirror. "And don't forget the infamous Elliot Monroe."

"Elliot Monroe..." Cammie repeated. She had definitely heard the name before.

"He skated pairs with his wife, Felicia, about ten years ago. Right, Mom?" Sonia appeared wearing tight black pants and a light blue sweater.

"One of the most beautiful couples I've ever seen," Leanne said quietly. "What a tragedy!"

"Elliot never really got over it. At least he's finally performing, though as a singles skater. He won't hear of another partner." Jarod sounded sad.

"What happened?" Cammie looked at the three of them.

Sonia averted her eyes.

"Felicia fell from a lift and died," Jarod said curtly. "Unfortunately, skating accidents happen. That's why you girls need to be extra careful."

Cammie shivered. Could someone really die from a skating accident? How terrible! Skating was supposed to be fun. It was beautiful, uplifting.

Jarod stood up. "We'd better go eat. Are you sure you won't change your mind, Cammie?"

Cammie smiled and shook her head. "Thank you very much, but I promised Mrs. Page I would have dinner with her tonight."

"Okay. Enjoy your meal. We'll see you tomorrow at the show, then," Jarod said cheerfully.

Leanne nodded slightly as she walked out of the room, Sonia by her side. Cammie waited for the door to close behind the Harrisons. Then she lowered herself on the floor and started unlacing her skating boots. She wanted the day to be over. Perhaps tomorrow would bring her something good. She would see a show, and watching famous skaters would take her mind off her lack of progress. Cammie's mind went back to Elliot Monroe, who had lost his wife in a skating accident. Now that was a tragedy. Not moving up to the novice level was nothing compared to the death of a loved one.

Cammie changed into her old jeans and a sweatshirt. She should probably go downstairs for dinner. Yet, although it had been hours since she had had lunch, she had no desire to eat. She jumped into bed and pulled the covers over her head.

On Sunday afternoon, at four thirty, Cammie and Sonia took their seats in the front of one of the top rows facing Main Square Rink. Skateland authorities had anticipated a big turnout, so it had been decided that the *Magic on Ice* show would take place outside, on Main Square. As Cammie looked around, she realized that the houses encircling the square had been turned into grandstands. As far as she could see, there were bleachers. The seats rose to the tops of the buildings. They encircled the small stores. Some of the benches were so close to the ice that the fans would probably be able to shake the performers' hands without even getting up.

"Yes, those seats are closer to the ice, but we will be able to see the skaters better from here," Sonia said. "Trust Dad. He knows how to choose the best seats."

"Your dad is so cool!" Cammie wrapped her coat tighter around her body. "Did your parents win any medals at the Olympics or the worlds?"

"Dad medaled at the nationals as a singles skater a few times. He never got a medal at the worlds, though. Mom was an ice dancer. She did win a few international competitions with her partner, but they didn't get to go to the worlds or the Olympics."

"It must be great to have professional skaters for parents," Cammie said.

Sonia sighed. "Yes and no. Of course, they always give me good advice. Yet, there's a lot of pressure too. For Mom, skating is all about hard work. Dad is different. He believes it's important to loosen up and have fun."

"Hey, here they are!"

Cammie turned around. Alex and Jeff were pressing through the crowd, approaching them.

"Where were you yesterday? I was looking for you." Alex sat down to the right of Cammie. His face was pink from frosty air, and his green wool hat brought out the color of his eyes.

"Don't you know?" Cammie asked glumly.

"What're you talking about?"

"Coach Ferguson wouldn't let me take my freestyle test." She sighed. "I'm still having problems with my jumps."

"So what? There is always next time. Just practice more."

If there was one thing Cammie liked about Alex, it was his nonchalant attitude. She wished she could take defeats with patience and grace. Last year, for example, her friend had come in fifth at a qualifying competition, missing the nationals by just one spot. Yet Cammie had never heard Alex complain.

Down below, the electricians were testing spotlights. A black-and-yellow Zamboni glided across the ice. Mr. Walrus must have recognized the four of them, for he lifted his gloved hand in a sign of greeting.

The sun slid below the horizon. The darkening sky was trimmed with crimson streaks.

Jeff rubbed his hands. "Hmm. It's nice up here but colder than I thought."

"Hand, head, and boot warmers anybody?" a female voice sounded from Cammie's right.

Cammie turned around and saw a slender, middle-aged woman holding what looked like ordinary wool mittens and gloves.

"Aren't you cold, ma'am?" Alex asked.

As Cammie took a closer look, she realized that the woman was definitely underdressed. All she had on was a thin wool turtleneck and blue jeans. Of course, she also wore a bright red wool hat and matching mittens.

"I'm actually hot," the lady replied with a grin. "And it's all because of my calorific clothes."

Cammie wrinkled her forehead. "Calo-what?"

The woman loosened her red scarf. "Do you guys see my hat, scarf, mittens, and boot covers? Those are calorific clothes, Mr. Reed's latest invention. They have built-in batteries that keep the fabric hot for hours. Of course, you need to recharge the batteries by placing the clothes on the radiator every night."

"Awesome! How much do you want for them?" Jeff took a twenty-dollar bill out of his pocket.

"Just five dollars apiece. It's a fifty percent discount because of the show," the woman replied with a wink.

"I have enough." Sonia reached for her money. "I want everything in yellow please."

"Our rink signature color, huh?" Jeff studied the display on the woman's tray.

"There's no way all of us will wear the same color. So it'll be black for me." Alex handed the money to the woman and replaced his own hat with the new black one. "Hey, it feels like a heating pad!"

"Okay. I'll wear navy blue." Jeff pulled the covers over his skating boots.

"What about you, Cammie?" Sonia put on her yellow mittens. "They are warm!"

"Purple, please," Cammie said with determination.

Sonia's eyes sparkled. "What happened to the pink?"

Cammie faked a sigh. "I'm getting too old for that." As she got into her new calorific clothes, she realized that they were worth every penny she had spent. Pleasant warmth spread all over her body. She felt as though she sat in a hot tub. She let out a sign of relief and looked around.

The grandstands were filled with people of all ages. Right across from Cammie, on the other side of the rink, there was a brightly lit display window advertising skating clothes. A few people sat inside in folding chairs. Light poured out from every window of the apartments above the store, and Cammie could discern dark figures of people looking outside.

"Programs, anyone?" A girl of about eighteen waved a stack of brochures in their direction.

"How much are they?" Sonia reached for her purse again.

"A dollar." The girl handed Sonia a brightly colored booklet.

Alex patted his coat pocket. "I'm broke."

Cammie and Jeff nodded in agreement.

"Don't worry. We'll take turns," Sonia said. She quickly flipped through the pages and then passed the program to Cammie.

The front and the back of the booklet were decorated with pictures of the show participants. Cammie thought she would have more time to study those later and turned the page. "*Magic on Ice* is an engaging show that combines impeccable skating technique with exquisite artistry and storytelling." Cammie moved to the next page. "*Magic on Ice* is giving an interpretation of the story The Snow Queen." Even though Cammie had heard of the fairy tale, she had never read it before. She decided to go over the summary, hoping that knowing the story line would help her to concentrate on the skaters' performance better.

The fairy tale was about a boy and a girl who were good friends. The boy's name was Kai, and the girl's name was Gerda. One day, the boy got a piece of ice in his heart and became mean and cruel. Then he was kidnapped by the evil Snow Queen. So Gerda went to look for her friend. On the way to the Snow Queen's palace, she met an old woman who could do magic, a princess, and a gang of robbers. Finally, as the girl reached the Snow Queen's palace, she kissed Kai. The piece of ice in the boy's heart melted, and he became his old self again.

"Nice story," Cammie said as she passed the program to Alex.

Before Alex had a chance to open the booklet, the lights dimmed, and then a bright spotlight shot out from the dark. A small figure clad in a long, black dress glided to the middle of the rink. Cammie recognized Wilhelmina Van Uffeln, the president of Skateland.

"Dear fellow skaters, coaches, parents, and guests," Wilhelmina said in her slightly husky voice. "It's my great pleasure to welcome all of you to the performance of *Magic on Ice*. Let us give a warm Skateland greeting to the participants of the crew."

The audience burst out with applause.

"Yes!" Jeff shouted.

Alex whistled loudly.

Wilhelmina smiled into the grandstands, her hair sparkling silver. "While a lot could be said about *Magic on Ice,* I'm sure the best thing would be to let the music and skating speak for themselves. Let the show begin!"

The spotlight went off, and then a tiny, pinkish beam of light glided across the ice. A boy and a girl sat in the middle of the rink amidst bright flowers. As the boy and the girl stood up to perform a waltz, Cammie realized that they were very advanced skaters.

"Those are Allison Yang and Griffin Walton, junior national champions," Sonia whispered.

Now Cammie recognized the couple too. Of course, she had seen them on Kanga's media player. As the show moved on, Cammie found herself more and more involved in the story. The Snow Queen appeared, riding a sparkling white sled.

Sonia pressed Cammie's hand. "That's Karen Ballock."

Cammie had recognized the famous skater even before Sonia mentioned her name. The woman had won the nationals five times, and she had medaled at the worlds more than once. Mesmerized, Cammie watched the woman take off the ice in a huge triple salchow followed by a double toe loop. None of the skaters Cammie had seen before seemed to have Karen's outstanding springing ability. Somehow, the woman made triples look like simple waltz jumps. She looked perfectly relaxed and light as a feather.

Jeff turned to Sonia. "You aren't any worse!"

"Are you nuts?" Sonia squeaked.

"Shh!" an angry male voice said from behind them.

Down on the ice, Gerda, who was looking for Kai, was forced to stay in the house of an old woman who could do magic.

Cammie felt Sonia squeeze her elbow. "That's Mom!

"Oh!" Cammie craned her neck. As much as she disliked Sonia's mother, she had to admit that the woman was amazing. She glided across the arena noiselessly, and her twizzles seemed endless.

"What part is your father playing?" Cammie asked Sonia.

To her surprise, Sonia chuckled. "Let's see if you'll recognize him."

As the show moved on, Cammie didn't see any skater who looked like Jarod Harrison. The prince was a tall, dark-haired man, definitely not Sonia's father. The princess who gave Gerda some clothes and sent her to look for Kai in a sled was a beautiful blonde. The sled was later attacked by a gang of robbers led by an old woman, who looked a little like the Witch of Fear. The gang leader skated around the rink, brandishing a knife. Her lipstick was bright red.

"That's Dad, "Sonia said.

"The first robber on the left? The one with a bow and arrows?" Cammie asked.

Alex leaned across Cammie to face Sonia. "No. That guy is Asian. Sonia's father is second from the right, the one with a sword and a shield."

Sonia giggled. "Nope."

"I know, but I won't tell." Jeff folded his arms on his chest, looking amused.

Cammie leaned back. "Okay. I give up."

"The gang leader." Sonia pointed to the wild-looking woman who was doing a camel spin in the middle of the rink.

"What?" Cammie strained her eyes, unable to believe.

"He's a terrific skater!" Alex exclaimed.

"And he's a great actor too," Sonia said. "I wish he could do more shows. But he's too involved in coaching."

"Oh, wow!" Alex rose in his seat. "Look at that beauty!"

Cammie followed his stare. There was a petite girl in the middle of the ice. She wore a brown leather skirt and a vest trimmed with fur. Cammie realized that the petite skater was playing the part of the Little Robber Girl. The girl did a perfect split jump, touching her toes with her hands.

Jeff slapped himself on the knee. "She sure is flexible and cute too."

"Wow!" Alex said again.

"That's Celine Bouchard, the daughter of Karen Ballock and Gaston Bouchard," Sonia said. For some reason, she sounded annoyed.

"I've never seen anyone as beautiful as her!" Jeff leaned forward.

"Actually, she isn't that good. Her jumps are—" Sonia said.

"Not good?" Alex shouted. "What do you understand? She's incredible!"

"Young people, if you don't behave, I'll ask security to escort you out!" the man behind them croaked.

They cringed in their seats.

"Hey, that guy isn't bad," Alex whispered as he pointed to a tall man wearing a reindeer costume. He was performing an intricate footwork on ice. Suddenly, he lifted himself in the air in a beautiful double axel.

Alex exhaled loudly. "I can't believe the height he's getting."

"That's Elliot Monroe!" Sonia said. "Dad says it took them all a while to talk Elliot into performing with *Magic on Ice*. He's still—"

"Wait!" Cammie jumped to her feet, her heart somewhere in the bottom of her stomach.

"Sit down!" the man behind her hissed.

"No, it's…he's—"

Alex pulled her down. "Did you see a witch?"

The reindeer pulled the sled in which Gerda sat, waving good-bye to the robbers.

"It's him!" Cammie cuddled her cheeks in her mittened hands, her eyes fixed firmly on the man who was moving in a fast combination spin. The skater rode out of the spin, and Cammie saw the familiar blue eyes, the perfectly shaped nose, and the dimple on his chin.

"This is the man who rescued me the night of the snowstorm!"

She felt joy bubble within her. It warmed her up. She didn't need her calorific clothes anymore. That was it. She knew who her rescuer was. It was Elliot Monroe, a famous skater. She had found her Prince Charming.

"Cammie, wake up!" Someone shook her by the shoulder.

Cammie blinked. "What?"

"The show is over," Sonia said.

Alex jumped from his seat. "The skaters are going to sign autographs. Come on. We might be able to talk to Celine Bouchard."

"Right!" Jeff clapped his hands.

"Guys!" Sonia gave them a look of reproach. The boys ignored her. Sonia turned to Cammie. "Can you believe it?"

"Sure. Let's go talk to the skaters," Cammie said quickly. If she was lucky enough, she might be able to get Prince Elliot's attention. Would he recognize her? Cammie's hands got sweaty with excitement. She took off her purple mittens.

Down on the arena, the skaters were making a final round, waving to the audience.

"Bravo!" the people cheered.

Alex rummaged through the pockets of his parka. "It would be nice to give Celine flowers or something. Do you have any money left, Cammie?"

"No. I've spent everything on my calorific clothes," Cammie said.

Alex clicked his tongue. "Darn!"

They were forced to move very slowly. Everybody around them seemed to be anxious to get down to the arena. Cammie kept watching Prince Elliot as he stroked around the rink. What would she say to him? "You're a terrific skater?" No, that would be too childish. "I liked your spread eagle?" Hey, who was Cammie to judge the accomplished skater's moves? "Do you remember me?" And why would she want to ask him that? If he still remembered her, he would surely mention it. Okay, how about, "Mr. Monroe, I love you!" Gosh! Cammie felt hot as though she was walking through fire. She quickly unzipped her parka.

"The Champion Flowers store presents every show participant with a specifically designed bouquet!" a woman's voice came from the speakers.

A group of ladies wearing bright calf-length coats skated to the middle of the rink. Each skater received a huge bouquet. Bright multicolored flowers were intertwined with snowflake garlands.

Jeff groaned. "They're ahead of us!"

Alex sighed gravely.

"Sweet Blades is happy to honor every performer with newly made candy called *Royal Blades*."

"Oh, here's their AD!" Sonia pointed to a flashing sign across the street. It pictured transparent hard candy shaped like a blade emblazoned with a crown.

"And another special prize for the show participants, something that will restore their strength after the tiring performance." The voice sounded at the very top of the grandstands, directly behind Cammie. She looked up, but she couldn't see the speaker.

"Ice Spiced Soda!" the man shouted.

The crowd was very thick. People jostled Cammie from all sides. Someone brushed against her head, causing her calorific hat to slide off. Cammie tried to adjust the hat, but her arms were pressed tight to her body.

"Excuse me! Coming through! Do you mind letting me in?"

Cammie turned right and finally saw the man who had been advertising Ice Spiced Soda. He was tall and young, probably in his twenties. He carried two cartons filled with small crystal bottles.

"I need to get these down." The man appeared lost. There was no way he could break through the crowd.

"Why don't you just pass these down?" a short, elderly woman suggested.

"Uh…okay. Do you guys mind?" The young man handed his cartons to the people around him.

Cammie watched the crystal bottles travel from hand to hand, all the way down to the rink. Karen Ballock got her drink and mouthed a quick thank-you. Celine Bouchard raised her bottle over her head, saluting the crowd. Sonia's father took a swig from his bottle and gave the vendor a thumbs-up.

"And here's the last one." Someone put a bottle in Cammie's hand. It felt pleasantly heavy. The blue liquid inside bubbled and sparkled.

This soda must be terrific, Cammie thought as she gave the bottle to Sonia, who then passed it to the young woman in front of her. Cammie saw that Elliot Monroe was the only skater who hadn't received his drink yet. She rose on her toes to see the man accept the bottle. Yet five minutes passed, and the last bottle of Ice Spiced Soda still hadn't reached its destination.

"Where is it?" Cammie hopped on her skate guards, trying to locate the missing drink. The crowd blocked her view. Before Cammie had a chance to ask Alex if he could see something, a bloodcurdling shriek shook the air.

"What?" Instinctively, Cammie covered her ears with her hands.

"There was poison in that bottle. Now I'm going to die. Help me, please!"

"It's Winja!" Alex shouted.

Cammie squeaked and grabbed Alex's hand. So there were witches at the rink. But the cops had promised Wilhelmina there would be tight security during the show. Now it looked as though Winja had attacked someone.

"Look!" Jeff yelled, pointing to the ice.

Cammie looked down, and her mouth opened wide. A woman lay on the snow close to the edge of the rink, writhing in obvious pain. Her long, bandaged arms flailed erratically. She was kicking the ice with her left blade. Two crutches sat in the snow next to the witch.

"What's wrong with her?" Cammie felt confused.

Winja, which was short for the Witch of Injuries, was known for inflicting terrible injuries on talented skaters. She had attacked Jeff twice. Last year, the Witch of Injuries had cursed Cammie, causing her to break her ankle. Now, however, Winja acted as though she was in pain. What was going on?

"Everybody step aside. Police!" Captain Greenfield appeared from the crowd and bent over the screaming witch.

Most of the people hurried away. Some stayed where they were, hungry for further news. Alex grabbed Cammie's hand, and the two of them pushed their way forward. Jeff and Sonia followed.

"Get the ambulance, Lieutenant. Now!" Captain Greenfield said to a dark-haired young man.

Before Cammie knew, two strong-looking men showed up. As Winja was transported to a stretcher, she kept whining. "My insides are burning. Ouch. Can't you be gentle? Oh my gosh. Am I going to die? I know who did it to me. It's the Witch of Destruction for sure. And I wouldn't put it pass the Witch of Fear either. Ah-ah-ah!"

"Why would the witches attack one another?" Cammie whispered to Alex.

"Beats me." His eyes were fixed on the taillights of the emergency icemobile.

"It's skaters they hate. So—"

"All right, people! Move on! Show's over!" Captain Greenfield said.

"Oh!" Cammie looked back at the ice arena. Perhaps it wasn't too late to say hi to Prince Elliot. But it was indeed too late. The rink was empty, except for Mr. Walrus's Zamboni, which was slowly making its way out from one of the side streets.

COACH FERGUSON'S SECRET

"If I don't make it as a professional skater, I'll definitely become a reporter," Jeff said. "What can be easier than that? Just write what you want and the readers will buy every stupid thing."

"I'm with you, buddy!" Alex stuffed the rest of his dark chocolate skating boot into his mouth and gave Jeff a high-five. Cammie and Sonia giggled over their glasses of crossover cocktail.

The four of them sat at a window table at Sweet Blades. They still had an hour before their afternoon practice, so instead of heading to their dorms to rest, the four of them decided to talk about what had happened the night before. They simply couldn't keep their thoughts to themselves. The whole day at Skateland School had been filled with speculations and suppositions.

"This stupid reporter has absolutely no doubt the attacker was after Winja." Jeff unfolded the last issue of *Skateland Daily News*. Almost half of the paper was filled with the accounts of yesterday's attack during the *Magic on Ice* show.

Cammie looked at the paragraph Jeff had underlined.

> Our reporter stopped by the hospital to talk to the victim. At the sight of Wanda Hopkins, the poor woman's eyes lit up with joy. A moment later, however, tears clouded Winja's beautiful, powder blue eyes. "It's so nice to be talking to someone who cares! Visitors? Of course not. My fellow witches want me dead. That's for sure. Of course, I know who did it to me. The Witch of Destruction has been plotting to get rid of me for years. She sabotaged me at competitions; she has ruined every chance I ever had to get into a professional skating show. Why? Well, she just hates me too much. She is jealous of my exquisite skating style. You must have seen her. The Witch of Destruction has absolutely no technique; she pulls off those doubles on pure strength. And she is nothing but a muscular oaf; she has no grace whatsoever. You've got to help me! I'm sure the Witch of Destruction isn't going to give up."
>
> Skateland community hopes Skateland authorities will assign the poor woman a bodyguard to ensure her protection.

Sonia smirked. "What do you expect of this Wanda woman? She never checks out the facts."

"Oh, that's for sure!" Cammie exclaimed.

She knew the author of the editorial too well. Last year, Wanda had interviewed Cammie after her golden performance at Skateland Annual Competition. Cammie had been so happy that she had slightly exaggerated her skills, telling the woman she was working on her triple salchow. The woman had blown Cammie's words out of proportion, writing in her articles that Cammie had already landed all of her triples. Coach Ferguson hadn't been too happy.

"Oh, look! There is a comment from a doctor!" Sonia pointed to a small article in the bottom of the page.

> The toxicology test confirmed that the bottle of Ice Spiced Soda was filled with Raal, an extremely toxic substance. Apparently, the attacker injected the solution into the bottle. The expertise confirmed that the lid had a tiny hole. Raal is a deadly poison. No individual who has taken even a small dose of it is expected to live. It appears that Winja is an extremely lucky woman. I'm still not quite sure how Winja managed to survive the deadly attack. At this point, her condition has stabilized, and I believe that she will make a complete recovery.

"Amazing!" Jeff said. "Winja has messed up the career of so many skaters, yet she ends up healthy even after taking a deadly poison."

"But Winja couldn't have been the target of the attack," Sonia said.

"Of course. Winja probably got thirsty, so she stole the last bottle. And now she's trying to make it look like whoever put that poison in the bottle was after her," Jeff said.

Alex nodded. "That Ice Spiced Soda wasn't even meant for Winja. There were only enough bottles for the show skaters."

"It means the attacker wanted to kill someone from the show," Jeff said slowly.

"But who?" Sonia whispered.

Cammie grimaced at the cold grasp of fear inside her. The truth was too scary to digest.

"It could have been anybody," Alex said.

"My parents!" Sonia shuddered.

"Celine!" Alex said meaningfully.

Jeff raised his index finger. "That's right!"

"But…but the only skater who didn't get his bottle of Ice Spiced Soda was Elliot Monroe!" Cammie looked at her friends' grim faces. "Isn't it obvious the last bottle was meant for him?"

"Hmm. That's a possibility," Jeff said.

Alex shook his head. "That's too much of a coincidence. How could the attacker be sure Elliot Monroe and not someone else would get the bottle?"

"Elliot Monroe was the last in line," Cammie said.

"I don't think it was in the script." Sonia creased her forehead. "Elliot just happened to be at the very end of the line."

"Can you ask your parents if skaters do their final round in certain order?" Alex asked.

Sonia shrugged. "Of course, but I'm pretty sure they skate around in random order."

"Well, if that's the case, the attacker didn't care which of the show participants would get hurt," Jeff said. "He or she simply wanted to kill a top skater."

"How about the vendor who sold Ice Spiced Soda?" Sonia asked.

Jeff flipped through the pages. "He's completely cleared. Listen. 'The owner of the store To Skater's Satisfaction confirms that he personally handed the bottles to the man and they were all right.' No, it looks like the attacker bought his own bottle and filled it with poison."

Alex raised his head. "That's right. He must have stolen one of the bottles from the vendor and replaced it with his own, the one with the poison."

"But who did it?" Sonia's baby blue eyes shifted from one face to another.

"Who but the witches?" Cammie asked. "I can't understand why Wilhelmina hasn't thrown them all out of Skateland."

"I guess you're right. Look here." Jeff showed them an article on page two.

> Mrs. Van Uffeln, the president of Skateland, isn't pleased with the security measures that were imposed during *Magic on Ice* show. On Sunday night, she invited Captain Greenfield, the head of Skateland police department, and Seymour Dawson, the security chief to her office.
>
> "I believe my people did their best," Mr. Dawson said. "We checked everybody who went into the grandstands. I can assure you: none of the witches were among the spectators."

Mr. Greenfield, however, seemed to disagree. "I personally scanned the audience at the end of the show and I saw at least seven witches there."

Cammie almost spilled her cocktail. "Seven?"

"That's what is written," Jeff said.

"I always knew that those cops were a bunch of idiots." Alex smirked. "Especially that dork Lieutenant Turner."

Cammie kept reading. "'That same night, Skateland witches were brought into the police headquarters for questioning. Each of them denied playing any part in the attacks during the show.'"

Alex clicked his tongue. "What do they expect the witches to do, confess?"

"'While no arrests have been made, the witches are still our primary suspects,' Captain Greenfield said. 'The investigation is still on going.'"

Jeff folded the newspaper and put it in his skating bag.

"Well?" Cammie said.

Sonia stared at her.

"What're we going to do?" Cammie asked.

"I guess we'll leave the whole thing to the cops." Alex finished his cocktail with a big slurp and stood up.

"Anyway, who cares if the witches kill one another?" Jeff jumped off the chair and stretched. "Got to go."

Sonia glanced at her watch. "Oh, yes. We barely have enough time to make it to practice."

"But what if the witches try to poison someone else?" Cammie exclaimed.

"I guess we have to be careful with what we eat and drink," Alex said. "Don't accept anything from strangers, and watch your back. Anyway, let's go."

Outside, Cammie watched as the three of them headed in the direction of the Yellow Rink. Then she pulled on her gloves and sprinted to her Green Rink.

The green-painted lobby of the rink was deserted, which worked in Cammie's favor. Ignoring the readings of the clock that said 4:30 p.m., she sprinted across the carpeted floor in her skate guards and pulled the door leading to the arena. A blast of music pounded her eardrums. The tune was vaguely familiar, and Cammie recognized it as *I've Got a Feeling*. She couldn't possibly imagine Coach Ferguson letting her skaters warm up to a modern hit.

Cammie put her skate guards on the boards and skated to the middle of the rink. Now, what was that? George was doing hip hop moves on his toes. Angela and Rita stood next to him, cheering and clapping. A few younger kids played in the far corner. The only skater who seemed to be practicing was Dana.

Liz waved at Cammie. "It's your lucky day. Ferguson's late!"

"She is?" That was good. At least Cammie wouldn't get in trouble for coming late. Although... Cammie slowed down, thinking hard. What if her coach's absence had something to do with yesterday's attack? What if the woman was hurt too?

Before Cammie could finish her thought, the door opened and a couple walked in. First, Cammie took them for skating parents from the Yellow Rink.

Mothers and fathers of most top skaters rode expensive icemobiles and wore designer clothes. Yet, as the woman removed her ice guards and walked onto the ice, a collective *ah* rolled across the rink. It was Coach Ferguson, but she didn't look her usual self. Instead of being pulled up, her hair streamed down her shoulders in perfect ringlets. Coach Ferguson had also replaced her usual green parka with a silvery gray fur coat.

"You look so pretty today, Coach Ferguson!" Angela sang.

"What a gorgeous coat!" Rita echoed.

"Is today your birthday?" George boomed, his face sweaty from his hip hop exercise.

Coach Ferguson tossed her head back and laughed. "Thank you for the nice words, girls! And, George, no, today isn't my birthday, though I do have an important announcement to make. But first, I'd like to introduce someone to you."

Coach Ferguson offered her hand to someone behind her. A tall man in a long cashmere coat stepped onto the ice. He wore rental skates, and by the tentative way he glided forward, Cammie realized the man wasn't a skater. He smiled at the puzzled kids, and Cammie couldn't help thinking that his teeth were too big and white.

"This is Mr. Deelan, skaters!" Coach Ferguson said. "He's my fiancé."

It became very quiet at the rink, and not only because someone turned off the CD player.

"I'm sorry, you guys, but I won't be able to coach you anymore," Coach Ferguson said. "I'm moving to San Diego."

Sonia shook her head. "Just like that?"

"Yes. And the man isn't even a skater. He's a book accountant," Cammie said bitterly.

"So who'll be in charge of the Green Rink, Coach Yvette?"

"Yes, her. But wait. It gets worse. Coach Yvette won't have time for all of us. So all Green Rink skaters are going to have an audition tomorrow."

Sonia looked puzzled. "What kind of an audition?"

"Ferguson said it was Wilhelmina's decision. 'Some of you might have outgrown the Green Rink and are in need of a change,'" Cammie quoted. "Urgh!"

"Gosh. It is terrible." Sonia's eyes darkened. "Tomorrow?"

"Yep. Right after morning practice. We'll have to cut school."

"But it gives you guys no time to get ready!"

"That's it. Who cares!" Cammie pounded her pillow. "That's exactly what I need now, when my jumps are off."

"Oh, you'll do fine. You're a good skater, and everybody knows it," Sonia said. "Did Coach Ferguson tell you who would be there to judge you?"

"All Skateland coaches. 'You guys can use an extra opportunity to perform in public.'" Cammie quoted her coach again.

"It does sound scary." Sonia grimaced. "Still, don't worry, Cammie! I'm sure they'll love you. Hey, you know what? You're almost a novice skater. What if Coach Darrel agrees to take you? Wouldn't that be great?"

That would be fantastic! Cammie thought of Darrel Johnson, the head coach of the Yellow Rink, the man who had worked with several Olympic and world medalists. Cammie had dreamed of working with the man even before she moved to Skateland. Of course, it wasn't news to her that Coach Darrel only took the best skaters.

For a kid who was lucky enough to be picked by the legendary coach, a medal at a major competition was almost a sure thing. Sonia, Jeff, and Alex had been working with Coach Darrel for over a year already. Of course, they were much better than Cammie. They could do triple jumps.

"Sonia, maybe you can ask Coach Darrel to take me," Cammie whispered. "Just tell him I'll work really hard."

Sonia stared at her as though Cammie showed up at a competition wearing shorts and boxing gloves. "Are you out of your mind? No one can just come up to Coach Darrel and ask him to take on a student. It's something he'll have to decide himself."

"Oh well." Cammie grabbed her bathrobe and headed for the bathroom. "I guess I'll have to do my best tomorrow."

Sonia gave her a reassuring look. "I'm sure everything will go well."

That night, Cammie didn't sleep well. She wished she had passed that novice freestyle test. As a novice skater, she would have moved to the Yellow Rink automatically. Would Coach Darrel want to work with someone who was only at the intermediate level?

Cammie pulled her covers over her head. She needed rest to pull off a good performance at the audition. The west wind howled outside, adding to her nervousness. Cammie rolled on her back, listening to Sonia's soft breathing. A clock ticked loudly from the wall.

I need to land my jumps perfectly tomorrow, Cammie thought.

When she finally fell asleep, she believed everything would be all right.

AUDITION

Cammie bent over and massaged her calves. She was the next to skate, so she was desperately trying to loosen up. Dana was on the ice, looking slimmer than she had in weeks and very determined. The girl's jumps still looked sloppy, though she had managed to land a couple of doubles.

Across from the entrance to the ice, Skateland coaches sat at a long table. Coach Greg from the Pink Rink whispered something to Coach Betsy, who worked at the Blue Rink. Coach Joanne, who was on the Yellow Rink staff, sat with her arms folded across her chest. She didn't seem to be interested in Dana's performance in the slightest.

Coach Darrel sat next to Wilhelmina, looking stylish. Today, he was dressed in a black velvet sport coat over a beige pullover and a white shirt. For Cammie, all the coaches were strangers. Coach Ferguson hadn't showed up. Either she didn't care about her former students' destiny or, which was more likely, she was already on her way to San Diego.

She's probably kissing Mr. Deelan now, Cammie thought angrily. *Isn't she afraid the man might bite her tongue off with those long, sharp teeth?*

Dana stepped off the ice looking red-cheeked and ruffled. Cammie moved over to let the girl pass.

"Cammie Wester!" the speaker announced.

Already? Cammie's heart dived into the pit of her stomach. She glided to the middle of the rink and moved her feet in the T-position, her arms over her head. Her knees buckled, and before she realized it, she sat on the ice.

The stands exhaled in a loud *ouch*. Her face hot, Cammie stood up awkwardly. Gosh, how could she fall before her music even started?

It's not going to work, she thought, feeling panicky.

The music was already playing, her *Romeo and Juliet* theme, but Cammie was so upset that she skidded off the beginning backward pivot. Suddenly, she couldn't remember what she was supposed to do next. She was painfully aware that everybody in the arena was watching her. Even though it was Tuesday, the news about the audition had spread around Skateland, bringing in quite a few curious spectators. They were probably laughing at the awkward girl who, for some ridiculous reason, pictured herself as a figure skater.

Okay, Cammie! Get a grip!

She did her best to focus. The first jump of her double salchow-double loop combination came out single. Before she realized what had happened, she was behind the music.

Forget the combination!

Her spiral sequence was next. Cammie arched her back and raised her leg as high as she could. Her extension had greatly improved during the last couple of years. She moved into her camel spin. It felt smooth and secure. She made sure her head was turned in the direction she was spinning. People's faces in the bleachers rushed by faster and faster.

As Cammie rode out of the spin, she glanced at the bleachers again. What? She couldn't believe it. Seated in the third row, just behind the coaches, was Elliot Monroe. Their eyes met, and Cammie could swear the man smiled at her. Miraculously, she felt her body relax. No, she wasn't giving up. She was a skater, for crying out loud. Now she would show them all what she could do. Cammie moved into backward crossovers, picking up speed, setting up for her double lutz.

"I can do it!" she said out loud.

The sound of her voice chased away the creeping fear. *Yes!* The jump came out high and secure. The music carried Cammie forward like a magical icemobile. Her footwork was smooth. Cammie sailed through her rockers and Choctaws as though they were nothing. She slightly two-footed her double flip, but she didn't care. The important thing was that the girl who moved across the ice was no longer a gangly scared skater but Juliet, a young, innocent girl who had fallen in love for the first time. Cammie landed a huge double loop. It might have been under-rotated, but it didn't matter. As she completed her change-foot spin, joy rose within her. She had done it. Her program hadn't fallen apart.

Breathing heavily, Cammie stepped off the ice. She took a seat in the front row and grabbed her water bottle.

Dana, pale and sickly looking, leaned over Liz to squeeze Cammie's hand. "Not bad."

"Thanks. You were good too."

Cammie glanced at the coaches, who were deeply involved in a discussion of some sort. Coach Greg was scribbling on a piece of paper. Coach Darrell appeared to be listening to Wilhelmina. Yet, as Cammie lifted her eyes to the third row, she realized that Elliot Monroe wasn't there anymore. Why had he come to the audition in the first place?

What if he wanted to see me skate? A voice whispered in her ear. *What if... what if he likes me?*

"What're you smiling at? You think Darrel will want you?" Dana hissed.

Cammie touched her burning cheek. "Uh... nothing."

"All right, skaters. We have made our decision," Wilhelmina spoke into a microphone. "First of all, I'd like to congratulate all of you. You've made wonderful progress, so whatever happens, don't consider yourself a failure."

Green Rink skaters exchanged panicky looks. What decision was Wilhelmina talking about? And why had she used the word *failure*?

"The following skaters are going to stay at the Green Rink and work with Coach Yvette: Angela Myers, Rita Gray, Jane McNeil, Bob Lovett..." Except for Rita and Angela, the skaters Wilhelmina had named were at the pre-juvenile and juvenile level.

"George Belgrave will work at the Blue Rink with Coach Betsy for some time. Your moves in the field are still sloppy, George." Wilhelmina looked at the boy over her glasses.

George groaned and lowered his head on his folded arms.

"Liz Tong will move to the Yellow Rink to work with Coach Darrel," Wilhelmina said.

"Okay!" Liz clapped her hands.

"Come on, Darrel! Take me!" Dana whispered.

Me too, Cammie thought. *Please!* She closed her eyes. There were no more announcements. Cammie opened her eyes again.

Wilhelmina put the list away, removed her glasses, and fixed her unblinking eyes on Cammie and Dana. "As for you two, Cammie and Dana, no decision has been made so far. We'll leave the issue pending for a while."

Dana raised her hands and turned to Cammie. "Pending? What's she talking about?"

Cammie felt her eyelids twitch. Did Wilhelmina's words mean that no one wanted to coach Dana and her? So what was next? Was Cammie supposed to practice without a coach, on her own? A nasty buzz was starting in her ears; she was afraid she was going to faint.

Across from them, the coaches were already on their feet, gathering their things. Feeling humiliated, Cammie stood up and dragged her heavy feet in the direction of the exit. Even though she tried to look perfectly straight, she did catch a few curious looks.

"Skaters, don't forget your music!" the sound equipment man called from the left.

Cammie sauntered down, picked up her CD, and headed toward the lobby. There were a few people there standing in tight groups, talking and laughing. Keeping her head down, Cammie started walking in the direction of the exit when she heard a voice that sounded vaguely familiar.

"Coach Darrel, if you only give Dana a chance, you'll never regret it."

Cammie turned her head. A tall, blonde woman in a beige leather coat stood next to Coach Darrel, looking as though she were about to grab the man by his tie.

"I'm sorry to disappoint you, ma'am, but I don't see the makings of a good skater in your daughter," Coach Darrel said calmly.

The woman's nostrils flared up. "That's ridiculous. Dana made it to nationals last year."

Coach Darrel lowered his head. His hair looked as though he had just stepped out of a barber's shop. "She might have gotten lucky once. Still, she isn't champion material."

"But she landed all…okay, most of her jumps today!" Dana's mother clasped and unclasped her hands.

Coach Darrel sighed heavily. "Dana doesn't have the right body for multi-revolution jumps. Her spins are slow too. But even that's not the issue."

"So what is the issue?" Dana's mother was almost shouting.

"A skater might have sloppy technique, but even so, people can't take their eyes off her. Dana, however, doesn't quite connect with the public."

"I don't even understand what you're talking about!" Dana's mother roared.

"I do! I understand him all right!" Dana had just approached her mother and Coach Darrell. Her face looked white. "So you don't believe I can become a champion, huh? Well, you're wrong." Dana glared at the staring crowd.

"Just give me one more chance to prove myself. Please. Let me skate my new short program and you'll see I'm not that bad."

The man turned around as though looking for a way to escape. "I think I've seen enough, Dana."

"One last chance. Please!"

Coach Darrel checked his watch then took a step in the direction of the arena. "I'll give you two minutes."

"Thanks!" Dana took off, her blonde ponytail slapping against her back.

Coach Darrel cast an uncertain glance at Dana's mother and followed Dana. Cammie went after them, wondering if Dana's plot would work. At the arena, Dana was talking to the sound man. Then she slid a CD into the player and skated to the middle of the rink. Dana's eyes sparkled as she took her starting position.

She has surely lost a lot of weight, Cammie thought.

Dana's music sounded like nothing familiar to Cammie. It was neither slow nor fast but something in between. Dana did a bunny hop followed by a lunge and then went into a Mohawk. The melancholy sound of a violin almost made Cammie's skin crawl. A cello started playing. Tiny needles pricked Cammie's neck and lower back. Drums blasted. Cammie felt her heart squeeze. For some weird reason, she had a strong desire to pull Dana off the ice immediately.

Dana landed a sloppy double toe loop and went into a spin entrance. She swirled faster and faster…

That's enough! Cammie wanted to shout, but only a whisper came out of her mouth.

There was a loud blast, and Dana was lifted off the ice. Her body flew about ten feet forward and slammed hard against the boards.

"Stop the music!" Coach Darrel shouted.

Cammie saw him stand up and rush down the steps toward the ice.

The music stopped abruptly. There was a short silence and then a very loud high-pitched voice screamed, "Dana! Dana!"

Dana's mother was on her feet, running across the arena to the spot where Dana lay prostrate, her eyes closed. The girl didn't move.

"Everybody, please step aside! The girl needs air," an authoritative voice came.

Cammie saw Captain Greenfield bend over Dana's still body.

Lieutenant Turner broke through the crowd. "The ambulance is on its way."

"Baby, please open your eyes!" Dana's mother sobbed, sitting on the ice next to her daughter.

"You'd better not touch her, ma'am," Captain Greenfield said. "Not until the doctors find out what's wrong with her."

"She's been starving herself for months," Liz's dull voice came from Cammie's right. "She's been trying to lose weight."

Captain Greenfield turned to Liz. "Now that's something you need to let the paramedics know, miss."

"Careful! Coming through!"

The people blocking the entrance to the rink stepped away to let in four young men with a stretcher. As the paramedics gently lifted Dana, she still looked limp, her eyes closed. Fear shot through Cammie. Would Dana be all right?

"All right, everybody. I have to ask you to clear the facility. The auditions are over," Captain Greenfield said.

As the crowd started thinning out, Cammie caught snatches of conversation from all directions.

"An obvious case of anorexia."

"Sure, the girl did gain a lot of weight lately."

"Well, she didn't look too bad today. So whatever a diet she was on must have worked."

"You call that working? It looks like a terrible injury."

"Gosh. Will she be able to skate again?"

"She's alive. That's all the paramedics told us."

The rink and the bleachers were completely empty. Whatever voices Cammie heard were coming from the lobby. She rubbed her face and stood up. There was nothing she could do at that point. She could only hope Dana would have a complete recovery.

As Cammie stepped into the aisle, something white sitting on the floor next to the sound system caught her sight. She walked up to the boards and picked up the small square object. It was a CD, and the name *Dana Deraco* was written in Dana's handwriting. Cammie pocketed the CD. She would return it to Dana once she was back in the dorm.

Although... Wait a minute! Cammie didn't remember anybody taking the CD out of the player. After Dana's scary fall, everybody at the rink rushed to the entrance to see how she was doing. So how had Dana's CD ended up on the floor?

With trembling hands, Cammie opened the CD player. Yes, there was a CD there already. That had to be the music Dana had skated to. Gosh. What was that supposed to mean? Had Dana skated to somebody else's music, then, without knowing it? Or had there been a last-minute switch? But why? Once you worked on a program, the music got so engrained in you that it became your second nature. No skater would ever want to change music right before an important performance. And for Dana, the audition had meant everything, especially her last number, the one she had intended to impress Coach Darrel with.

"What're you doing here, Cammie?"

She swirled around. Captain Greenfield was slowly coming down the steps.

"Uh...someone forgot the music." She handed the man the CD she had just extracted from the CD player.

Captain Greenfield swirled the silvery disc in his hands. "Hmm. You must be right. Okay. I'll make sure the skater gets it back. Now why don't you go back to your dorm, Cammie? It's not safe to be at a rink alone, not at times like this."

Cammie faked a brave smile. "There weren't any witches here today. Dana didn't get attacked, did she?"

"Probably not. The security made sure none of the witches sneaked in. Still, it's not good for a young girl to wander around alone." He gave her a warm smile. "Do you need a ride to your dorm?"

He's really nice, Cammie thought. "No thank you. It's still light. Captain Greenfield, do you think Dana'll be all right?"

The man's hazel eyes saddened. "I hope so. Such a young girl! What a tragedy! I'll keep you informed of your friend's condition. Okay?"

Cammie nodded.

"I'll be seeing you, then. Now go back to your dorm."

Cammie left the building, her mind still on Dana's unfortunate performance. Really, why had she skated to a wrong piece of music? She must have put in a wrong CD by mistake. But if so, could the blunder have had something to do with Dana's falling?

Cammie squirmed as she thought of the piece Dana had skated to. The music had really sounded eerie. Cammie simply couldn't imagine any skater choosing it for her number, unless it was... Cammie slowed down. A thought stirred up in her mind. Of course! The music of death. Hadn't Mr. Dulcimer, their music teacher, said that certain pieces of music could minister life to listeners while others...hmm. The teacher had

113

mentioned the music of death, though he had refused to elaborate.

You don't want to know. That had been Mr. Dulcimer's answer to the boys' question.

Cammie stopped completely as she tried to gather her thoughts. The music Dana had skated to was weird enough to throw anybody off. The wailing violins, the mourning cellos, and a sudden blast at the end. Cammie might have fallen too if she had been forced to skate to that piece. Now, if that was true, there was another question: where had that ghostly music come from? It obviously wasn't Dana's or any other skater's. Somebody else must have brought it to the rink. So who was it?

"Ha! Do I even have to ask?" Cammie said out loud. The question was quite obvious: the witches.

Of course, Captain Greenfield had assured her none of the witches had managed to come to the Silver Rink this afternoon. How could he be sure, though? The witches were sneaky, and they were masters of disguise. Yes, the situation was obvious: Dana had been attacked by the witches.

The sudden realization took Cammie's breath away. She hopped in place, looking around. The street was empty. Everybody had to be at work or at practice. But Cammie had to share her theory with someone, and the sooner the better. Alex! Of course! Who else would understand the whole situation better than Cammie's friend? She would find him right now. They would go to Sweet Blades and talk.

Cammie turned back and almost headed toward school when she remembered to look at her watch. It was ten after four. Alex was already at practice at the Yellow Rink. Perhaps Cammie should go to the Yellow Rink too. That way, she would be able to catch her friend right after his afternoon freestyle session. Cammie groaned and shook her head. No, that wasn't a good idea. Somehow, Cammie had completely forgotten that her own predicament was perhaps only a little better than Dana's. Cammie had failed her audition. No coach had selected her. The decision about her future training was pending. What was she going to do?

Tears rolled down her cheeks. Immediately, her skin began to sting. The cold air had made her tears freeze immediately. She wiped her face with her mittens. As much as she wanted to talk to Alex, she couldn't show up at the Yellow Rink all splotchy and distressed. All of her friends would be asking questions.

Cammie could picture Sonia's concerned face expression. "Oh, Cammie! It's terrible! What're you going to do?"

"What *am* I going to do?" Cammie asked loudly.

As though on cue, her cell phone started ringing. Cammie took it out of her pocket and looked at the monitor. It was her mother.

Cammie pressed the off button. The conversation with her mother would have to wait until Cammie figured something out. What could she think of, though? A skater couldn't train without a coach, period. So what was next? Would they tell her to leave Skateland, go home?

"Oh no!" She pressed her hands against her cheeks and began to cry.

A woman with a small boy appeared at the end of the street. Immediately, Cammie skated away. She didn't want to be seen crying. Cammie looked around. She was in the middle of Axel Avenue, the street that led directly to the dorm. The tall trees of the Icy Park stood like sentinels on her left. Without even thinking, she stepped off the ice path and trudged through the deep snow into the park. She had nothing to lose. If the witches attacked her, well, so be it. If she couldn't train in Skateland anymore, she didn't care about getting hurt.

She plunged into the thicket, enjoying the silence that enclosed her in a tight cocoon. A small, circular pond appeared from among the trees. Cammie recognized the place. It was there that she had practiced her triple salchow a year ago, the jump that had caused her a broken ankle. Of course, it hadn't been just Cammie's mistake. She had been attacked by Winja. For a moment, Cammie thought of turning back. Then she shook her head stubbornly. Nothing mattered anymore if her skating career was over.

She found a lonely bench partially hidden among bulky fir trees. Good. She would stay there until she figured out what to do with her life. Cammie swept the snow off the wood surface and sat down on the bench cross-legged. Luckily, she was wearing her calorific clothes from the show, so she wouldn't freeze.

She sat watching the snow weave an intricate pattern of white lace atop of the dark gray ice. The sky above her was slowly darkening. A bell clanked nearby, followed by a scuffing sound. Startled, Cammie raised her head. The cops must have found her after all. Gosh. Could a person have a little privacy? She thought of lurching into the thicket when she heard a male voice that didn't belong to any of the cops.

"How well do I remember the statue, Mrs. Van Uffeln! But it no longer looks the same. What is it, old age?"

A slightly husky female voice chuckled. "If you're old, what am I supposed to be? And please, Elliot, call me Wilhelmina. You're not my student anymore, though that might change."

Cammie turned her head slightly and peered through the heavy branches that partially blocked her view. Wilhelmina stood next to s silver icemobile, looking chic in a gray fox coat. Holding the older woman's elbow was Elliot Monroe. He wore black jeans and a matching parka. His blond hair was uncovered.

"Really, Wilhelmina, what happened to the statue?" he asked. "When I grew up here, the figure of the beautiful skater stood for everything good about figure skating. The attitude position, the multicolored petals representing different rinks. I found it so inspirational."

"Everything changes," Wilhelmina said curtly.

"There are things that must never change. A woman with an evil smile and crooked legs can't be the symbol of Skateland. Who ever thought of replacing the original statue with this abomination?"

Wilhelmina waved at the man. "No one did it on purpose, Elliot. The problem is there is too much evil in the Icy Park. The witches are getting out of hand. And at some point, the statue got a full blast of the witches' curse. It's as simple as that."

Cammie hugged herself tightly and lowered her head, hoping she wouldn't be seen. She knew better than anyone what had caused the transformation of the beautiful skating statue into a witch. A year ago, Alex and she had buried Winja's crutch under the statue. When they had come back a few days later, the elegant skater was gone. Instead, there was an evil woman with gnarled limbs. Even after the crutch had been removed, the statue had never returned to its original beauty. Not that the whole thing had been Cammie and Alex's fault, but Cammie still didn't want the charming show skater to find out that she had been somehow involved in destroying his delightful figure skating symbol.

"Are you saying that the witches are as active as ever, Wilhelmina?" Elliot asked.

Wilhelmina grunted. "Isn't today's attack evidence of that?"

"So…it was an attack," the man said slowly.

Cammie pressed her hand hard against her mouth to suppress a gasp. Wow. So she was right.

"Well, at first, I thought Dana simply got dizzy. She has had problems with anorexia lately. But you see, as soon as the girl started skating, I couldn't get rid of a weird feeling that something wasn't right. And then I realized that it was wrong music. I talked to Dana's mother in the hospital, and she did confirm that wasn't the piece her daughter usually skated to."

"So what're you saying?" Elliot asked.

"Someone must have replaced the girl's music with a cursed CD," Wilhelmina said gravely.

"Do you have any idea who that someone is?"

"The obvious supposition would be the witches," Wilhelmina said slowly, "although I'm not quite sure."

"You're not sure."

"Something doesn't line up. I have to give it more thought. The whole pattern of attacks looks a little weird to me."

"What do you mean?" Elliot asked.

Cammie held her breath, trying not to miss anything.

"First, someone tries to kill a show skater. I hope you understand Winja wasn't the target."

"I think so. And the witch is alive anyway."

Wilhelmina gave out a throaty laughter. "The only reason she survived is because she is a witch. The evil inside the woman protected her from the lethal effect of Raal. You might want to put it this way. Winja's evil made her partially immune to poisonous substances."

"So which of the show skaters was the attacker after?" Elliot asked.

"The attacker probably didn't care. The death of any elite skater would have satisfied his desire to kill. What happened today, however, is completely out of line. You see, Dana isn't a promising skater."

"Yes, I could see that."

"So why did the attacker choose her? I can't understand it."

There was a moment's silence while Wilhelmina and Elliot seemed to be deeply in thought. Snow kept falling in long, thick threads.

"Well, we'll get to the bottom of this," Wilhelmina said. "Now let's talk about something more cheerful. Elliot, I'm so happy about your decision. You're a true well of knowledge and experience, and I know our little skaters will learn a lot of good things from you."

A bashful smile appeared on Elliot's full lips. "Oh, well—"

"I especially appreciate your willingness to help me to get Christel's skating career back on track," Wilhelmina said. "You see, Christel is way too young to be my personal cook and nurse. And you saw her at the peak of her career, so you know what she's capable of. I believe it's not too late."

Elliot shrugged. "Wilhelmina, honestly, I don't think I'll be able to ever skate pairs again."

Wilhelmina raised her arms in the air. "Son, who's talking about competitions? Perhaps a show number or two—"

"Wilhelmina, no!"

"Look, why don't we talk about performing later? Just help Christel get in performing shape again."

"Uh…let me think about it."

"Elliot, Felicia would want you to do it. Yes, don't look away. She wouldn't be happy about you burying your gift in the ground. She wouldn't want you to give up."

"Wilhelmina, I—"

"Elliot, you're tough. I know you can do it."

The man groaned and lowered his head. His blond hair covered by snow looked almost white. "Well… all right."

"Good!"

Cammie had slid off the bench long ago, inching herself closer and closer to where the two adults were standing. She found the whole conversation extremely interesting. So it looked like Prince Elliot would stay in Skateland. He was going to skate pairs with Wilhelmina's daughter, Christel. How cool! So Cammie would be seeing the handsome man on a regular basis.

I've got to do my best to stay here, Cammie thought.

She kept getting closer until at some point, she lost balance and fell right on the dark gray ice. She kicked her right blade to stabilize herself. Instead, the impact sent her forward, and within the next couple of seconds, she found herself face-to-face with Wilhelmina and Prince Elliot.

Wilhelmina's eyebrows arched over her deep gray eyes. "And what're you doing here in the snow, Cammie? Shouldn't you be in the dorm?"

"I…" Cammie tried to think of an excuse, but her mind refused to work. Instead, she stared at Prince Elliot.

His face was slightly pink from the frosty air, and he was actually smiling. "Well, hello, Cammie Wester. See? We meet again."

Wilhelmina's penetrating eyes shifted from one face to the other. "So the two of you know each other."

"We met," Prince Elliot said.

He turned to Cammie. "I saw you at the audition. You're good."

"Oh!" Despite the frost, Cammie felt as though she were on fire. She pulled off her calorific mittens.

"Anybody can have a bad day." Prince Elliot brushed the snow off his hair. "But you're light on your feet, and you definitely like what you're doing. Am I right, Wilhelmina?"

The older woman nodded. "See how many young skaters need you here, Elliot?"

The man turned to Wilhelmina. "What're you trying to say?"

"Cammie is between coaches at this point," Wilhelmina said.

"Well, I'm aware of that." Prince Elliot smiled at Cammie. His eyes were like huge sapphires. "Would you like to work with me, Cammie?"

Cammie tried her best to keep her mouth from opening, but her lower jaw dropped. Ah-ah-ah. She heard herself squeak. She pressed her hands to her chest. Did Prince Elliot want to coach *her*? But it couldn't be right. It was too good to be true. The man tilted his head. "I didn't hear you. Sorry."

"Y-yes!" Cammie stuttered.

"I'm glad everything worked out." Wilhelmina winked at Cammie. "Well, I think you, Cammie, should stay at the Green Rink until you pass your novice freestyle test. You should aim at that."

Cammie nodded enthusiastically.

"Well, Cammie, I'll see you at the Green Rink at five tomorrow." Coach Elliot's smile was warm.

The Icy Park was no longer wintery dull but silvery white and glistening. The tall fir trees spoke of Christmas, of joy and hope. Cammie could no longer suppress her excitement. Humming loudly, she skated in the direction of the dorm.

PRESTO

Cammie tugged on her new green dress and cast a nervous glance at the entrance to the rink. Coach Elliot was due any minute, and Cammie hoped he would see how dazzling she looked in her new outfit.

"It's not a practice dress," Sonia had said when Cammie had proudly shown her the dress in their dorm room.

"But I love it," Cammie had said. She knew the dark green dress with a velvet skirt trimmed with lace, tight sleeves, and sequins on the chest was just right for her. It showed off her slim figure and made her eyes appear shamrock green.

In the middle of the rink, Coach Yvette was giving Rita a private lesson. The girl kept falling from her double flip, but she seemed unperturbed by her mistakes. She would land on her backside, smile, get up, and start over again. And Coach Yvette seemed way too relaxed and careless for Cammie's taste. Cammie was used to Coach Ferguson's no-nonsense attitude.

No little mistake like slipping off the edge had ever escaped the woman's inquisitive eye.

On the contrary, Coach Yvette appeared nonchalant. During their morning moves-in-the-field practice, Coach Yvette had played country music instead of Coach Ferguson's classical pieces. It wouldn't have been an issue if it hadn't been for the fact that the coach had plain ignored Cammie, as though Cammie hadn't been part of the Green Rink anymore, as though she wasn't even a skater.

"And I know my moves were good," Cammie protested as she circled the rink in alternating crossovers.

"Hi, Cammie! I see you're working hard."

Cammie went to an abrupt stop and looked up. Yes, there he was, her Prince Elliot, looking like a movie star in his black skating clothes and a black-and-white bandana. But the best thing about him was his smile, genuinely warm and caring. Although Cammie couldn't but notice that even though the man was grinning, his eyes remained slightly withdrawn and sad.

"Have you tried any jumps today, Cammie?"

She suppressed a sigh. She had been struggling with her jumps, but she hoped Coach Elliot wouldn't notice. Oh, how she wanted to impress him!

"Don't worry. We'll fix them. At the beginning, however, let me see some of your moves in the field."

That wasn't what Cammie had expected. "But, Coach Elliot, I passed my novice moves-in-the- field test."

"Nonetheless." His eyes flashed aquamarine blue. It had to be the reflection of the ice.

Cammie shrugged and went into her bracket pattern. She thought she was doing all right, but her coach looked pensive.

"I think you can do better than that. Let me show you." He did the same step sequence, and Cammie noticed regretfully that she wasn't half as good as she had believed. Coach Elliot seemed to float across the ice, and he also managed to gain much more speed.

"Wow!" Cammie said sincerely. From the corner of her eye, she could see Angela gawking at the man.

"When you do everything right, even the most difficult pattern becomes easy. Okay. So we'll keep working on that. Now let's do some jumping. What's the most difficult jump you've ever worked on?"

"Triple salchow," Cammie said quickly.

It was only half truth. She had really tried a couple of triple salchows a year ago, but she had never been successful. But she had to make a good impression on Coach Elliot. Almost every girl her age was at least working on triples already.

"Triple salchow, huh? Okay. I want you to put this on." Coach Elliot skated to the edge of the rink and took something out of his bag.

When he handed the item to Cammie, she saw that it was a black elastic unitard with lots of zippers and silver buckles. "Put it on."

"But why?" She was slightly disappointed. Didn't the coach like her new green dress?

"I'll explain later. Just put it on."

Cammie stepped off the ice and pulled the unitard on top of her dress. The pant legs went all the way down and over her skating boots, and the sleeves had gloves attached to them. The outfit fit Cammie like a glove. She actually felt comfortable. She even thought she could feel slight vibration coming from the fabric, but it was probably her imagination.

"Let me show you something here, Cammie." Coach Elliot pushed a metal button on Cammie's chest pocket.

To her great surprise, the pocket flipped open, revealing a small screen and a keyboard. Ignoring Cammie's gasp, Coach Elliot typed in *triple salchow*.

"Now we press *enter* and…"

The screen came to life, and a message appeared: "Triple salchow: skater not ready."

"Aha! Well, as you see, Cammie, this jump is too advanced for you."

"What is this thing?" Cammie ran her finger against the soft fabric of her sleeve.

"This is a magical unitard developed by Mr. Reed," Coach Elliot said. "It's called Proper Rotation Enhancing Self Training Outfit, PRESTO for short. It has tiny electrodes built into the sleeves and pants. The electrodes make the skater's hands and feet pull in just as much as she needs to pull off a certain jump. It will also help you to reach proper height in the air. You can program the unitard to perform any jump you're ready for. The device automatically adjusts to the skater's height and weight, and it adds enough force to your spring. This way, you don't have to worry about falling. And, of course, if you don't have enough muscle or coordination for a specific jump, PRESTO will let you know."

"Oh, so it's just like self-spinning boots!" Cammie exclaimed. "You know, Mr. Reed invented those too. I actually tried jumping in them some years ago."

Coach Elliot shook his head. "Self-spinning boots are different. They are more suited for recreational skating than serious training. Self-spinning boots will throw you up in the air, make you spin, and then bring you down correctly, no matter how crooked you are in the air. Therefore, they do nothing to develop a skater's jumping technique."

"But Mr. Reed skates in them all the time."

"He only does it for fun. This unitard, however, will give you a hundred percent mastery of the jumps." Coach Elliot pointed to Cammie's outfit.

"A hundred percent?" Wow. That sounded almost too good to be true.

"You don't look convinced, Cammie. Okay. Let me show you something. Do you mind taking PRESTO off for a minute?"

Cammie obeyed, wondering what Coach Elliot was up to. The man put on the unitard. Amazingly, it fit him too.

"It's one size fits all," Coach Elliot said. "Okay. Here is the thing. I never landed my triple axel. This isn't a mandatory jump for pairs skaters. But I'm probably ready to work on it. See…let me type it in…here. You can take a look!"

Cammie bent over to see the monitor. It really said, "Triple axel. Ready."

"Now watch me." Coach Elliot skated around the rink, picking up speed, and then jumped off his left forward outside edge. It was a textbook perfect triple axel.

"Y-yes!" Cammie clapped excitedly. "You've got to go to the Olympics, Coach Elliot."

The man's eyes darkened as he took off the unitard. "I don't think you understood me right, Cammie. What the device is saying is that I'm ready *to work* on my triple axel, which I have no intention of doing actually. Just the fact that I landed the jump wearing PRESTO is nothing. It's—"

"Elliot! For goodness sake, that's you!"

Cammie and Coach Elliot looked back almost simultaneously. Waving at them from the entrance was Mrs. Page, all smiles and dimples. The woman wore a plaid coat and a purple beret.

"Leonora, it's so great to see you again!" Coach Elliot skated to the boards and gave Mrs. Page a bear hug.

Mrs. Page beamed. "I haven't talked to you since your graduation ceremony. So you're coaching Cammie now. That's great. See, I was so worried about her. One of the girls told me that Cammie had failed her audition. And Cammie wouldn't talk to me last night, so I decided to stop by the rink this afternoon to check on her. And now you're here. How wonderful!"

It was Liz, Cammie thought angrily. *She blabbed everything to Mrs. Page. Gosh. Why can't the stupid girl leave me alone?*

"There's nothing to worry about, Leonora. Cammie's doing just fine." Coach Elliot winked at Cammie.

"Good. Because you know what's going on here." Mrs. Page took off her beret and shook her brown curls with streaks of gray. "That poor Dana! They say her condition has stabilized, but the girl is still in the hospital. Actually, I'm on my way there. I've got to see how the poor girl is doing. And you—"

"Look, Leonora, as much as I feel like catching up, now is not a good time," Coach Elliot said. "Why don't we get together one of these days?"

"Oh, of course. I'm so sorry!" Mrs. Page readjusted her beret. "I'd better go, then."

"Although…you know what? You can actually help us here. Do you have a couple of minutes?" Coach Elliot asked.

Mrs. Page smiled somewhat uncertainly. "Me? What can I do?"

"Do you mind stepping onto the ice? Yes, and you'd better take off your coat."

"Sure." Mrs. Page shook off her long coat and jumped onto the ice.

"Are you warmed up?" Coach Elliot asked.

"Well…I skated here."

"Okay. Then put this on." Coach Elliot handed the woman the magic unitard.

Mrs. Page cackled as she pointed to her wide thighs and protruding belly. "Don't you think it's a little small for me?"

"Trust me."

Still muttering under her breath, the woman pulled on the unitard and zipped it up. Cammie had to admit that Mrs. Page looked rather good. In fact, the black tight fabric slimmed her down a little.

"Okay. How about we go for a single axel?" Coach Elliot tapped a few keys.

"What's this?" Mrs. Page asked with obvious curiosity.

"Ah! It does say, "Single axel, ready." Okay, Leonora. Do an axel for us."

"Are you nuts?" Mrs. Page shrieked.

"Go ahead."

"No way. I haven't done it in years. In fact, Dick Button tried it after years of not practicing and ended up in a coma."

"PRESTO says you're ready."

"What's PRESTO?" Mrs. Page asked.

"I'll explain later. Go ahead."

Mrs. Page looked around, obviously flummoxed. By that time, all activity at the arena had stopped. The skaters were watching Mrs. Page intensely. By the worried creases on the woman's forehead, Cammie could tell that Mrs. Page wasn't looking forward to being accused of cowardice.

"Ah, what the heck!" Mrs. Page waved her hand. "But if I break my neck, you, Elliot, will sit by my side 'til my complete recovery."

"Oh, sure." The man's eyes were laughing.

As Mrs. Page started skating around, Cammie couldn't help but admit that the woman was quite a decent skater. There came a Mohawk, fast backward crossovers. The woman bent her knee and soared up in the air. She turned around once, did another half a rotation, and landed solidly on one foot.

"Bravo!" the girls behind Cammie screamed.

Cammie jumped up and down. "Mrs. Page, you rock!"

As Mrs. Page skated up to them, she wore an expression of dumb disbelief. "But how...why?"

Coach Elliot put his hand on the woman's shoulder. "We'll talk about it later. Okay? Now could Cammie have the unitard, please?"

Panting, Mrs. Page pulled the zipper down. "All I can say, Cammie...hmm...you've got just the right coach by your side."

Cammie put the unitard back on, feeling encouraged. If Mrs. Page had managed an axel, surely, she—

"You'll have to do the jump several times wearing PRESTO," Coach Elliot said. "Eventually, your body will memorize the exact motions. Then you'll be able to land the jump on your own."

"But it says I'm not ready for the triple salchow," Cammie said sadly.

"Can you land all of your doubles consistently?"

"Well, actually...sometimes."

Coach Elliot nodded. "They aren't consistent, are they? Now we'll let PRESTO determine what we should start with."

Cammie frowned as she saw the man type in "single axel." Come on. Did her coach think she was a beginner? She had mastered her axel years ago. Okay, there was PRESTO's answer: "jump mastered." Cammie let out a sigh of relief.

"All right. How about double salchow?"

The unitard confirmed that Cammie's double salchow and double toe loop were good too. Yet when Coach Elliot typed in "double loop," the message said "ready."

Cammie felt slightly hurt. "But I land my double loops most of the time."

Coach Elliot flipped the monitor closed. "When you say you have the jump down, it means you can land it in your sleep or in front of judges."

"But everybody makes mistakes. There is no such thing as a hundred percent consistency."

Coach Elliot grinned. "That's what PRESTO will give you, a hundred percent consistency. All right. Why don't you try your normal double loop for me?"

Cammie started circling the rink obediently. She got on her backward outside edge, waiting for the right moment. One, two, three... She felt like a surge of current. It was coming from the unitard. Her right knee bent on its own, and when she was thrown up in the air, her arms and legs pulled in automatically.

"Ah!" Cammie breathed out. The height she had reached was tremendous. Her landing edge was deep and clean. She didn't remember ever executing such a powerful double loop. Cammie skated up to Coach Elliot, her arms spread. "Did you see it? It was incredible!"

The man nodded. "See how PRESTO works?"

"So it wasn't me?" Cammie didn't even try to hide her disappointment.

"Not yet, but you're getting there. Don't you worry, Cammie. As you keep landing double loops wearing PRESTO, you'll develop the muscle memory you need for the jump. Time will come when you are able to land consistent double loops on your own."

"Oh!" Cammie thought for a moment. "But when exactly will it happen?"

Coach Elliot shrugged. "Every skater learns at her own pace."

"But how will I know that I no longer need PRESTO?"

Coach Elliot winked at her. "Isn't it obvious? The device will tell you."

"Coach Elliot, if PRESTO is so great, why isn't everyone using it?"

He ran his hand through his hair, appearing pensive. "That's a good question, Cammie. When Mr. Reed invented PRESTO, there was a big article about it in Skateland Sensations. Of course, Mr. Reed made sure everybody understood that you couldn't use PRESTO at a competition. That would be considered cheating. That made most coaches skeptical; they thought that wearing a special suit in practice could make a skater dependent on it."

"Oh!"

He smiled, though his eyes remained sad. "Don't worry, Cammie! Mrs. Van Uffeln used PRESTO many times when she coached my partner and me. It worked well. Besides—"

"Well, well, well! I'll bet my best blade brakes as well as my icemobile if it's not Elliot Monroe!" a male voice said from the entrance.

Cammie did a quick pivot and saw Captain Greenfield leaning against the boards. Lieutenant Turner slouched behind, his bushy eyebrows almost knit together.

"I beg your pardon, officers?" Coach Elliot looked slightly confused.

"Now don't tell me you didn't recognize your main rival. Remember Junior Nationals in nineteen eighty five?"

"Hmm…" Coach Elliot rubbed his cheek.

"The novice level, dude. Who beat you then?"

"Oh!" Coach Elliot's eyes were deep azure. "Could you…no. It's impossible. Are you…Gilbert Greenfield?"

"Same old me." Captain Greenfield stepped onto the ice.

Cammie watched the two men hug.

"So you're a policeman now." Coach Elliot looked at Skateland logo emblazoned on the officer's chest pocket.

Captain Greenfield lowered his head. "Indeed. I'm a man of the law who's working hard to protect these rising stars from evil witches."

Pleasant warmth spread through Cammie's body. So she was a star in the officer's eyes. What a nice man he was!

"So the witches still keep the authorities busy," Coach Elliot said.

"I see you're skating again, Elliot," Captain Greenfield said.

Coach Elliot shrugged. "Well, Mrs. Van Uffeln talked me into doing some coaching. And…uh…I might try skating a few numbers here and there."

"Ah. I see."

"How about you?"

"No," Captain Greenfield said firmly. "Ensuring the safety of promising skaters is my solemn duty. That's where I'm needed most."

There was a short pause. In the middle of the rink, Angela was skating her program to a Beatles medley.

"Well, don't let me interrupt," Captain Greenfield said. "We only came here to make sure the rink is clear of witches. Have fun, Elliot. Good luck, skaters!"

Cammie watched the officers' gray-clad figures disappear through the exit.

"Coach Elliot, do you know Captain Greenfield?" she asked quietly.

A distant look appeared in the man's eyes. "I did years ago. He was quite a promising pairs skater."

"He's really nice."

Coach Elliot swept his hand against his face as though chasing away an unwanted memory. "All right, Cammie. Let's get back to work."

CELINE BOUCHARD

Cammie practiced her double loop wearing PRESTO for the next two weeks. She couldn't even tell how many repetitions she did. One hundred? Two hundred? Three hundred? She lost count. At least PRESTO made sure Cammie didn't crush onto the ice after each unsuccessful attempt. Finally, Cammie mastered her double loop and they moved to her double flip.

Lessons with Coach Elliot were never dull. The man was good at demonstrating every difficult move to Cammie, and his strong technique strengthened her desire to become a better skater. If PRESTO determined that Cammie wasn't ready for a specific jump, Coach Elliot would give her preparation exercises. He made Cammie practice her moves in the field over and over again.

"I used to neglect them myself when I was younger," Coach Elliot said. "That slowed down my jumping progress."

They spent hours on brackets and counters perfecting every edge, polishing every turn. Cammie could feel that her quality of skating was improving dramatically.

At the beginning, Cammie thought that with the help of PRESTO, she would get all of her jumps back in no time. Unfortunately, that wasn't the case. As her coach had explained to her, the magical device was only good for the final stage of mastering a difficult jump. Before PRESTO pronounced her ready for a certain jump, Cammie had to do a lot of preparation exercises. And Coach Elliot made sure Cammie worked extra hard. The man turned out to be as hard as he was nice.

Coach Elliot was nothing like the pairs coach from the White Rink. The woman never let her students spend even a moment of precious practice time off the ice. But when Coach Elliot saw that Cammie was getting tired, he would entertain her with stories about the foreign countries he had visited as a competitive skater.

"Are you travelling a lot with *Magic on Ice* too?" Cammie asked.

Coach Elliot shook his head. "I only did a couple of performances with them."

You should perform more, Cammie wanted to say. *You're the best skater in the world!*

But she knew better than saying something like that to her coach. He would think Cammie was only a silly little girl. And she wanted to portray the image of a serious, mature skater.

On top of everything, Coach Elliot was really cool. He showed up at the Green Rink wearing stylish pants and sweaters. His blond hair was usually covered with multicolored bandanas or caps from all over the world. Cammie often caught jealous glances coming from other girls.

Coach Elliot worked with nobody else at the Green Rink. He appeared at their rink every day for only half an hour, only to give a lesson to Cammie. That very fact gave Cammie satisfaction. Prince Elliot skated to the Green Rink just for her. It was almost like…a date.

"That's not fair. Why did he choose *her*? No other coach thought she had potential," Cammie once heard Angela whisper to Liz at breakfast.

Liz had really distanced herself from the other girls in the dorm. The only person she ever acknowledged was Sonia. Cammie knew it was because Sonia trained at the Yellow Rink too.

"Perhaps that Elliot Monroe is a special coach for losers," Liz said.

Cammie turned her burning face away. What did stupid Liz know?

"He looks like a terrific coach," Angela said, shaking her head. "I wish he would coach me too. I've been having problems with my double flip lately. Coach Yvette just told me to lay off the jump for some time."

"Uh, it sucks," Liz said. "Once you lose a jump, it's hard to get it back."

"She is getting her jumps back." Angela pointed to Cammie. "You know what? I'll ask my mom to call Wilhelmina and ask her to give me Elliot too. If she deserves him, why don't I?"

"Oh, could your mom ask Wilhelmina to let me work with Elliot too?" Rita screeched.

"Please!"

Cammie put her unfinished toast on the plate and stood up. Did those stupid girls have to be so mean? If they had problems with their jumps, why couldn't they work harder instead of criticizing another skater? In spite of all the snide remarks, she didn't really feel upset. Her jumps were coming back, and they had already put all of her doubles back in Cammie's *Romeo and Juliet* program. And after school, she would see her prince Elliot again.

"All right. Let's see what PRESTO will say about your double flip," Coach Elliot said after Cammie completed her bracket pattern.

They had only worked on Cammie's double flip for two days, so she expected dozens and dozens of repetitions.

"O-okay, how about that?" Coach Elliot showed her the monitor.

Cammie felt her eyes widen. The words on the screen were "double flip mastered." Cammie read and reread the message several times and then stared at Coach Elliot.

The man's eyes laughed. "Go ahead."

"What?"

"Take PRESTO off and do a double flip."

"Hmm. Are you sure I'll land it?"

Coach Elliot folded his arms on his chest. "I remember you trying to tell me you had doubles down pat."

"Uh...well, I thought I did. And—"

"And now you have mastered the double flip."

"But—"

"Go ahead."

As Cammie skated into the jump, she felt confidence streaming through her body. Her muscles knew exactly what to do. Her timing was perfect up to the last second. She sprung up. It was magnificent. She wished she could stay in the air for hours.

"All right! What did I tell you?"

Clapping her hands, Cammie skated up to her coach. "I did it!"

"Sure you did." His eyes were now sky blue. "Okay. Your double lutz is next."

"Really?"

"Let's try it wearing PRESTO, shall we?"

Cammie bunny-hopped along the dark streets. She didn't remember ever feeling happier. Within only two weeks, she had gotten two of her double jumps back. That was awesome. She was almost back to her previous level. Now she needed her double lutz, and then they would start working on her triples. Finally!

Cammie slowed down and readjusted her scarf. Well, of course, she would have to practice her double-double combinations first. And even when they did start working on her triples, it would probably take longer than relearning the jumps Cammie had been able to land before. But she was ready for more challenges.

I'll still show everybody what I can do, she thought.

Cammie smiled at Mrs. Page, who had opened the door for her. Nothing could be finer. Today was Friday,

140

the last full day of the week. Saturdays were easy. One long public session at the Silver Rink and they would be free. And the session started at one o'clock, so Cammie would be able to sleep in. There were voices coming from the living room, and they didn't sound excited. As Cammie looked inside, she found most of the girls sitting on couches and armchairs, looking slightly subdued.

"What's up?" Cammie asked brightly as she folded her calorific scarf.

Liz gave her a dull look. "Dana is leaving."

"What? Leaving where?"

"Her parents are taking her out of Skateland. She's going home," Sonia said.

"Actually, Dana's going to some prep school," Liz said. "Her parents want her to get ready for college."

Rita looked at Liz, wide-eyed. "But how about skating?"

"Skating, skating," Liz mimicked her. "She's quitting, okay? She's retiring!"

Retiring. That was the word people normally used in relation to accomplished skaters who had decided to put an end to their competitive career. But those were adults, people in their twenties and thirties. Most of them were champions. And Dana was a fourteen-year-old girl who still yet had to win a major competition.

"Her parents stopped by to get her things." Sonia dried her eyes. "Mrs. Page told me."

"Her mother says Dana's had enough. She almost killed herself skating, so it's not worth it."

"But it was an attack!" Cammie exclaimed.

Angela gave her a weird look. "Attack? No. It was anorexia. That's what the doctors diagnosed her with."

Cammie shook her head. "I don't think so."

Sonia interrupted her. "Who cares?" Her eyes were red and swollen.

"Darn!" Cammie slapped herself on the thigh. When she first moved to Skateland three years ago, she didn't really like Dana. She had thought of the girl as too self-confident, too judgmental. But a year ago, the two of them had become good friends. Of course, because of Dana's obsession with weight, she had hardly talked to Cammie or anybody else lately. But Cammie really cared about Dana. And now Dana was gone.

"They're expecting a new student. I guess she'll live with me." Liz stood up. "I'm really tired. I'd better take a bath."

One after another, the girls walked up to their rooms. Halfway up the steps, Cammie heard them actually wondering who the new girl would be.

"I think it'll be Megan Ligovski," Sonia said. "She's had a good year."

"Megan says she'll never leave her New York coach," Liz said. "No, I'm sure it'll be Linda Sanchez."

"What're you talking about? She can't even land her double flip," Angela said.

Cammie wasn't listening anymore. *If it weren't for Coach Elliot, I might have to leave Skateland too.* She stopped to catch a breath.

Sonia looked back. "Are you all right, Cammie?"

"Fine. I'm fine. Go ahead."

Sonia joined the rest of the girls.

142

I'll never give up, Cammie thought. *I'll never let the witches get the best of me!*

Dana's leaving and the arrival of a new student was the topic of every conversation at the Silver Rink public session. At some point, Cammie got tired of speculating what had really happened to Dana and who would become Skateland's new star. She moved to the center of the rink and did a few double loops and double flips. The jumps were high and solid.

"Not bad!" Alex skated up to her.

"Thanks!"

"I'm sorry they didn't move you to the Yellow Rink," Alex said.

Cammie waved her hand. "I'm actually happy with Coach Elliot."

"Oh yeah. The show guy. He coaches a novice pair and a junior pair too."

"He does?"

"Yes, and he is working on a number with Christel Van Uffeln."

Cammie wrinkled her forehead. "Who?"

"Don't you remember Wilhelmina's daughter?"

Cammie stared at him. "You know what? I think I heard something…"

Of course! When Cammie had overheard Prince Elliot talking to Wilhelmina in the Icy Park, the woman had actually talked about the possibility of her daughter skating with Coach Elliot.

"Isn't Christel kind of old?" Cammie asked.

Alex shrugged. "They're not going to compete. They'll probably do a couple of shows. That's it."

For some reason, Cammie felt a stab of pain in her chest. Christel Van Uffeln was so beautiful. And she had to be a terrific skater. With a mother like Wilhelmina, the woman couldn't be just average. *I wish I could skate pairs too*, Cammie thought. *Perhaps Prince Elliot could become my partner. Maybe it's not too late to try.* Yet when Cammie remembered Christel's petite frame, she let out a deep sigh. At five feet five inches tall, Cammie couldn't become a pairs skater. That was absolutely out of the question.

"What's wrong?" Apparently, Alex had noticed Cammie's frustration.

"Ah, nothing. I'm just worried about my jumps," Cammie lied.

"They look much better," Alex said.

"Oh, Coach Elliot is terrific."

"Would you like to hang out tonight? You could tell me about his coaching."

"I can't," Cammie said sadly. "The new girl is coming tonight, so Mrs. Page wants us all to give her a warm welcome."

"Ah!" Alex smoothed out his blond hair. "Any idea who it is?"

"Nope."

"Okay. Have fun. See you."

The public session was over, and most of the skaters had already walked out into the lobby. Cammie exchanged her yellow skating dress (she couldn't stop dreaming of the Yellow Rink) for warm black pants and a white sweater. She rushed out of the Sport Center, zipping up her parka as she skated in the direction of her dorm. She was tired and looking forward to a delicious dinner. The smell of barbecued chicken hung in the lobby when Cammie walked in.

Cammie sniffed. "Could we eat already, Mrs. Page?"

"In about ten minutes. Go talk to the girls in the living room," the dorm supervisor said.

The girls sat on the couches, some still in their skating clothes.

"Mrs. Page made a cheesecake for dessert." Rita patted her stomach.

"You'd better watch your diet, squirt. No wonder your double flip isn't there," Angela said.

Rita's light brown eyes flashed. "I do eat right."

Before Angela could say something else, the doorbell rang. They heard Mrs. Page pad to the lobby. The lock clicked. "Come in, Celine! Welcome to our dorm!"

The girls looked at one another. Celine? Where had Cammie heard that name before?

"Everybody's waiting for you." Mrs. Page appeared in the living room with a very small girl by her side. Lieutenant Turner's sulky face loomed behind them. The young man carried two huge red suitcases.

"Okay, girls. This is our new student, Celine Bouchard. I'm sure you know her from the show *Magic on Ice*." Mrs. Page looked excited.

Now Cammie remembered where she had heard the name. Of course, Celine Bouchard had played the part of the Little Robber Girl in the show.

Everybody sat staring at the newcomer. Celine, however, didn't seem intimidated by all the attention. "Hi, kids. I bet you're excited to see me, huh? It's not often that you get to hang out with show skaters."

Sonia cleared her throat.

Celine fixed her violet eyes on Cammie's roommate. "Oh. Hi, Sonia. It's been a while."

"It's nice to see you too, Celine," Sonia said flatly.

Celine let the strap of her bag slide off her shoulder. The bag fell on the floor, and Celine stepped over it. Cammie couldn't but notice how classy she looked in her white fur jacket and red leather pants. Her chin-length blonde hair was streaked in red.

"Your room is on the third floor, Celine," Mrs. Page said. "You'll be staying with Liz."

Celine wiggled her fingers in Liz's direction. Her fingernails were also crimson.

"Are these your suitcases, Celine?" Mrs. Page exclaimed.

Celine cocked her head. "Actually, they call them *valises* in France."

Mrs. Page gave Lieutenant Turner a pleading look. "They look awfully heavy. Could you give us a hand here, Bob?"

"Sure," Lieutenant Turner grumbled. Apparently, he didn't think carrying the showgirl's things was part of his job description. He picked up the suitcases he had just put down on the floor and headed up the steps.

"I'll see my room later. Okay? I'd like to get to know everybody first." Celine gave Mrs. Page a shiny smile as the woman retired to the kitchen. Celine's teeth were small and round, like two strings of pearls.

Cammie found it a little strange that the girl was wearing bright red lipstick on an ordinary day.

"Please sit down." Angela stood up from her armchair.

"Thanks!" Celine took Angela's seat and started unlacing her skating boots. "Picture this: they made me put on my skates at the entrance. I told them I wasn't going to a competition or a practice session, but they wouldn't listen. I mean, hello! Are they out of their minds?"

"Here, in Skateland, we skate everywhere," Sonia said coldly.

Celine glanced at her. "What do you mean *everywhere?*"

"To the rinks, to school, to stores, you name it."

Celine's face expression changed from surprise to concern. "But why?"

"Mrs. Van Uffeln says skating everywhere develops your stamina and builds up your muscles," Cammie said.

Celine raised her hands in the air as though shielding herself from Cammie. "Hey, don't give me that! The last thing I want is huge, bulky muscles. I've got to do something about it."

She jumped off the armchair and ran to the lobby in her red socks. "Bob? I need to talk to you for a minute."

Cammie heard Celine say something softly to the young man. Lieutenant Turner didn't sound very excited, though Cammie couldn't distinguish the words. The girls looked at one another, wondering what it was all about. The front door slammed.

Celine returned to the living room and sat down on the floor, cross-legged. The girl looked disappointed. "What a dork! I wanted him to take me to practices and to school in his police icemobile. I offered him five dollars a ride. I was only doing him a favor, of course. I mean, how much does a cop make? What?" She must have noticed the expression of shock on the girls' faces.

"You have to skate everywhere in Skateland. It's a law," Liz said.

Celine ran her hand through her hair. "Laws only exist to be broken."

Sonia narrowed her eyes. "Why did you come to Skateland if you don't like the way we do things here?"

Celine looked at her askance. "And why do you think? It was my folks' idea. 'It's the best skating facility in the world. They'll make a champion out of you.'" Celine made a very good imitation of a father counseling his young daughter.

Cammie couldn't suppress a giggle.

Celine smiled at her. "Like I need those silly games to become a champion. In fact, the whole place is crazy. Pink Rink, Green Rink, skating cookies. How much more stupid can it get? Mom even told me about skating witches. Is it true? Has anybody met them?"

"I'll be sure to introduce you to them," Sonia said coldly.

The room erupted in laughter.

Celine rolled her eyes. "I'm sure I'll be able to find them myself if I get bored. Mom trained here for eighteen years. She knows the place like the palm of her hand. She actually passed on some secrets to me."

"Why did you leave the show?" Rita asked breathlessly. She seemed mesmerized by the presence of a celebrity.

Celine twirled her gold pendant shaped like a palm tree. "Isn't it cute? I got it in Florida. Well, let me see. The show is touring Japan now. So Dad said there was no way I could travel with them. 'How about your practices, sweetheart? And school?' Ha! Give me a break, Daddy!"

More laughter followed. The girls obviously liked Celine, all except Sonia, who still looked grim. Personally, Cammie didn't know what to make of the girl. Though definitely a rebel, Celine looked quite cool.

"Ready for some souvenirs?" Celine asked excitedly. She unzipped her shoulder bag, and out spilled a few multicolored pens and notebooks, all carrying the logo *Magic on Ice*. She passed the goodies around. Cammie got a red pen and a matching notebook.

"Here's more." Celine gave them all tubes of lipgloss and some jewelry.

Cammie's silver pendant read *Magique sur Glace*.

"We did a tour in France, and they made those for us," Celine said.

Sonia, however, turned down Celine's gifts politely. "I'm fine. Thank you."

"Come on, girl! Loosen up!" Celine almost forced Sonia to accept a blue pendant shaped like a flower. "It'll look great with your eyes."

Sonia sighed gravely as she put the pendant on. "Thank you."

"Time for dinner, girls!" Mrs. Page announced, and everybody went to the dining room.

"Why don't you like Celine?" Cammie asked Sonia as the two of them got into their beds later that night.

Sonia fluffed her pillow. "What's there to like? Celine is the biggest showoff I've ever met."

Cammie had to admit that Sonia was right. "I guess anybody would be. After all, she skates with *Magic on Ice*."

"I wonder why," Sonia said sarcastically.

Cammie rose on her elbow. "I don't understand."

"You think she's part of the show because she's a terrific skater? No way. She's only average. You'll see. They only used her because her parents are famous."

"But…" Surely Cammie didn't want to hurt Sonia. "Your parents were champions too."

Sonia pulled her knees to her chest. "But my parents never give me a break. I started skating at two, and I've never stopped ever since. And in case you forgot, I'm a junior national champion. Yet my parents have never let me skate with *Magic on Ice*, not once. Celine, however, has never really worked hard. She never went to an important competition. She likes being in the center of attention, but she hates pressure. Did you see how upset she got when she found out she would have to skate everywhere? She even wanted to bribe the cop."

Cammie chuckled. "Well, it didn't work. She'll have to skate to places, just like everybody else."

"You don't know Celine. Believe me. She'll think of something. Okay. We'd better get some sleep. It's getting late."

As Cammie lay in the dark, she couldn't stop thinking about Celine Bouchard. What a lucky girl! Cammie wondered what it felt like, skating in a famous show, touring the world, being on the first-name basis with champion skaters. Of course, Celine knew Prince Elliot too.

"What rink are you going to practice at, Celine?" Sonia asked at breakfast.

Even though the question sounded perfectly innocent, there were unmistakable notes of sarcasm in Sonia's voice. Cammie knew why. While everybody else in the dining room wore their rink signature colors, Celine showed up in a red warm-up jacket over black skating pants with red cylindrical stripes. Of course, red wasn't the official color of any of Skateland's practice rinks.

Celine yawned. "I think they assigned me to the Yellow Rink. Any idea where it is?"

"We can go together," Liz said as she pushed the sugar bowl closer to Celine.

"What level are you anyway?" Sonia asked.

"Novice." Celine buttered her toast. "But Dad is putting pressure on me to move up to juniors. 'You're fifteen, honey, so time is running out.' Ugh!"

"Are you really fifteen?" Cammie thought Celine wasn't a day older than thirteen.

151

Sonia interrupted her. "You're only supposed to wear yellow if you train at the Yellow Rink."

Celine blinked. "Why?"

"It's a rule."

"Not today." Celine fluffed her red-streaked blonde hair. "I would look garish in yellow."

The girl's remark sent the girls into a long fit of giggles. Even Sonia smiled.

"Are you going to work with Coach Darrel, then?" Sonia asked.

"No. With Elliot." Celine took a sip of her tea and pushed the cup back with a scowl. "It needs more sugar."

Cammie's spoon slid out of her hand, sending a blob of oatmeal to the carpet. "Coach Elliot?"

"Yeah. Mom says he can help me with my triples, unless we kill each other first. I'm temperamental too, you know."

"Temperamental?" Cammie echoed. She didn't know what Celine was talking about. Coach Elliot was really nice.

"Time to go!" Sonia stood up.

Liz too jumped to her feet.

Celine glanced at the clock. "But it's only a quarter after six!"

"The Yellow Rink is twenty-five minutes away." Liz wrapped a scarf around her neck.

Cammie knew she was running late too, but for some reason, she couldn't get up. Celine was going to train with Prince Elliot.

Celine pushed herself away from the table. "Do you guys really skate all the way to the rink?"

"That's a rule." This time, Sonia sounded almost nasty.

Celine's violet eyes shifted from Sonia to Liz. "But...but won't you be too tired to practice once you get there?"

"You'll get used to it," Sonia said coldly. "Come on. We'll be late."

Celine knelt on the floor next to her skating bag. "You guys go ahead."

"How about you?" Liz's hand moved away from the door handle.

"Don't worry about me. I'll get a ride." Celine extracted a small gold cell phone from her skating bag and flipped the lid open.

Sonia stared at Celine for a moment and then walked out. Liz followed, though she kept looking back at Celine. A puff of cold air rushed into the lobby, and the door closed with a bang.

"Who're you calling?" Cammie stood up and took her parka from the hanger. So what if she was running late? Coach Yvette didn't care anyway.

"Wait!" Celine whispered. "Hello, this is Celine Bouchard. Yes, that's right, I'm Karen Ballock's daughter. Yes, I'm excited to be here. Oh, she does. She told me about you so many times. Yes! Mr. Spiegler, I have a huge favor to ask you. It's my first day in Skateland, and I'm really tired. Could you please take me to the Yellow Rink? You can? Oh, thank you so much! I'm at the intermediate and novice dorm. Yes. Okay. I'll be ready."

She hung up and gave Cammie a thumbs-up. "That was the Zamboni driver from the Yellow Rink. He knows my mom, of course. Well, who doesn't?

He's picking me up in five minutes. Do you want to come along?"

"I train at the Green Rink." Cammie shook her head. Celine was really something else. "But Elliot Monroe is my coach too," Cammie added.

"Oh, really? So what do you think of him?"

"He's terrific."

Celine picked up her skating bag. "Good. See, I know him from the show, of course, and he's a cool guy, most of the time."

"Not all the time?" Cammie wondered what Celine was trying to say.

"He's still grieving over his wife. I mean, it was fourteen years ago!" Celine shrugged. "So now he won't look at any other woman."

"I understand," Cammie said softly. Prince Elliot was still in love with his wife, even though the woman was no longer with him. Prince Elliot was real. For him, love was the way it had to be…forever.

"Don't feel sorry for him, though." Celine must have noticed Cammie's sad face. "A man like Elliot won't stay alone for the rest of his life. He's smart, and he has good sense of humor. And he's cute too."

"Cute?" That wasn't the word Cammie would use to describe Prince Elliot.

"Sure. So don't take him too seriously. He'll like you. He likes me already." Celine winked.

"He does?" For some reason, Cammie felt hollow inside.

A horn honked from the street.

"Oops. That's for me. Okay, I'll see you…what's your name?"

"Cammie."

"Okay, Cammie. Have fun with old Elliot!"

The front door slammed, leaving Cammie alone in the lobby. She glanced at the clock that already showed six fifty-four, sighed, and reached for her backpack. She skated along Axel Avenue with her head down, not knowing whether the tears in her eyes were caused by the blasts of the cold west wind or by the lump in her throat.

She realized she was being silly, yet she couldn't help thinking that Prince Elliot definitely liked Celine more than her. The showgirl was much better looking than Cammie. She was also a higher-level skater, someone who had already started working on her triples. If only Cammie hadn't broken that ankle a year ago. If only she hadn't grown three inches that last year. If only…

The trees and the houses looked dim. The tears prevented Cammie from seeing clearly. She tripped on the ice path and barely stayed on her feet. But that was ridiculous. She needed to get a grip on herself. Apparently, there was nothing she could do about Celine, so why even think about the showgirl? At that point, the most important goal was to get her jumps back.

Cammie took a deep breath and skated forward, picking up speed with each step. If she wanted to get better, she would need every minute of her ice time.

At dinner, Cammie sat across from Celine, taking in every word. She hoped the showgirl would share the impressions of her first lesson with Prince Elliot. Yet Celine didn't seem interested in discussing her skating technique. Instead she talked about the clothing style of the skaters at the Yellow Rink: "So plain!" She mentioned a few Yellow Rink boys: "So gauche!" And she even spoke about the way skating parents criticized their kids for not working hard enough: "So rude!"

Come on! Talk about Prince Elliot! What's the matter with you? Cammie thought.

"On the positive side, there were some cute boys there. Two gave me flowers and some candy." Celine showed the girls two chocolate blades. "Do any of you want those? See, I prefer Swiss chocolate."

"Oh, I've never tried those." Liz took a bite of one of the blades. "It has peanut butter inside. I like it."

"Who gave them to you?" Sonia asked warily.

"This is from the sweet curly head named Jeff." Celine pointed to the peanut butter chocolate blade.

"And this is from the blond guy. I believe his name is Alex." She raised a white chocolate blade. "I believe it has mint flavor. At least that's what Alex said."

So Alex had finally managed to get Celine's attention. Well, Cammie couldn't blame her friend. If she were a boy, she would probably fall in love with the showgirl too.

"I thought Jeff had better taste," Sonia said later when she joined Cammie at the desk in their room.

Cammie lazily flipped through the pages of her math book. "Didn't you see it coming? Alex and Jeff wanted to shower Celine with gifts even at the show. So they finally had their chance."

Sonia hissed like an angry cat. "That's what boys are like. So okay, she has nice outfits, and of course, she flirts like crazy. So what? She's not a good skater at all. You should have seen her double axel. She keeps landing on both feet, yet she claims she has it. What a fraud!"

"Oh really?" Cammie felt a little better. Maybe Celine wasn't that advanced after all. Perhaps, with the help of PRESTO, Cammie would get her double axel back soon. Then she would be ahead of Celine.

But then Cammie realized that Coach Elliot would probably be using PRESTO during his lessons with Celine too.

I've got to see what kind of a skater she is, Cammie thought as she lay in bed that night.

She wondered when Celine's private lessons were scheduled. Coach Elliot gave Cammie her lesson at five o'clock every afternoon. Sonia would probably know. They worked for half an hour, which gave Cammie another half hour to practice on her own. Six o'clock brought an end to the official freestyle session.

"Coach Elliot starts working with Celine at six, after the end of freestyle session," Sonia said as she packed her skating bag the following morning.

"During public sessions?" Cammie couldn't believe it. Public sessions were always so crowded. There was no way you could practice doubles, let alone triples.

"But we don't have public sessions at the Yellow Rink," Sonia explained. "The facility is for high-level skaters only, remember? The coaches teach there all the time, not only at official freestyle sessions. Everybody wants private ice time anyway. For example, my lesson is at three o'clock."

Cammie knew what she was going to do. She would sneak to the Yellow Rink after her own freestyle session and watch Coach Elliot work with Celine. As Skateland resident, Cammie had access to every practice rink. Of course, the idea of visiting the Yellow Rink didn't seem particularly appealing. Cammie had been there last year during her recuperation process, and she had found the skaters too smug and their parents too patronizing.

Well, who cared? This time, she wasn't going to skate there. She would just sit in the bleachers and watch Celine's practice. Actually, watching her coach work with another skater could be beneficial for her own progress. When she was on ice herself, she was so focused on her own performance that she barely saw what was going on around her.

Cammie's private lesson went really well that afternoon. PRESTO finally pronounced her double lutz mastered. Cammie raced around the arena, landing one double lutz after another.

After about the twentieth time, Coach Elliot raised his hands. "Don't you think it's enough for today?"

Cammie skated over, her head swimming with joy. "I did it! I did it!"

"Good job!" He patted her gently on the back. "Now get some rest. Tomorrow we'll start working on your double axel."

Double axel! That was the last jump Cammie had landed before getting injured last year. She had almost made it. She was almost back to her level.

Cammie stepped off the ice and grabbed her skate guards from the boards. Coach Elliot waved at her and walked out into the lobby.

Cammie ran to the locker room and changed into black polyester pants and a thick black sweater. She hummed happily as she skated along the evening streets. Still warm from her intense private lesson, Cammie made it to the Yellow Rink in record time. She showed her ID to the security guard and walked into the brightly lit lobby. The expansive facility looked busy. Most of the Yellow Rink skaters were leaving.

Somebody took Cammie by the hand. "What're you doing here?"

Cammie looked back. Sonia had approached her, and her roommate's blue eyes were narrowed suspiciously.

"Nothing," Cammie said.

Sonia's eyes flicked from Cammie to the rink entrance and then to Cammie again. "Ah. I see. Have fun!"

"Sonia, wait. I just need some help with my double axel. See, when I'm on the ice, I can't really see—"

Sonia waved at her. "See you at the dorm."

How come Cammie hadn't thought that other people might consider her behavior weird? Really, who in his right mind would show up at a strange rink after two long practices just to watch another skater? Oh

159

well. Cammie walked up higher and higher into the stands. She would take a seat in the back row so nobody would see her and ask her more questions.

Cammie sank into a plush yellow seat and let out a sigh of relief. The temperature was warmer than at the Green Rink, so she took off her hat and unbuttoned her parka. Yet when Cammie looked around, she saw that she wasn't the only spectator at the arena. Seated about ten seats to the right of her was Alex. Cammie recognized the striped yellow-and-black scarf that her friend wore between practices.

"Alex! What're you doing here?" Cammie walked in Alex's direction and took a seat next to his.

The moment Alex's green eyes spotted Cammie, his face turned pink. "Ah. Well…I just thought of maybe getting some tips from Coach Elliot. They say he's great with jumps."

Cammie clapped her hands. "He is! You won't believe it. I got all of my doubles back already. We're about to start tackling the double axel."

"I thought you could do it before."

Cammie felt her friend stiffen a little. As she looked down, she saw Celine taking off her skate guards.

"Sure I did, but I lost all of my doubles after my injury, remember?" Cammie turned her head to look Alex in the face, but he didn't look like he was listening anymore. His gaze was fixed firmly on Celine. Finally, the girl was dressed up to the standards of the Yellow Rink—in a canary yellow T-shirt and black imitation leather leggings. Even the red streaks were gone from her hair.

"She's gorgeous, isn't she?" Alex breathed out.

Cammie barely had time to admit that Alex was acting a little weird when Coach Elliot joined Celine on the ice. Next to each other, they looked like father and daughter. As Prince Elliot laughed at something, squeezing Celine's hand, Cammie's heart throbbed in her chest.

The coach and the student moved around the rink, picking up speed with each stroke. Cammie sighed, realizing that Celine was a natural. Of course, the girl had started skating before she had even learned to walk properly. Cammie glanced at Alex, fearing he had heard her jealous sigh. Yet her friend seemed to be oblivious to her presence altogether. His eyes were taking in Celine's delicate frame and her liquid, catlike moves on the ice.

After a brief warm-up, Coach Elliot started working on Celine's triple toe loop. He walked the girl through the jump and had her land a few singles and doubles. Finally, he helped Celine to get into PRESTO. As Celine pulled the pant legs over her skating boots, Coach Elliot held her gently by the elbow. For some reason, Cammie felt there wasn't enough air in the arena. She started breathing hard with her mouth.

Alex's cold fingers clasped tight around Cammie's wrist. "She could have put that thing on herself."

"Exactly." Cammie squeezed Alex's hand, signaling that she understood.

Wearing the unitard, Celine landed several triple toe loops. Each time the girl completed the jump, Prince Elliot skated up to her to explain something. The man's hands flew up and down. Celine responded with equal flare. Each time their hands touched, Cammie felt as though the Witch of Fear's long crooked fingers tightened around her throat.

Next to Cammie, Alex coughed several times. "Do you have any water with you?"

Without taking her eyes off the ice, Cammie reached for her bottle in the backpack and handed it to Alex. Down on the ice, Coach Elliot signaled for Celine to take off the unitard. Then he put his hands on the girl's elbows and showed her how to pull in correctly. Celine nodded and skated around the rink faster and faster. A split second later, she soared up in the air in a huge triple toe loop.

"Bravo!" Alex clapped hard.

"Not bad!" Coach Elliot shouted. He did the same jump that was way bigger than Celine's.

"Great!" Cammie cheered.

The two skaters must have noticed that they weren't alone. They looked up into the stands simultaneously. Cammie saw them grin and wave at Alex and her. A moment later, Coach Elliot hugged Celine and led her off the ice. The lesson had to be over.

Alex sprung off his seat and ran down, his skate guards clomping against the steps. Cammie followed.

"See you tomorrow, Celine," Coach Elliot said. "Bye, guys." The man waved at Cammie and Alex and walked out into the lobby.

Alex already stood in front of Celine, looking very poised and erect, as though he was about to start skating his free program. "You're a wonderful skater, Celine. Would you like to go out with me tosweblads?"

At the end of the sentence, Alex was completely out of breath, so Cammie could only guess that the last words had been *to Sweet Blades*.

Celine's thin eyebrows arched over her violet eyes. "Oh, that's so sweet. Where did you say we're going, Jeff?"

From her spot behind Alex's back, Cammie could see the boy's ears turn orange. Even Alex's perfect posture seemed to have collapsed somehow. "Uh…my name is Alex. Alex Bernard, remember?"

Celine rubbed her forehead. "Oh sure. See, there're so many good skaters at this rink, it's hard to keep them straight. What do you think?"

"Well…" Alex shuffled his feet. "Anyway, we could go to Sweet Blades. It's a skating bakery, you know."

Celine put on her black warm-up jacket decorated with the logo *Magique sur Glace*. "Here's the deal. I'll check out your sweet bakery, but only after you let me grab a hot dog or something on the street. That monster almost worked me to death."

Before the shock of hearing Coach Elliot called a monster could register in Cammie's mind, Celine took Alex by the hand. The two of them marched straight past Cammie. Alex's mouth was open, and his eyes were slightly glazed. Cammie remembered seeing the same stunned look on Alex's face after he had been fiercely attacked by the Witch of Pride two years ago.

The glass door opened and closed. The couple was gone. Cammie was alone at the rink. For a few seconds, she stood in her spot, her lower jaw hanging almost to her chest. So Alex had taken Celine out and left Cammie at the Yellow Rink alone. Some friend he was! And she had hoped the two of them would go to Sweet Blades and have a nice, long talk. She was dying to share all the details of her lessons with Prince Elliot. She also wanted to discuss Dana's leaving, talk about Celine… She was interested in whatever was new in Alex's life. No luck. Alex had chosen the showgirl. So that was the real reason why Alex had stayed at the arena after his practice, to see Celine. Forget everything he had been telling Cammie about tips from Coach Elliot. She would never believe Alex again.

Cammie stared at the shimmering yellow ice. It looked almost golden in the light of the lamps. She felt morose. Now she would have to skate all the way to the dorm alone. So much for a friendly shoulder to cry on.

Cammie crossed the empty lobby, staring wishfully at the walls decorated in different shades of yellow and gold. She had always dreamed of training at the Yellow Rink with its swimming pool, fitness center, ballet rooms, and a huge snack bar. A year had passed since Cammie had first visited this place, and she wasn't even a step closer to her goal. She hunched her shoulders, lowered her head, and headed for the exit, hoping that none of the elite skaters would spot her.

Cammie stood on the porch, putting on her gloves, when she heard a familiar voice. "Cammie!"

She turned around. Coach Elliot was right next to her, a black-and-white ski hat in his hand. "So your friends left you alone."

Cammie did her best to appear nonchalant. "Coach Elliot, I guess they needed some privacy."

His eyes sparkled dark blue. "Naturally. Well, I hope you're not skating to the dorm alone. It's already dark."

"I'm used to it."

"So it looks like we have to work on another bad habit of yours." His smile seemed to have lit up the place. She couldn't think of an appropriate response. She merely stood gazing into the deep ponds of his eyes.

"Choctaw and I will accompany you to the dorm," Coach Elliot said as he tightened the straps on his backpack.

Cammie barely suppressed an excited *yes*. So he cared about her. Spending time with Prince Elliot outside the rink was much better than feasting on chocolate skating boots at Sweet Blades. She would pretend Prince Elliot and she were on a date. No, even better, they would be two famous skaters returning home after a successful performance. They both skated with *Magic on Ice*; they were husband and wife, and Choctaw was their dog. At that point, Cammie felt so hot that she quickly pulled off her wool hat. She also took the green scrunchie out of her hair, letting long heavy locks stream down her back. She wanted to look more mature.

Coach Elliot walked up to a lamppost, and Cammie saw that Choctaw's leash was wrapped around it. The man let the dog off the leash. The husky barked appreciatively, shook himself, and took a few laps around the block.

"It must be boring for him to sit like this for a long time." Cammie watched the dog sniff at the shrubs.

"I'm sure it is. But I never leave him at home alone. We go everywhere together. Choctaw is my best buddy. Hey, Choctaw!" Coach Elliot whistled and patted his knee.

Immediately, the dog was by his side, his mouth open, steam coming out of his dangling tongue.

"Good boy! Here." Coach Elliot held out his hand, offering the husky a dog treat.

Cammie noticed that even the creamy-colored dog cookie was shaped like a spiral. Choctaw gently accepted the treat. The cookie crunched between the dog's sharp teeth.

"And where's your sled, Coach Elliot?" Cammie looked around.

"My sled? Oh, it's far from here, in the Icy Park. I don't use it on Skateland streets. So we're skating to your dorm. And by the way, young lady, put your hat back on. It's freezing."

Cammie obeyed, feeling slightly disappointed. They skated in silence for a while. Cammie expected her coach to critique her technique, but the man was quiet.

"Do you live in the Icy Park, Coach Elliot?"

That was something Cammie couldn't understand. Most Skateland residents preferred settling down far away from the dark trails of the park. So far, Cammie could only think of one person living in the Icy Park, Mel Reed. Of course, she wasn't counting the witches.

"Not really. My cabin is deep in the forest. It's actually outside Skateland, though not very far."

"But why?" Cammie cringed, fearing Coach Elliot might think she was prying.

"It's quiet there," the man said simply.

Quiet? So what? How could Prince Elliot like the silence of the forest more than the busy life of Skateland, with its music and noise? Yet somehow, Cammie felt she had no right to ask the man those personal questions.

They skated along Cross Roll Street past small houses with ivy streaming down the walls and Christmas lights winking at them from the roofs. Next to a statuette of two lions, three little kids played tag. The little girl not older than five chased the boys, her blades screeching violently.

She needs to work on her edges more, Cammie thought. She glanced at Coach Elliot and noticed that the man was smiling.

"I came to Skateland when I was only six. It was the first time that I got the gold at the Annual Competition, so Mrs. Van Uffeln talked my parents into leaving me here. I spent the best years of my life at Rainbow Rinks."

The best years of his life. Did it mean he wasn't enjoying life anymore? "Did you always want to skate pairs?" Cammie asked, just to say something.

"No. I used to think I would do well in singles. But I was tall for my age, even in my childhood. So they paired me with Felicia when I was twelve and she was ten. We started winning right away. Felicia was so small and light. We always went for the hardest lifts."

Coach Elliot's voice suddenly became flat, as though drained from all emotion. Darkness seemed to have thickened around them. Choctaw barked loudly and ran after a tubby cat. The cat flew up a tree then hopped to the roof of the nearby house.

"You've got to be very careful when you skate, Cammie," Coach Elliot said in the same monotonous voice. "I want you to promise me that you'll never take any unnecessary risks."

So he *did* care about her. "Sure."

"And never, and I repeat *never* try any difficult jumps without me."

"I won't." That was a lesson Cammie had already learned.

"You remind me of Felicia." Coach Elliot's looked at her with a faint smile. "She didn't really look like you. She was a redhead, and she was smaller than you. But I see the same joy in you when you skate. That's what counts the most. Everything else can be taught."

If that wasn't a compliment, what was? Cammie felt her lips spread wider. "I would do anything to become a good skater."

"You're already doing everything."

They skated along Axel Avenue. The dorm building was straight ahead. Cammie could see light in the living room. Dinner was probably over. That was okay. Mrs. Page would never let Cammie go to bed hungry.

"Mrs. Page must be worried about you," Coach Elliot said.

"Sonia probably told her where I was." Cammie hesitated for a moment. "I just wanted to get some tips from your lesson with Celine."

"That was smart of you. Celine is a talented skater, but she needs to practice harder. Actually, she could learn work ethic from you, Cammie."

He likes me more, Cammie thought happily.

They were already at the entrance. Choctaw rubbed his nose against the steps and finally sat down next to Prince Elliot. Snowflakes sparkled like sequins on the dog's thick hair.

"I'll see you tomorrow, Cammie. Have a good night." Coach Elliot gently nudged Cammie toward the front door and skated away, Choctaw trotting by his side.

TRIPLE AXEL

Melvin Reed called Cammie early on Saturday morning. "I have good news for you, Cammie. Your Kanga bag is ready."

"Oh, thank you, Mr. Reed!"

She stopped by the skate sharpener's cabin on her way to the Silver Rink. Her skating bag looked brand new. Kanga's fur appeared washed. It felt soft and smooth. Cammie quickly loaded the bag with her change of clothes, skate guards, water bottle, and a snack. Now she wouldn't have to carry all that stuff on her back. And tonight, she would watch Grand Prix final on Kanga's media player. Life couldn't be better. Of course, Kanga's alarm clock would wake her up at five again on Monday morning. But that was okay. Humming with joy, Cammie skated in the direction of the Sport Center.

Saturday afternoon public sessions at the Silver Rink always reminded Cammie of skating exhibitions. Skaters didn't merely practice; they watched one another, and they judged, critiqued, compared. Public sessions were energizing, challenging. And yet since her injury, Cammie had somehow lost interest in Silver Rink public sessions. With most of her doubles gone, she knew she looked very much like a beginner. She hated people's sympathetic looks. She had grown tired of whispers behind her back.

"She's done."

"Yeah, I always knew she was just a fluke."

"Cammie Wester? Give me a break. She is past her peak. That's for sure."

Today, I'm going to show them what I can do, Cammie thought as she put on her new outfit—a purple T-shirt over a black skirt.

Perhaps after practice, Alex would be willing to hang out with her. The two of them could go to Sweet Blades. For crying out loud, they hadn't talked for quite a long time. They could invite Jeff and Sonia too.

Yet when Cammie stepped onto the silver ice, she realized Alex's plans for tonight were different. Dressed in tight black skating pants and a white shirt, Alex glided along the perimeter of the rink with a girl by his side. The girl, of course, was Celine. She wore a hot pink skating dress with so many sequins that the original fabric was only barely seen. Celine had also added some pink streaks to her hair to go with the dress. Cammie had to hand it to the girl. She looked stunning. However, were good looks the only thing that mattered?

Alex separated himself from Celine. The moment he let go of her hand, Jeff rushed to Celine's side.

"A circle of love," Sonia said as she skated past Cammie.

Cammie watched Alex perform a set of difficult steps in the middle of the arena. Cammie recognized the senior test pattern, the one Sonia had been struggling with. Then Alex went around the rink in fast backward crossovers. He stepped forward and bent his left knee. Cammie realized that her friend was going to attempt a triple axel. She crossed her fingers, wishing for him to succeed. No, even though Alex had managed to complete the rotation, there simply hadn't been enough height. He crushed onto the ice.

Celine laughed. "You blew it."

Alex stood up, his face red. "I can do it."

"No. It's my turn." Jeff rushed forward, perhaps a little too fast. He sprung off his left forward outside edge. No, it was only a double axel.

"Is there a man here who can do a triple axel?" Celine spread her arms, looking as though her whole life depended on someone executing a clean, three-and-a-half-revolution jump.

"I think I can make the lady happy," Michael said. He set himself up for the difficult jump.

Cammie could tell the boy was trying hard, but he wasn't even close. He only completed two revolutions and landed on both feet.

Alex tried again, and he was almost successful. He completed three and a half revolutions then teetered precariously on his blade, flailing his arms. Finally, he fell down again.

"Not bad!" Cammie shouted, but the boys ignored her.

"My turn." Jeff tried again and fell.

Michael didn't even go for another attempt. He skated away and started working on his camel spin in the corner.

Kyle, the reigning junior national champion, skated up to Celine. "I see you want a triple axel, Little Robber Girl. So be it."

Kyle's skating was secure. The boy really took his time preparing for the tough jump. He completed three and a half revolutions easily and landed softly on his blade, his free leg perfectly extended behind him.

"Now that's a real skater!" Celine hopped in place, her arms high in the air.

Apparently, Celine expected Kyle to stay by her side, maybe do a couple of laps around the rink with her. The boy, however, smiled at Celine and joined Brittany Stein, a seventeen-year-old senior skater. Even if the rejection shocked Celine, she didn't show it. She merely fluffed her pink-streaked hair and glided smoothly forward. Halfway across the rink, she raised her leg in a high arabesque. The boys cheered. Cammie wondered why they were all so excited over such a basic move. Her own spiral wasn't any worse.

"Hey, what's he doing?" Michael shouted from the corner.

Cammie followed the directions of Michael's hand. What she saw made her gasp. Within about forty feet of her, Lieutenant Turner was doing backward crossovers, his blades cutting deep into the ice. The young cop set himself for the axel entrance then took off his forward outside edge. It looked like Bob Turner aimed at a double axel. Yet the jump came out awfully under-rotated, and the young man collapsed onto the ice.

"Don't even try!" Kyle shouted as he shot by with Brittany by his side.

Lieutenant Turner glanced quickly in Cammie's direction. She saw his clasp his fists stubbornly and circle the rink one more time. He jumped up. That time, he did a decent single axel.

"That was okay," Cammie said just to cheer him up a little. Her last words got drowned in an avalanche of whistles and catcalls.

"A single axel! Oh my God!" Brittany was doubled over with laughter.

"I would step off the ice if I were you, Officer," Kyle said, faking seriousness.

"How's he going to get better if he leaves?" Alex asked innocently. He winked at Celine, who was grinning by his side.

"I'm sure a few lessons at the Pink Rink could really help," Jeff said.

"Leave him alone!" Cammie shouted.

Immediately, she felt shocked at her outburst. The truth was she had never liked Lieutenant Turner. She actually hated him. Sour and smug, the young man always found ways to annoy her. Yet this time, the young cop was being bullied unmercifully, and that was wrong. So what if he couldn't do a double axel? Lieutenant Turner wasn't a competitive skater anymore; he couldn't be expected to be in perfect shape. Cammie shivered at the silence around her.

"Watch out, people. Cammie has a crush on our valiant officer," Celine said in a sugary voice.

The girls clad in multicolored dresses giggled. Jeff averted his eyes. For a split second, Cammie thought she noticed Alex's sympathetic look, but then her friend looked away.

"She's right!" Sonia shouted. "We must never look down on other skaters. Because—"

"Because if we do, we're on our way to becoming witches!" Cammie blurted out.

Before the rest of the skaters had a chance to digest her words, a loud whistle came from the stands. Captain Greenfield stepped onto the ice.

"Lieutenant Turner, you're here to ensure the skaters' safety, not to show off. I suggest you leave the ice immediately."

"Yes, sir." Bob Turner hung his head so low that Cammie was concerned his long nose would pull him down onto the ice.

Captain Greenfield gave the skaters a cheerful wave. His gray uniform was perfectly pressed. "Enjoy your practice, champions!"

The session resumed, though Cammie's festive mood had somehow abated. She was no longer looking forward to demonstrating her newly acquired doubles to the crowd. On top of everything else, she felt tired. She might as well head to the dorm and catch up on her homework.

On her way back home, Cammie couldn't help thinking of Celine. What was so special about the showgirl that she had somehow managed to capture the heart of every Skateland boy, even Lieutenant Turner? For it didn't take a rocket scientist to understand what had prompted the young cop to show off his skills at the Silver Rink. He too was a victim of Celine's charm.

In the dorm, Cammie took a quick shower and put on her old, worn-out sweatshirt and loose, faded leggings. She wanted to be as comfortable as she could. She picked up the biography of Dorothy Hamill and plopped on her bed. Their English teacher had assigned them a book report. Out of the famous skaters, Cammie had picked out Dorothy Hamill, but she still hadn't had a chance to get started.

Cammie read till the sky outside turned dark gray. She got up and flipped the light switch. Outside, it was snowing again, but Cammie's room was warm and comfortable.

The door opened, and Sonia walked in, her face red. "Oh, here you are. Why did you leave early, because of Celine?"

Cammie turned a page. "Because of everybody, actually. Why're they all so smug? Okay, Turner isn't a good skater anymore. He had to quit. So what? It can happen to all of us."

Sonia's face became serious. "True. I guess people don't understand it unless it really happens."

"I do," Cammie said sadly. "Last year, I got injured and lost all of my jumps."

"They're coming back, though, right?"

"Yes!" Cammie jumped off her bed. "I got all the doubles already. We're starting to work on my double axel on Monday."

"Oh, Cammie, that's wonderful!" Sonia hugged her.

"But Celine!" Sonia grimaced. "You saw what she's like."

Cammie nodded. "A showoff."

"And all the guys are drooling over her. I thought Jeff had more sense. We've been friends all our lives, you know. I thought friendship meant more to him. Now he's gone totally nuts."

"Alex too," Cammie said. "But I don't care."

"I thought you liked Alex."

"Sure I like him. But only as a friend, not as... you know."

"Really? Because I thought—"

The door opened, and Liz peeped in. "Hey, what're the two of you so serious for? Come to our room. Celine has something fun for us to do."

"Thank you. We're fine," Sonia said.

Liz tossed her dark hair behind her shoulder. "You won't regret it. I promise."

Cammie quickly looked in Sonia's direction and saw her friend shrug.

"We're coming," Cammie said. She wondered what Celine had thought of.

When Liz left the room, Sonia made a few nasty faces at the closed door.

"Look, it would be good for us to take our minds off skating for a short time," Cammie said.

Still looking sour, Sonia followed Cammie to the room across from theirs. The lights were out. Except for a lonely candle positioned in the center of the room, it was completely dark. Celine and Liz sat cross-legged on the floor, leaning against a stack of cushions.

"Oh hi. Take your seats." Celine, bright-eyed, dressed in a pink tracksuit, pointed to the multicolored cushions strewn all over the carpet.

"Thanks." Cammie threw herself on the floor.

Sonia leaned against the wall and pulled her knees to her chest.

"Okay. Here is what I want to tell you, girls." Celine beamed at them, revealing two perfect dimples. "Does it ever occur to you that while we work our buns off here, life is passing us by?"

Cammie saw Sonia lift her eyebrows slightly.

"Just tell me the truth, everybody. How many real dates have you had?" Celine asked.

Wow. That was a blunt question. Cammie found herself wondering what could qualify as a real date. Okay, last year, she had danced at the Main Rink with Kyle. Yet he hadn't even walked her home, and it was after midnight—

"Well, your silence probably means you haven't had any. Too sad. How do you expect to convey the true meaning of music on ice, and that's what Mr. Dulcimer wants, if you don't know anything about love?"

Wow. She's probably right, Cammie thought. With a few exceptions, most pieces of music spoke of love, of perfect harmony, of passion. Perhaps the very fact that Cammie had never been in love explained why she couldn't fulfill Mr. Dulcimer's requirements and become one with the music.

"So are you suggesting that you know everything about love?" Sonia demanded, staring straight at Celine.

The showgirl fluffed her hair. "*Everything* would be too much to say, of course, but, well, I've had a few dates, perhaps even too many."

Liz's lips formed a perfect circle, as though the girl was saying, "Oh."

"Which brings me straight to the point," Celine said. "There are quite a few cute guys here, in Skateland, and they all like me, but still…" She made an exaggerated sigh. "I have to confess something: I feel totally miserable."

"Miserable?" Liz looked incredulous.

"Of course. See, chances are that one of those guys is the love of my life, right?" Celine looked around, apparently waiting for the girls to agree with her. When no one spoke up, Celine went on. "But I have no idea who it is. That's what."

Everything became quiet. The only sound Cammie could hear was the distant music in the hallway. The younger girls were probably watching television.

"Would you all like to know who is meant to be your man, your husband?"

Celine's last questions sent chills down Cammie's body. The truth was that Cammie already knew the answer. Prince Elliot! *Just let me not blush. I don't want anyone to notice,* she prayed silently. Her heart fluttered in her chest like a startled bird. *No one is supposed to know. It's my secret.*

"There's a way to find out," Celine said.

Liz rose on her knees. "How?"

Sonia didn't say anything, but by the sparks in her eyes, Cammie could see that her friend was definitely interested.

"You know that my mom trained here too when she was a child," Celine said. "So she told me about this magical rink in the Icy Park. It's called the Fortune Rink. If you look at the ice on a night of a full moon, you can see the man who is destined to be yours."

The darkness spun around Cammie, and then the candlelight formed a perfect round shape like the moon. Coach Elliot's face loomed in her mental vision. Yes, he was her man.

"Cammie! Do you hear me?"

"Ah. What?" Cammie rubbed her forehead.

The three girls were staring at her.

"Are you coming or what?" Celine asked. "Because tonight the moon is full, so…"

"Tonight?" Cammie exclaimed.

"And why not?" Liz switched sides and pulled her wool socks up higher.

"Personally, I can't wait." In the reflected light of the candle, Celine's eyes looked like two amethysts. "My mom visited the Fortune Rink when she was fifteen, just like me, and she saw Dad's face there."

Was that really possible? "Uh…I'd like to come," Cammie heard herself say.

"How about you, Sonia?" Liz asked.

Sonia played with the cuff of her sweater. "Sounds like fun."

"Definitely." Celine clapped her hands. "Mom says the Fortune Rink is perfectly round, and the ice is transparent. So during the day, you can see the reflection of the trees and the sky, but when the full moon is out—"

"Dinner's ready!"

The door opened. Startled, Cammie raised her hand to protect her eyes from the bright light from the hallway.

Rita's slightly pudgy figure stepped in. "What're you guys doing in the dark?"

"Would you mind closing the door, Rita?" Though quiet, Celine's voice had unmistakable authority.

There was a squeak, and the door was shut.

"We don't want those Green Rink girls to know what we're up to," Celine said. "Oops. Sorry, Cammie. We didn't mean you, of course."

Cammie was glad the darkness provided a perfect cover for her flashing cheeks.

"How far is the Fortune Rink?" Sonia asked.

"I have the directions right here." Celine patted the pocket of her velvet hoodie. "I don't think it's very far. If Mom made it easily, why can't we?"

"Can we go right now, then," Sonia asked, "before it gets too late?"

Celine shook her head violently. "Of course not. It has to be done at midnight. That's when the gates of destiny are open."

The light of the candle flickered. Again, Cammie felt the chills of excitement rush through her body. The gates of destiny. Tonight, she was about to unveil the mystery of her future.

"But how about our morning practice?" Sonia asked uncertainly. "If I don't get enough sleep, I'll be sluggish and Coach Darrell will kill me, so—"

"It's not Coach Darrel you need to be afraid of, Sonia," Celine said.

Sonia's eyes flashed a question.

"It's your fanaticism that will get you into a mental institution one day." Celine sounded almost concerned.

For a moment, Sonia stared at the showgirl, and then her mouth cracked a smile.

"For your information, tomorrow is Sunday," Celine said.

"Oh!" Sonia's smile widened. "I completely forgot."

"See? That's the first stage of mental degradation." Celine shook her finger at Sonia.

That time, all of them laughed. The door opened again, and Mrs. Page walked in, her hands on her hips. "Do you expect me to heat up dinner for you three times?"

"Oh. We're sorry, Mrs. Page," Celine said.

"We'll be right down," Liz added.

Mrs. Page's silhouette bent forward as though surveying the room. "And what're you sitting in the dark for?"

Cammie glanced at Celine, wondering what excuse the girl would come up with.

"Just girls' talk, you know," Celine said importantly.

Mrs. Page raised her head. "Ah. Okay. Well, you don't want your tilapia to get cold."

There was a click and the room plunged into darkness again.

"Wow. That was cool, Celine," Cammie said.

The showgirl shrugged. "Be my guest. See, half-truth is always the best. This way no one can accuse you of lying, and you still get to keep your secret."

At dinner, the four of them tried to keep their voices down. Cammie felt so excited, tilapia with mashed potatoes didn't look particularly appealing.

"I would finish the meal if I were you. You need strength to skate through the Icy Park," Celine said.

Cammie picked up her fork. "I have one concern. What if the cops show up?"

"Oh!" Sonia pushed her glass of ice tea away.

Celine appeared to be thinking hard. "They say the best defense is a good offense, right? So to prevent a possible intrusion, let's ask Bob Turner to join us."

"No!" The three of them shouted.

"Be quiet and finish your meal!" Mrs. Page snapped. "What's the matter with you three?"

Cammie lowered her voice to a whisper. "We're not taking this idiot with us, okay?"

"And why not?" Celine asked.

"Are you afraid you'll see Lieutenant's face in the Fortune Rink?" Liz asked.

"You're nuts!" Cammie's hand brushed against her plate, sending it to the edge of the table.

Sonia caught the plate just in time before it fell on the floor.

"Now I won't have this in my dining room!" Mrs. Page approached their table, her lips pressed in a tight, angry line, her eyes flashing. "One more sound from this table and none of you are getting any dessert."

Celine folded her hands on her chest. "Oh, Mrs. Page, you can't be that cruel!"

The showgirl was quite an actress. If Cammie hadn't noticed the quick smile on Celine's lips, she would swear the girl was going to cry.

Mrs. Page smiled back and went back to the kitchen. There was a clanging sound of the stove opening and closing, and then the unmistakable smell of baked dough wafted into the dining room.

"Actually, it would be better to take the dessert with us," Celine whispered.

"Why?" Liz asked.

"Well, if we get tired or cold, a snack will be quite useful. Yes, and we need to take some hot tea with us in a thermos."

"We don't have a thermos, Celine, and I doubt Mrs. Page will lend us one." Liz looked at the dorm supervisor, who had brought in a tray filled with what looked like perfect snowballs.

"It's my new promotional item. Snowball rolls," Mrs. Page said with unmistakable pride. She walked around the dining room, offering the rolls to the girls.

"Wrap it up in a napkin and put it in your pocket!" Celine hissed.

The freshly baked roll looked divine. Reluctantly, Cammie stuffed hers in her pocket and sipped her tea. The plain hot liquid tasted dull. Cammie reached for the sugar bowl.

"We have a thermos in our room, Cammie," Sonia said softly. "Remember how you and Alex poured tea in it when we worked on my jumps in France?"

"That's right!"

Sonia was talking about the time when she had been kidnapped by the witches and taken to 1936 Paris by Wilhelmina's magic *Skating History* book. To deliver the girl from the curses, Cammie and Alex had had to help her relearn all of her doubles and triples. Mrs. Page had done her share of assistance by providing food and a thermos of hot tea every day. And, how great, the dorm supervisor had never asked for the thermos to be returned to her.

"Okay, Sonia. Give the thermos to Liz and she'll fill it up with hot tea," Celine said.

Liz bolted up. "Why me?"

"Because you have more guts than these snow maidens!"

Before Cammie had a chance to rebuke Celine, the showgirl stood up. "Be ready at eleven o'clock. And dress warm."

THE FORTUNE RINK

Cammie would never have imagined that Sonia would be such a nervous wreck. As the two of them tiptoed along the hallway, Cammie's roommate kept casting nervous glances at the closed doors. "What if someone hears us? Ouch!"

"Be quiet!" Cammie snapped.

"I stubbed my toe. Ugh! It hurts!"

Cammie bent over and picked up a skating boot. The blade was still wet. "That's Angela's. She never puts her stuff away."

Sonia put her own skates on the carpet and sat down, rubbing her toe. "How am I going to skate?"

"Just like you normally do. Push forward with one foot and then with the other."

"I don't think it's a laughing matter!"

They sprinted down to the first floor, and Cammie lifted the sliding glass of the window at the end of the hallway. "Come on."

Sonia laced up her boots and leaned out of the window. "But the ground is too far down!"

"Don't worry. I've done it before. Let me go first." Cammie swung her leg and saddled the windowsill. For a couple of seconds, she clung to the frame, her legs dangling, and then she let go.

"Are you all right?" Sonia squeaked.

"Sure. The snow is deep. Go ahead."

Sonia curled into a tight ball and jumped, sending snow into Cammie's face. "Wow! It's soft!"

"Calm down, you two!" Liz's angry voice came from the ice path.

Brushing the snow off her gloves, Cammie hurried forward. Celine and Liz already waited for them in the middle of the street.

"We made it!" Sonia said happily.

"It's a big surprise that the cops aren't here already with all the racket you're making," Liz said angrily.

Celine put her hands into the pockets of her silvery mink jacket. "It's a beautiful night, girls."

Cammie squinted at the perfectly round pearly moon. The night was unusually clear with clusters of stars strewn across the deep, black sky.

"Where exactly are we going, Celine?" Cammie asked.

Celine glanced at a small piece of paper clutched in her hand. "Straight into the park and then right."

The four of them moved forward, bending their knees deep to stay warm. It wasn't windy, but the frost nipped Cammie's cheeks and nose.

"Have you ever been to the Fortune Rink yourself, Celine?" Cammie picked up speed to catch up with the girl.

"Never. So I'm as excited as all of you. I wonder whom I'll see." Celine slowed down a little. "See, Alex is good-looking, and Jeff is cute too. Michael...well, I like his rebellious spirit."

Cammie felt Sonia stiffen behind her.

"But I hope it'll be Kyle," Celine said. "Did you guys see his triple axel?"

"What does the boy's jumping technique have to do with anything?" Sonia asked.

Celine went into a quick T-stop. "Would any of you want to date a guy who's not championship material? Liz?"

Liz hopped across a frozen limb. "Never."

"Cammie?"

"I...I don't know." Of course, Prince Elliot was a champion already, so Cammie didn't have to worry about that part.

Sonia coughed. "What matters is for the boy to be nice, and kind, and—"

"Good-looking!" Liz said.

"I think Jeff fits the description." Celine touched Sonia's arm.

"And what does Jeff have to do with anything?" Sonia snapped.

Before Celine had a chance to answer, Liz raised her hand. "Hush! Did you hear it?"

"What?" Celine asked in a small voice.

Liz put her finger against her lips. The four of them listened in silence, but all Cammie could hear was her own deep breathing.

"I think there's someone over there." Sonia's trembling hand pointed in the direction they had just come from.

Cammie straightened her eyes. The moonlight illuminated only the first thirty feet of the ice path. Whatever was beyond that was drowned in thick blackness. And then the sound came, soft but clear. Someone was making his way through the forest, someone wearing skates.

"Run!" Cammie mouthed and dashed forward.

The rhythmical whooshing of the blades on both sides told her that the other girls were following. They skated deeper and deeper into the park. The tall trees gathered around them allowed only occasional glimpses of silvery light.

"Wait!" Celine did a hockey stop.

The rest of them froze by Celine's side.

"I think we lost him," Liz said.

"Definitely." Whoever the stalker was, Cammie could no longer hear him.

"But who could that be?" Sonia's face was unusually pale.

Cammie sighed. "The witches. Mrs. Page. The cops. I'm not even sure who would be the worst."

"No!" Sonia's wide-open eyes darted back and forth between the thicket and Cammie. "I wish I hadn't come with you! I wish—"

"Do you mind shutting your mouth? I can't think!" Celine studied her piece of paper.

"You don't know how strict they are about breaking rules here," Sonia whined. "If they catch us, they'll tell my parents. And then—"

"Okay, we went a little too far," Celine said, ignoring Sonia's whimper. "We have to go back about a quarter mile and then—"

"Didn't you hear what I said?" Sonia cast another scared look at the coppice behind her.

Celine shrugged. "Whoever our pursuer was, our little trip isn't a secret anymore. So why not finish what we started?"

Cammie smiled at the showgirl's logic. Actually, Celine was right. If they had been chased by Mrs. Page or the cops, they would be in trouble no later than tomorrow. But if they had been spotted by the witches, chances were that they could still escape freely. At least their pursuer seemed to have lost them.

"I think we should head to the Fortune Rink," Cammie said. "It's too late to turn back at this point."

"I'm all for it," Liz said.

"But girls…" Sonia clasped and unclasped her hands.

"It looks like you're in the minority here, Sonia," Celine said. "Of course, you can go back. We won't keep you."

Sonia's chin twitched. "Me going back to the dorm alone? No way."

"Then follow me." Celine was already heading for the thicket behind them.

The three girls joined her, Sonia still fussing about the possible repercussions.

"Here it is!" Celine shouted.

Cammie caught up with the showgirl and clapped her hands in amazement. They stood in front of a perfectly circular pond with ice so smooth that it looked like glass. The ice was neither gray nor white. It was like clear water, perfectly transparent. Small trees grew around the pond. Their branches were glazed with packed snow, which gave them an almost enchanted look. Even the sky arching above the Fortune Rink didn't look dark but silver. The distant stars seemed to be winking in encouragement.

"Well, it's time for revelations." Celine knelt in front of the pond, studying the ice.

Liz dropped her backpack on the snow. "So who goes first?"

"Sonia, how about you?" Celine asked.

"Wait. Are you going to look at my man too?"

"And why not?"

Sonia shook her head. "It's private. Cammie, tell her."

"Absolutely," Cammie said.

"You think we don't know your little secrets, girls?" Celine asked.

She can't know anything, Cammie thought, hoping the showgirl wouldn't notice her burning cheeks. *I only told Sonia about Prince Elliot, and she would never tell.*

"I have no secrets from my friends," Liz said.

"Look!" Cammie didn't even know what she was going to say.

Celine glanced at her gold wristwatch. "You know what? I think we'd better scatter around and do it separately."

"But why?" Liz appeared genuinely disappointed.

"We don't have much time. And it might take a while before the Fortune Rink reveals its secrets to us. Mom said she had waited for about an hour."

"That long?"

Without saying another word, Celine stepped on the clear ice. The moment her blade touched the surface, the ice responded with a soft clinging sound, reminding Cammie of a little bell.

"What was that?" Sonia smoothed the ice with her glove.

Liz bunny-hopped onto the ice, causing it to jingle even louder. Celine did a few toe taps accompanied by more tinkling. It was as though a sled pulled by a reindeer glided by. Cammie joined the rest of the girls. For a few moments, they tried to outdo one another, making the ice play different rhythms.

"Okay. Back to business!" Celine finally said. "Look, this spot is mine."

The showgirl knelt on the ice in the middle of the pond and stared into the depth. Liz took a spot closer to the edge. Cammie and Sonia shrugged and moved to the opposite sides of the rink.

Following Celine's example, Cammie knelt over, brought her face close to the ice, and peered into the frozen water. She saw absolutely nothing except for an interplay of gray-and-white shadows. She was sure it was the light of the moon that created the impression.

"I can't see anything!" Liz's voice came from Cammie's right.

"Don't look away! Concentrate," Celine said.

"Do you see anything, Celine?" Cammie asked.

"Of course." The showgirl sounded smug.

"How about you, Sonia?" Cammie turned left.

"Stop talking! It destroys the magic," Celine exclaimed.

Cammie groaned and stared at the ice so hard that her eyes began to sting. Still, she could see nothing except moving shadows of varying degrees of white and gray.

She didn't know how much time had passed. At the beginning, she was cold, and then she didn't feel uncomfortable anymore. The shadows swirled and then scattered to the sides. There was a long corridor leading somewhere to the bottom of the pond. Something moved at the very end of the passage, someone looking like a human being.

Cammie moved closer to the ice, afraid that if she looked away, the vision would disappear. No, it was still there, and now she could clearly see that it was a man. Yes, the very person she had hoped to see. It couldn't be a mistake. She definitely recognized the tall, slender figure and the blond hair brushing the collar of his black sweater.

"Aha! That's what I thought!"

"Ouch!" Startled, Cammie felt her hand slip. She lost balance and fell to the side. Something brushed her cheek, and the next thing Cammie saw was Celine's white glove on the ice next to her. Cammie looked up. Celine was leaning over her chosen spot. "You can't look at that!" Cammie stretched her hands to push the girl away, but Celine ducked easily.

"Really, Cammie! I haven't seen anything new!"

"You can't!" With the corner of her eye, Cammie could see Sonia still deeply immersed in the study of the surface in front of her.

Cammie threw herself onto the ice, trying to shield her spot from the showgirl.

"I think I'll eliminate this one from my list of eligible man, then," Celine said.

"Who is the guy?" Liz looked as though she was done with her fortune telling. Cammie saw her approach Sonia's spot.

"Sonia, watch out!" Cammie shouted.

"Go away!"

"Oh, that's interesting." Liz bent over.

With a loud shriek, Sonia pushed Liz on the side, sending her down to the ice. Liz responded with a blow on Sonia's shoulder.

"Get her off me!" Sonia screamed.

Before Cammie had a chance to say anything, a loud whistle came from the narrow path they had come from. A figure dressed in gray crossed the snow-covered lawn and stopped on the edge of the Fortune Rink. The young man with a long nose and a pout smiled at them. "Having a good time, lawbreakers?"

Lieutenant Turner. So it was he who had been following them. Of all the possible stalkers, he was surely the worst. Cammie gritted her teeth in frustration. If they had to face the cops, Cammie would definitely prefer Captain Greenfield.

"Good evening, Bob! It's such a pleasure to see you," Celine sang.

Cammie was so shocked that she forgot she was supposed to be mad at the showgirl.

"I assume you're here to give us all a ride back to the dorm," Celine said. "How very charming!"

The showgirl really had the guts.

Lieutenant Turner's nose now looked like a hot pepper, perhaps because of the frosty air. "I could arrest you all, you know, especially this one. She already has a criminal record."

Cammie flinched as the cop nodded in her direction.

Celine's smile widened. "So you're a felon, Cammie."

Cammie rolled her eyes.

"I kind of suspected you have a crush on Cammie, Bob. You know what? Just take us back home and she's all yours," Celine said.

"What?" Cammie yelled.

Bob's face was now deep maroon. "That's not the issue. I—"

"It's okay, Officer. We understand." Celine was all sweetness, but as she turned to Cammie, her eyes were like burning coals.

"Be nice to him!" Celine said through clenched teeth.

"You're nuts. You know what?" Cammie jerked her hand away from Celine's grasp.

"Cammie just told me she'd really appreciate your help, Lieutenant Turner." Celine gave the young man a playful tap on the arm.

"Celine!" Cammie was afraid she was going to cry. She had never been humiliated like that.

Lieutenant Turner took off his hat and ran his hand through his hair. His hand shook slightly. "Well, I...

hmm. Of course. Let's go to the icemobile, then. It's parked right there, close to the trees."

Behind the man's back, Liz gave Celine a thumbs-up. Celine smiled and smoothed out her jacket. The moon made the gray fur sparkle as though it was decorated with sequins.

The four of them followed Lieutenant Turner to the police icemobile. Everybody, including Sonia, looked relieved. Cammie tagged along in the back. *Just wait 'til he files an official report*, she thought. *You can't trust this dork, Celine! No way!*

Bob Turner cleared his throat. "It's not safe to be in the park at this hour, you know. Something bad is happening in Skateland now."

As though we don't know about the witches.

"The witches are really nasty, aren't they?" Sonia too sounded as though she was trying to keep the conversation going.

Bob Turner shook his head. "It's not that." He opened the back door, waiting for Celine, Liz, and Sonia to get inside.

"Hey, wait for me!" Cammie's hand brushed against the closed door.

"You can sit in the front, Cammie!" Lieutenant Turner smiled at her.

Cammie would feel better if the cop kept insulting her the way he had done before. That sort of behavior would have been familiar and, therefore, less threatening. The kind, sweet Bob Turner was something Cammie wasn't used to. Cammie sank onto the soft leather cushion on the passenger seat, trying to stay as far away from Lieutenant Turner as possible.

"Look, girls. I won't report you if you promise to stay away from the Icy Park," the young cop said.

"What else is dangerous there?" Sonia asked. "You said it wasn't the witches."

Lieutenant Turner spread his arms. "At this point, everything is in the realm of suppositions. But there are definitely strange creatures in the park, and believe me, they are much more dangerous than the witches. You girls are no match for them."

Without waiting for any of them to say a word, Bob bent over the dashboard. "Intermediate and Novice Dorm."

The icemobile shot forward. As it took a sharp curve into the thicket, the gravity pushed Cammie against Lieutenant Turner's side. She gritted her teeth and grabbed the handle, desperately trying to move away. She could almost feel Celine and Liz exchange winks in the back. For crying out loud, how she wished Captain Greenfield had come after them himself instead of sending his cocky assistant.

The ride to the dorm seemed short. Celine had to be right. The Fortune Rink wasn't that far away. As the icemobile came to a stop in front of the dorm building, Lieutenant Turner offered Cammie a hand, which she ignored.

"Thank you, Bob!" Celine blew the young officer a kiss.

"Hmm. May I ask you a question, Lieutenant Turner?" Sonia spoke up.

Cammie looked back, interested.

"How did you know we were in the Icy Park?"

"I saw the four of you jump out of the dorm window," the young man said.

What?

"Why were you next to our dorm in the middle of the night?"

"Just doing my job. It's my solemn duty to ensure the residents' safety." Bob Turner's brown eyes seemed to be escaping their inquisitive looks.

"Or one particular resident's safety," Celine echoed, glancing straight at Cammie.

"You know what? Give me a break!" Without waiting another second, Cammie bolted forward. She rose on her toes, reaching for the sliding glass. She pushed it up. When safely inside the building, she removed her skates and tiptoed to the third floor.

When Sonia walked into the room, Cammie was taking her pajamas out of the closet.

"Is the freak gone?" Cammie fluffed her pillow.

"Yup. He rode away. Cammie, you can kill me on the spot, but it looks like the cop really likes you."

"Oh, Sonia, please! Not you too!"

"I know, I know. At least he won't tell on us, and that's good." Sonia put her skates away and lowered herself on the carpet.

"What?" Cammie could see her roommate was about to ask her something.

"Cammie, did you see anything in that ice?"

Cammie hesitated for a few moments and then nodded.

"Me too." Sonia took the scrunchie out of her hair. "And you know what? I think it was Jeff."

"But you didn't need the magical rink to find out you liked Jeff," Cammie said.

"I guess not. " Sonia rolled on her stomach and looked up at Cammie. "May I ask you who you saw?" Silver stars danced in Sonia's eyes, as though the Fortune Rink had somehow left an imprint there.

"Prince...I mean Coach Elliot." *What a beautiful name,* Cammie thought. *It sounds just like the jingling bells, like the ice at the Fortune Rink.*

"Really?"

Cammie wondered what was so surprising about that.

"But...but he's so much older."

"My grandma says twenty years' difference isn't that much for a man and a woman to be together." Cammie looked at the dark sky outside the window. The full moon was still out, and suddenly Cammie felt very, very light.

"Let's go to bed. Okay?" Cammie quickly changed into her pajamas and pulled the covers up to her chin. As she smiled, thinking of what had happened that night, she was sure she would never be able to fall asleep. But the moon covered her with its silver blanket, and before Cammie knew, it was already morning.

A MYSTERIOUS ATTACK

"You're doing much better, Cammie," Coach Elliot said at the end of Monday afternoon practice.

Cammie glanced up, surprised.

He grinned at her from under the bill of his baseball cap. "Of course, you still need more consistency on your double axel, but it's coming along nicely. You're even getting the hang of your triple salchow. We'll definitely put difficult jumps in your program."

Cammie's head spun. After an hour of doing double-double combinations, she felt a little dizzy. The green walls of the rink danced around her. For a moment, she pictured herself and Coach Elliot in the middle of a roaring sea.

"I think it's time you performed up to your potential, Cammie," Coach Elliot said. "Do you think you're ready to do a double axel in your show program?"

A green wave lifted Cammie and carried her forward. The walls tilted. She swayed and would have fallen if Coach Elliot hadn't grabbed her hand. "Are you all right?"

"Do you...do you mean St. Valentine's show?"

St. Valentine's show was supposed to be a big thing that year in Skateland. As far as Cammie knew, everybody had come up with some kind of a love theme for their programs. Her own *Romeo and Juliet* would fit right in. And with all those difficult jumps, her program would be definitely a hit. And yet...St. Valentine was only two weeks away. Would two weeks be enough for Cammie to start landing her double axel consistently?

"You can do it, Cammie." Coach Elliot's look was so warm that she wasn't afraid anymore.

Cheer up, Cammie! If he is sure you can land all doubles, what's there to worry about? She knew she was beaming when she looked him in the eyes. "I'll do my best."

"Yes, you'd better." He seemed to be thinking hard. "Both of us are taking a risk here, which means we need to work harder."

"But I..." Was Coach Elliot suggesting that Cammie hadn't been practicing hard enough?

"You'll need a few more lessons with PRESTO," Coach Elliot said. "So I got us some extra ice time at the Silver Rink. Can you get there tomorrow right after school? I would say around two thirty?"

That meant Cammie would only have time for a very quick snack. No big deal. She would grab something from the snack bar at the rink.

"Of course!"

"Celine is coming too," Coach Elliot said.

Oh no! So it wouldn't be just the two of them. What a bummer! Oh well. After all, Prince Elliot had said before that Cammie could teach Celine work ethic.

The following afternoon, Cammie changed into her skating clothes in the school locker room during the lunch break. The last class was supposed to be music interpretation, not Cammie's favorite. Especially today, when she was facing a rigorous jumping practice, she wasn't looking forward to waves of emotion, vibrations of the tone and rhythm, putting her heart and soul into her performance—boring stuff, really.

So far, no one in Cammie's class had managed to meet Mr. Dulcimer's requirements. If she could believe her teacher, they all skated like jumping machines. They merely went through the motions. Their hearts were anywhere except in the pieces they were supposed to interpret. Furthermore, the only thing they had on their minds was trying to beat one another. Cammie was actually tired of listening to that stuff. Well, perhaps Mr. Dulcimer was right in a way. But today, Cammie wanted to feel like a real athlete. Perhaps if she came to the Silver Rink early enough, she might even get a few minutes of practice on the wonderful silver ice.

Cammie liked skating at the Silver Rink. The huge arena, the long rows of seats going almost all the way up to the ceiling, almost seemed to bring her Olympic dream closer. At one o'clock in the afternoon, the huge lobby of the rink was deserted. Most skaters were either at school or in the dorm, trying to relax before the afternoon practice. Cammie got herself a cup of strong Tea Position and a chocolate chip cookie. She replaced the water bottle in Kanga's paws with the teacup, took a bite of her cookie, and pushed the heavy door leading to the rink.

Her first feeling was that of disappointment. The arena wasn't empty. A couple skated fast in the middle of the ice. The lights were dimmed, so Cammie couldn't tell who they were. So much for extra practice. On second thought, watching the couple might be interesting. Cammie didn't get to see a lot of pairs skating or ice dancing. Trying to make as little noise as possible, Cammie jogged up the steps and took a seat in the tenth row. The Silver Rink was much warmer than the other practice rinks. Cammie shook off her parka, picked up her teacup, and got ready to watch.

"Oh no!" Hot tea spilled all over Cammie's knee, but she ignored it.

Gliding across the ice in a beautiful spread eagle was Prince Elliot himself. Of course, Cammie had seen the man skate before, and she had a pretty good idea at how accomplished he was. What surprised her, however, was the fact that her coach wasn't practicing alone. Next to him was a woman, her leg raised high in a graceful spiral position. Yes, Cammie was pretty sure it was a woman, not a girl. Cammie stretched her neck and squinted, trying to see the skater's face. The woman bent her knee, and Prince Elliot lifted her easily. *The lasso lift*, Cammie admitted, automatically thinking that all the effort spent on that history essay had proved handy after all.

Now that the woman was moving across the rink, Cammie could see a narrow face, dark gray eyes, and a small, straight nose. Cammie rose up in her chair.

Of course! It was Christel Van Uffeln, Wilhelmina's daughter. Cammie remembered the Skateland president asking Prince Elliot to help her daughter with her skating. It looked like he had taken the offer seriously. Cammie had to admit that Christel looked very classy on ice. So far, Cammie had only seen her in Wilhelmina's house two years ago, right before Skateland president had sent Cammie and Alex to the past to look for Sonia. Back then, Christel had always looked sour, and her long hair had hung loosely down her back. Today, Christel's brown locks were pulled up in an elegant French twist, and her pale green skating dress made her look younger.

Cammie let out a sigh as she watched the couple do side-by-side triple toe loops. Christel was a decent skater—a very good one, actually. And Cammie could tell that Coach Elliot was a perfect partner. He led Christel across the ice gently, gracefully. When he offered his hand to the woman, there was an unmistakable expression of pride in his shining eyes. He made Christel look special. No wonder she enjoyed skating with him.

Someone clapped from the aisle. Cammie looked down and saw Wilhelmina leaning against the boards. "That was very good, Elliot and Christel. Would you like to try this part to the music?"

The next thing Cammie saw was Wilhelmina's gray head bend over the DVD player. Today, the older woman was wearing a dark purple dress. As Cammie looked around the stands, she could see quite a few people scattered around the arena, sitting alone or in tight groups of three and four. Two aisles farther, Captain Greenfield stood talking to Mr. Dawson, a tall African-American security head. And surprise! Celine sat in the second row, dressed in a white fur coat. The coat was unzipped, revealing a bright orange skating dress.

Music started playing, and Cammie recognized the familiar tune from the musical *Notre Dame de Paris*. The couple skated forward, gaining speed with each move. Coach Elliot put his hands on Christel's waist and spun her around in a throw lift. Their throw jump came next, a double salchow, which Christel landed perfectly. They glided next to each other in side-by-side spirals. Christel's extension was amazing.

Cammie clasped her hands as she watched the couple's death spiral. She had always wondered how the woman managed to keep her back almost parallel to the ice. Perhaps Cammie could try it one day too. Maybe Coach Elliot would be willing to show her that.

At some point, Cammie forgot about the steps, the jumps, and the spins. A story was unfolding on the ice, and Cammie leaned forward, trying not to miss a thing. Coach Elliot was playing the hunchback from the musical, a miserable guy who was madly in love with a beautiful woman. Somehow, the man managed to create ugliness with a tilt of his head, with his arms bent at unnatural angles. His wide-open mouth pleaded for mercy. His eyes were focused longingly on Christel. He lifted her carefully, showing off her fragile beauty, her long, graceful limbs.

Cammie's heart must have swelled to an enormous size, for there wasn't enough room in her chest. She wrapped her arms around herself. So that's what love was like. It wasn't all about joy and beauty. It could be ugly too; it could tear a person apart. The ice sparkled under their blades. It helped them. They belonged together.

What if Prince Elliot is in love with Christel? Cammie suddenly thought. No, that was ridiculous. It was his deceased wife that the man loved.

And then everything was over. The music was still playing, but the couple had stopped midway through the program and skated over to the boards. Cammie felt disappointed, even robbed. The story called for further development. She wanted to know what was going to happen next. Would those two people ever be together? Cammie squeezed the edge of her seat so hard that her knuckles began to sting. Wilhelmina sat in her usual wheelchair, her gray fur coat wrapped around her arthritic legs.

Coach Elliot drew a quick circle in the air. Christel waved her hand as though disagreeing with whatever her partner was suggesting. Wilhelmina seemed to be listening to both of them. Bits of conversation reached Cammie's ear. Once, she was sure she had heard Wilhelmina say *throw triple salchow* and *star lift*, but the rest of the words were drowned out by the music. The dramatic *Belle* tune still swirled across the ice.

Wilhelmina clapped her hands. "Moving on. Let's do your Appassionato number."

The skaters returned to the middle of the rink. The music still blasted from the speakers.

Wilhelmina slapped herself on the forehead. "Oh, I forgot to change the CDs. Somebody. Yes, Celine, do you mind slipping in the blue CD? There it is, to the right of the player. Thank you, dear."

Cammie watched the showgirl replace the *Belle* piece with another CD. The couple took their opening posture in the middle. That time, they leaned against each other, holding hands, their free arms arched. They started with side-by-side axels. Cammie had no doubt they would eventually move up to doubles. She grimaced. The music sounded a little weird. It seemed to be tripping over unseen rocks. Cammie wondered who had picked out such a jerky piece for the lyrical couple. It had to be Wilhelmina, of course. Perhaps it was the woman's idea of originality. Cammie's hands clammed up. For some reason, she found herself struggling for breath. Gosh. What was wrong with her?

Down on the ice, the skaters were getting ready for a lift. Coach Elliot's hands were placed on Christel's waist.

"Stop! Stop right away!" Wilhelmina shouted.

Coach Elliot's hands slid off Christel. She collapsed onto the ice. She would have hit her head if Coach Elliot hadn't caught her.

Now there was hardly any melody coming from the speaker, just a series of banging and hissing. The lights went off for a split second and then came back. Thunder blasted.

"Somebody turn that music off! Now!" Wilhelmina had half risen from her wheelchair.

Christel stood up awkwardly but a split second later was thrown against the boards by some invisible force.

Cammie saw Coach Elliot jump between the woman and the boards.

"No!" Cammie opened her mouth wide, but no sound came.

The man looked as though he had hit his right side hard. He rolled across the ice, rubbing his ribs, and then rushed to Christel.

The DVD player spat out scraping sounds like steel rubbing against glass.

"The music!" Wilhelmina made a groaning sound and jumped off her wheelchair. Her small, wrinkled hand reached for the off button, and the arena plunged into silence.

Cammie had a weird impression that she was staring at a photograph. Everything seemed to have frozen, Christel sitting on the ice, her eyes glazed, Coach Elliot lying on his side, his knees bent.

"Get off the ice, you two!" the older woman shouted.

Cammie saw Wilhelmina's hands grip the boards, her chest rising and falling rapidly. Captain Greenfield and Mr. Dawson jumped onto the ice at the same time. Cammie held her breath as she watched the policeman lift up Christel. Mr. Dawson said something to Coach Elliot. Leaning on the security man's hand, Coach Elliot finally got up. Mr. Dawson raised his walkie-talkie to his mouth, and almost immediately, two paramedics rushed over to the skater with a stretcher on wheels.

One of the paramedics, a young man, bent over Christel. "Are you okay, miss? Let me help you onto the stretcher."

Christel shook her head. Loose brown strands hung across her cheeks. "No, thank you. I'm fine. Mom?"

The Skateland president was already by her daughter's side. "Where does it hurt? Talk to me!"

"I'm okay. What was it?"

"Not now." Wilhelmina straightened up. Though petite, she seemed to be towering over the four men by her side.

"Elliot, what's wrong?"

Coach Elliot was bent over, and from his pale face and his raspy breath, Cammie could tell he was in a lot of pain. "I just need…rest."

"I think he needs a doctor, Mrs. President," one of the paramedics said.

Wilhelmina nodded. "Absolutely."

"But Mrs. Van Uffeln…" Coach Elliot coughed and grimaced as his hands clasped his side.

"We'll talk later, Elliot. Now you need medical help."

"Mr. Monroe, if you let us help you." The paramedics nudged Coach Elliot in the direction of the stretcher.

The lights in the arena dimmed in front of Cammie as she saw the stretcher being wheeled out.

Captain Greenfield approached Wilhelmina, his head lowered. "Mrs. Van Uffeln, what an unfortunate incident! I hope Elliot will be all right."

"Thank you, Gilbert. I'm sure he'll get good care at the hospital. What I want you and Seymour to do now is raise the security level."

Mr. Dawson's black coffee eyes rounded. "So it wasn't an accident."

"It was definitely an attack," Wilhelmina said firmly.

Cammie's hand shot to her mouth. An attack? But who—?

"No extracurricular activities for students, nine o'clock curfew, skating to school and practices only under adult supervision."

"Consider it done, ma'am," Mr. Dawson said.

"Good. Now, if you'll excuse me…" Wilhelmina motioned for Christel to come closer.

Captain Greenfield cleared his throat. "Mrs. Van Uffeln, as an officer of the law, I'm happy to inform you that the felon has been apprehended, and my colleague and I will bring her to justice right now."

"And who might that be, Gilbert?"

"Here." Captain Greenfield took a step to the side, and Cammie saw Lieutenant Turner holding by the elbow a very ruffled-looking Witch of Pride.

As dismayed as she was, Cammie couldn't help grinning as she registered the changes in the witch's appearance. She remembered the Witch of Pride as a classy woman, always wearing furs and expensive jewelry. The witch had always worn her long, thick hair down, running her manicured hand over the shiny locks. Now, however, the Witch of Pride was dressed in bulky black pants and a long, black cardigan. She wore no makeup and no jewelry. But the most amazing thing was the witch's hair that was now cropped even shorter than Wilhelmina's. Last year, Cammie and Alex had spent three weeks in the Witch of Pride's mansion, and they had never seen her look so drab.

Cammie clenched her fists. So it was the Witch of Pride who had caused Christel and Elliot to fall.

Weird, though. Injuring people was usually Winja's job. The Witch of Pride normally attacked by stealth and flattery. Besides… Cammie rubbed her forehead, thinking hard. From what she remembered, there had to be some physical contact for a curse to be inflicted upon a skater. And Cammie hadn't seen the Witch of Pride at the rink today. There had been quite a few people, but Cammie could swear the Witch of Pride had just showed up.

"Mrs. President!" The Witch of Pride touched her cropped hair, looking miserable. "I swear I'm innocent. You know me. I'd never attack a coach."

"Yes, like the skater's reputation has ever mattered to you!" Captain Greenfield barked.

"But I wasn't even at the rink!" the witch wailed.

"Mrs. Van Uffeln, the witch was arrested at the entrance to the Sport Center," Captain Greenfield said.

"I was on my way home from the hairdresser!" the witch exclaimed.

"Somehow, your hairdo doesn't have an overly professional look!" Christel spoke up for the first time, looking livid.

"Well, I burnt it last month as I was adding pink streaks," the witch said. "So the hair dresser tried to do her best to reverse the damage. Hey, you know her. It's Mrs. Sepper from Skaters' Super Styles. You can ask her."

Captain Greenfield rolled his eyes. "I've heard that before. Anyway, Mrs. Van Uffeln, I think this woman needs to be incarcerated. It will send a clear message to the other witches and protect the skating community from further attacks."

Wilhelmina twisted the diamond ring on her middle finger without looking up. "Just do what you think is right, Officer."

"But…" The Witch of Pride opened her mouth and spread her arms.

"Blade brake her, Lieutenant, and escort her to the police icemobile!" Captain Greenfield boomed before the witch could say another word.

Out of his pocket, Lieutenant Turner produced two metal skate guards with rubber patches at the bottom. Within a few seconds, the witch's blades were trapped. Now she could only walk very slowly. The two cops led the whimpering witch away.

"Mrs. Van Uffeln…" A very concerned-looking Mr. Dawson approached the president. "I think it's some kind of mistake. There were no witches in the arena. My guys and I, we checked the whole area, I swear. We—"

"It's okay, Seymour. I know you did your best. If you will excuse me, I need to talk to my daughter in private."

"Uh…of course, but…" Shaking his head, Mr. Dawson walked away.

Wilhelmina swiveled in her wheelchair and then stopped abruptly. "Oh yes. One more thing." The woman's gray eyes scanned the arena. For a split second, they rested on Cammie's face, making her flinch. But the next moment, Wilhelmina looked away.

"Celine! Could you please come to my office too?"

Cammie saw Celine shrug. The showgirl buttoned her fur coat and followed Wilhelmina and Christel. Cammie frowned. Why did the Skateland president want to talk to Celine?

A few minutes later, the Silver Rink was empty again, as though nothing had happened, as though there had been no enchanted music, as though no one had gotten hurt. The silver walls seemed to blend with the ice, and as Cammie looked at the sparkling surface, she battled a strong urge to cry. Was Coach Elliot badly hurt? Would he be all right? But as she thought about Celine again, the tears dried off. Really, why had Wilhelmina invited Celine to her office? Did the Skateland president suspect that somehow the showgirl had been involved in the attack?

THE ICY PARK MONSTER

Cammie knew she was supposed to head to the Green Rink for her afternoon practice, yet working on her technique was the last thing on her mind. Her legs were still weak from shock, and she couldn't shake off the feeling of unreality. There had just been another horrible attack, and Prince Elliot was hurt. What had caused Christel and Elliot to fall? Would Elliot be all right? And why, really, why would somebody want to attack a coach?

As Cammie crossed Main Square, she almost skated into a tall guy. The wind played with his blond hair, and a black-and-yellow scarf slapped him on the back and the sides.

"Alex!" Immediately, Cammie felt tremendous relief. Alex was exactly the person she needed at the moment. He would definitely have answers for her. Together, the two of them would surely figure something out.

"Hey, what's up?" Alex slowed down but didn't stop.

"A terrible thing just happened."

She told him about the attack on Christel and Coach Elliot, interrupting herself occasionally to catch her breath.

Alex whistled. "I bet you're scared. Any idea who did it?"

"Nope. But I'm sure Wilhelmina has a theory. She took Christel to her office. I tried to eavesdrop, but the door must be soundproof."

"What exactly did Wilhelmina say?"

"Not much. What surprised me, though, is that she didn't look like she believed the Witch of Pride was involved."

"Well, it must have been a witch."

The huge building of the Yellow Rink—all chrome and glass–was already close. Alex picked up speed.

"Did Mr. Dulcimer tell you guys about the music of death?"

The ice screeched under Alex's blades. "What?"

"Well, there is music of life. It makes people happy. And there's music of death that causes skaters to fall and get hurt or even die. At least that's what Mr. Dulcimer said. Now the music Christel and Elliot skated to sounded really weird. It definitely wasn't the piece they had prepared. You see, the music gave me that creepy feeling. I couldn't even breathe. And Wilhelmina knew something was wrong, so she told them to stop. And then Christel fell, and Elliot rushed to her rescue and fell too—"

The wind caught Cammie in her throat, causing her to cough.

"Hmm." Alex appeared to be thinking hard.

"And I think Wilhelmina suspects Celine. She took her to her office too, and—"

"What?" Alex finally went to a complete stop.

"Well, I kind of see her point. Celine was the one who put that CD in the player, so—"

"Are you completely out of your mind?" Alex shouted so loudly that Cammie had to cover her ears.

"Look, Alex. I'm not saying that Celine actually attacked them, but—"

"Think before you talk, then!"

"Come on. No one's accusing Celine yet."

"Aha. Not *yet*! Thank you very much!"

"Alex, please be reasonable!" Cammie didn't remember ever feeling so desperate. She couldn't get through to her friend. It was as though the two of them were speaking different languages.

"So now you're asking *me* to be reasonable. Right after Wilhelmina and you accused Celine of attacking your coach?"

"Alex, Wilhelmina probably wanted to talk to Celine about that cursed CD. That's all."

"I thought you said it was Wilhelmina who had asked Celine to put that CD into the player."

"Wilhelmina probably had a different CD in mind."

Alex smirked. "So Celine was supposed to read Wilhelmina's mind. Nice one, Cammie."

"Alex!"

She didn't even know what to say to him. She felt as though she was talking to a complete stranger. For the first time in her life, she couldn't get through to Alex. What was going on, anyway? Alex had always understood her. Even if he hadn't agreed with her ideas, he had always had a good piece of advice for her. Many times, Alex's theories had allowed Cammie to look at situations from a different angle. Together, they had always been able to find a solution, except now.

"You're probably jealous of Celine because she's a better skater than you," Alex said.

Cammie felt as though he had slapped her hard on the face. She bit her lip and looked away. For crying out loud, did everything have to be blamed on jealousy? Celine was really a better skater than Cammie, but she was older and she had been skating much longer. So Cammie wasn't jealous of Celine at all; she actually enjoyed the showgirl's company. Celine was nice, funny.

"I wonder where that music of death came from," Cammie said, just to change the subject. "You see, when Dana got injured, wrong music was playing too, and it was actually similar."

"And, of course, it was Celine who put the CD into the player again," Alex said sarcastically.

"Oh, don't be an idiot!"

Alex's eyes cut through her like sharp blades. "So *I* am an idiot now? And let me tell you something. You're a complete fool to think that a girl like Celine could even think of attacking somebody."

"Alex, I'm not—"

Too late; he was skating away.

"Alex!" Cammie rushed after him. "What I'm saying is, perhaps someone is using Celine or...hang on. Maybe it was a prank of some kind, but instead—"

Alex turned around and glared at her, his eyes like two frozen swamps. "Cammie, I'm warning you. Get your head examined. And if I hear you say one more nasty word about Celine…"

He didn't even finish his sentence. He glided in the direction of the rink, his scarf tagging behind him like a threatening finger.

"Some conversation," Cammie said under her breath.

She turned around and skated in the opposite direction, not really knowing where she was heading. Actually, she had no place to go to. No one was waiting for her. There would be no private lesson because her coach was injured. Well, it meant Cammie had work cut out for her, even if Alex wasn't about to help her. Something wrong, something terrible was happening in Skateland, and Cammie had to get to the bottom of it.

Cammie reached the dorm in record speed. There was a clutter of dishes in the kitchen, which meant that Mrs. Page was cooking dinner. Cammie rushed upstairs to her room, trying to make as little noise as possible. She wasn't in the mood to talk to the dorm supervisor about the attack. Before nightfall, Mrs. Page would know everything anyway.

In her room, Cammie plopped on her bed with her cell phone. She quickly dialed Information and found out the number of the hospital.

"Skateland Hospital. How may I help you?" a high female voice answered.

"Could you please tell me how Mr. Elliot Monroe is feeling?" Cammie asked.

"Are you family?"

"Well, no. I'm his student."

"I'm sorry, but we only give information about patients' health to family members."

"Yes, but—"

"Have a nice day, miss."

The phone went dead in Cammie's hands. She twisted the small device and then threw it away. What a bummer! She didn't even have the right to know how Prince Elliot felt. For a couple of minutes, she toyed with the idea of calling Wilhelmina and then shook her head. How was she going to explain to the Skateland president that she cared about Prince Elliot, that the man wasn't just her coach, that he was her Prince Charming?

The door opened, and Sonia ran in, her face red. "Oh, Cammie! I'm so sorry!"

"So you already know," Cammie said.

"They raised the security level. Coach Darrel took Liz and me to the dorm. And then Mrs. Page told me what happened. Anyway, that's what everybody's talking about downstairs."

Cammie raised her head. "Is Celine there too?"

"Well, yes. Cammie, wait!"

Cammie bolted off her bed and sprinted to the hallway in her socks. Celine had just walked up the steps and was approaching her room.

"Celine, what?"

The showgirl slowly unbuttoned her coat. "Look, I don't know what happened."

"What did Wilhelmina talk to you about?"

"She asked me if I had seen who had brought that CD to the rink. I said I had no idea."

"And then?"

Celine removed her orange gloves. "And then Bob Turner brought me home in his icemobile."

"Is Coach Elliot hurt badly?" Cammie tried to sound calm, but she could feel her voice shaking.

"Wilhelmina called the hospital, and they say he broke two ribs. He'll be fine, though. He'll have to stay off the ice for three weeks. Actually, we could use a vacation." Celine pushed her door.

"I don't need a vacation. I have a program to work on. My triple salchow—" Cammie cried out.

"Don't you care about our poor coach's health?"

"Of course I do, but—"

"Look, I'm really tired. Can we talk later?" Without waiting for Cammie's answer, Celine closed the door behind her.

Her head down, Cammie returned to her room, where Sonia was changing into her bathrobe. "Did you talk to Celine?"

"She doesn't know anything. And Coach Elliot will have to stay off the ice for three weeks." Cammie plopped on her bed again. "I can't figure out who wanted to attack him and Christel. And Alex won't talk to me."

She told Sonia about her conversation with Alex.

Sonia nodded sympathetically. "I know what you're talking about. Jeff barely talks to me too. And it's all because of Celine, of course."

"So do you think Celine could be involved in the attack?"

Sonia's baby blue eyes registered surprise. "What? No. Of course not. What an idea! Celine is a big flirt, but she would never attack another person."

"Well, all right."

There had to be reason in what Sonia was saying, but Cammie still wasn't sure. So far, Celine was the only person who had touched the CD with the music of death. At least Cammie had seen no one else.

Cammie called the hospital every day, but she never managed to get any information about Coach Elliot's condition. The receptionist was persistent; only family members had the right to know the details about patients' progress.

The tightened security made life in Skateland really boring. Students weren't allowed to go anywhere, even to school and practices, without being accompanied by an adult. For that reason, Cammie found herself spending a lot of time in the company of Coach Yvette and Mrs. Page. None of the ladies seemed particularly happy about having to chaperone the girls as they skated around. Needless to say, any extra trip other than to the rink or to school was absolutely out of the question.

"Don't you think I have enough on my hands already?" Mrs. Page snapped when Celine asked her if she could go shopping.

Celine pouted, but a minute later, she was all happy and bubbly again. During the last week, Cammie had been watching the showgirl closely, trying to figure out whether Celine had really been somehow involved in the attack against Christel and Elliot. Yet, so far, nothing suggested that Celine was the culprit. First of all, Cammie couldn't think of a motive. There was no way Celine would ever compete against Christel or Elliot. Besides, Christel was a successful skater. The experience of performing with *Magic on Ice* had gained her fame and a reputation that stretched far beyond the boundaries of Skateland. And, of course, if Celine had really attacked the couple, she would surely be wondering about Coach Elliot's condition. Yet Cammie never heard Celine even mention her coach's name, let alone wonder if the man was going to be all right. The showgirl seemed to be truly enjoying the unexpected break, giggling with other girls in the living room, changing her clothes three or four times a day, and sending messages from her cell phone to her numerous friends all over the world.

Cammie practiced at the Green Rink alone. She felt sluggish and bored. All of her doubles up to the double axel were solid, but she was afraid of working on her triple salchow on her own. What if she fell and got injured again? That would terminate her skating career forever. No, she would wait for Prince Elliot. She missed him so much, his encouraging smile, his support, his advice. She felt so lonely at the Green Rink! Coach Yvette usually ignored her, and Angela and Rita treated her like an over-age student who had been compelled to repeat the school year due to poor performance.

On Saturday afternoon, right after the public session at the Silver Rink, Cammie ran to the locker room and dialed the hospital number again. She hoped that another receptionist would answer the phone, someone who wasn't such a stickler for rules.

Her guess had been almost right. The minute she mentioned Coach Elliot's name, the lady cut her off.

"Mr. Monroe has been discharged."

"Oh! Is he all right?"

"Young lady, our doctors would never let a person go unless they were sure he was out of danger."

"Thank you!" Cammie said to the dead phone. She put the small device in her pocket and smiled widely. Okay, so Prince Elliot was doing fine. How awesome! She would probably see him on Monday, and everything would be all right again. But how could she wait two whole days until Monday? And poor Prince Elliot. How bored he probably was all alone, with no one but Choctaw to talk to.

Cammie stood in the middle of the locker room with her green parka in her hands. Prince Elliot lived alone. What if he needed help? He had just been released from the hospital, so he probably wasn't strong enough to take care of himself. Cammie remembered her own injury. After being discharged from the hospital, she had gone home to spend time with her family. Her parents had doted over her, pampering her, spoiling her, making sure her needs were met.

Cammie put on her parka and walked slowly into the lobby. She pictured her coach in a lonely cabin far in the woods. She shivered. How come he didn't have any family or friends who could visit him?

He has me!

Suddenly, Cammie had an idea. What if she paid a surprise visit to her coach? She would ask him if he needed something. There was nothing wrong about that. Of course, Prince Elliot's house was probably far from Main Square, but Cammie had her Kanga bag. Getting anywhere in Skateland wouldn't be a problem.

"Cammie, where're you going?" Sonia ran up to Cammie, her face sweaty. "Mrs. Page will be here in ten minutes. She told us all to wait in the lobby."

"Oh sure!" Gosh. Cammie had completely forgotten that they weren't supposed to skate to the dormitory on their own. It meant her wonderful plan wasn't going to work. Cammie sank her fingernails into her skin. Why on earth wouldn't it work? Hadn't she managed to bend rules many times before?

And you got injured, remember? a nasty voice spoke in her mind.

Ah! Stop it! I'm not going to practice any difficult jumps on my own, Cammie thought.

The road to Prince Elliot's house is through the Icy Park, the voice reminded.

"I'm perfectly aware of that! Thank you!" Cammie said angrily. She remembered she didn't know Coach Elliot's address. Well, that wasn't a problem. Her Kanga bag had not only a built-in navigator but also the list of all Skateland residents with their addresses.

Cammie waved her hand. "Don't wait for me!"

"What?"

Out of the corner of her eye, Cammie saw Celine walking in the company of Alex, Jeff, and Michael. She was carrying a pink teddy bear and two paper bags.

Sonia nodded in Celine's direction. "More gifts from Miss Bouchard's admirers."

Cammie shrugged. "Who cares?" She really wasn't interested in what Alex was doing anymore. Her former best friend had proven to be nothing but a nincompoop whose reasoning abilities had been completely wiped away by the presence of a skating celebrity.

"Okay, girls! Let's get going!" Mrs. Page's voice announced from the front door.

Cammie grabbed Sonia's hand. "Sonia, you've got to cover for me. Tell her I already left. Wait. Tell her I went to the library to do my literature report. Yes, that'll work. *Skating Mysteries,* a perfect topic."

Sonia stepped backward, her face twisted in an expression of complete shock. "Cammie, you can't."

"I've got to. Listen. I'll explain later. Just tell her I'm gone. See you!" Cammie dived around the corner, making sure her skate guards didn't clomp too hard against the floor. Her heart pounded loudly in her chest. She still couldn't believe she had skipped off just like that.

Well, I can't just sit and wait, she told herself.

Prince Elliot could still be in danger. After all, the attacker had injured him only slightly. Dana's attack, for example, was different. The girl had had to give up skating altogether. And Winja had been poisoned. Had the person for whom Ice Spice Soda had been intended drunk it, he would have surely died.

"The soda was for Coach Elliot!" Cammie said out loud.

Of course. Whoever the attacker was, Prince Elliot had been the target. The villain was sly. He had definitely planned his attacks well. He had been watching the show skaters. He had seen that Prince Elliot was the only skater without a drink. And he had slipped him the poisoned bottle.

The attacker was coming back. And unless Cammie warned her coach about the danger, the villain's next attempt could be successful. Breaking a silly rule meant nothing if a human life was at stake.

Without giving the matter another thought, Cammie crossed the lobby.

"Cammie, I think Mrs. Page is waiting for you at the entrance." Captain Greenfield had appeared as if from nowhere.

Cammie stifled a groan. "Bathroom."

"Ah. Sure." He stepped back to let her pass.

That was close, Cammie thought as she watched the policeman walk back in the direction of the arena. She clenched her teeth stubbornly. *I'm going to visit Coach Elliot anyway, and no one will stop me.*

Cammie left the building through one of the back doors. There was still plenty of light outside, which meant Cammie would be perfectly safe in the Icy Park. To make sure she wouldn't bump into her friends accompanied by Mrs. Page, Cammie took the road to the left leading toward Counter Alley. When she was sure no one leaving the Sport Center could see her, she positioned Kanga in front of her, grabbed the handle with both hands, and said softly but distinctly, "Elliot Monroe's place in the Icy Park."

The bag moved forward, first slowly, lazily, as though trying to figure out the shortest way to the designated address, and then faster and faster. Wind whistled in Cammie's ears as she glided past the long row of houses. They were about to enter the Icy Park. Cammie felt her feet moving through deep powder snow. A couple of seconds later, the bag steered into an ice path again. The statue of a skater holding a multicolored flower whooshed by, still looking very much like a witch.

The path winded past a small circular pond with scratched ice. Cammie figured local kids had been using it as a playground. They moved along a wide alley with gazebos and ice figures of swans. Then Kanga took a sharp turn to a narrow path waving around oak trees. They passed a frozen pond with sky blue ice and plunged into the thicket. The treetops closed above Cammie's head. Immediately, everything became dark. Cammie fidgeted slightly. She hated skating in the woods all by herself. She suddenly realized how she missed the sun. For weeks, Skateland had seen nothing but falling snow and the west wind. The minute Cammie thought about the weather, snowflakes rushed into her eyes and her mouth. She wiped her face with her glove, almost losing her balance.

"Easy now, Kanga!"

The bag was now shooting straight through the park, moving so fast that Cammie could discern nothing but gray limbs. There was a slight decline, and then the path went up. Kanga slowed down a little, and it gave Cammie an opportunity to study the area.

It was the most miserable place Cammie had ever seen. The trees standing on both sides sprouted crooked gnarly limbs. Some of the trees looked dead. Twice, Cammie had to bunny-hop across fallen logs that blocked her way. They passed a swamp with dark green, almost black ice. The surface was littered with dried leaves and acorns.

I can't believe Coach Elliot lives in such a dreary place.

Kanga slowed down even more, its blades screeching loudly against the hard ice.

"Move on!" The gloomy atmosphere was getting to Cammie.

Instead of picking up speed, the bag slowed down even more and then came to an abrupt stop, almost causing Cammie to fall forward. "Easy now!"

She peered into the coppice ahead of her. There was a long row of trees growing so closely to one another that the whole structure looked more like a fence than a natural growth. A narrow strip of clear ice stretched along the fence. Cammie wondered what it was for. Surely the patch wasn't big enough to be qualified as a rink. She let go of Kanga's handle and jumped on the ice. The minute she did it, a thought flickered in her mind that the ice might be cursed. But it was too late already. Her blades made contact with the smooth surface. Miraculously, nothing happened.

"Well, the entrance has to be here somehow," Cammie said out loud, just to hear the sound of her voice. She still couldn't understand why Coach Elliot had chosen to live in such a ghoulish place.

She studied the natural fence very carefully, inch by inch. She hoped for some sort of an opening or a handle that would reveal a hidden door, but there was none.

"But Coach Elliot does enter the property somehow. Right, Kanga?"

There came no response from the skating bag. Cammie grimaced. The eerie atmosphere was making her more and more uncomfortable.

"How about we—"

There was a sound of heavy footsteps behind the pine trees. A hopeful thought flashed through Cammie's mind that maybe it was Coach Elliot returning home. She wondered what would be the best way to explain her presence next to his property.

Cammie shifted her feet and looked back. A bulky figure emerged from between the trees. It surely wasn't Coach Elliot. No, it wasn't even a human being. The creature was huge and hairy, though he moved on his back paws, stretching its front limbs ahead of him. Two scarlet eyes with slits for pupils glittered below eight sharp horns.

"No, no, no!" Cammie stepped back, her hands stretched forward as though this simple gesture could keep the monster from coming closer. She had definitely seen that creature before, in her dream perhaps. No, of course, it hadn't been a dream. Cammie had already met the horrible beast in the Icy Park on the night of the snowstorm, when she had got lost skating from the library.

The monster advanced on her, its eyes burning holes in her face.

"Help!" she shouted, but her voice sounded weak. She knew nobody would come to her rescue. Even Coach Elliot was probably miles away. Kanga must have taken Cammie to the wrong place.

The beast opened its mouth. Its teeth were sharp and uneven. In a minute, it would rip her to pieces. She would die. She would never see her parents again. She would never have another chance to skate. Everything was over.

The beast stopped about twenty feet away, its body swaying. Its mouth opened again, and another rumbling sound came out of the creature's throat. As scared as Cammie was, she realized that the monster was laughing.

"Please!" She pressed her fists against her eyes. Purple circles appeared in her field of vision. She was afraid to look up.

"Cammie, are you there? Cammie!"

Somebody was calling her name. Was it Alex? He was still her friend. He had come to her rescue after all. No, the voice wasn't Alex's. It had a funny twang that sounded familiar. She let her hands drop and opened her eyes.

The monster must have heard the voice too, for its posture showed confusion. The beast's claws scraped the ice. He pirouetted and thumped back into the darkness of the forest.

"Cammie!" The nasal voice was now really close. There was a grazing of the blades next to her. A gray figure braked. There was a man's face with a long nose.

"Are you all right?"

Cammie tried to push herself up, but her body still shook feverishly. A strong hand grabbed her elbow. She felt herself lifted up. She looked the man in the face.

"Lieutenant Turner!"

"You can call me Bob." The young man wiped his forehead with his glove. "Did you see—"

"There was a monster. He went right there." Cammie's hand still shook as she pointed into the thicket.

Bob Turner's full lips curved. "I saw him too."

"You did?" So the beast wasn't a figment of her imagination.

"Fur like a bear's, sharp teeth," the young man said.

"And six horns..."

"Eight," Bob Turner corrected. "I counted them."

"Does it matter six or eight?"

He shrugged.

"Who is he?" Her mouth found it hard to form words.

"How would I know?" The young man looked in the direction in which the monster had disappeared. "But I've seen him before in this side of the park."

Cammie peered into the coppice, but the snow-covered trees were perfectly still. All she could hear was eerie silence. She glanced at the young policeman. His hands were deep in his gray coat pockets, his head turned away.

"Okay. You win. You can take me in now."

Bob's bushy eyebrows twitched. "Excuse me?"

She spread her arms. "Take me to the police station, send a report to my coach, to the president, my parents...what else? I'm not supposed to skate in the park alone, am I?"

"I guess not. But I'm not going to do that."

"You aren't?"

Kindness was the last thing Cammie expected from Lieutenant Turner.

"Let's get out of here." Bob took Cammie's hand.

She jerked herself free. "I can walk on my own, thank you."

"Suit yourself." He waited for her to brush the snow off Kanga and take the ice path slightly ahead of him.

They skated in silence for a few minutes. Cammie kept straining her eyes, fearing to see the monster leap at her from between the trees, but they appeared to be alone in the forest. She wondered if Lieutenant Turner had scared the beast away.

"I just saved your life, you know."

"I appreciate it. Bob!" Cammie said the last word, trying to put as much sarcasm in her voice as she could. How she wished it was Alex who had found her in the park.

Bob Turner looked insulted. "He would have killed you."

They passed the swamp with dirty ice. Cammie wondered how far the police icemobile was.

"Why were you following me?" Cammie asked.

"Isn't it obvious? You're in trouble."

And you'd be a much better cop if you spent your time chasing real criminals, not intermediate-level skaters! She wanted to shout. Really, there had been three attacks in Skateland already, and instead of looking for the culprit, Lieutenant Turner was stalking Cammie. Before she could say something, a branch creaked on their left and a loud voice shouted, "Freeze!"

The two of them looked back. Captain Greenfield slowly approached them. Right behind him was the glossy outline of the police icemobile.

"Did I hear somebody screaming?" The man's gray eyes studied their angry faces.

"She went to the park. I was concerned for her safety. I followed along, sir," Lieutenant Turner said.

"Without the icemobile."

"I thought you needed it," Bob said.

"There was a monster over there!" Cammie pointed to her back.

"I beg your pardon?"

As she described the horrible creature, Captain Greenfield appeared more and more concerned. "Cammie, are you sure you're all right?"

"What, you don't believe me?" she asked. "Bob saw the beast too."

"So the two of you are on a first-name basis now."

What was he talking about? "Captain Greenfield." Cammie tried to sound as convincing as she could. "That creature was real. I saw him before, on the night I got lost in the park."

"It's quite common to have nightmares after a long exposure to cold."

"But I saw him too," Bob said.

"Well, I didn't. Anyway, Lieutenant, I suggest that you curb your initiative a little and stay within the realm of your responsibilities."

"But he did save my life!" Cammie exclaimed.

Captain Greenfield waved his hand. "He wouldn't have done it if you had obeyed the laws. Now, Lieutenant, I want to make sure Cammie's dorm supervisor and her coach know about her misbehavior."

During the whole trip back, no one said another word.

BAD CONSEQUENCES

When Cammie entered the dining room on Sunday morning, Mrs. Page ignored her completely. However, the clanging of the kettle against the stove and the dorm supervisor's loud sniffs were sure signs that the woman was in a foul mood. Most of the girls averted their eyes at the sight of Cammie. Liz studied her with interest, and Celine kept smiling enigmatically.

Feeling uneasy, Cammie took her seat at the table next to Sonia, Liz, and Celine. Mrs. Page approached with a bowl of oatmeal. Beads of perspiration dotted her forehead, and one of the straps of her apron hung loose.

"I spoke to your mother this morning." There was unusual coldness in Mrs. Page's normally kind voice.

Cammie's hand jerked, causing her glass of orange juice to turn over. "What?"

"You're officially on probation, Cammie. It means one more violation, and you're out of here."

Mrs. Page marched back to the kitchen, leaving Cammie with her mouth agape. Unable to move, she watched the bright orange liquid drip to the floor.

Sonia dived under the table and dabbed on the wet spot on the carpet with a napkin.

"What did you do in the park at night anyway?" Liz asked.

Celine spread butter on her toast. "Is it too hard to figure out?"

Cammie felt her whole body seize up. She jumped off her chair, sending it to the floor. As she ran out of the kitchen, there was a collective sigh and Sonia's weak, "Cammie!" She flew up to the third floor, skipping steps. In her room, Cammie threw herself on the bed, shaking with sobs.

She only realized Sonia was by her side when she felt her roommate's warm hand on her shoulder. "There, Cammie. Everything will be all right."

"Nothing is going to be all right!" Cammie wiped her nose with her sleeve and sat up.

"You know Mrs. Page. She never stays mad very long."

"She was mad long enough to ruin my whole career," Cammie said bitterly. "My mom has been talking about taking me out of Skateland for months anyway. Now all she needed to hear was that I'm no longer welcome here."

She accepted a tissue from Sonia and blew her nose loudly.

"But, Cammie, Mrs. Page isn't the one to make a decision about your staying or leaving."

"But still." Cammie folded her tissue in half and then in quarters and in eighths. "It's all those cops. I hate them. Why can't they just leave me alone? First, that dork followed me all the way—"

"Lieutenant Turner." Sonia spoke as though she already knew the answer.

"Exactly. Though he kind of wanted to cover up for me until his boss showed up."

Sonia's eyes sparkled like two aquamarines. "He does like you."

"Oh shut up." She bit her lip for a moment before summoning her courage for another question. "Look, Sonia. Does everybody know why...that I—"

"That you went to the Icy Park to see Coach Elliot?" Sonia asked.

"Of course not!"

Cammie looked up. "Really?"

"Cammie!" Sonia moved up closer. In the light of the morning sun, her long red locks looked as though they were on fire. "Nobody knows you like Coach Elliot. Celine told everyone that you had gone to the enchanted rink. Somehow, she's sure you're like her, trying to find out who's the love of your life."

"Oh!" Immediately, Cammie felt a lot better.

"Of course, Mrs. Page is sure you went to the Icy Park to practice. She says you're obsessed about moving up to the novice level. She also kept telling everybody this sort of zeal was really unhealthy."

Cammie smiled. "I'll take that."

Sonia looked around as though to make sure no one was listening to them. "So...did you get to talk to Coach Elliot?"

Cammie sighed. "No."

As she told Sonia about her trip to the park, her friend nodded sympathetically. When Cammie mentioned the monster, Sonia let out a loud shriek. "It must have been the Witch of Fear. She likes scaring people like that."

Cammie nodded. "She did the same to me in her castle last year and in the Icy Park during that terrible storm."

"You must have been scared to death!" Sonia groaned. "Gosh, Cammie. You could have gotten seriously hurt."

"Well, I didn't," Cammie said angrily. "It was Coach Elliot who broke two ribs. And someone had to visit him, you know."

"I understand," Sonia said in a small voice.

They sat in silence for a few minutes. The sparkling snow outside made Cammie's story about dark alleys and monsters appear almost unreal.

"You know, Cammie, I'd come to the park with you, but…," Sonia whispered.

"I understand. St. Valentine's show. Junior Worlds."

That year, Sonia had taken the bronze at the Junior Nationals and was facing her second Junior Worlds. Cammie, however, hadn't even managed to qualify for the national competition. It was all because of her injury, of course.

"How about Alex?" Sonia asked. "With his sixth-place finish at the nationals, he's not going to the worlds. So he could probably visit Coach Elliot with you."

"No, he couldn't. He has Celine, remember?"

"How could I forget?"

"Look, let's not talk about it now. I only hope Captain Greenfield hasn't said anything to Wilhelmina yet. If only he waits before Coach Elliot comes back, then I'm sure Coach Elliot will ask them not to expel me. Perhaps he could tell them I've been really improving lately."

"They won't expel you," Sonia said. "Mrs. Page did say *one more violation*. And Captain Greenfield is really nice. He wouldn't want to hurt you."

"You should have seen him yesterday. He looked mad."

"So will you tell Coach Elliot why you went to the park alone?" Sonia asked.

Cammie felt herself blush. "Gosh no! Let him...let him think I went there to work on my jumps."

They spent the whole Sunday catching up on their homework. In the afternoon, Mrs. Page took all the girls out to see the movie *Blades of Glory*. Yet Cammie refused to leave her room even then. She had a lot of homework to do, thank you very much. The truth was, she didn't feel like talking to anybody. Her mother called just before dinner, and Cammie had to endure another shouting session. Her mother's condemning words made her cry even more. Why, why had Mrs. Page squealed on her?

Cammie didn't sleep well that night. She kept wondering if she would even be allowed to stay in Skateland. If only Coach Elliot would come back tomorrow. He wouldn't let them expel a promising skater. Cammie's eyes got sore from staring into the dark. She fell asleep.

"Mrs. Van Uffeln wants to see you in her office," Kelly said when Cammie showed up at the Green Rink for her afternoon practice.

Cammie's heart did a double flip.

"Did...did she say why?" Right, as though Cammie didn't know.

Kelly, who had just finished lacing up her skating boots, stood up. "She probably forgot to give me all the details."

Cammie sighed in resignation. "What time is my appointment?"

"Now. Forget the practice. President Van Uffeln is waiting for you in her office at the Silver Rink."

She wouldn't worry yet. After all, she had been in trouble before, and Wilhelmina had always been able to understand her. After all, Cammie had done nothing wrong. She had merely wanted to help Coach Elliot. After showing her ID to the Silver Rink security guard, Cammie asked him where Wilhelmina's office was.

"On the third floor," the tall, sandy-haired man said lazily.

Cammie had never been on the third floor of the Sport Center. She passed a classy-looking VIP bar and turned around the corner. The hallway ended in an alcove with a dark wood door. The silver plaque read "Wilhelmina Van Uffeln, Skateland president."

Wondering why there was no secretary to announce her arrival, Cammie knocked on the door.

"Come in."

Cammie pushed the hard door. The air in the room was warm and smelled of perfume. Wilhelmina sat behind a big mahogany desk, dressed in a long beige dress. Cammie was surprised to see Christel slouching in an armchair next to the president's desk. The younger woman wore a purple tracksuit, and her long hair was gathered in a loose ponytail. When Cammie managed a faint hello, Christel simply nodded and looked away.

"Oh, there you are!" Wilhelmina slapped the desk with her hand. "Good. We can go now."

Cammie stared at her. "Where?"

Wilhelmina closed the file she had been reading. "To see Elliot, of course. Isn't that where you were headed when the police found you?"

So she knew. Cammie wasn't even surprised. You couldn't hide anything from the Skateland president.

"Yes, I'm aware of your enthusiastic effort, Cammie!" The older woman's smile appeared genuine. "You reached Elliot's property. At least, Kanga took you there. But then you failed to get past the security fence."

Wasn't Wilhelmina going to rebuke her for skating in the Icy Park on her own?

"Elliot doesn't want any unannounced visitors, so he had a security fence installed. You need a password to get through." Wilhelmina tapped her fingers on the desk. "Actually, your technique might have been sufficient, Cammie. Yet coming to somebody's house uninvited wouldn't have been very polite. What do you think?"

241

Was it a veiled attempt to tell Cammie she had done wrong? Cammie peered into the older woman's dark gray eyes.

The Skateland president's face expression remained calm. "Today, however, I contacted Elliot, and he's expecting us."

Cammie felt as though she had been dipped in a scalding bathtub. "It's...great!"

"Let's move on, then. I'm ready." Wilhelmina stood up. "Don't forget to put the bags in the icemobile, Christel."

Christel rose from her armchair, and Cammie saw three heavy-looking plastic bags sitting on the floor.

"You can take one of the bags, Cammie," Wilhelmina said as she rolled forward in her wheelchair.

Cammie grabbed a white plastic bag emblazoned with *Skaters' Supermarket* logo. She could barely lift it off the floor.

"I'm sorry, but Elliot has no food in his house," Christel said. She picked up the remaining bags and followed her mother down the hallway.

The familiar silver icemobile was parked near the back entrance. The black letters on the side of the vehicle said "Skateland President." Wilhelmina rose from her wheelchair and took the driver's seat. Cammie couldn't help feeling amazed at how light and fluid the older woman looked. If Cammie didn't know the Skateland president had a bad case of arthritis, she would never even suspect Wilhelmina of having even a minor health problem.

Cammie helped Christel load the folded wheelchair in the back of the icemobile. Then the two of them positioned the food bags on the floor next to it. Christel took the front passenger's seat next to her mother, and Cammie settled in the back.

They didn't talk during the ride. As usual, the icemobile glided along the streets of Skateland with incredible speed. Cammie wrapped her scarf around her neck and hugged herself tightly to protect herself from the ghastly wind. Halfway through the trip, snow started falling. Cammie didn't mind the blizzard so much. The only thing she slightly feared was the Icy Park monster. Although, she figured, the beast was unlikely to make its appearance with the Skateland president around. And yet as they drove through the park, Cammie peered into the dark labyrinth of limbs and logs, ready to close her eyes the moment the monster showed up. Part of her even wished they would see the monster after all. As the president, Wilhelmina had to know what tricks the Witch of Fear was capable of.

The icemobile hit a mogul and careened to the left. Wilhelmina turned the steering wheel to the right, straightening the vehicle. Cammie clasped her hands around the leather seat to steady herself. Her head and shoulders were completely covered with snow. A few turns later, Cammie recognized the swamp covered with dirty green ice. The blades of the icemobile squeaked, and the vehicle stopped, facing the familiar thicket. The monitor in front of Wilhelmina came to life. The words *destination reached* ran across the gray background.

"All right. Here we are." Wilhelmina's voice sounded calm, as though she were in her office, away from the wind and snow. "Christel, go get the password."

Cammie watched the younger woman get off the icemobile and bunny-hop across the dry logs blocking the way. From a distance, Christel could easily pass for a teenager. She stepped onto the clear patch of ice stretching along the thicket. Cammie saw her bend over and nod, as though she had read something inscribed on the ice.

When Christel came back, there was an unmistakable smile on her face. "It's double loop-double loop combination, Mom. Do you want to do it?"

Cammie wondered what was going on.

Wilhelmina, who had been busy brushing the snow off her fur coat, stopped midway and chucked. "Are you kidding me? Even in my competitive years, the double loop was the best I could do."

"You?" Christel's dark eyes were now fixed on Cammie's face.

"Am…am I supposed to do a double loop-double loop combination?" Cammie's voice was dry.

Christel shrugged. "That's the password."

"Uh…I could try."

Deep inside, Cammie wasn't so sure. Thanks to Coach Elliot, her double-double combinations had gotten significantly better. But to do one on the spot without proper warm-up would be a huge challenge. What if she failed? The three of them might not be able to get to the other side of the thicket.

"Go ahead, then, Christel." Wilhelmina opened the door and swung her arthritic legs to the side. Judging from her calm demeanor, the older woman had no doubt that her daughter was ready for the difficult combination.

Christel stepped onto the clear ice again, did a few strokes, changed direction and glided backward. Her double loop-double loop combination looked easy, as though there had been no effort involved. Cammie didn't even try to contain a groan. Would there ever be time when she wouldn't have to worry about landing difficult jumps?

The thicket spread open like a curtain on a stage, revealing a passage covered with ice.

"Okay, girls. Get the bags." Wilhelmina stood up, using the icemobile door to steady herself. "No, Christel. I won't need the wheelchair once we're inside."

Cammie saw the older woman take a few tentative steps in the direction of the ice. The moment Wilhelmina's foot touched the glassy surface, her very appearance changed. No longer was there a tired old woman; instead, a poised and confident skater glided across the patch of ice.

"What are you waiting for?" Christel called. She stood on the ice next to her mother, two bags in her hands. Only then did Cammie notice that the thicket in front of them had spread, revealing a circular pond and a small log cabin with a slanted roof. The snow packed on the roof looked like icing. The door and the shutters were deep purple, and there were lights in the high arched windows. Cammie was also surprised to see that the house was perched on the edge of a cliff. High mountains towered behind the house, their tops almost blending with the swirling snow. Thick purple-and-white clouds rolled alongside the mountains.

"I didn't know there were mountains in Skateland," Cammie said quietly.

"Coach Elliot actually lives outside Skateland. The thicket we just crossed marks the boarder of Skateland."

Cammie looked around again. The place had its own wild beauty, yet for some reason, she couldn't shake off the feeling of uneasiness. She simply couldn't understand why Coach Elliot had chosen to live so far away from other people. "Mrs. Van Uffeln, I—"

"You can save your questions for inside, Cammie. I'm freezing, and besides, Elliot is expecting us promptly at five. It's not good to be late."

And with those words, the Skateland president crossed the pond, walked up the snow-covered steps, and rang the doorbell.

COACH ELLIOT'S CABIN

The door opened. A wedge of warm light appeared from the inside, and a moment later, Cammie felt Choctaw's furry head pushing her palm.

"Hi, Choctaw!" Cammie hugged the dog's neck. His hair smelled faintly of snow and pine.

The dog let out a few happy barks and stared at her with his eyes, the color of roasted chestnuts.

"Cammie, what a pleasant surprise! I'm happy to see all of you ladies." Coach Elliot stood leaning against the doorframe. Dressed in dark jeans and a navy blue sweater, he looked thinner and paler than Cammie remembered him.

When the three of them walked into a small foyer, Coach Elliot kissed Wilhelmina's hand, gave Christel a friendly pat on the back, and finally hugged Cammie.

"Well, how's my girl coping?" His eyes were midnight blue, but as he smiled at Cammie, they turned the nice shade of cobalt.

For the first time that week, Cammie felt relaxed and happy. "I'm fine, Coach Elliot. How are you?"

She desperately wanted to throw her arms around him and tell him that she missed him so much; that without him, the rink wasn't the same; that she cared about him. "Oh, I'm so much better." He ran his hand across his left side. "I could probably work already, but the overbearing doctor insists I take it easy another week."

"I second that. And you probably should be in bed, Elliot," Wilhelmina said sternly. She let him take her coat and smoothed her short hair in front of a mirror.

Coach Elliot grinned, though as usual, his eyes remained sad. "Believe me. I've spent more than enough time in a supine position already."

"That's exactly what you need." Wilhelmina waited for Elliot to hang Cammie and Christel's parkas in the closet and walked along the short hallway as though she was perfectly familiar with the layout of the cabin.

Coach Elliot winked at Cammie. "Come on. We'll have tea in the living room. I only have Skating Animal Crackers to go with it, though. Sorry about that."

Cammie liked the living room. Warm and bright, it probably was the biggest area in the house. She admired the paintings with winter landscapes. The glass wall gave an unobstructed view of the snow-covered trees and the mountains standing behind them like silent guards. The green fir trees made the stone fireplace with creaking fire even more welcoming.

"It's really quiet here. I often see deer walking on the lawn," Coach Elliot said.

Cammie grinned. "Doesn't Choctaw chase them around?"

Coach Elliot offered a chair for Wilhelmina to sit down. "That's probably his biggest dream, but I don't let him roam on his own. Come take a seat, Cammie, Christel."

As Cammie faced the fireplace, she found herself staring at the picture of a very beautiful woman gliding across the ice in a spiral position. The interplay of light and shadows made it appear as though the skater was laughing at all of them.

"It's my wife, Felicia," Elliot said softly.

Before Cammie could think of something appropriate to say, Christel spoke up. "I'll be in the kitchen, making dinner."

Coach Elliot's cheeks turned slightly pink. "Oh, you don't have to, Christel."

Wilhelmina looked amused. "I've never met a man in my life who would turn down a good meal. Go help her, Cammie."

Coach Elliot's kitchen was sterile clean, and it was obvious that he barely had any food in the house.

"How can he even survive on these?" Christel shook her head as she opened one cabinet after another. The shelves were half filled with cans of Campbell's soup and boxes of cereal. In the refrigerator, they found half a carton of milk and a loaf of whole grain bread. Christel popped open the freezer door and snorted at the assortment of TV dinners.

"I'm glad I got him some take-out from Skater's Finest Food. There, Cammie. Hand me the plates from the top shelf."

Cammie helped Christel to heat up some steaks and garlic mashed potatoes. Then she poured club soda into tall glasses and added lemon.

"All right. Tell them we're ready." Christel put silverware and napkins on the kitchen table.

Cammie found Coach Elliot and Wilhelmina deeply engrossed in a conversation. When she walked in, her coach stopped midsentence and glanced at the Skateland president.

"I have no secrets either from Christel or from Cammie," Wilhelmina said firmly. "Unfortunately, the latest events involve everybody in Skateland. However, because Cammie is probably going to tell us that dinner is ready, whatever I have to say will wait."

In the kitchen, Coach Elliot sniffed the delicious aroma of sizzling steaks. "I can't believe you brought all that food. You shouldn't have. I'm doing just fine."

Wilhelmina made a cackling sound. "If you were a student at Skateland, I'd give you one of my famous lectures on the importance of nutritious food for an athlete in training. But since you're a coach, I'll spare my effort for the ones who still need it."

She threw a quick look at Cammie. Cammie responded with a grin. She was hungry, and it took her only a few minutes to polish off her plate. Elliot seemed to be enjoying the dinner as well. By the time he finished his steaks, his cheeks appeared less hollow. He even had some color in his face.

"That's better. Thank you, Christel and Cammie," Wilhelmina said.

"I'll serve tea in the living room. Okay, Mom?" Christel asked.

"That'll be nice."

Surely the two of them are acting as though they're at home and Coach Eliot's their guest, Cammie thought.

Yet Coach Elliot didn't seem to mind. In fact, he looked quite happy and even teased Christel about not being able to do her triple toe loop if she kept eating that much.

"Was that the reason you came up with that novice-level password? She, for example, wasn't up to it." Christel nodded in Cammie's direction.

Man, why did she have to say that? Cammie fidgeted in her seat.

Coach Elliot's brow creased. "I thought you had that combination down, Cammie."

"But I'd have to warm up first."

"Ah, well. In time, you'll be able to do those combinations the moment you step on the ice. Anyway, that password is enough to thwart the witches away. They can't do double-doubles. So far, I haven't had any visitors, except for the three of you, of course." Coach Elliot smiled warmly.

Wilhelmina's chair creaked as she turned to face Cammie. "By the way, Cammie, I keep forgetting to ask you. How're you doing in Mr. Dulcimer's class?"

Cammie looked up, surprised. "Music interpretation?"

"Well, the last time I checked, that was the only subject Mr. Dulcimer taught."

"Well…" With all eyes fixed on her, Cammie felt very uncomfortable.

"Don't try to come up with a good excuse, Cammie," Wilhelmina said. "From what Mr. Dulcimer told me, I know that none of his students have managed to interpret a piece of music correctly."

"I loved music interpretation," Coach Elliot said. "It was Mr. Dulcimer's first year of teaching, and he gave us some good pieces to work on. Most of them were classical, of course, but he let us do rock and disco a few times."

"He did?" That was something Cammie would never have expected.

"From this moment on, I want you to really concentrate on music interpretation, Cammie. Do you hear me?" Wilhelmina said sternly.

"Well, sure." Cammie wondered why Wilhelmina was making such a big deal out of it, especially knowing that all the students had come short of Mr. Dulcimer's high requirements.

"I want you to promise me that, Cammie," the Skateland president said. "At this point, nothing is more important than learning how to interpret music correctly."

"But why?"

"Why? Because it's a required course. That's why."

"Well, let's get down to the most important issue," Wilhelmina said as she took a bite of her chocolate croissant filled with almonds.

Cammie was already finishing her third croissant and was seriously worried about her practice tomorrow.

"I want you all to listen carefully to what I'm going to say." Wilhelmina pushed her cup away and looked at them with her deep penetrating eyes.

For some reason, Cammie felt a cold draft rushing at her from the corner. She clasped her hands tight to keep them from trembling.

"The latest events have led me to believe that Skateland has been attacked by Mavet."

Who on earth was Mavet? From Coach Elliot and Christel's puzzled face expressions, she could tell that they had no clue either.

Wilhelmina swirled a small diamond ring around her crooked finger. "Let me explain. Mavet is an evil spirit, a monster whose name means *death*. He's extremely dangerous, and I regret to tell you that I've seen him lurking around the Icy Park twice this winter."

Cammie couldn't contain a squeak. A split second later, everybody's eyes were fastened on her.

"What was that, Cammie?" Wilhelmina asked.

"But...I saw a monster in the Icy Park too," Cammie said feebly. "I thought it was one of the Witch of Fear's tricks."

"Would you like to tell us what the creature looked like exactly?"

Cammie began to speak, trying to keep her teeth from clanging. For a moment, she felt as though darkness had thickened around her. The monster's scarlet eyes with narrow slits glistened threateningly from the corner. Coach Elliot's living room no longer felt safe and cozy.

"Easy now, Cammie!" Coach Elliot's eyes glistened a reassuring shade of sapphire. "Brown fur and eight horns. Is that what you're saying? Of course, it's one of the witches' pranks. I saw that beast too a few times."

"I thought it was a bear." Christel smiled somewhat nervously. "So I ran for it."

Wilhelmina clicked her tongue. "How come I didn't hear about those encounters?"

Christel added hot water to her tea. "Are you really interested in witches' scare tactics, Mom? Personally, I think the witches have been getting too much attention lately."

"Skateland community was in denial about the existence of witches for years," Wilhelmina sniffed.

"Well, that's preposterous, of course, but I think Christel is right," Coach Elliot said. "When I was a student here, the witches tried to attack me many times, the Witch of Fear especially. Whenever I passed her castle, she would try to intimidate me with images of skeletons, gargoyles, chimeras. What else?"

"Ogres, dragons," Cammie whispered.

Coach Elliot smiled at her. "I worked hard. I stood my ground, and finally, they left me alone."

Cammie shifted in her seat, feeling a mixture of awe and jealousy. How Coach Elliot had managed to come out of the witches' attacks unscathed was a mystery to her. Neither she nor her friends had been particularly successful. Almost everybody Cammie knew had received their share of assaults. What had Coach Elliot said anyway? Practicing hard, standing your ground… But Cammie had tried, hadn't she?

"As interesting as your discussion might seem, folks, this isn't my point at all," Wilhelmina said. "Right now, I'm talking about Mavet, not the witches. And let me assure you, Mavet is not a witch or a prank. Neither is he a vision or a hallucination. Unfortunately, the monster is quite real, and the attacks that have recently taken place are true evidence of his presence in Skateland. And Cammie and Elliot, the monster you met in the park was undoubtedly Mavet. I'm sure about it because, as I said before, I saw him many times myself."

"How do you know his name?" Christel asked. "I doubt he introduced himself to you."

"His name is written on the middle horn, the one that's right above his forehead. *Mavet* is a Hebrew word, and it means *death*."

No one spoke up.

"Mavet is much more powerful than the witches, and he is much more dangerous. Unlike the witches, who aspire to destroy promising skaters' careers, Mavet is out to kill."

A log cracked in the fireplace, and the west wind outside howled.

"Mavet is an evil spirit, yet he has the power to make himself visible to humans," Wilhelmina said. "What you have all seen is the monster's true nature. He has the body of a beast, and his eight horns represent Skateland's official rinks. Mavet is ruthless and cruel, and his yearning to destroy lives is insatiable."

Christel stirred in her armchair. "How exactly does he kill? I mean, Mom, do you know anybody who was actually murdered by this...by Mavet?"

"Well…" Wilhelmina closed her eyes for a moment. "I wish you could enjoy your skating life rather than worry about the imminence of death. Unfortunately, we can no longer deny Mavet's presence, and it would be in our best interests to do whatever we can to protect ourselves from the impending danger. Now speaking about his killing methods…" The older woman folded her arms on her chest and gazed outside, where the wind threw handfuls of snowflakes against the window. "As I already mentioned, Mavet is an evil spirit. He has control over the weather. Actually, he has been sending the west wind over Skateland. And if you've been listening to the news, you know about avalanches in the mountains."

Cammie vaguely remembered the reporter talking about mountain climbers getting lost.

"Only this winter, two people were killed by avalanches," Wilhelmina said.

Cammie brought her hand to her mouth to conceal a gasp.

Coach Elliot, however, looked skeptical. "But, Wilhelmina, there is nothing supernatural about the west wind and avalanches."

Wilhelmina turned her angry face in his direction. A pouch of loose skin under her chin dangled furiously. "Not unless we have them forty straight days in a row."

Coach Elliot didn't say anything, but by the raised corners of his lips, Cammie could tell he still didn't believe the Skateland president.

"Anyway, inclement weather conditions are only an opportunity for Mavet to express his rage," Wilhelmina said. "When it comes to harassing skaters, his methods are much more subtle. The worst thing about this evil spirit is his power to possess a human being. Once Mavet indwells a person, the individual is under the monster's complete control. While on occasion, Mavet shows himself to people in his true monsterlike form, he might walk by you every day, looking like someone you know. The worst thing is that it's very difficult, if not impossible, to see the beast behind the familiar façade of an individual that you consider your friend."

The room swayed in front of Cammie. This time, she didn't even try to suppress a shriek. The monster could be hiding behind someone she knew, a friend? Wilhelmina had to be kidding. Christel and Coach Elliot appeared to be equally flabbergasted.

"Come on, Mom!"

"Wilhelmina. Hmm. I don't know." Coach Elliot coughed politely. "As much as I value your opinion, don't you think it's a little far-fetched?"

"Not, it's not!" Wilhelmina put on her glasses and glared at Coach Elliot through thick lenses. "And if you have a modicum of respect for me and my experience, you'll hear what I'm trying to say, for your own protection, Elliot. And for those around you."

Wihelmina's heavy glance shifted from Coach Elliot's face to Christel's and then to Cammie's.

Looking a little sheepish, Coach Elliot muttered that he was sorry, that he didn't mean— Wilhelmina cut him off with a swift wave of her hand. "Mavet lives in a cave in the mountains. Right there, if you want me to be exact." Wilhelmina pointed outside at the invisible cliffs.

Another gust of wind hit the house. The snow thickened. Coach Elliot stood up and added more logs to the fire.

"This is the reason we all saw him in the Icy Park. Why here? I'll get to it in a minute. However, I'm pretty sure Mavet has another home, the place that belongs to whoever he has chosen to possess this time."

"But who is it?" Christel cried out. "Who exactly does Mavet possess?"

"How I wish I knew that! Unfortunately, I don't."

The small bronze chandelier clanged, causing Cammie to jump.

"And this is the very reason I wanted to talk to all of you," Wilhelmina said. "Many minds are better than one, and the truth is usually established in the mouth of two or three witnesses. Now I want you to remember, Mavet's attacks are not something we see or experience every day. In fact, in my lifetime, I have only witnessed the monster's presence three times. And that, I dare say, has helped me to come up with a sort of pattern."

They all stared at her. Cammie tried not to breathe, fearing she would miss something.

"I've never shared this with anyone before," the older woman said. "You see, I always thought that perhaps what I had experienced might have been a coincidence. Somehow, I didn't believe I had the right to pass judgment for fear of getting the wrong person. So when the first attack happened, I merely dismissed it as random. The second time, I got worried. Now, however, I believe I have no right to hide the truth from others. It's my responsibility to protect Skateland from deadly assaults, for, I repeat, *Mavet is after skaters' lives.*"

Wilhelmina leaned back in her chair, and there appeared a distant look in her eyes. "The first time I met Mavet was almost sixty years ago. I was a young, promising skater seeking one of the spots on the US Olympic team. My programs were ready, and everybody thought I was the clear favorite to win the nationals. Until…" Skateland president toyed with a diamond snowflake pin on her chest.

"There was another girl at the competition, and she seriously thought she could beat me. Her hopes weren't unreasonable, to tell you the truth. Brenda, that was her name, was a big girl, and she was more athletic than me. While my true strength was in grace and artistry, Brenda was a natural jumper. I excelled in school figures, but Brenda hated them. Things like that happened a lot back then. Very few skaters managed to be equally good at compulsory moves and in freestyle. Some coaches even voiced opinions that those two were mutually exclusive, meaning that you could be either proficient at drawing good figures or jump and spin well. Either or, never both. Different groups of muscles, different technique. I don't know. Personally, I think the two complement each other. I loved drawing figures. They gave me perfect edge control and high speed. And as for jumps, well, I could land my doubles all right too. Actually, I found them pretty easy. The true mastery of edges always let me feel as though I owned the ice."

Cammie nodded as she remembered Wilhelmina's stellar demonstration of special figures during the History of Figure Skating Show two years ago. A few twists and turns and intricate drawings would appear on the ice, crosses, beaks, shamrocks, even spectacles.

"Brenda was older than me, already twenty-six, and it was her final season and the last chance at making it to the Olympics," Wilhelmina went on. "Four years before, she had failed to make the team. Apparently, she didn't want to leave it to chance, so she went after me."

Choctaw walked silently into the room and put his fuzzy head on Coach Elliot's lap. The man ran his fingers against the dog's hair, his eyes resting firmly on Wilhelmina.

"I was in first place after the compulsory figures," the older woman said. "Brenda was in fifth. At that time, however, school figures gave you two thirds of your score. So Brenda was desperate. The day of the free program, during lunch, she put sleeping pills in my iced tea."

Christel gasped loudly. Coach Elliot's hand flew off Choctaw's head.

"I passed out right before warm-up." Wilhelmina frowned. "By the time I came back to my senses, the competition was over. I didn't even know what was wrong with me."

"But how did you find out it was because of sleeping pills?" Christel asked.

"They gave me a blood test. See, if the pills had started working during my performance, I might have gotten seriously hurt. And if I hadn't felt the effect of the medicine 'til after the event, I would have failed the doping test. So either way, it would have been a no-win situation for me. Anyway, I missed the free program altogether, and Brenda came in second overall."

Coach Elliot spread his arms. "So if you had competed—"

"Brenda would have come in third and gotten the spot on the team anyway,"

"So why?" Cammie asked.

Wilhelmina shrugged. "She wanted to be sure. Of course, she denied playing any part in my passing out. She told my coach I had taken those pills myself because I had been having trouble falling asleep at night. We were roommates, you know. She even had the nerve to accuse me of being a nervous wreck. My coach knew it was a lie, of course. But he couldn't prove it. And neither could I."

Cammie raised her hand. "But...but you won silver at the Olympics anyway. Or was it four years later?"

Wilhelmina smiled triumphantly. "Oh, it was that year all right. You see, the federation decided to give me another opportunity to prove myself. So they invited Brenda and me to skate at a pro-am competition. School figures weren't included, so Brenda thought she had the gold in her pocket. And yet..."

Skateland president crossed her legs. "I won fair and square. Actually, I never skated that well, not even at the Olympics. I didn't make any mistakes; every jump felt easy. And of course, instead of merely going through the motions like Brenda, I let the music carry me forward. I skated to *Ave Maria*, and it was a truly magical experience."

Cammie pictured Wilhelmina as a young woman, looking a lot like Christel, floating gracefully across the ice.

"How did Brenda do?" Coach Elliot asked.

"She got silver. Actually, the judges liked her athleticism. So as you see, all of her evil plotting was for nothing. Except she didn't do particularly well at the Olympics; she only came in seventh. I, however, got the silver medal."

"So?" Christel asked impatiently. "I still don't see how Mavet could be part of it. Things like that happen all the time. Skaters perform well at their national competitions, yet they choke at the worlds or at the Olympics."

Wilhelmina's normally gray eyes were now charcoal. "I saw the monster hovering in our hotel·room both the night before the compulsory figures and the free program. Actually, that was the reason I couldn't sleep."

"It might have been a nightmare!" Christel blurted out.

"That's what I thought too," Wilhelmina said, "until the pills appeared in my tea."

"Still, you had no proof Mavet was involved," Christel said stubbornly. "Brenda went berserk, so what's the big deal?"

"See, that's the very reason I never shared it with anyone." Wilhelmina drummed her fingers on the table. "Christel, do you really think I would be coming up with those terrible stories even now if I weren't a hundred percent sure? Besides, what I shared with you wasn't the end. Ever since Brenda lost the Olympics, she was never the same. She might have looked fine on the surface. She did commercials. She skated in Ice Follies. She even got married. But now that I look back, I see that there was always that evil drive in her, that burning desire to get to me, to revenge."

"But what did you do?" Coach Elliot exclaimed. "You skated better than her, you medaled. Isn't that what skating is about? How can a skater hate another athlete for merely doing her job?"

"Now you understand it right, Elliot! Thank you very much! Do you think I disagree with you? I'm merely telling you what happened."

Wilhelmina took a deep breath. "Everybody around Brenda thought she was mean and cruel. But now I know that at that time, Mavet already possessed her. As I mentioned before, I saw the monster a few times around me again, and it always happened when Brenda was around, skating in the same show with me. Mavet owned her; he was the one who made her do evil things."

"But…why did Mavet possess her?" Cammie asked.

"Good question." Wilhelmina nodded. "Mavet will always look for a weakness in a person. A certain flaw will become an entrance through which the evil spirit will take a hold of the person's soul. Brenda was obsessed with hate and jealousy, and that opened the doorway for the evil spirit to come in."

Cammie's stomach clenched. She felt as though the world was crumbling around her. That wasn't the way things were supposed to be. Skating was supposed to be beautiful; it had to engage the audience in the swirl of grace and music. Yet there was a skater who was ready to commit a serious crime only to reach her questionable goal. If that was true, there was no point in skating altogether.

"Brenda didn't stop at that point," Wilhelmina went on. "She wanted to ruin my career. Only she didn't realize that by doing so, she terminated whatever chance she had to a happy and productive life. Anyway, she attacked me again. By that time, I had already retired from amateur skating and became part of the Ice Capades. One day, I was on the road, trying to make it to practice in time. It was a bright winter day, and the highway was perfectly clear, no snow or ice. However, at some point, I felt I was losing control of the car. It was weird. I started going around and around as though doing a scratch spin on the highway. I tried to straighten out the car, and it wouldn't cooperate."

"It must have been the brake," Coach Elliot said. "They say if it happens—"

"There was nothing wrong with the car!" Wilhelmina barked. "Didn't I tell you? I took it to the repair shop afterward; they ran every test, and everything was fine."

Christel stared at her clenched fingers.

"The car swerved to the right. It was the exact feeling of exiting a spin. I remember thinking how funny it was that I felt like a skater even on the highway. But next thing I remember was the car slamming into a pole. I was jammed inside. The pain was excruciating. But before I passed out…" The older woman's eyes appeared huge as she peered at the three of them. "I saw Brenda's face leering at me. She just stood staring at me. And then she actually smiled and said—I'll never forget that voice; it was dripping with venom. She said, 'That Olympic medal won't do you any good now, huh? Well, have a safe trip to hell!'"

Cammie felt as though there was no air in the room. Choctaw lifted his head from Coach Elliot's lap and approached her. She buried her face in the dog's fleecy hair, choking on her own tears.

"I woke up in the hospital with thirty-six broken bones," Wilhelmina said huskily. "It took me a year to even start walking again. But the next day after I managed to put one foot ahead of the other, I put on my skates. And you know what? I found out that skating was easier than walking, at least for me. Within a few months, I was almost back to my normal skating level. Almost," Wilhelmina repeated as she slid her eyes over their faces. "Unfortunately, I started developing arthritis shortly after the accident. So here I am."

Cammie looked at the woman's crooked fingers and the long hem of her dress covering her arthritic legs. When Wilhelmina sat in her wheelchair, people saw a sick old woman. Yet as soon as the Skateland president's feet touched the ice, the woman magically transformed. Her skating technique was still impeccable. You simply couldn't take your eyes off her.

Coach Elliot cleared his throat. "So you think Brenda had something to do with your accident, don't you?"

Wilhelmina nodded. "Absolutely. Well, don't get me wrong. A human being couldn't have made a car spin like a skater on a perfectly clean highway. It was all

Mavet's doing, for at that time, the evil spirit already possessed Brenda."

Cammie squirmed and pulled the sleeves of her warm-up jacket over her hands. It was probably getting colder outside.

Wilhelmina rounded her shoulders. "This unusually cold temperature is also a sign of Mavet's presence."

"Is he…is he there somewhere?" Cammie felt her throat constrict.

Christel scowled but moved her chair closer to the table. "In this case, I'm not getting out of this house. You'll have to put up with us for the night, Elliot."

The man added more logs in the fire. "Be my guests."

"Actually, we don't have to worry about making it back home," Wilhelmina said calmly.

Christel folded her arms on her chest. "And why's that?"

"Because Mavet isn't after us."

THE MUSIC OF DEATH

"Gosh, Mom. Can you be a little more explicit?"

Christel picked up a spoon and swirled it nervously in her long fingers.

Wilhelmina took the spoon away from her and rested it on her saucer. "I thought you might have figured it out by this point, Christel. Mavet's current target is Elliot."

Cammie's heart pounded in her chest, sending hot terror all the way to her limbs.

"What?" Christel gasped.

Coach Elliot, however, looked calm, even slightly amused. "Me?"

"And I expected more shrewdness from you too, Elliot," Wilhelmina said. "Remember the night of the show and the poison in Ice Spice Soda? You were the only skater who hadn't received his drink. Now don't tell me that this fact didn't get you to think."

Coach Elliot rubbed his forehead. In the light of the chandelier, his hair appeared golden. "Well, I'll be honest with you, I gave that matter a thought. It seems unlikely, however. Who on earth would want to kill me?"

Cammie nodded in agreement. How somebody could hate a man as nice as Coach Elliot was beyond her imagination.

"I'm sure it was a coincidence," Christel said.

Cammie saw the younger woman exchange smiles with Coach Elliot.

Wilhelmina, however, appeared unperturbed. "Okay. Now how about what happened at your last practice? You can't deny the obvious fact that switching CDs was a deliberate attempt to take Elliot's life. I mean, I didn't bring that CD to the rink. Did any of you?"

"But whoever switched CDs could have been after me too!" Christel exclaimed.

Wilhelmina shook her head. "Christel, you're not the type of skater who would evoke so much hatred. Don't get mad at me now, but you never made it to the podium."

The younger woman's face reddened. "I'm perfectly aware of that, Mom. You don't have to insult me. Sorry for not meeting your expectations."

"And again, you've completely missed the point. What I'm trying to say is that Mavet hates Elliot because he made it to the top." Wilhelmina nodded in Coach Elliot's direction.

"But Felicia and I never medaled at the worlds or the Olympics," Coach Elliot said. "We won two national titles, but there are many skaters who did the same. That's no big deal."

"That's right, Mom. Mavet can't possibly be after Elliot," Christel said.

"Cammie," Wilhelmina said, "could you kindly bring your Kanga bag in here?"

"What?" Now that the four of them were in the middle of a serious discussion involving deadly attacks, the Skateland president wanted Cammie's skating bag?

"Just bring it in!"

Cammie went to the foyer where she had left her bag and pressed the button that replaced Kanga's blades with wheels. As she entered the living room again, pulling the bag behind her, Wilhelmina sat in her chair, facing Elliot.

"Elliot, I presume you've never figured out how Felicia died."

Blood drained from Coach Elliot's face. His fingers closed around the edge of the table. "Excuse me?"

"Elliot, do you have any idea what really happened?"

"You know what happened. I dropped her from that lift."

"Yes, you always thought the accident was your mistake. That's not true, Elliot. You didn't drop Felicia because you were weak or there was a flaw in your technique. It was Mavet's job."

Coach Elliot's face was the color of fresh snow. "I don't understand."

"Turn your Kanga bag to media player mode, Cammie," Wilhelmina said.

Cammie quickly obeyed, wondering what the older woman was up to.

"Kanga's media player has videos of every skating competition that ever happened in history. Since the time video equipment appeared, of course," Wilhelmina said. "All right, Cammie. We will need the nineteen ninety-two US Nationals, pairs' free program."

"Wilhelmina, no!" Coach Elliot half rose from his chair.

"You have to see it, Elliot."

"Please! I can't face it again."

"I'm sorry, but you need to understand. And so do they." Wilhelmina nodded at Cammie and Christel.

Kanga's monitor lit up royal blue, and words ran across the screen: "1992 US National Competition: Pairs Free Program." Next came the names of skaters listed in the order of their rankings after the short program. Cammie saw at once that Felicia Monroe and Elliot Monroe had come in first after the short program, which meant they were going to skate last.

Cammie relaxed in her soft chair, ready to watch. Skating competitions were never dull.

"Now we'll fast forward to Felicia and Elliot's performance," Wilhelmina said.

Cammie pressed the fast forward button obediently.

Felicia and Elliot stood in the middle of the rink. Elliot's bright blue shirt matched the color of Felicia's dress. Cammie recognized Coach Elliot's wife immediately. Felicia's auburn hair was pulled up, but it still looked as though there were dozens of shades of red in it. As Elliot offered the woman his hand, Felicia beamed at him. There was absolutely no mistake; the two of them were in love.

Felicia rested her head on Elliot's shoulder, and the two of them glided close to each other in smooth crossovers. They started with side-by-side triple toe loops followed by a throw triple salchow. Cammie admired Felicia's arms that seemed to have a life of their own. One moment, they were arched gracefully, and then Felicia spread them, letting her wrists and her shoulders form a perfect line. Cammie would never have thought a skater's arms could convey such a wide range of emotions.

Felicia shook her flaming hair, a teasing smile on her lips. Even with incredibly strong technique, there was genuine, almost childlike playfulness in her. *Do you like me?* Felicia's smile seemed to be asking. And then she raised her arms, as though embracing everybody at the arena. *Everybody loves you, but you're mine*, Elliot answered as he gently scooped her from the ice. His strong hands closed around Felicia's hands. Now she was in the air, soaring high above her husband's head. And then... Elliot only held her by one hand, and his feet tapped the ice in a series of steps.

The music coughed. Was there something wrong with the sound system? The melody was choking. It sounded as though the musicians were struggling for breath. Felicia's hair soared over Elliot's head. There was a wailing sound, like the cry of a wounded animal, and Felicia started falling strangely, slowly, so Cammie hoped that somehow, somehow Elliot's hand would reach Felicia's. Surely, he would be able to rescue her. He was strong. He was a man. No!

Felicia lay prostrate on the ice. It was the first time the skaters had come apart. Elliot was kneeling next to his wife, his hands over Felicia's torso. Elliot touched Felicia's face. She didn't move. And then he fell onto the ice next to her. The music wasn't playing anymore. There was silence on the ice.

The silence of death, Cammie suddenly thought.

"It looks like Felicia Monroe is seriously hurt. She's not getting up." The commentator's worried voice appeared as if from nowhere.

"Turn it off!"

Cammie glanced in Coach Elliot's direction. His head was buried in his knees, his fists resting on top of his head.

"Elliot!" Wilhelmina took a few tentative steps in the man's direction. "Elliot, I didn't want us all to see that video to hurt you. Now…" The older woman hugged Coach Elliot tightly.

"Now the paramedics are taking Felicia to the hospital," the commentator said.

"Cammie, turn it off!" Wilhelmina's dark gray eyes flashed in Cammie's direction.

"Oh!" Cammie reached for the *off* button. Her hands shook so hard that she missed it twice. Coach Elliot raised his ashen face from his knees. He ripped the collar of the white shirt that he wore under a navy blue V-neck pullover. A button came off and rolled on the floor. Cammie picked it up and put it gently on the table next to Elliot's chair.

"It…it was the same music!" Christel muttered.

Wilhelmina nodded gravely. She was still patting Elliot on the back, whispering something into his ear.

"But who?" the man blurted out. His eyes were red.

"That's what we need to find out." Wilhelmina returned to her seat. "What we have just seen and heard is a typical example of the music of death. I don't want to get too scientific here, but our bodies function according to certain rhythms. Our hearts beat regularly. Our breathing follows a certain pattern too. This is the very reason people enjoy music. When we hear something that conforms to the natural rhythm of our bodies, we reach out to it, we like it. Talented composers have managed to come up with masterpieces that are able to penetrate the soul deeply, making people laugh or cry." Wilhelmina went on. "A composer who pours true love into his music is able to create a piece that will make listeners feel better, even heal their diseases. This is what we call music of life."

Cammie raised her head at the sound of a familiar phrase. "Mr. Dulcimer told us about the music of life. He even played a piece for us."

"That's right. Mr. Dulcimer's love for music and skating is so genuine that he comes up with true masterpieces. And if a skater who uses the music of life truly performs from her heart, miracles might happen."

For a split second, Cammie felt the Skateland president's eyes rest on her face.

"Unfortunately, there is a down side to everything," Wilhelmina said gravely. "Just like there is music of life, the opposite exists, something known as the music of death. We all get used to certain patterns and tempos. Once the structures we perceive as normal are disrupted, we might become sick or even die. Music of death causes human bodies to stop functioning properly. A person's heart diverts from its normal rhythm, the beating becomes erratic, the heart weakens and eventually stops. Actually, some African tribes who worship the devil are known to be able to use music as a weapon against their enemies. As the spirit of death, Mavet, of course, has a true mastery of disruptive, potentially lethal patterns."

"Now...wait a minute." Christel sounded almost scared. "Are you saying that music may work like... hmm...poison?"

Wilhelmina nodded. "That's right. When a skater performs his program, he attunes to the musical pattern of the piece. A certain connection is created. So that's what happened at that national competition, Elliot. You weren't the problem; you didn't merely drop Felicia. Someone who hated the two of you managed to replace your music with the music of death. So please stop blaming yourself, Elliot. You could have done absolutely nothing to prevent the fall. Once you started skating to that piece, the two you were doomed. One of you was destined to be hurt. Or it could have been both. I don't know."

Coach Elliot shook his head. *He probably wishes the music of death had killed him instead of Felicia,* Cammie thought.

"I have absolutely no doubt that the person who messed up your music in nineteen ninety-two tried it again two weeks ago," Wilhelmina said. "Only this time, he went after you, Elliot, although he didn't care that Christel might have gotten hurt too."

Cammie looked at Christel, who sat awkwardly on the edge of her chair, one leg tucked under the other.

"Mrs. Van Uffeln, the same kind of music was playing when Dana got hurt during her audition," Cammie said.

Christel and Elliot stared at her, but Wilhelmina gave her a nod of approval. "Exactly."

"Oh really?" Coach Elliot glanced at Wilhelmina. "But I wasn't skating then. So it wasn't an attack against me."

"And besides, Dana wasn't even one of Elliot's students." Christel's dark gray eyes searched her mother's face.

"Well, I have to admit it's a little glitch in my theory," Wilhelmina said with obvious reluctance. "However, just because I still haven't managed to establish a connection between Dana and Elliot doesn't mean that there isn't any."

"Dana might have been attacked by mistake. You know, instead of Coach Elliot," Cammie said.

Wilhelmina raised her index finger. "Good thinking, Cammie!"

Coach Elliot, however, looked pensive. "But Wilhelmina, who...who on earth could hate Felicia and now...me?"

Wilhelmina leaned forward. "Think. Think hard, Elliot. Someone had to execute those attacks. Although I'm sure the person didn't come up with the idea himself. I recognize Mavet's handwriting. He obviously possesses the individual who hates you, Elliot."

Coach Elliot shook his head. "I can't think of anyone who would even be interested in my skating anymore, let alone hate me."

Wilhelmina pressed her lips. "Don't tell me you don't have enemies. Everybody does. And unless you think hard, it might take us a while to find out—"

"It was Celine Bouchard who put that CD into the player!" Cammie was shocked at herself for saying those words.

Everybody's eye was now on her.

"Cammie, that's ridiculous," Coach Elliot said.

Wilhelmina, however, nodded. "I wouldn't eliminate Celine from the list of possible suspects. Thank you, Cammie."

Coach Elliot spread his arms. "You really surprise me Wilhelmina. Do you seriously think a child could attack me? Besides, in nineteen ninety-two, the girl wasn't even born yet."

"Maybe her parents tried to finish you off," Christel said eagerly. "And then they handed the torch to their daughter."

Wilhelmina pushed herself away from the table. "We've got to go. Elliot, concentrate on getting better. But I also want you to remember that your life is in jeopardy. Be very careful."

"Now wait a minute, Wilhelmina." Coach Elliot stood up too. "Suppose you're right and there's really a demon-possessed person in Skateland who hates my guts. So wouldn't it be better for me to get out of the spotlight altogether?"

"Hey!" Christel clapped her hands.

"I mean it, Christel." Elliot looked at his partner. "If Wilhelmina's right, and as long as I've known her, she's never been wrong, there's someone dangerous in Skateland, and that individual is after me. Until he kills me, he causes all those terrible thunderstorms and avalanches. Or if Cammie's theory is correct, innocent people get hurt by mistake." He paused for a moment, apparently expecting them to say something, and then went on. "Why don't I just retire? Everybody's life will be easier. I can move farther away to the mountains with Choctaw and—"

"And hand over the victory to Mavet and to whomever he possesses, right?" Wilhelmina roared. "Let me tell you something. That's exactly what he wants. You and Felicia were terrific skaters twenty years ago, so he killed her. Now you finally went back to the ice, you skated in shows, you're coaching—"

"For crying out loud, Wilhelmina!" Coach Elliot exclaimed. "So why not let him get what he wants? I'll retire, and that's no big deal, and Skateland residents will be safe."

The diamond snowflake on Wilhelmina's chest caught the light of the chandelier as she slapped herself on the knee. "Wrong. Totally wrong. We must never succumb to the enemy's evil schemes. Because if we do, he will win. And he won't stop at that. Believe me. Oh no. He'll want more. Eventually, he'll take Skateland over completely. And if he does, Skateland will no longer be the same. Besides, Elliot. Think of all the young and talented skaters who need you here."

No one spoke for a few minutes. Outside, the west wind whined and whistled.

"Okay." Coach Elliot looked a little calmer. "You're right. I'm not quite ready to throw in the towel. And I'm sure…I'm sure Felicia wouldn't want me to give up. I'm only worried about Christel's safety. Because if she skates with me—"

"I have a say in it too, don't you think?" Christel jumped from her seat. Her hands in her pockets, the woman stared at Elliot with an unfazed look.

"Naturally, we'll do our best to prevent future attacks," Wilhelmina said. "We'll have to be very careful when we put CDs in the player. So each time you play your music, please check and double-check whether it's your CD, the one you brought to the rink with you. And as you all already know, keeping ourselves in good shape and working on the basics never hurts. Finally, let me remind you to look around and think who might be plotting those evil attacks. We need to think logically here. The attacker definitely knows a lot about music."

They were already getting in the icemobile. Coach Elliot stood in the doorway, leaning against the frame. Wilhelmina bent down to the dashboard to give her destination to the icemobile then turned back to Coach Elliot.

"Elliot, one more thing. When you make up a list of possible suspects, don't forget to include your closest friends!"

MUSIC INTERPRETATION CLASS

"So who do you have on your list?" Sonia asked Cammie as the two of them skated to school after their morning practice. Sonia, who trained at the Yellow Rink, had caught up with Cammie on Inside Edge Street that led right to Skateland School.

Cammie's piece of paper fluttered in the wind. "Well, of course, I started with Celine because she did put that CD with the music of death into the player."

Sonia nodded. "Good thinking."

"Celine's parents are also under suspicion. Because when Felicia got killed, Celine hadn't even been born yet. However, her parents might have had some grudge against Felicia and Elliot."

Sonia skipped a step. "That's right! They've known one another for years."

"Unfortunately, Celine's mom and dad didn't compete against the Elliots. If they had, I would be a hundred percent sure they were behind those attacks."

"True." Sonia sighed. "It's incredible what people will do to win. Okay. Who else?"

"Next is Lieutenant Turner. Oh, don't look at me like that, Sonia! That guy is all over the place. I'm tired of bumping into him every day. Remember how he followed us to that Fortune Rink? And that other time, when I tried to reach Coach Elliot's property and saw the monster, Turner was there too. What if he was the monster? What if he had transformed back into a human being right before he called me?"

"Hmm. It's a possibility, of course," Sonia said. "But Lieutenant Turner couldn't have killed Felicia. He was still a baby in nineteen ninety-two. I think Turner follows you everywhere to protect you from the attacker. He really likes you, Cammie."

"He hates me!" Cammie shouted.

Nikki and Liz, who walked ahead of them, turned around and stared at her. Cammie glared back.

Sonia grabbed her hand. "Wait! Let them pass."

The two of them stood shivering in the cold wind for a couple of minutes and then resumed their stroking.

"What's our first class?" Cammie asked.

"Music interpretation." Sonia shivered. "At least it isn't snowing today. I would hate to skate in a blizzard. Why can't we have music interpretation at an indoor rink?"

"Beats me." Cammie looked at her paper again. "Speaking about music interpretation, I also have Mr. Dulcimer on my list."

Now it was Sonia's turn to yelp. "No way!"

"Wilhelmina told us to look for an expert in music. And who but Mr. Dulcimer—?"

"But all choreographers are musically trained!" Sonia exclaimed. "Come on, Cammie. Mr. Dulcimer absolutely can't be the attacker."

"And why not? He's old enough. He probably knew the Monroes. He could have killed Felicia easily."

"I don't think a person who writes the music of life can also come up with a piece that can kill somebody," Sonia said firmly.

"Well, you might be right, but Wilhelmina told us to look at everybody, even friends."

Sonia shivered again. "It's hard to believe your friend can kill someone you care for."

"I think so too. Well, that's all I have so far." Cammie folded her piece of paper.

"I would go with Celine," Sonia said. "Her parents must have hated the Monroes, so they killed Felicia. And now they want to get rid of Elliot too. But it would be difficult for them to get to him, so they asked Celine to do it. Hey, that must be the reason they sent her to Skateland!"

Cammie thought for a moment. "You know what? You might be right. But I still think we need to keep an eye on Turner. We don't know his parents. They might have hated the Monroes twenty years ago."

They turned around the corner of the school building and approached the rink. The ice was badly ripped, gutted with ruts and holes. Most of the ninth-graders stood close to the edge of the rink, talking loudly.

"I'm not even stepping on this ice. It'll ruin my blades!" Nikki whined.

Liz put her hands into her pockets. "Me either."

"Who did they have here anyway, a bunch of hockey guys?" Michael made an exaggerated imitation of a hockey player chasing a puck. His facial expression was so ferocious that Cammie giggled.

"Good morning to you all!" a deep baritone called from behind them.

As Cammie looked back, she saw the familiar black-and-yellow Zamboni with Mr. Walrus at the steering wheel. In spite of the cold, gloomy day, Mr. Walrus was his usual joyful self.

"Sorry, guys. I'm a little late. I had to clean the Main Rink. There must have been a party there 'til dawn. The ice was all torn."

"This ice isn't much better." Jeff scraped the dark gray surface with his blade.

Mr. Walrus's beard twitched. "Hey, you're right. It looks like there had been a party at the school rink too last night. I think it's the witches' job."

Michael sniggered. "You're kidding, right?"

"Not at all, young man. Not at all. Anyway, you may relax for a while, skaters. The ice will be ready in a few minutes."

Groaning and complaining, the students trudged up the steps to the bleachers. Cammie and Sonia, however, stayed at the edge of the rink.

"I think I'll turn into an icicle if I sit down at least for a moment," Cammie said, her teeth cluttering.

Sonia hugged herself. "Yeah, me too. Hey, what did he say about the witches' party?"

"I have no idea. But you know when the witches party, it usually means that they are plotting another attack."

Sonia glanced in the direction of the Icy Park. "That's right! Look. Maybe Mavet has nothing to do with those attacks anyway. Maybe it was all the witches."

Cammie shook her head. "Wilhelmina thinks it was Mavet. And she's never wrong, you know."

There came a soft rumble of the Zamboni moving across the rink. Mr. Walrus looked as though he was really enjoying himself. As the Zamboni approached Cammie and Sonia, they realized that the man was singing at the top of his lungs.

> It's every skater's cherished dream
> To swirl, and roll, and glide.
> So on the ice, so smooth and clean
> I'm dying to abide.
>
> Now move my feet:
> I'll try to skate
> Much faster than before.
> Who cares if it's dark and late?
> I'll stay and skate some more.

"Wow. That's nice," Sonia said.

"Sonia!" Cammie grabbed her friend's hand. "It's Mr. Walrus!"

Sonia took a step away, looking concerned. "Of course it's Mr. Walrus. Are you feeling all right, Cammie?"

"No. Mr. Walrus. He's Mavet."

"What?" Sonia cried out and then lowered her voice. "No way!"

"And why not? Wilhelmina told us to watch out for a musically talented adult. Mr. Walrus writes and sings songs, so—"

"You're out of your mind, Cammie! Mr. Walrus would never attack anyone. He's nice, he's dedicated, he's—"

"Wilhelmina told us to look for the attacker among our friends," Cammie said.

"Well, I don't know, Cammie. There still need to be people in our lives whom we completely trust, like Wilhelmina, and Mr. Walrus, and Mr. Reed."

"But Wilhelmina said—"

"We still need to trust somebody. Because if we don't"—Sonia said the last sentence almost in a whisper—"then the witches and Mavet have reached their purpose."

They were quiet for a while as they watched the Zamboni make its final round across the ice.

"Bye, ladies!" Mr. Walrus waved his hand at them, his bright blue eyes sparkling on his pink face.

"Bye, Mr. Walrus!" Cammie and Sonia said in unison.

"Time to get to work, girls!" Mr. Dulcimer's familiar voice called, and the two of them hastened to take their seats in the bleachers.

"Watch the CD player!" Cammie mouthed to Sonia as the two of them walked up the aisle. She just remembered that Wilhelmina had told them to make sure no one would slip a suspicious-looking CD into the player.

"What? Oh, yes." Sonia cast a surreptitious look at the big, black CD player that sat on the snow. There were also four speakers positioned around the rink.

Mr. Dulcimer appeared on the ice, panting, his reddish brown goatee ruffled at the edges. The flannel shirt that he wore under a leather vest wasn't tucked in, and his Levi's were wrinkled. Cammie also noticed that the teacher had some dark smudges on his cheeks and on the tip of his nose.

"All right, people. I want you all to excuse me. There is an emergency situation that requires my immediate attention. I'll have to leave you for about twenty minutes."

"Yes!" the students shouted excitedly.

"However!" The teacher raised his hand. "I don't expect you to waste your time gossiping in the freezing temperature. Instead, I want all of you to go down to the ice and do some warm-up exercises. Let me put on some music."

The students rose from their seats, moaning and smirking. Cammie watched the teacher take a CD from his briefcase and then slide it into the machine. She looked at Sonia, sending her a silent message, *Watch out!* Her friend too leaned forward, her neck craned.

Music began to play, something jazzy. *Oh yes!* Cammie recognized the piece. It was "Take Five." She glanced at Sonia again and saw her nod.

So far so good, Sonia's eyes seemed to be saying.

"I hope he'll be away long enough so we won't have to do that stupid interpretation thing," Nikki said cheerfully. With her bright yellow parka and tight leggings, the girl looked like a little chick. Yet Cammie had seen Nikki perform with her partner, and she knew what a strong skater the girl was.

Sonia sighed. "I wish I could go to the Yellow Rink and work on my short program."

"What keeps you from practicing here? The ice is good now, and I like this music." Jeff jumped onto the rink and did five twizzles.

Cammie followed Jeff and Sonia to the ice and warmed up with alternating forward and backward crossovers. She tried a few spins and then did all of her single jumps. When she was sure she was warm enough for her doubles, Nikki stopped in the middle of the rink.

"You know what? I think Dulcimer wants to turn us all into show skaters." Nikki took off her gloves, blew on her hands, and then put the gloves back on.

"I'll do show numbers when I'm a hundred years old," Liz said, smirking. "And there'll be nothing but forward edges and two-foot spins in that program."

Liz glided forward on her left outside edge, waving her arms dramatically and jerking her chin.

The students erupted in raucous laughter.

"Well done, Tong! And you just won the top award!" Michael jumped onto the ice next to Liz, lowered himself on his knee, and handed the girl a CD.

Liz twisted the black-and-purple disc in her hands. "What's that?"

"Some nice hip hop songs. There, Liz. Let me put it in." Michael took the CD from the girl's hand and glided in the direction of the player.

A CD. He was going to play that CD. And what if...what if Michael was the attacker? What if he was going to play the music of death?

"No!" Cammie darted forward past the startled Liz.

The CD was already in the machine. All Michael had to do was press the *play* button.

"No. Don't press it!" Cammie coughed as the wind blew ice-cold air in her throat.

"What's your problem, girl?" Michael's finger froze on the *on* button. "We just want to have some fun here. That's all."

Sonia skated up appearing out of breath. "You ... can't...play...this...CD!"

"You too, Harrison?" Michael's dark eyes narrowed. "Who are you, the music police?"

Liz laughed loudly behind them.

"Come on, Sonia, a little bit of hip hop will help us warm up!" Jeff hugged Sonia from behind.

Sonia jerked forward. "Let...go...of me!"

"Okay. That's enough." Michael tried to push the *play* button again, but Cammie grabbed his hand.

"What's wrong with you two?" Jeff's chocolate brown eyes were rounded as he looked at Cammie then at Sonia.

"You know what, Jeff? I got it. They're simply jealous because of Celine," Michael said nastily.

Sonia's pink face turned white. She stepped back. "What?"

Cammie was so shocked that she let go of Michael's hand. At that same moment, he pressed the *play* button. The sound of drums rolled across the rink.

"Don't! Everybody off the ice!" Cammie shouted.

"You can't skate to this music!" Sonia yelled.

"I don't think I'm supposed to take orders from you, suckers!" Michael said with a nasty grin.

"Sonia, it's okay. We'll just have a little fun. Mr. Dulcimer won't say anything." Jeff reached for Sonia's hand.

"Get off the ice!" Cammie rushed between Liz and Nikki, trying to stop them.

"Now *you* get out of here!" Liz went into a hockey stop. Her eyes were like two hot coals.

"I want to be a billionaire so freaking bad…" the singer announced.

"Please don't skate!" Cammie's voice was already husky from too much shouting. "This music will kill you!"

"Hey, you're even worse than my mom. She hates hip hop!" Michael exclaimed as he glided past her in a gorgeous spread eagle.

"You know, Sonia, not every hip hop song is for the witches!" Grinning widely, Jeff whooshed past Sonia, who had been trying to stop him.

All of their classmates now skated happily, jumping, spinning, doing steps. Sonia looked at Cammie, her eyes rounded with horror. Cammie clasped her hands not to allow angry tears to stream down her cheeks. What did they all know? She cringed as she listened to the fast song, expecting the familiar wailing sound to come any moment. And then her friends would collapse on the ice and hit their heads. And perhaps someone would die.

"Please, stop!" Sonia sounded as though she was crying.

"It's the music of death!" Cammie whined.

Jeff stopped abruptly. "What?"

"Please, everybody. We know what we're talking about!" Cammie looked around, not even trying to hide her tears anymore.

Her classmates froze in the middle of their performance, staring at her. The music was still playing.

"Do you remember what Mr. Dulcimer told us about the music of death? Well, that's it!" Cammie pointed at the CD player.

The students' eyes followed the direction of Cammie's hand.

"No!" Jeff smiled.

"You're kidding, right?" Nikki wrinkled her nose.

"It's true!" Sonia said.

"You know what? I think these two went nuts," Michael said with exaggerated seriousness. "My mom told me about those things that happen to skaters who practice too hard and don't eat right."

"Oh please!" Cammie groaned.

"So it's hip hop time, guys?" a deep voice came from the far end of the rink.

Cammie looked back, and to her great relief, Mr. Dulcimer skated up to them, his usual briefcase in his hand. The man looked definitely better than at the beginning of the lesson. He had even changed into a clean pair of blue jeans, and the dark smudges were gone from his face.

"Well, there's nothing wrong with hip hop, as soon as it's helping you to relax," Mr. Dulcimer said with a smile. "Actually, this is the best performance I've ever seen from you guys."

The students exchanged happy grins.

"So it's not the music of death, right?" Jeff sounded dead serious, though Cammie could see the corners of his mouth twitch.

Mr. Dulcimer spread his arms. "The music of death? Of course not. Who gave you that ridiculous idea?"

Nikki pointed to Cammie and Sonia. "They did."

The first song had just ended. The song that was playing now was "We'll Be Alright."

"But…but we thought…" Sonia lowered her head. All Cammie could see was the bright red tip of her nose. Cammie too felt so hot that she seriously considered taking off her parka.

"No, no. These songs are perfectly all right," Mr. Dulcimer said. "Please don't think that hip hop music is bad. Absolutely not. You've got to understand it, guys. Death isn't in the genre. A villain who creates a deadly melody or beat may work within the framework of classical music, rock, pop, disco, anything. Okay. Why don't you all take your seats? We have just enough time to do a little interpretation."

As Cammie walked up to her usual spot in the third row of the bleachers, she felt the weight of her classmates' stares. She hated herself. What had she been thinking? Why on earth had she thought of the music of death? As though the attacker would have dared to kill a student in front of the whole class! Besides, as Wilhelmina had said, Mavet was after Coach Elliot.

Yes, but Wilhelmina also told you to watch all CDs, a small voice said in Cammie's mind. Cammie looked at Sonia. Her roommate stared firmly ahead, her cheeks cherry red.

"Remember, the most important thing is sincerity," Mr. Dulcimer said. "So today, I encourage all of you to do your best. And I have a prize for the best performer."

"It must be a disc with Mozart's symphony," Michael growled behind Cammie.

"Okay. Michael Somner, I want you to come down," Mr. Dulcimer called.

As usual, the students received earphones with the musical pieces the teacher had chosen for them. One by one, Cammie's friends performed to the tunes they had listened to. From what Cammie could tell, none of them even bothered to portray the character of the music. All they did was spin and jump.

I don't feel like interpreting any music today, Cammie thought sadly.

In fact, her only desire was to get as far away from the school rink as possible. Her classmates still cast weird glances at her. Three or four times, she heard her and Sonia's names spoken in a whisper. A few girls giggled.

"Sonia Harrison, your turn!" Mr. Dulcimer called.

Sonia rose from a seat in the front row, where she had been listening to her piece. Cammie closed her eyes. *Please, may the lesson be over before my turn comes,* she prayed silently. *Because I feel so bad, I'm definitely not in the mood to interpret any music.*

Remember what Wilhelmina told you, the familiar voice popped up in her mind.

Wilhelmina? What did Wilhelmina have to do with music interpretation? And then Cammie remembered. Of course! Right before the Skateland president had started telling them about Mavet, she had said, *From this moment on, I want you to really concentrate on music interpretation, Cammie.*

But I don't feel like it. Not now! Cammie pleaded silently. And Wilhelmina's voice spoke again in her mind, as clearly as in Coach Elliot's cabin the day before, *At this point, nothing is more important than learning how to interpret music correctly.*

"Cammie Wester!" Mr. Dulcimer said.

Cammie stood up obediently.

Michael laughed from behind her. "You'd better be careful, honey. What if it's the music of death?"

Jeff sniggered next to him.

Cammie's greatest desire was to give both jerks a good kick. No, she couldn't do that, not in front of a teacher. She would be in so much trouble. The idiots weren't worth it. What did they know? If Michael and Jeff hadn't spent most of their time trying to impress Celine, perhaps they would be paying more attention to what was happening right under their noses. And Alex... At the thought of Alex, Cammie's fingers clasped into tight fists. Some friend he was! To think that just a couple of months ago, Cammie could have talked to him about anything. Now, in Alex's mind, the whole world revolved around Celine.

Cammie looked up at Mr. Dulcimer.

"Now listen to your music, Cammie."

It took her only a couple of seconds to recognize the piece. It was *Totentanz* by Listz. She had seen a few elite skaters perform to the same piece, and she had always felt carried away by the wild interplay of sounds. Well, she would show all those nincompoops how to skate right. She would give them just the message they needed. And the message was, *Beware! Be alert, skaters, for there's an enemy in our midst. And he's very dangerous.*

"Go ahead, Cammie!"

That was it, her time to skate. Cammie bent one knee and planted the toe pick into the ice. She stretched her arms ahead of her, her fingers spread. She would show all of them what righteous anger looked like. The music started playing, and it carried Cammie forward. It was easy. Cammie understood exactly what the composer had been trying to say.

You are in danger. Stand up and fight!

She felt her body leave the ice and spin twice, but she didn't even realize what jump she was doing. Her feet tapped the ice. Was that the footwork from her program? No, of course not. The steps were huge and angry. The music roared across the rink. Cammie picked up even more speed. Her final spin, and there she was sitting on the ice, her head bent over her knee, her arms over her head.

She didn't hear anything for a few seconds. Her mind was blank. Then someone sighed loudly. Someone clapped. More people applauded. She heard a faint, "Bravo!" And suddenly, someone whistled; and as

293

Cammie looked up, all of her classmates were on their feet, clapping loudly.

Cammie blinked, shook her head, and glanced at Mr. Dulcimer. Was it a dream, or was she really getting a standing ovation? To her greatest surprise, the teacher clapped too, and there was a clear expression of disbelief written all over his ruddy face.

The man skated up to Cammie. "Now, everybody, this is exactly what I wanted from you all. This is what I call music interpretation. Good job, Cammie! It was a pleasure watching you. Am I right, you guys?"

"That was awesome!" Sonia clapped harder.

"Yeah! Well done, Cammie!" Jeff shouted.

Michael appeared flabbergasted. He only shook his head.

"Well, the performance was really outstanding. And I think you, Cammie, deserve more than just an A. Take this."

There were more sighs as the students bent over to see what the teacher had given Cammie. She blurted a quick thank-you and accepted a small, flat object. As she looked at it closer, she realized it was a CD case. Nested inside was a sparkling silver-and-blue CD with the title of the piece written around the perimeter, *Music of Life*.

Mr. Dulcimer bent his head to look closer at Cammie. For a moment, his brown eyes studied her flushed face. "This piece is very precious, Cammie. Use it wisely."

TRIPLE SALCHOW

Cammie took Wilhelmina's assignment of watching the people on her list very seriously. So far, Cammie and Sonia had agreed that Celine was their primary suspect; therefore, Cammie's eyes never left Celine. Cammie rushed to the Yellow Rink after her own practices so she would catch Celine gliding around the arena. Even though Coach Elliot was still on sick leave, chances were that the showgirl would attack someone else.

Spending a whole hour in the bleachers of the Yellow Rink was tiresome. Every night, Cammie had to stay up way past her bedtime to finish her homework. During her own practices, she felt exhausted, yet she hadn't noticed anything suspicious so far. But she never thought of the extra hours at the Yellow Rink as a waste of time. If that was what she had to do to protect the Skateland community from vicious attacks, she didn't mind the fatigue that much.

Cammie also made sure she was close to Celine during school recesses. Seeing Celine in the company of

Alex, Jeff, and Michael was a heartbreaking experience. No wonder Sonia plain refused to stalk Celine during school hours.

"Jeff might think I'm watching him," Sonia explained to Cammie one particularly blistery morning. "And I don't want to give him the satisfaction. If he likes Celine more than me, so be it!"

Cammie agreed with Sonia. If Jeff preferred hanging out with Celine over Sonia, he was an idiot. If Cammie were in Jeff's shoes, she would choose Sonia hands down. So what if the showgirl wore Bebe T-shirts, Dolce & Gabbana pants, Juicy Couture tracksuits, and Louis Vuitton bags? Under all that glamorous veneer, the girl was as shallow as a saucer. Just one silly competition that Celine organized for her admirers would have been enough for Cammie not to ever look in Celine's direction again. Sonia, however, was smart, and talented, and...

"And pretty too," Cammie said as she heard Sonia make nasty noises while she looked at herself in the mirror.

"I have freckles," Sonia groaned.

"So what? They're pretty. Besides, there are tons of concealers on the market."

Eventually, Cammie and Sonia decided that Cammie would limit her stalking to school hours, while Sonia would watch Celine during practices at the Yellow Rink.

"If the showgirl even comes close to the CD player, I'll be on her faster than bees on honey," Sonia said menacingly. "And I'll pretend Jeff isn't even there."

Honestly, Cammie hated to see Alex in his current state of obsession too. The guy made sure Celine carried fresh flowers every morning. Cammie suspected Alex of spending most of his allowance on roses, tulips, and carnations from the Fresh Flowers for Skaters' store on Main Square. Jeff did his best too by giving Celine an endless supply of candy and cookies from Sweet Blades. Michael, however, didn't look as though he bought anything for Celine, yet he lingered by her side all the same. Each time Celine and Cammie's eyes met, Celine would stare at Cammie with innocence, so sweet, so genuine that Cammie would have to suppress a strong desire to gag.

"Can you believe it, girls? I still can't decide on Mr. Right," Celine would say at dinner, flashing her violet eyes and dimples. "I like all those guys."

"And whom did you see in the Fortune Rink?" Liz would ask.

Celine would lower her eyes, batting her long lashes. "Oh, well…I think I saw a few guys there, not just one."

Cammie wished she could follow Celine on her way to school and the rink too. What if Mavet decided to strike while Celine skated to the dorm after her evening practice? Unfortunately, it would have been impossible. Celine never skated anywhere. Every morning, when the girls from the intermediate and novice dorm left the dorm building, there was a shiny black-and-white Zamboni waiting outside.

"Your limousine is here, Celine!" Sonia once said as she looked outside through a window in the lobby.

The girls giggled.

Celine, however, kept her cool. "Thank you, Sonia. Do you mind telling the driver I'll be right out? Thank you!"

Cammie would have laughed, but she was afraid to make Sonia even more upset. Her roommate already looked as though she was going to murder Celine any minute. In fact, each time Celine appeared in the living room, Sonia would emit a serious of angry *sh-sh-sh's*.

"That's Celine. She's a shallow show shuffler, sh, sh, sh," Sonia explained to Cammie.

And Cammie quite agreed with Sonia. Riding a Zamboni was probably exciting, yet Cammie couldn't understand why somebody would rather pay five dollars to a Zamboni driver than skate to practices on her own.

No wonder Celine's still struggling with her triples, Cammie though as she studied Celine's petite frame and her long limbs with virtually nonexistent muscles.

For some stupid reason, the showgirl thought that muscular girls looked ugly and totally non-feminine. That, of course, was sheer nonsense. For all Cammie knew, all elite skaters had very strong, tight bodies. And if muscles were necessary to nail difficult jumps, Cammie would never neglect her off-ice workout.

It looked as though Lieutenant Turner was doing an investigation of his own. At least, he made sure Cammie was under constant police supervision. Each time Cammie looked back, she would see his nimble, catlike figure skating about thirty yards behind. Of course, Cammie tried to lose him many times. Yet no matter how much speed she picked up, trying to separate herself from the crazy cop, the distance between them always remained the same. As much as Cammie despised Bob Turner, she couldn't deny the obvious fact that he was quite a decent skater.

"You've got to agree with me, Sonia. Turner totally fits the profile," Cammie said to her roommate once. "Wilhelmina said that Mavet would only enter a person if he made an entrance for the evil spirit to come in. And you know what Turner is like. He's mean and bitter."

Sonia looked up from her calves that she had been massaging. "True, but even nasty people may fall in love."

"Oh, give me a break!" Cammie moaned.

And finally, finally, a week after Cammie started watching Celine and Bob Turner, Coach Elliot came back. Cammie was happy to see that there was no trace of fatigue in him. In fact he looked better than he had before the assault. It was as though the danger of being attacked by a mysterious killer had somehow breathed new life into him. Gone was the quiet, slightly distant look of resignation. Coach Elliot's face expression now spelled determination. And as always, Prince Elliot's eyes shone bright blue, and his blond hair fell along his cheeks in a casual manner.

"Excellent, Cammie! I'm so proud of you," Coach Elliot said as he watched Cammie land all of her doubles with confidence and ease. "Now how's your triple salchow progressing?"

"Uh, well, I had to lay off it for a while," Cammie mumbled. "I couldn't use PRESTO without you."

"Let's try it, then." Coach Elliot bent over to help Cammie zip up the unitard. "Oh!"

"What?"Cammie tilted her head to see the reading on the monitor.

"Never mind, never mind." Coach Elliot slipped the protective cover over the monitor. "Go ahead!"

Cammie circled the rink, setting herself up for the triple. She got on a deep edge, she bent her knee, she was up, one, two…

"Yes!" She kept her exit edge long, her free leg high behind for extra flare.

Coach Elliot's eyes were laughing. "Way to go, champ!"

"Well, it was PRESTO that did it, not me." Cammie sighed.

"Take the unitard off, then, and try another triple salchow," Coach Elliot said lightly.

Cammie shook her head. "I don't think I'm ready."

She definitely needed more repetitions wearing PRESTO. Cammie smoothed out the unitard on her right side. The smooth, silky fabric felt pleasant under her fingers.

"Do you want to see something?" Coach Elliot opened the monitor again.

Cammie squinted and read, "'Triple salchow, jump mastered.' Come on! It's not true!"

Coach Elliot furrowed his eyebrows. "PRESTO isn't a human being, so it never lies. However, if you don't have trust in your technique, this kind of attitude might ruin your performance. So are you going to believe the evaluation PRESTO just gave you?"

Cammie thought for a moment. The triple salchow was the jump she had fallen from a year before. The fall had resulted in a very nasty injury. Cammie really wasn't looking forward to another two months of recuperation, not even counting all the time she had spent trying to get her doubles back.

"Don't think too hard! Just do it!" Coach Elliot said firmly.

He's here to help me, Cammie thought. *He isn't even afraid of Mavet, even though his life is obviously in danger. So what am I scared of? The triple salchow is only a jump. I'm not going to get injured again. Last time, it was Winja who caused me to fall. This time, she isn't even here.*

Cammie raised her head and scanned the bleachers. No witches. There weren't any spectators at all.

"Okay." Cammie skated away from Coach Elliot and started circling the rink.

She bent her knee. She was on her left backward inside edge. *Don't jump too soon!* she told herself.

"Now!" Coach Elliot shouted, or was it Cammie's thought?

She jumped, pulling in as tightly as she could. She seemed to spin forever, but the feeling was amazing. She didn't remember opening up and bending her right knee before her blade touched the ice. Her edge felt deep, secure. Everything was perfect! As she skidded to a stop, the silver walls still swirled in her field of vision.

She put her hand on her chest to slow down her racing heart. "Did I—?"

"Congratulations! You landed a triple on your own." Coach Elliot hugged Cammie.

"Yes!" She squealed so loudly that novice pairs skaters stopped in the middle of their footwork to gawk at her.

"Good girl!" Coach Elliot looked happier than she had ever seen him. "So are you ready to do a triple salchow in your program?"

Cammie frowned. "In my new program? Do you mean next year?"

"Oh no. I'm talking about your current *Romeo and Juliet* routine. This way, you can try the triple during your show performance."

The St. Valentine's show.

"But, but, C-Coach Elliot, the show is only a week away," Cammie stammered.

He patted her on the shoulder. "You're ready, Cammie. All you need to do is substitute your double salchow for a triple, and you'll be all set. We'll work on it tomorrow, okay?"

Well, if he thought she was ready. "Sure!" She smiled at him.

Coach Elliot's handsome face was so close to her. She could even discern a faint smell of his aftershave.

I wish I could kiss him, a thought popped up in her mind. *Just once.*

The silver walls spun around her. *Just once, just on the cheek,* she thought again. His face was so close. He was so gorgeous. She loved him.

His ocean color eyes widened under the arched brows. Apparently, he expected her to say something. But what could she say? Suddenly, she couldn't remember a single word. But she had to say something or he might think she was stupid.

Just kiss him on the cheek, girl! Now!

"Elliot!" a woman's voice came from the entrance.

Another flash of blue eyes, and he looked away at Christel, who smiled at him from the edge of the rink. Wilhelmina's daughter wore a bright red skating dress decorated with silver lining under her breast. Apparently, Christel needed that detail to give credit to the dress code of the Silver Rink.

Cammie watched Coach Elliot skate up to the entrance and kiss Christel's hand.

"You look great today, Christel," he said. "Is it a new dress?"

Christel looked happier than she had in years. "Yes. Mother made it for me. She thinks the red will go well with our *Belle* program."

"Definitely. Shall we start, then?"

"In a minute. How're you feeling anyway, Elliot?"

"Oh, just fine, like I've never been injured. Come on. Let me show you a new sequence I thought of yesterday." Coach Elliot led Christel away.

A moment later, they were on the other side of the rink, forty yards away from Cammie. And Coach Elliot's mind was apparently even further away from Cammie's aching heart.

Nobody even cared that Cammie was still on the ice. They skated by without looking at her, chatting, laughing, enjoying themselves. Their blades made deep, secure curves on the ice.

And suddenly Cammie didn't care anymore. She turned around abruptly and skated away. Luckily, the locker room was empty. Cammie took her seat on a bench facing her locker and stared miserably at her hands. She had polished her fingernails silver. After all, she was going to the Silver Rink, right? And had Prince Elliot noticed her fingernails? Nope.

In her skate guards, Cammie ran up to the floor-length mirror and stared at her gloomy reflection. How come Coach Elliot had noticed Christel's red dress, yet he hadn't said anything about Cammie's new outfit, a black-and-silver unitard? She had bought it at Skateland Super Styles, the most expensive store in Skateland. At the beginning, Cammie's mother had even refused to talk about it. But Cammie had been dreaming of a new practice outfit for months, something nice and classy and, if possible, with silver lining.

"But I thought your rink required green," Cammie's mother had said.

Well, Cammie already had a few green skating dresses and blouses. And, of course, Coach Elliot had seen her in green about a thousand times. Now as soon as Coach Elliot had brought her to the Silver Rink for extra practices, it would have been silly not to use the opportunity to come to her private lessons in sparkling silver. Besides, Celine showed up at almost every lesson wearing a different outfit.

So after Cammie had gotten into all the trouble of getting a new and expensive unitard, Coach Elliot hadn't even noticed it. What a bummer!

He likes Christel more than me, Cammie thought bitterly. *But why? Why?*

Well, of course, Christel was closer to Prince Elliot in age, and she was a much advanced skater.

"But I'm getting there!" Cammie told her reflection in the mirror. "I even landed a triple."

The sad-looking girl in the mirror shook her head, as though saying, "But Christel is so much prettier than you."

Cammie brought her face closer to the mirror. She wasn't that bad looking. Her eyes were green, and when she was in a good mood, they sparkled bright, like two emeralds. But perhaps Coach Elliot didn't really like the green color that much. He probably preferred Christel's eyes, a beautiful shade of gray, just like Wilhelmina's. So when Christel was in a gloomy mood, her eyes looked dark, almost black. And when the woman was happy, her eyes glittered like silver coins.

"Christel looks better at the Silver Rink! That's for sure!" Cammie said loudly.

Gosh, what a silly thought it was! What did the color of the rink have to do with people liking one another?

Cammie slowly pulled off her unitard and changed into her street clothes. Okay. Prince Elliot liked Christel more. But Cammie wasn't going to give up. She would do her best to look prettier. A little makeup would surely help. Perhaps she could ask Celine to give her a few tips. Celine liked makeovers. At some point, the showgirl had actually said that if it weren't for her parents, she might consider the career as a cosmetologist.

And if Christel's skating technique was better than Cammie's, even that wasn't a reason to give up. Cammie would work harder than she had worked before. She would land all of her triples, go to the nationals and to the worlds, perhaps even to the Olympics. Why not? Christel, however, would never be able to compete at those major competitions. She was way too old. And for starters, Cammie was going to pull off such a terrific performance at the St. Valentine's show that Prince Elliot would have no choice but to notice her.

ST. VALENTINE'S SHOW

February came, bringing with itself strong gusts of the west wind. Yet Skateland residents barely paid attention to the rough weather. All show participants, from Snowplow Sam students to adult skaters, were completely immersed in polishing their show numbers. As always, Mr. Reed promised them a few special effects that would make the performance even flashier.

For starters, the show was supposed to begin at three in the afternoon, while it was still light. As it got darker, Mr. Reed would be adding more and more artificial illumination. The audience would be able to see Main Square in broad light, during twilight, and finally, in the dark. Knowing Mr. Reed's ingenuity, Cammie had no doubt the show would be a big hit. Her parents had already booked seats in the third row. As Cammie spoke to her mother on the phone, her mother seemed to be really excited.

"So you're doing a solo number this time, aren't you, Cammie?"

Cammie smiled at the phone. "That's right, Mom. It'll be my *Romeo and Juliet* program."

"Oh, it'll be terrific. I love that music. Just be extra careful, Cammie. Don't get sick or injured right before your performance."

Cammie laughed. "No, of course not. Coach Elliot is watching me like a hawk."

"Well, that's good."

Cammie hadn't been quite truthful, of course. The only time her coach saw her was during her private lessons. That was if she didn't count the time she spent in the Silver Rink bleachers, watching Elliot and Christel's practices. But as February 14 drew nearer, Cammie started leaving the rink immediately after her lesson. She wanted to make sure her homework was finished in time so she wouldn't have to stay up late. Her mother was right; she needed plenty of rest to avoid colds and injuries.

Cammie even cut the time she spent stalking Celine down by half. Cammie still suspected that the showgirl was somehow involved in the bad things that had recently happened in Skateland. And there was no guarantee Mavet wouldn't strike again. Therefore, Cammie did her best to make sure Celine wouldn't slip an unrecognized CD into the player. But time went by, nothing happened, and Cammie felt herself relax a little. She didn't have to worry about keeping an eye on Lieutenant Turner, because he kept following her to the dorm, show or no show. Cammie ignored the nosy guy. She had more important things to think about.

Cammie's triple salchow was consistent. As Coach Elliot had promised, they put it in the beginning of her show program. The first time Cammie skated her routine with the triple salchow in it, she felt tense and nervous. Yet she somehow pulled off a decent performance, and from that time on, her fears were gone.

"I knew you had it in you, Cammie!" Coach Elliot said at the end of their last lesson before the show. "Just wait. You'll have all of your triples in no time."

"Oh!" Cammie was so overwhelmed with joy that she didn't even know what to say. Perhaps she had to thank Prince Elliot for what he had done for her. Or she could tell him that she loved him. But her tongue wouldn't move, and before she knew it, Prince Elliot was gone. A few long strokes and he was on the other side of the rink, talking to Christel, who was wearing a stunning black-and-yellow dress.

Well, you can't have it all, Cammie thought as she skated toward the exit.

On February 14, at two thirty in the afternoon, Cammie stood at the end of one of the side streets leading to Main Square. The other show participants were there too, talking loudly and stomping their feet to keep warm. From her spot, Cammie could see the smooth, light gray surface of the Main Rink and the grandstands filled to capacity. Women dressed in long, white coats and red scarves skated around, offering everybody cups of hot chocolate and skate shakes. Non-participant skaters glided by delivering valentines. All of them wore red-checkered vests over white sweaters complete with nametags that said "Mail Deliverer."

"Here's one for Celine Bouchard!" A boy from the Blue Rink handed Celine a white envelope.

"Thanks!" Celine rewarded the mail deliverer with a charming smile and then made quite a performance of opening the envelope.

As Cammie came closer, she saw that inside was a card with a bright red rose on the cover. Celine opened the card and read the message out loud: "You are the best; don't doubt: it's true. This rose is pretty, just like you!"

"Hmm, that's sweet." Celine twirled the card in her gloved fingers. "I wonder who it's from. It's not signed. Well, my guess will be Jeff. That's his style."

Cammie felt Sonia stiffen next to her then stare at something at the edge of the rink.

"Just ignore her!" Cammie whispered in her friend's ear.

"I'm not even thinking of this stupid card," Sonia said. "Actually, I've been admiring the decorations. Aren't they adorable?"

There were wreaths and clusters of flowers hanging all around the Main Square Rink. Cammie recognized roses, tulips, forget-me-nots, and white lilies. There were also other kinds of flowers whose names Cammie didn't even know. The flowers looked so real that Cammie had to squeeze a petal between her fingers to find out it was actually artificial.

"Boys, take the girls' hands, please," a familiar voice said behind Cammie.

As she looked back, she recognized Coach Greg from the Pink Rink. A blonde girl of about six reached for a pink carnation.

"Don't touch the flower, Cindy!" Coach Greg said.

"But I want to put one in my hair. My dress is pink, so—"

"I want a yellow flower because my dress is yellow!" another girl, who looked exactly like Cindy, squeaked.

"Girls, no!" Coach Greg said. "Those are decorations for the show."

"But more flowers will grow," Sandy said with charming seriousness. "Mom says—"

Coach Greg shook his head. "They aren't real, Sandy."

"Real flowers couldn't grow in this cold. Right, Coach Greg?" Cindy asked importantly.

"That's right." Coach Greg turned around, and his small, dark brown eyes rested on Cammie. "Cammie Wester! What a pleasant surprise! So? Are you still afraid of bunny-hops?"

Cammie felt herself blush. The little skaters from the Pink Rink giggled simultaneously.

"Bunny-hops aren't scary at all. Do you need help?" Cindy asked excitedly.

"I can teach you a toe loop and a salchow!" Sandy exclaimed.

Now it was Sonia's turn to chuckle.

"Last year, Cammie couldn't do bunny-hops because she had an injury," Coach Greg said patiently. "She's a much better skater now. She can do all doubles. Am I right, Cammie?"

311

"I have a triple salchow in my program!" Cammie didn't mean to boast, but the words just flew out of her mouth.

Cindy and Sandy's bright lips formed perfect circles. "Oh, wow!"

Music began to play, something light and airy. Cammie recognized Tchaikovsky's *Waltz of the Flowers*.

"It's our number, pinkies. Follow me!" Coach Greg led the gang of little skaters dressed in multi-colored dresses and shirts to the ice. Their appearance was greeted by an enthusiastic applause.

Sonia turned to Cammie, looking terrified. "We're supposed to watch the CD player!"

"I've been watching it all the time," Cammie said. "Wilhelmina put all the CDs with the show music next to the player herself. I saw that."

"How about...you know?" Sonia bent her head slightly in Celine's direction.

"She didn't even approach the player. And Turner is over there." Cammie looked to the right.

The young cop stood about a hundred feet away from the show participants, his sour look fixed firmly on Cammie.

"What does he want?" Cammie muttered angrily.

"Relax! It's actually for the best. With a cop around, you'll never get hurt."

"Yeah, unless he's the attacker. But I've been watching him too. He's been here all the time."

"Well, okay, then."

"A valentine for Celine Bouchard!" Rita, who wasn't skating in the show, stopped next to the showgirl.

Celine opened the envelope. Her new valentine turned out to be a music card. As a cheerful melody played, pink candles shimmered against the dark background.

Celine wrapped herself tighter in a white fur coat. "O-okay, this must be from Alex. It's cute."

Cammie and Sonia exchanged looks of deep skepticism and walked away.

"I w-wonder h-how many m-more cards Celine'll get." Cammie's teeth clattered. As always, she was dressed too lightly. Perhaps her green parka did provide some warmth for the upper part of her body, yet her legs covered by nothing but thin tights were beginning to complain.

"I can't stand this cold anymore!" Sonia moaned. "Let's go to the locker room."

"But...but who'll be watching the CD player?" Shivering, Cammie looked at the rink.

Sonia rose on her toes, staring ahead of her. "Yes, all the security guys're standing beside the player. Captain Greenfield is there too."

"Ah. It's okay, then." At the sight of Captain Greenfield pacing the arena with cool confidence, Cammie felt calm and secure.

Cammie and Sonia walked about thirty yards to a small fitness center. The building stood on a side street in close proximity to Main Square. For that reason, the owner of the center, Mr. McGraff, usually kept the place open during show performances, allowing skaters to use the facility as temporary locker rooms. As they walked inside the small, one-story building, warm air enveloped them. They felt better immediately.

"Look. There's tea." Cammie poured herself a cup of hot, steaming liquid from a teakettle on the table.

Sonia still looked glum.

"Forget Celine, Sonia. You're a much better skater."

"I think everybody's better than Celine. She's such an airhead." Sonia helped herself to tea too and then lowered herself on the carpet and stretched into a split.

Cammie did the same. "I hope I'll land that triple salchow. It's the first time I'm going to try it in the program, you know."

The door opened, and a cold draft of frosty air swept in. "Shut the door!" Cammie and Sonia shouted.

George from the Blue Rink walked in, his face red from the cold. "A valentine for Cammie Wester!"

"Oh!" Cammie took the envelope from the boy's hand. Inside was a card picturing a tall wine glass that stood on a pond with clear ice. The message read, *To your skating! Your biggest fan.*

"Who do you think it's from?" Cammie handed Sonia the card.

"Hmm. Alex, perhaps?"

"I don't think so. We haven't spoken in weeks," Cammie grunted. "Besides, he's still Celine's slave."

"Well, I wouldn't know who else—"

"Sonia!" Cammie grabbed her friend by the hand. "I know. It's from Coach Elliot."

Sonia froze in a lunge position. "You've got to be kidding!"

"I'm telling you, it's him. He's been so nice to me. And look what it says: 'your biggest fan.' Who else cares about my skating more than my coach?"

Sonia still didn't look convinced.

"Look—"

Before Cammie could think of another reason, the door opened and in walked Lieutenant Turner. With a nasty scowl, Cammie pressed the card against her chest and folded her arms to cover it.

"That's where the two of you are," the young man said. "The kiddies are done skating. There'll be a dancing number now, and you, Miss Harrison, are next."

Sonia gasped and grabbed her coat. "I've got to go!"

Cammie still sat on the floor.

"You'd better join your friend, Miss Wester. Van Uffeln and Elliot's number is after Miss Harrison's, and then it's your turn."

"I have the schedule, thank you very much," Cammie said coldly.

She took the piece of paper with the skating order from the pocket of her parka. That year, the choreographer of the show, who was Wilhelmina, of course, had deviated from the traditional principle of starting with lower-level skaters and keeping the best performance 'til the end.

"St. Valentine's is a holiday of love," Wilhelmina had said a week before. "Therefore, I don't want to turn our show into a technical competition, where performances are judged on the basis of the complexity of jumps and spins. This year, we will focus on the harmony of music and movement. So when I decide on the order of your numbers, I will be thinking of the way musical themes complement one another."

When all show participants received their schedules, Cammie was surprised to find out that she would skate after Prince Elliot and Christel. There would be a few pre-prelimiary numbers afterward, then senior dancers, novice pairs, a few adult skaters. The pre-juvenile skater, Heather Reese, whom Cammie had met in the hospital the year before, was going to skate last.

Sonia was already approaching the Main Rink. Cammie ran after her, trying to stay close. Someone coughed behind her, and a familiar voice asked, "Did you like your valentine, Cammie?"

Cammie clenched her teeth, turned around, and glared at Lieutenant Turner. "I don't think reading private messages is on your job description, Lieutenant."

The young man's nose was almost purple from the cold. "But—"

But Cammie was already far from him. She stood by the entrance to the rink. Sonia had already stepped onto the ice, looking like a flaming torch in her bright orange dress. At the first sounds of Sonia's piece, *The Firebird*, Cammie looked at the CD player. Everything seemed to be all right. Celine, who was supposed to skate after Cammie, hopped on the spot next to Liz. Lieutenant Turner was, of course, behind Cammie. And the stack of CDs by the player appeared to be well protected by four security guards and Captain Greenfield. As Cammie glanced at the officer, he gave her a cheerful wave.

"Oh no!"

Cammie turned back to see Christel standing on one foot next to a very concerned-looking Coach Elliot.

"What's wrong, Christel?" the man asked.

"It's…it's my left blade. See? The screws are loose." The woman grabbed her blade and turned it around twice.

"You need to get it fixed immediately," Coach Elliot said quickly. "Where's Mr. Reed?"

"Mrs. Van Uffeln and Mr. Elliot, your turn!" Mr. Frascatti, a former ice-dancer who now worked as a coach, bowed his head slightly.

Coach Elliot shook his head. "We can't skate now. Christel needs to get her blade fixed."

"But it's your turn, guys!" Mr. Frascatti cried out, his Italian accent much more pronounced. "The program—"

"All we need is a couple of minutes." Coach Elliot pointed to Christel. Mr. Reed was by her side, already working on her blade.

Mr. Frascatti spread his arms. "I don't know."

Sonia stepped off the ice, her face red with excitement. "It was awesome, it was—"

"Cammie, can you skate your number now?" Coach Elliot asked quickly.

What? Now? But she wasn't ready!

"And we'll skate after you." Coach Elliot smiled at her.

"Well, I don't know—"

"Go! I believe in you. You're my best student." Coach Elliot raised his hand, and the two of them exchanged high-fives.

As in a daze, Cammie walked to the edge of the ice.

"And now, ladies and gentleman, we will watch a number that is a tribute to the victory of life over death," Mr. Frascatti's voice magnified by the speakers announced. "Let's give a warm welcome to Cammie Wester! *Romeo and Juliet.*"

Cammie glided to the middle of the rink, a ripple of applause following her. Coach Elliot had just called her his best student. He believed in her.

She froze in her starting position, her arms arched over her head. The grandstands loomed around her with rows and rows of seats. Hundreds of eyes watched her every move. Suddenly, she couldn't wait for her music to start. She was excited. Coach Elliot liked her. Now she was a hundred percent sure. It was he who had sent her the valentine. Her music started, a languid love theme. Cammie began to move, first slowly and then faster and faster. A warm wave washed over her as she remembered that Coach Elliot was watching her too. He believed in her. That is why she was going to skate her best.

Her feet were light. She skimmed the ice in blinding speed. There! She landed her triple salchow. There was no time to get excited. She had to nail her double lutz-double toe loop combination. Perfect! The music played inside Cammie. She felt as though she had become one with the melody. She went through a series of Choctaws and half jumps, a stag and a fallen leaf. She felt great. She wished her program would never end.

Her combination spin was next. Cammie performed six revolutions on the camel spin and lowered herself into a sit spin. Wow. She didn't remember ever spinning so fast. She rose from the sitting position. The speed increased even more. Fine. She could handle it. She would hold her spin as long as she could. Perhaps she would even be able to hit a hundred revolutions, like Wilhelmina.

The world shrank around her. It was reduced to a whirlwind of bright colors and sounds. Oh no. The colors weren't bright anymore. They were the color of dark rags. All she could see was gray ice. Why was she still spinning?

Come on. I don't want to spin anymore! Stop!

The ice rushed her in the face, and then everything went black.

"Will she be all right?"

"Her eyes are still closed. Is she unconscious?"

"Don't worry. She's breathing on her own."

"Did she hit her head?"

"It looks like it."

Who were those people talking about? Oh, it had to be Dana. Of course! Dana fell during her audition and had a bad concussion.

"Cammie, can you hear me? Cammie!"

Someone was talking to her. It was probably Sonia. Cammie must have overslept for her morning practice again. Kanga hadn't awakened her. It was all because of the witches. They had infected Cammie's Kanga bag with a virus.

"We need to put her on a stretcher. We don't want her to catch a cold."

No, it wasn't Sonia talking to her. The voice belonged to a man. And he was right. Cammie's back and thighs did feel cold. Kanga had probably pulled the quilt off her. Plus, she had a terrible headache. She must have really caught a cold.

Strong arms picked her up and put her on something soft. She opened her eyes but closed them again instantly. The bright light hurt her eyes. All she managed to see was something black-and-white.

"Look. She opened her eyes!" The voice sounded like Cammie's father.

"Cammie!" That was definitely her mother.

Cammie opened her eyes again. She lay on a stretcher. There was a group of people around her, and they were spinning fast.

"Ugh. Why're…spinning?" Her tongue barely cooperated.

"Let's get her in the ambulance icemobile," a man's voice said.

Cammie felt the stretcher move.

"Cammie, you'll be all right. Do you hear me? Everything'll be fine."

Even in her weird condition, Cammie could never mistake that voice for anybody else's. "Coach Elliot!" she moaned without opening her eyes.

"Coach Elliot, thank you very much!" her father's voice spoke up.

"If it hadn't been for you…" Her mother sobbed next to her.

They were probably talking about Coach Elliot's saving her life in the Icy Park. Her mother was right. If it hadn't been for Prince Elliot, Mavet might have killed her. Someone must have just told her parents about it.

She heard a door slam. She realized she was in an ambulance icemobile. The vehicle moved forward, picking up speed.

Cammie must have fallen asleep, for next time she opened her eyes, she was in bed. Bent over her was the familiar face of a man with pink cheeks and glasses.

"Hi, Cammie. Do you remember me?"

"Dr. Eislaufer," she whispered. Of course she had recognized the doctor who had operated on her ankle a year before.

"What happened to me?" Cammie asked feebly. Her head throbbed with pain each time she moved, so she tried to lie perfectly still.

"You fell during your performance, but you're getting better. You have a slight concussion, but everything will be all right." Dr. Eislaufer patted Cammie on her clammy hand.

"When can she go home?" a familiar voice asked.

Ignoring the pain, Cammie turned her head slightly to the right. "Dad?"

She was shocked to see that her father had aged in just one day. His cheeks were lined with creases Cammie hadn't seen before.

"I'd like to keep an eye on her for about a week," Dr. Eislaufer said. "Not that she's in any danger, but in the dorm, she won't be able to get all the medical attention she needs."

"We're taking her out of Skateland," Cammie's mother said firmly.

Cammie turned in the direction of her mother's voice and tried to sit up, but a fit of nausea threw her back on the pillow.

"Skating is taking her nowhere. So we've had enough!" Cammie's mother was talking to Dr. Eislaufer as though Cammie wasn't even in the room.

"I think it'll be better to discuss Cammie's future when she gets better," Dr. Eislaufer said softly but firmly. "In the meantime, she needs to rest."

Cammie's mother sighed and brushed the tears off her eyelashes. "Just relax, sweetie!" She bent over to kiss Cammie.

"I'm not giving up skating!" Cammie tried to put as much strength into her voice as her current condition allowed. "Dad?"

"Shh! Shh! Sleep. Everything will be all right." Cammie's father stroked her hair gently. The door shut behind her parents. Cammie accepted a blue pill from the nurse and fell asleep before she knew it.

When she woke up, the sun poured through the tall window, leaving bright spots on the white walls and an IV bag next to her bed. Someone sat on a hard chair next to the IV stand.

Cammie blinked a few times and recognized her dorm supervisor. "Mrs. Page!"

The woman looked up quickly. "Oh, Cammie, please! I don't think you should move yet."

"But…I think I'm fine." Cammie sat up slowly and let her eyes roam around the room. She saw a bare window, an IV stand, a radiator, and two doors. One of them probably led to the bathroom and the other to the hallway. So she hadn't been dreaming; she was really injured.

"I have good news for you!" As Mrs. Page smiled, fine lines ran from her eyes all the way to her cheeks. "You can go back to the dorm in three days. That's what the doctor said."

Cammie licked her dry lips. "But…when will I be able to skate again?"

Mrs. Page averted her eyes. "Well—"

"Please! I need to know."

Mrs. Page opened and closed her mouth a few times. "Cammie, there's nothing seriously wrong with you healthwise. Actually, Dr. Eislaufer is sure you'll be able to go back to practices in a week."

A week. Well, she could probably handle that.

"What happened to me?"

"You fell during your performance at St. Valentine show."

Now Cammie could really remember everything: the shimmering flowers around the Main Rink; hundreds of faces watching her from the grandstands; the gray, slightly scratched ice; the spin.

"I fell from my combination spin!" It was ridiculous, of course. Spins had always been Cammie's strength.

"That's right!" Mrs. Page's face brightened. The woman suddenly looked younger. "So you don't have any memory lapses. The doctor says it's a really good sign, because—"

"How could I fall from a spin?" In her mind, Cammie saw herself entering her camel spin and then swinging her free leg around and bending her left knee. Okay, everything had been fine up to that point. She rose up, she spun, and she couldn't stop.

Mrs. Page kept clasping and unclasping her hands, looking extremely uncomfortable. "We thought something was wrong, you know. Coach Darrel says you went into that spin too fast. But I still don't understand how it could happen. Normally, skaters run out of speed at the end of a spin. In your case, it was just the opposite. And that music. I don't know. I heard your *Romeo and Juliet* theme many times, and it was all right. Something was probably wrong with that CD player. First, there was some background noise on top of your music, and then we could hear nothing but hissing and wailing. Cammie, what's wrong?"

Cammie fell down on her pillow. "The music! The music!"

Mrs. Page's face blurred in front of her. Her mind barely registered Mrs. Page's running out of the room. She heard the woman's panicked voice.

"Nurse? Over here!"

She remembered swallowing another pill, and then she fell asleep for a very long time.

Nobody talked to her about the accident anymore. Even Dr. Eislaufer plain refused to answer any of Cammie's questions, insisting that at that point, Cammie had to concentrate on getting better. Yet Cammie didn't need anybody to explain to her what had really gone wrong. She had already heard hissing and wailing on top of skating music twice before. First, it had happened during Dana's audition. And there was the second time, or perhaps it would be better to call it the first one, because Felicia's accident had taken place eighteen years ago. Felicia had died, of course, and Dana had had a concussion. But both ladies had skated to the music of death. And now Cammie had experienced the same thing.

Cammie rolled on her belly and took a glass of water from her night stand. Her dizziness had subsided, and if it were not for slight weakness, Cammie was sure she could step on the ice immediately. Well, she could wait a few days if that was what the doctor wanted. A week away from skating was nothing. She wouldn't even lose any of her jumps and spins.

Okay, what had she been thinking now? Her combination spin. She hadn't been able to stop because someone had slipped in a CD containing the music of death. So the attacker had come to the show after all. As hard as Cammie and Sonia had watched the CD player, making sure no one would tamper with the CDs, it had happened anyway. And Cammie was the victim.

Okay, but why did Mavet go after me, not Coach Elliot?

Actually, it wasn't hard to figure out at all. Cammie had skated at Christel and Elliot's appointed time. The screws on Christel's skating boot had come loose. Coach Elliot had asked Cammie to skate her program a little earlier.

"Mavet had already put his CD into the player," Cammie said out loud. The music of death had played on top of her *Romeo and Juliet* theme. Well, the attacker had obviously managed to activate both tracks of the player simultaneously. The person whom Mavet possessed had to be not only musically but also technically minded.

But who is it?

Cammie sat up in bed, making sure she wouldn't disconnect her IV. Sonia and she had been watching Celine like a hawk. Right before Cammie's performance, Celine had been on the side street with the rest of the performers. She hadn't been anywhere close to the CD player. Lieutenant Turner, of course, had come to the fitness center to tell Cammie and Sonia to hurry up. So he hadn't been tampering with the CDs either. Then who? Cammie had to admit that slipping in a deadly CD would have been an incredibly difficult, if not impossible, task. After all, the security personnel had been guarding the sound system during the show.

Cammie's head got heavy. Perhaps, all that thinking was too much for her. Determined to find the solution at any cost, Cammie closed her eyes and sank into a deep, dreamless sleep.

On the day of Cammie's discharge, Dr. Eislaufer walked into Cammie's room looking rose-cheeked and excited. "All ready for the big day?"

She beamed at him. "Of course!"

Her tote bag labeled *Green Rink* was already packed. It contained her black-and-silver performance dress and cards from her friends. Dr. Eislaufer hadn't allowed any visits except from her parents and Mrs. Page. Yet almost everybody she knew had sent her a get-well card. Safely tucked at the bottom of the bag was a card from Coach Elliot. It said, "Skate from your heart and never lose courage! Coach Elliot." Cammie felt warm and cozy on the inside each time she reread Prince Elliot's card.

"Can I go to practice tomorrow?" Cammie asked. She couldn't wait to see Prince Elliot.

Dr. Eislaufer cleared his throat. "Actually, your parents don't want you to continue skating competitively. No! Wait!" He raised his hand protectively. "Don't jump down my throat, Cammie! Your concussion wasn't that serious. In fact, you passed out not because of the brain injury but because you got dizzy and scared. I assured your parents that there are absolutely no counter indications for your skating. You didn't fall because you were sick. It was merely an accident."

Cammie nodded. "That's right. So I'm not quitting! No way!"

Dr. Eislaufer took off his glasses, squinted at one of the lenses, and then put them back on. "Cammie, please understand that I'm on your side. Unfortunately, you're still a minor, so your parents are your legal guardians. You can't make decisions about continuing or quitting skating on your own. However…" The doctor raised his index finger as though anticipating Cammie's protests. "Your official discharge day is tomorrow. Yet, I'm letting you go to the dorm today. Tomorrow morning, Mrs. Van Uffeln wants to see you in her office. I'm sure she'll find a way to get your parents to change their mind."

"Uh…thank you!" Cammie believed in the Skateland president's powers, but she knew her parents too.

"Okay. The ambulance icemobile will take you to the dorm. And I suggest that you get a good night's rest before tomorrow's practice."

When Cammie entered her dorm room, Sonia yelped and jumped off from her chair to hug her. "Cammie! Oh my God! How are you?"

"I'm fine, I'm fine." Cammie hugged her friend and looked around the familiar room, feeling elated. How come she had to go to the hospital to realize how much she loved her dorm?

"Oh, Cammie, I've been so worried about you! I wanted to visit you in the hospital, and so did other girls, but the doctor said absolutely not. Only family and, of course, Mrs. Page. But you did get her cookies, right?"

"Sure."

Mrs. Page had given Cammie an assortment of her trademark cookies: chocolate pretzels, mitten cookies, skating bear cookies, Kanga cookies, and, finally, snowball rolls.

"Cammie!" Sonia grimaced as though from pain. "It was an attack, wasn't it?"

Cammie smiled sadly. "Do you have any doubt?"

"No, of course not." Sonia sighed deeply. "When I heard that music, I knew Mavet was involved. So I ran to the player, but the security guards wouldn't let me come close. I begged them to turn the music off, but they looked like they didn't have a clue."

"Oh!" Cammie rubbed her forehead. The headache that had left her in the morning was coming back.

"And you kept spinning and spinning!" Sonia's eyes glistened with tears. "And Wilhelmina shouted something to Captain Greenfield, but he just stood there, staring at you."

Cammie slowly sat down on the edge of her bed. "So…how exactly did I fall?"

"Well, at the beginning, everybody was impressed with your spinning ability. But when you wouldn't stop, I started getting worried. It didn't look right, you know. And, of course, the music of death." Sonia stopped mid-sentence. "It was creepy."

Cammie wasn't even sure she wanted to hear the rest of the story. It was like reliving the terrible experience again.

"After probably a hundred revolutions, you got lifted in the air, and I thought you would slam into the announcer's booth head first. Yes, that's what would have happened if it hadn't been for Coach Elliot."

Cammie looked up. "Coach Elliot?"

"He rushed to the ice and caught you halfway to the booth. And then you both fell, and your head smacked against the ice. But now everybody is saying that if Coach Elliot hadn't broken the fall, you would have died for sure."

A wave of excitement washed over Cammie. She didn't even try to conceal a happy smile.

"What's so funny? Cammie?"

Cammie stared dreamingly at the patch of gray sky outside the window. "So Coach Elliot saved my life."

"Don't tell me you didn't know!"

"I didn't."

How come everybody had been talking about her endless spin, almost making it look as though Cammie had merely tried to show off? And even from the words of the few people who had mentioned the attack, Cammie had assumed that Mavet's attempt had been successful. He had managed to get her injured. And nobody had bothered to tell her the most important thing. Coach Elliot had been there for her. He had saved her life for the second time. Cammie felt her smile spread almost all the way to her ears.

"Cammie, what're you smiling at?" Sonia said impatiently. "I thought you would be upset. You've lost almost a week of practices. When can you start skating again, by the way? Cammie?"

Cammie knew her smile probably looked silly. Really, she had had a very close brush with death. And the whole experience meant that Mavet was on the loose for sure. No matter how hard Cammie and Sonia had watched the CD player, he had managed to sneak in his music of death. Yet Cammie had never felt happier. Prince Elliot was her knight in shining armor. And tomorrow, she would see him again. He would help Wilhelmina convince her parents that Cammie belonged in Skateland. She would live here and train with Prince Elliot for the rest of her life. It was so wonderful that Prince Elliot had rescued her.

"How did Coach Elliot and Christel do?" Cammie asked. "They skated after me."

Sonia gasped. "Are you kidding? Nobody skated after you. They ended the show right after you had been taken to the hospital."

Sonia brought her freckled face closer to Cammie's. "But really, who was the attacker? Do you have any idea?"

Cammie shook her head slowly. She wished she knew. "Perhaps Lieutenant Turner somehow snuck by the security guards and put that CD in?"

"No!" Sonia said with determination. "He didn't even come close. He trailed us all the time."

"Yes, I saw him too. How about Celine?"

Sonia shook her head, causing her fiery locks to cascade down her shoulders. "She never even looked in the direction of the CDs. And even if she had…actually, the security people guarded the player pretty well."

"Could it be one of the security guys, then?"

Sonia waved her hand. "Of course not. They aren't even skaters. What could they have against Coach Elliot?"

"True." Cammie was disappointed. She had experienced the music of death, and all for nothing. They weren't any closer to solving the mystery of Mavet than before the show.

"Do you have any idea who put all the CDs next to the player?" Cammie asked, doubting that Sonia would know this important detail.

To her great surprise, Sonia answered right away. "It was Wilhelmina. I saw her position all the discs neatly on the stand next to the player right before the beginning of the show."

Surely, Wilhelmina hadn't slipped in the music of death. Although…

"Wilhelmina was the one who told us to look for the attacker among our friends," Cammie thought out loud. "So what if it was a trick? What if, by suggesting it, she was trying to take our minds off of herself?"

"What?" Sonia shrieked. "Cammie, you're nuts."

"I know. But—"

"No buts. There have to be people we trust a hundred percent, Cammie.

They didn't talk about the attacker anymore. During dinner, the rest of the girls gathered around Cammie. Cammie was forced to hear the story of her unfortunate fall and Coach Elliot's bravery a few more times. As unpleasant as the whole experience had been, the fact that Coach Elliot had rescued Cammie had created a bond between the two of them. Before the show, they had been a coach and a student. Well, of course, Coach Elliot had also found Cammie in the Icy Park during the snowstorm before. But even so, their relationship afterward had been purely businesslike. Now, however, Cammie felt that they were almost…hmm…a couple.

The interesting thing was that none of the girls seemed to have noticed that Cammie's *Romeo and Juliet* piece had been overridden by the music of death.

"They couldn't even organize the show properly," Celine said as she cut her baked chicken. "The skaters had to wait for their numbers outside in the cold. And that CD player is absolutely horrible. Did you hear all that noise and static during your performance, Cammie?"

All Cammie could say was, "Oh!"

"That's right! All that hissing and wailing gave me the creeps." Liz raised her fork.

"Surely they can splurge on a better CD player," Celine said. "And those flowers around the rink, they were so tasteless. I mean, in *Magic on Ice...*"

Cammie and Sonia exchanged knowing glances. None of the girls had thought of the music of death, although it could be expected. After all, even Coach Elliot had not found out the truth about his wife's death until later.

Cammie went to bed early that night. She wanted to be strong for her lesson with Coach Elliot. She was a little worried about her technique. Skating was a tricky thing. Sometimes a couple of days away from the ice could mess up your balance. And Cammie had missed the whole week.

Yet after a few wobbly laps around the Green Rink during the morning practice, Cammie started feeling as though she had never even stepped off the ice. Everything came back. Today, she even felt stronger. The slight dizziness and nagging headache were gone. Cammie was ready for new challenges.

But first of all, she couldn't wait to see Prince Elliot. She thought of him during her morning practice. She pictured his handsome face during a long and boring geography lesson. The teacher, Mrs. Redner—an overweight and irritable woman—made them show the locations of all former world championships on the map. Cammie was as far away from the classroom as Washington, DC, was from Tokyo.

Cammie planned her conversation with Prince Elliot during her geometry lesson. The students were expected to calculate the ratio of the radii and perimeters of the concentric circles in a perfect spin. Naturally, Cammie missed the teacher's explanation. But that wasn't a big deal; after all, she could always study later. She didn't hear a word of what was said at her English and Spanish lessons either.

She rushed to the Silver Rink right after school without exchanging a word with her classmates. From time to time, she would catch occasional glances in her direction. Some students looked cautious in her presence. Others gave her cheerful smiles. Cammie didn't care about either of those. Of course, she realized that her spectacular fall during the show had turned her into some sort of a celebrity. Under different circumstances, she might have lived up to the expectations by chatting with her classmates. Today, however, she had more important things on her mind.

When Cammie was crossing the school lobby, she almost ran into Alex.

Alex stopped abruptly, his green eyes wide with concern. "Cammie, how are you? I heard—"

"Oops. Sorry. I'm in kind of a rush."

Without even slowing down, Cammie waved at Alex and ran out into the blizzard. The west wind lashed her cheeks all the way to the Silver Rink. By the time she ran into the empty lobby, she could barely feel her face. She pushed the door to the arena, immediately noticing that no one was skating on the clear ice. Hmm. That was strange. She expected Coach Elliot and Christel to be already there practicing. Well, maybe the time of their lesson with Wilhelmina had been changed.

Cammie ran into the locker room and put on her black-and-silver unitard. As she walked past the mirror, she glanced at her reflection, thinking that her face appeared a little pale but overall, she looked pretty good. She secured her ponytail with a silver scrunchie and walked out of the locker room. There was still nobody on the ice. She wondered if it would be a good idea to start her warm-up. She probably shouldn't. Two thirty was still Prince Elliot and Christel's time, so it wouldn't be nice to trespass. Perhaps, they would start practicing at three, so she would watch them from the bleachers.

"Cammie!"

She turned around. Wilhelmina stared at her from the top row, her hands grasping firmly the backs of the chairs. "Could I see you in my office, please?"

Cammie didn't even try to hide her disappointment. There it was. Obviously, her parents had already contacted Wilhelmina, telling her they wanted to pull Cammie out of the figure skating program. And there was absolutely nothing Cammie could do about it. She clenched her teeth in frustration and stood up. As she clomped up the steps in her skate guards, her heart was somewhere in the area of her stomach.

Wilhelmina was silent as she led Cammie to her office. The older woman walked slowly, leaning on a cane. For the first time, Cammie noticed heavy lids under Wilhelmina's eyes. Gone was the usual spark. The woman looked old and tired.

"Coach Elliot won't be here for your lesson, Cammie," Wilhelmina said after she took her seat at her desk.

Cammie froze. So that was it. Her parents had already talked to Wilhelmina, and she had supported their decision. But it wasn't fair! They couldn't forbid Cammie to skate just like that. It was her life too.

"Did you...Mrs. Van Uffeln, did you talk to my parents?" Cammie did everything she could to keep her tears inside. She had to be strong to win that battle.

Wilhelmina looked up at Cammie with her bright gray eyes, the only young feature on the old face. "Your parents? Oh yes, they did call. They wanted an appointment to discuss your skating career, but I told them it couldn't be today. Tomorrow, perhaps, or in a few days. They seemed okay with that. Ah. By the way, your mother doesn't want you to practice until she talks to me. I told her you could take a few more days off, especially considering the fact that your coach isn't here, so—"

"Uh, wait!" Cammie raised her hands, feeling totally confused. "Why isn't Coach Elliot here? Is it because of what my mom said? She doesn't want me to continue skating, so he thinks he can't work with me?"

Wilhelmina frowned. "Oh no, Cammie. Those two things are unrelated."

"Because I want to skate. Mrs. Van Uffeln, I—" She pressed her folded hands closer to her heart, thinking of the most convincing words to get Wilhelmina to understand that she wasn't giving up. She had actually been rehearsing her speech ever since Dr. Eislaufer had warned her that her mother might be dead set against Cammie's skating career. Yet now, staring into Wilhelmina's sparkling eyes, she couldn't remember any of her good points. *Come on. What was it I wanted to say? Ah yes. That skating is my life. So—*

Cammie barely opened her mouth when Wilhelmina interrupted her. "Cammie, let's not talk about your skating at the moment, all right? We both know that you're a talented skater and you were born to do it. We also realize that as unfortunate as it might seem, injuries are a big part of a skater's life. This is something we need to be ready for. And while an injury might set us back for a while, the important thing is not to give up. We need to believe that hard work and pain will eventually yield beautiful results."

Cammie nodded a few times, admiring the Skateland president's eloquence. If she could talk to her parents like that, maybe they would change their minds.

"Mrs. Van Uffeln, could you please tell all those things to my mom? Then, maybe—"

"I will," Wilhelmina said firmly. "Don't worry about it. At this point, there's another thing I wanted to discuss with you."

Cammie furrowed her eyebrows. Had she done anything wrong?

"How are you feeling, by the way?" Wilhelmina asked.

"Fine, like I never fell." Cammie shifted her feet. "I went to the morning practice today."

"Good. That's great," Wilhelmina said. "Cammie, take your seat. This might be a long conversation."

She pulled an armchair closer to the desk across from Wilhelmina and sat down.

"Is...is Coach Elliot sick?"

The moment Cammie said it, a realization struck her. Mavet had attacked Prince Elliot too, after all. Even though he hadn't managed to skate his number with Christel, the monster must have got to them somehow. Or perhaps Mavet had assaulted Coach Elliot alone.

"He got attacked, didn't he?" Cammie's voice cracked.

Wilhelmina shook her head. "No. He turned himself in."

"He did...what?" Cammie's lips barely moved, yet Wilhelmina seemed to have understood her.

"After your attack, I called for the end of the show immediately. Elliot and Christel were fine. And then this morning, I got an e-mail from him." Wilhelmina picked up a piece of paper and handed it to Cammie.

Cammie's hand shook so badly that the lines refused to stay in place. Finally, she rested the paper on the desk and bent over the letter.

> *My dear Wilhelmina,*
>
> *I can't say enough to let you know how deeply I appreciate everything you have done for me. You have given me a few months of pure joy, of the excitement on being back on the ice, of the freedom of movement. By encouraging me to skate and pairing me with Christel, you let me relive the most wonderful moments of my life. I wish things were different. Unfortunately, we have to accept life as it is. So as much as I respect your desire to see me perform again, it is just not meant to be. You*

338

can't deny the obvious fact that my very presence in Skateland poses a serious threat to young innocent skaters. Let us not deceive ourselves by hoping that Mavet will get tired of pursuing me. He won't give up until he gets the satisfaction he wants. And if this is the case, wouldn't it be easier to merely give him what he wants instead of endangering other people? I know you will resent my decision, Wilhelmina; yet as you ponder over it longer, you will accept it. I know you will because you are a woman of wisdom. So right after I finish this letter, I'll be heading for the mountains.

So it is time to say good-bye. I wish you all the best, my dear Wilhelmina. Please give my best wishes to Christel. I am sure a talented and beautiful skater as she is will have no problem finding a good partner. I would also like to send my best wishes to my students, Cammie, Celine, McKenna, and Dayne. I know they have great future ahead of them.

Again, thank you for everything.

Yours truly,
Elliot

"Oh!" Cammie tried to say something, but for some reason, she forgot all the words she had once known. She pushed the letter away as though it was a poisonous snake.

Wilhelmina nodded gravely. "So Elliot is gone."

"But…I don't understand. Where exactly did he go?"

Wilhelmina pulled on her glass chain. "He surrendered himself to Mavet."

"What?" The room swam before Cammie. "I don't understand. Why?"

The expression of deep sadness in Wilhelmina's face was replaced with anger. "That's exactly my point. Giving himself to the spirit of death, letting the evil one triumph over everything that is good, how much more stupid could he get? But that's Elliot for you, Cammie. As long as I have known him, he has never put up a fight. He's always been content to be nonconfrontational. He has always believed in reason and fair play. Well, it's not that he's wrong, but unfortunately, the world doesn't consist of good people only. We all have enemies, and they are like roaring lions trying to devour others. If you see evil around you, Cammie, never give up. Do you hear me? Never."

"But…" Cammie picked up the letter, scanned it, and put it back on the desk. "Are we going to do anything about it? I mean, we can't let Coach Elliot get killed like that. We need to rescue him. We—"

Wilhelmina put her both arms in the air, palms forward. "Now be quiet for a moment."

Cammie choked on her own tears.

"Here." Wilhelmina handed her a tissue.

Cammie dabbed her eyes and blew her nose. She took a few breaths and then looked back at Wilhelmina, trying to appear calm.

"That's better. Now, Cammie, of course, I'm going to, as you say, do something about it. Actually, at this particular moment, Mr. Walrus and Mr. Reed are getting ready to leave for the mountains."

The mountains? Ah. That was the place where Mavet lived.

"Is...is Coach Elliot there already?" Cammie asked. "Because if he's still in his cabin, perhaps we...you could talk him out of it."

Wilhelmina shook her head sadly. "I drove there right after I got the e-mail this morning. He's gone. Choctaw barked loudly from inside the house, but there was no one there to open the door for me. And then there was his key in the envelope on the steps."

Wilhelmina showed Cammie a big silver key shaped like a blade. "He also left a note asking me to make sure Choctaw would be taken care of."

Coach Elliot had locked Choctaw in the house. It meant he wasn't planning on coming back.

"Mavet's going to kill him!" Cammie exclaimed.

"The monster will also have to face Mr. Walrus and Mr. Reed."

"Do you know who Mavet is possessing?" Cammie asked.

Wilhelmina shook her head sadly. "Unfortunately, I don't. But the monster will reveal himself once Mr. Walrus and Mr. Reed are there."

"Mrs. Van Uffeln, can I come too?" As Cammie watched the woman's eyes narrow, she started speaking faster. "I faced witches before. Besides, I won't be alone. Please—"

Wilhelmina's face looked livid. "Cammie, for once, I ask you not to get involved. This mission isn't for teenagers."

"But Alex and I, we've done it before."

"The two of you battled witches, not Mavet. You are no match for the monster. Even the witches are afraid of him. By the way, Cammie, I don't know if you noticed or not, but there hardly have been any witches' attacks in Skateland lately."

"Oh!" Now that Wilhelmina had mentioned it, Cammie realized that it was true. "How about that poison that Winja took with Ice Spice Soda?"

"It was Mavet, of course. His target was Elliot."

The two of them were silent for a few minutes.

"Okay, Cammie. That's it for now." Wilhelmina stood up. "And don't you worry. Mr. Walrus and Mr. Reed will bring Elliot back."

Cammie decided to try one more time. "Mrs. Van Uffeln, please let me come too. I won't be in their way. I promise. I—"

"Cammie, do you have a hearing problem?" Wilhelmina's eyes shot darts at Cammie.

Cammie hung her head.

"If you're still not convinced, let me tell you something. Do you know that this morning after hearing about Elliot's decision, Mr. Dulcimer went after Mavet himself?"

"He did?" Cammie felt excited. Mr. Dulcimer was strong; he could probably deal with Mavet.

"Do you know what happened?"

Oh no! Was Wilhelmina trying to say that Cammie's music interpretation teacher had got hurt?

"An avalanche sent him tumbling down a mountain for hundreds of yards after he crossed the Skateland border. The poor man broke three ribs. Luckily, Captain Greenfield happened to be in the vicinity with his icemobile, and he was able to take Mr. Dulcimer to the hospital. I would ask him to join Mr. Walrus and Mr. Reed, but someone will have to make sure Skateland residents are safe."

"So let me go. Please!" How could Cammie make Wilhelmina understand that she had to be by Coach Elliot's side, especially after the man saved her life?

"Cammie, we're not playing games here. And if you seriously think even for a moment that a little girl like you could possibly challenge the spirit of death, we have nothing further to discuss." Wilhelmina pointed to the door. "You're dismissed."

"Mrs. Van Uffeln, please!" Cammie was crying openly.

"I want you to return to the Green Rink and do a freestyle session."

The woman had to be kidding. While Coach Elliot was probably being tortured to death, Cammie was supposed to practice her jumps and spins?

"And I promise that as soon as there's news about Elliot, I'll let you know."

The expression on Wilhelmina's face was crystal clear; the conversation was over. Cammie had to leave.

MR. WALRUS'S TRUE IDENTITY

Cammie trudged out of the Skateland president's office, bending over as though she wore a twenty-pound jacket. As she walked down to the first floor, her legs felt like putty, so she had to hold on to the banister to stay upright. Prince Elliot had turned himself in. She might never see him again. He was probably being tortured to death at the moment. And Wilhelmina had been so darn calm, so put together. How was it possible? How could the Skateland president go through her daily routine knowing that Coach Elliot was in mortal danger? Wilhelmina had actually had the nerve to send Cammie to her afternoon practice. How much more absurd could things get? What exactly had Wilhelmina said? "Mr. Walrus and Mr. Reed will be leaving for Mavet's residence in an hour." Yeah right. In a whole hour, for crying out loud, as though Mavet was going to wait for them to get ready. What if it was too late? And what if Prince Elliot was already dead?

Cammie stopped in the middle of the lobby to catch her breath. Tears clouded her vision. She wasn't even sure she was heading in the right direction. Evil Wilhelmina, what right did she have to keep Cammie from getting involved? That was so unfair!

The front door slammed. There was a ripple of laughter and then excited voices. Cammie spun on her toes and darted around the corner. She didn't want to talk to anyone. She had to make a decision. She pressed her fists against her teary eyes and took a few deep breaths. *Think, Cammie! Think!* But what was there to think about? Everything was crystal clear. She wasn't going to stay behind. She had to take the matter into her own hands. Because if Prince Elliot got killed, Cammie would never want to skate again. She knew it. At this point of her life, those two things were inseparable, Coach Elliot and her skating, her skating and Coach Elliot...

She wasn't about to stay behind. She would go after Mavet. Cammie paused, staring at the display of famous skaters' pictures on the wall. She wouldn't repeat Mr. Dulcimer's mistake, going after Mavet alone. Cammie felt awed as she thought of what her music interpretation teacher had done. What courage, what bravery! He had risked his life to save another human being. That was so cool. On the other hand, the man had underestimated his opponent's strength. Mavet was too strong, too dangerous. If even Mr. Dulcimer had failed to defeat Mavet, Cammie didn't have a prayer.

A much wiser course would be to simply join the rescue mission. She would plead Mr. Walrus and Mr.

Reed to take her along. Mr. Reed might side with Wilhelmina, but surely Mr. Walrus would understand that Cammie simply couldn't stay behind; she had to help her coach. Besides, she had battled a few witches before. She was trained in combat.

The decision made, Cammie felt better instantly. Even her tears dried up. Pressing her lips determinedly, Cammie crossed the lobby and walked into the first-floor office that had a computer with the directory of all Skateland residents. Fortunately for her, the room was empty. Cammie quickly typed in "Mr. Walrus," and the man's address appeared on the screen immediately: "74 Spiral Street." Cammie sighed with relief. She had been concerned that the computer would direct her somewhere far to the outskirts of Skateland. But she knew exactly where Spiral Street was; it was just off the long Toe Loop Street, just a few blocks north of Skateland School.

Though the name suggested a winding road, Spiral Street actually mimicked the shape of a tracing made by a blade when the skater performed a change-edge spiral. There was also Skating Bookstore on Spiral Street that Cammie had visited a few times to buy her schoolbooks. Yet she had never known that Mr. Walrus lived nearby.

Cammie returned to the locker room and replaced her fancy unitard with warmer clothes. She could only hope that her thick sweater and her parka would provide enough protection from the freezing air, especially in the mountains, where the west wind was at its strongest.

Cammie entered Mr. Walrus's address into Kanga's navigation system. To her great surprise, she reached Mr. Walrus's house in record time. She realized that Kanga had taken her through a shortcut. That was great; time was running out.

Mr. Walrus's house was made of light gray stone with teal window shutters. Although it was still early in the afternoon, all the windows were lit up. Cammie pressed the doorbell button. The doorbell responded with loud music sounding like one of the songs Mr. Walrus always hummed when he resurfaced the ice. Cammie waited for a few minutes, but the door remained shut. She knocked, first with her fist and then with her skate guard. There was still no response. Frustrated, Cammie walked around the house and stopped abruptly. Ensconced between two pine trees stood two Zambonis. Mr. Walrus was putting a huge backpack into the newer-looking black-and-white machine.

"Cammie, is anything wrong?" Mr. Walrus brushed the snow off his face. With snowflakes resting on his mustache and his eyebrows, the man looked like Santa Claus.

"Mr. Walrus, I—"

"I'm sorry, but I'm in sort of a rush." Mr. Walrus took a squeegee from the driver's seat and started brushing the snow off the Zamboni.

"Mr. Walrus, I'm coming with you."

The brush fell from the man's hand, leaving a deep indentation in the fresh, powdery snow. "I beg your pardon?"

"I care about Coach Elliot too, Mr. Walrus. Please take me with you. I promise I won't be a nuisance."

"Cammie!" Mr. Walrus looked at the sky that was almost indistinguishable from the snow-covered lawn. "Mr. Reed and I are on a very dangerous mission. I'm sorry, but it's not for kids."

"But I'm not a child anymore. Besides, I can actually help. Alex and I, we battled witches before."

Mr. Walrus rubbed his forehead, looking tired. "Is Alex with you?"

"No."

"Look, let's go inside and we'll talk. Okay?"

Cammie followed the man into the house obediently, though she didn't see any point in wasting time on small talk. The best thing would be to rush to Mavet's residence as quickly as possible. After all, the monster could finish off Prince Elliot any moment.

Okay. Be patient, she told herself. *Annoying Mr. Walrus won't help. You've got to have him on your side.*

"Let's have some tea. It's freezing outside." The dishes rattled as Mr. Walrus took cups and saucers out of the kitchen cabinet. "Why don't you go to the living room and warm up by the fireplace, Cammie? I'll bring the tea in once it's ready."

But we can't waste time! The words burned her mouth, eager to get out. She pressed her lips tight. *Just another minute or two, and we'll be on our way.* At least Mr. Walrus didn't look like he was dead set against Cammie's involvement. After all, he had invited her inside, not sent her back to the dorm.

She walked into a square room with fire cracking in a fireplace made of the same gray rocks as the house. Though pretty spacious, the room appeared small. When Cammie looked around, she realized that every inch of space was taken by a music instrument or by some music-related item. There was a speaker in every corner. Two microphones sat on the carpet next to a huge pile of CDs. A big Yamaha keyboard stood next to a computer. Two guitars and a flute sat on a small desk closer to the fireplace. Cammie bent down and picked up a glossy saxophone.

"Oh no!" Cammie tried to breathe, but she felt as though there was no air in her lungs. She bit her thumb hard to stifle a scream that was about to slip out of her mouth. Why on earth did Mr. Walrus have all those music instruments and CDs in his living room? He wasn't even a professional musician. Unless…of course!

Cammie moaned as she felt her legs buckle under her. She collapsed onto the carpet, the room spinning around her. How stupid had she been! Mr. Walrus was Mavet. He was the one who had orchestrated all those attacks in Skateland. A Zamboni driver, how very convenient! Mr. Walrus could access skaters' CDs easily, and no one would ever suspect him. And it was all because of his profession. Skaters were so used to ice resurfacing routines that in their minds, Zamboni drivers were practically invisible. In fact, skaters treated Zamboni drivers almost as inanimate objects, as part of the rink environment. The Zamboni drivers were simply there like hockey lines, the boards, the locker rooms. So no matter how hard Cammie and Sonia had been watching the stacks of CDs, hoping that they would notice any suspicious activity, Mr. Walrus could have slipped in a CD with the music of death easily. He could have been there, and Cammie and Sonia wouldn't have seen him. He was part of the rink, after all.

"Tea is ready!" Mr. Walrus's cheerful voice called from the kitchen.

Cammie squeaked and pressed her fist tight against her mouth. She had to behave as though nothing had happened, as though she hadn't discovered Mr. Walrus's secret. If he only guessed that Cammie had him all figured out, he would murder her right on the spot. Killing people was easy for Mavet. It would be naïve to think that he would spare a silly little girl.

"Cammie, you don't want that water to get cold!" Mr. Walrus' voice called, that time much louder.

Oh no! What was she going to do? How could she sit next to a monster, drinking tea as though nothing had happened? And she would always remember that in another hour or so, Mavet would go to the mountains to finish off Coach Elliot.

Mr. Walrus appeared in the doorway, tall and bulky in his white sweater and black parka. "Is there anything wrong, Cammie?"

"Ah...uh...I was just looking at those beautiful instruments. I didn't know you could play." Her voice sounded unnaturally high, like a five-year-old's.

Mr. Walrus pulled on his white beard to untangle a few knots. "Well, I'm not that good a musician, actually. It's sort of a hobby. Skating and music are closely related, don't you think?"

"I guess." Cammie cleared her throat, slightly surprised that she could speak almost normally.

"I wanted to become a musician at some point," Mr. Walrus said. "I took piano lessons in my childhood, but skating took most of my time, so I had to make a choice. But when I resurface the ice, I always make up my own songs. And whenever I have access to other instruments, I try to learn how to play them on my own. I could show you if you like. I've recently mastered this tenor saxophone, and as for the flute—"

"Mr. Walrus, you know, I think I'd better go back to the dorm now," Cammie said quickly. "It's so cold and windy today, and I…I'm still not feeling that great after my fall."

"Oh!" Mr. Walrus's baby blue eyes rounded in obvious concern. "It's probably not a good idea for you to skate to your dorm alone. Let me give you a ride. I still have about forty minutes before I have to head for the mountains, so—"

"No!" Cammie protested, perhaps a little too loudly.

Mr. Walrus looked puzzled. "But why? If you aren't feeling good—"

"Shouldn't you be on your way to rescue Pr…Coach Elliot?" Cammie hoped she didn't sound too sarcastic.

Mr. Walrus frowned slightly. "Don't worry about Elliot. There are stronger powers in the world than Mavet's curse. But we aren't going yet. Something needs to be done before we hit the road, so giving you a ride won't be a problem."

"I'll be fine, thank you." Cammie walked across the room on stiff legs. As she approached Mr. Walrus, she felt dizzy and had to lean against the wall to steady herself.

"Cammie, you do look sick. You can't skate to the dorm alone."

"I'm probably coming down with something." She put her hand on the latch, trying to turn it. The latch wouldn't move.

She realized that Mr. Walrus had approached her from behind when his warm hand brushed against her forehead then slid down her cheeks.

"Oh good. I don't think you have fever. Are you sure you'll be okay skating home on your own?"

"I'm positive. Thank you, Mr. Walrus!" She made another attempt at opening the door.

Mr. Walrus turned the latch easily. "Cammie, please rest assured that Mr. Reed and I will do everything possible to rescue Elliot. I know Mrs. Van Uffeln has told you everything."

Except that Wilhelmina had no idea who was Mavet! Cammie ran down the steps to the ice path, jumped onto it with her skate guards still on, fell, yelped, stood up. She looked back. Mr. Walrus perched on top of the porch, shaking his head. She spread her lips in a fake smile and waved back.

She should probably go back to Wilhelmina and tell the Skateland president what she knew, that Mr. Walrus was Mavet, that he had to be arrested…

Cammie paused, bending against the gusts of the west wind. No, she wouldn't tell Wilhelmina anything. If Cammie was nothing but a silly little girl in Wilhelmina's sight, so be it. Let the Skateland president figure everything out herself.

She would go to Mr. Reed's house. She would tell him what she knew. She would warn the man not to get into the same Zamboni with Mavet. Because after Mr. Walrus killed Coach Elliot, he would probably decide to eliminate the witnesses. It meant that Mr. Reed was in grave danger too. It would probably be a good idea for Mr. Reed to tell Mr. Walrus that they would have to postpone the rescue mission. Let Mr. Walrus go to the mountains alone and chill out a little.

No, wait! Cammie slowed down. What if Mr. Walrus really went back to the mountains and killed Coach Elliot tonight? They couldn't take any chances. Perhaps it would be better for Mr. Reed and Cammie to head to the mountains immediately, leaving Mr. Walrus behind. If they reached Mavet's cabin before Mr. Walrus got there, they would be able to take Coach Elliot home with them. Hey, they wouldn't even have to fight; the rescue mission would be perfectly safe. That was great. Now, once Cammie explained everything to Mr. Reed, the man would definitely allow her to come along. He would even compliment her on solving Mr. Walrus's secret.

Cammie skated along the darkening streets in the direction of the Icy Park, tripping over loose chunks of snow. When she finally got under the trees, stroking became easier. The heavy limbs provided enough protection from the thick snow. In the misty twilight, the purple rink next to Mr. Reed's cabin appeared almost gray. Just like Mr. Walrus's house, the skate sharpener's cabin greeted her with illuminated windows. "Mr. Reed's Skate Sharpening Shop" the sign over the front door proudly announced.

Mr. Reed opened the door at the first sound of the doorbell. Cammie's mind registered that he was wearing a light gray snow suit. So he was ready to leave for the mountains.

"I'm sorry, but the shop is closed for tonight." Mr. Reed pointed to the "Closed" sign on the door. "Please call for an appointment tomorrow."

"Mr. Reed, it's me, Cammie."

The man's steel blue eyes narrowed. "So? Why do you expect me to make an exception for you?"

"No, it's just—"

"Look, if there's a real problem with your skates, I could possibly spare you a couple of minutes. But I have an urgent mission to attend to."

"But that's the reason I'm here!"

"Come in, then!" Mr. Reed stepped aside and motioned for Cammie to follow him to the sharpening office.

The very sight of the familiar rooms filled with antique skates, skating figurines and books, skating clothes, and other paraphernalia filled Cammie with a longing desire to go back in time to the period when everything had been normal.

"You can take off your skates," Mr. Reed said without looking at her.

Cammie bent over and untied the knot on her right boot. "Mr. Reed, don't get in Mr. Walrus's Zamboni!"

The man whirled around as though hit from behind. "Excuse me?"

"Mr. Reed, Mr. Walrus is Mavet. He's the one who killed Felicia Monroe. And now he's after Coach Elliot."

THE WEST WIND

Cammie thought she sounded very convincing. Mr. Walrus was Mavet, and he had been working hard to destroy the Monroes, first Felicia and now Elliot. Now how about Mr. Walrus's motives? Well, Coach Elliot was a terrific skater. Even now, years after his official retirement from competitive sport, he could still skate in shows and coach. And he was good at whatever he tried. And who on earth was Mr. Walrus? A lowly servant, perhaps only a little higher in position than a street cleaner. Therefore, Mr. Walrus had every reason to be jealous of Coach Elliot.

As Cammie presented her arguments, she kept staring Mr. Reed in the face, trying to read the man's thoughts. Yet his face remained impassive, though Cammie thought she could discern a flicker of annoyance as she spoke of Mr. Walrus's jealousy.

"Now I understand why Mrs. Van Uffeln called me an hour ago."

Cammie blinked. "Excuse me?"

"Yes, she contacted me and instructed me not to succumb to your supplications concerning your involvement in the rescue mission."

"What are you—?"

"She also told me to make sure you went back to the dorm where you belong and stop distracting those who are doing their best to rescue the man in danger."

Anger shot through Cammie's body, hot and violent. "I'm not—"

"Can I trust you to return to your dorm on your own, or do you expect me to get into the trouble of calling the police so they will take care of you?"

What a jerk! Cammie thought. *What a nasty, stupid—*

"I didn't hear your answer, Cammie."

She was so upset that even her tears dried off. "I think I can handle the trip to the dorm, thank you."

"Good. Off you go, then." Mr. Reed opened the door to let her out.

She gritted her teeth. *Don't even think that I'll ever ask you to sharpen my skates again! I'll go to my old skate sharpener in Clarenceville, or I'll turn to Mr. Sullivan, the Zamboni driver from the Silver Rink.* As she thought of the Zamboni, she realized that Mr. Reed would end up in the same vehicle with the monster after all. With a deep sigh of desperation, Cammie looked back at the cabin. Should she return and make herself clearer? Mr. Reed was in grave danger.

"But I already told him everything!" she exclaimed. Snow whooshed by, muffling the sounds.

"Ah, whatever!" She did an exaggerated two-foot turn and skated away from Mr. Reed's property. So she was on her own. Everybody had abandoned her. Mr. Dulcimer was injured. Wilhelmina and Mr. Reed thought she was nothing but a silly little girl. Mr. Walrus turned out to be the vicious monster. Alex, the boy whom she had always considered her best friend, had dumped her for a showgirl. And now that her beloved coach was facing a painful death, there was nobody to help him, nobody but Cammie.

"So what am I waiting for?"

The snow fell heavily, but the park looked peaceful. There was absolutely nothing scary under the thick canopy of snow.

She would go to Mavet's cave herself. She would find Coach Elliot, and she would rescue him. There was no choice; she had to do it. And should Mavet put up a fight, she would strike back.

Okay, so where exactly was Mavet's property? She skidded to a stop and looked around. For a moment, she toyed with the idea of going to the hospital and talking to Mr. Dulcimer. No, that was a bad idea. First of all, she couldn't afford wasting any more time. Second, the chances that she would even be allowed to talk to her teacher were very slim. After all, she wasn't a family member. And even if she somehow managed to sneak into Mr. Dulcimer's hospital room, the man would probably give her the same humiliating instructions she had heard three times: go back to the dorm where you belong. *So forget Mr. Dulcimer. You'll have to find Mavet's residence yourself.* It wouldn't be a problem anyway; she had her Kanga bag.

"Hey, where's Kanga?" Only then did Cammie realize her bag wasn't gliding by her side. The bag was with her when she left the Silver Rink. She was perfectly sure of that. But did she have Kanga by her side when she rang Mr. Reed's doorbell? She stopped and stared at the path ahead of her. No. She would have had to drag the bag up to the porch, and she didn't remember doing that. Which only meant one thing: she had left her Kanga in Mr. Walrus's house.

"For crying out loud!" That was the worst. Surely Cammie could return to the monster's residence to claim her bag. Yet it wouldn't be wise, for this time, she might not be so lucky. Mavet would surely finish her off.

Cammie bit her lip so hard that she could taste blood in her saliva. Even Kanga had forsaken her. But she wouldn't turn back. No Kanga? Fine. She didn't need the bag anyway. It was unlikely that Mavet's address was in Kanga's navigation system. Yes, but where was she supposed to go?

And then it dawned on her: the west wind. Snowstorms and avalanches always came from the west. She stopped and did a few calculations, mentally thanking Mrs. Redner, her geography teacher, for giving them tips on figuring out where the sides of the world were. Okay. Mr. Reed's cabin was in the northeastern side of Skateland. It meant that instead of heading south, to the dorm, Cammie would have to turn right. And once she reached the mountains outside Skateland, she would simply follow the wind.

Cammie rubbed her hands, tightened the scarf around her neck, and skated forward.

The western part of the Icy Park differed greatly from the rest of the forest. The farther ahead Cammie skated, the more challenging the ice path became. It wasn't that the ice was rough. On the contrary, it looked pristine, as though nobody had ever skated there. And yet the pale gray ice lacked the smooth, shiny quality that Cammie was so used to. She had to be careful not to get on top of loose chunks of ice, ruts and holes, and twice, she almost tripped over the frozen logs that blocked her way.

It wasn't particularly dark, but the dense snow made the paths almost impossible to see. The tall oak and maple trees gave way to fir trees scattered among huge rocks. Cammie was approaching the mountain range. The ice path swerved around a log nestled on top of a huge rock. Cammie saw a sharp incline ahead of her. She was just wondering how she was going to keep her blades from gliding backward, when she felt her feet sink deep into the snow. There was no ice anymore.

"Oops!" Cammie stopped and examined the road leading up to the mountains. It was wider than an average ice path. Snow lay on the ground, thick like a quilt, and except for an occasional fir tree, the area was pretty bare. Cammie's heart tapped a warning in her chest: *pay attention*. The absence of ice could only mean one thing: Cammie was outside Skateland. It wasn't exactly a surprise. She had known all along that she would have to cross the border. Yet she felt insecure. With all of its witches and cursed rinks, Skateland was still her home. Now she was on unfamiliar ground, approaching Mavet's territory. Or was she on the monster's property already?

Cammie looked up and ahead of her. The road wasn't particularly steep. Under different circumstances, it wouldn't be a problem for Cammie to go all the way to the top. Now that she had her skates on, her blades appeared to be a nuisance. They cut too deep through the snow, making every step difficult. About thirty feet up the hill, Cammie felt sweaty, as though she had been practicing her junior moves in the field for three straight hours. She was thirsty, but she didn't have her water bottle with her.

"Great!" Cammie muttered. She bent over and grabbed a handful of snow and stuffed it in her mouth. If she had been more attentive leaving Mr. Walrus's house, she would have her Kanga now. Not only would she enjoy fresh spring water, but she could also feast on the snacks that she usually kept in one of Kanga's side pockets. She thought longingly of the half-full bag of Skating Animal Crackers and two JOBB energy snacks. The abbreviation stood for *Jumping Our Best Bars*. A little snack would definitely boost her energy. Cammie rubbed her hands and knees and cast a sad look at the road. Prince Elliot needed her.

She had only covered the distance of about a hundred yards when she needed another break. This time, she felt as though her legs were about to give out any moment. Unaccustomed to digging through deep snow, her ankles kept cramping up and her thighs throbbed with pain. On top of everything else, she was getting really cold. The daylight had almost faded. The brutal west wind hit Cammie right in the face as though cautioning her to stay behind.

Cammie stuffed her hands into her pockets and strained her eyes, trying to determine how much farther she had to go. All she could see was a swarming grayish mass. She cringed at the thought of all the stories about the avalanches catching travelers in the mountains. That was all Mavet's doing, of course. Cammie shivered. For years, she had trusted Mr. Walrus. The man had helped her so many times. She wondered why he hadn't killed her before. Surely there had been plenty of opportunities.

"Because he isn't after you, silly!" she exclaimed. "It's Coach Elliot he hates."

Yet once Mr. Walrus discovered that Cammie knew his true identity, he would definitely try to get rid of her. She had to move on; she couldn't wait any longer. Who knew how much more time was left before Mavet was ready to strike? And yet Cammie felt she couldn't take another step. Her legs gave way; she fell into the snow. It felt soft and not that cold anymore. Perhaps she was getting used to the freezing temperature. She was so tired that she could barely keep her eyes open. She needed rest. She would relax for a short time, and once she felt better, she would go to Mavet's cave.

"Cammie! Cammie, do you hear me?"

The voice came from somewhere far in the distance, and it was familiar. It had to be part of her dream. No one in the mountains knew her name. Well, whoever the person was, Cammie wasn't going to answer. She wanted to sleep badly.

"Cammie! Cammie!" There was a rumbling sound. The voice was much closer.

Can a person have a little rest here? Cammie thought. She felt something moving next to her, something huge. She opened her eyes. "No! Go away, go away!"

There was a black-and-yellow Zamboni that spewed steam right by her side. That was it; Mr. Walrus had found her. She was going to die.

"Cammie!"

"Go away! I know who you are! If you only touch me, Captain Greenfield will come and arrest you. I told Mrs. Van Uffeln and Mr. Reed that I was going here, and—"

"Cammie, it's me."

"Go away, Mavet!"

"Cammie, it's me, Alex."

What? Cammie raised her head.

Alex bent over her, his face pink with frost, his eyes huge and green. He had come after her; he hadn't abandoned her after all.

"Alex, what're you doing here?" Cammie had hard time speaking. Her lips were numb.

"Mr. Walrus let me borrow one of his Zambonis. He told me you had come to see him, and—"

"No!" Cammie screamed so loudly that Alex took a few steps back, looking startled.

"It's Mr. Walrus, he's the monster, the one who killed Coach Elliot's wife." The words barely came out of Cammie's throat. She felt as though even the air in her lungs had turned to ice. "And now he's after Coach Elliot." Cammie clutched her chest and coughed a few times. "Oh, you don't know any of those things."

Alex stared at her. "Now wait a minute. Of course I know all about Coach Elliot's wife and how the monster attacked Wilhelmina years ago."

"You do? Who told you?"

Alex shrugged. "Well, for starters, I've been doing a little investigation myself. And today, I talked to Wilhelmina, and that's when she told me about Mavet possessing her fellow skater."

"Oh! You see—"

"Look. Why don't we sit in the Zamboni? You must be awfully cold lying in that snow."

Cammie managed a weak smile. "It's not that bad once you get used to it. I was even falling asleep when you started calling my name."

"Cammie, don't you know anything?" Now his eyes were rounded in concern. "You aren't supposed to sleep out in the cold. You could have frozen to death!"

"Really? But it felt so good. I—"

"Now that's enough. Get up!" He stretched his hand.

Cammie made an effort to stand up, but her legs felt as though they were made of stone. She lost balance and fell back into the snow. "I can't move my legs!"

"Great! That's exactly what we need, frostbite. Here you go!" Alex lifted her easily.

Her cheek brushed against the cold fabric of his parka. Immediately, her cheeks turned warm. "Alex, you don't have to—"

"Shh! Grab my neck."

She obeyed, surprised at how good it felt. Now that Alex was with her, she believed everything would be all right. They would fight Mavet together and rescue Coach Elliot.

Alex lowered her onto the passenger seat of the Zamboni. "Take your skates off. Your feet must be freezing."

"I can't feel them at all." Cammie tried to wiggle her toes, but her feet felt like stone.

"Wait. I have an idea."

Cammie watched Alex walk around, picking up dry limbs and twigs. He arranged them in a neat pile on the snow, placing the smallest twigs at the top. Out of his parka pocket, Alex produced a cigarette lighter. As he clicked it, fire erupted from its end but went out instantly.

"Hmm. I need something to keep the fire going. Oh. I have an idea." Alex rummaged in his pockets again and took out a Yellow Rink flyer. He tore it in half and lit one of the sides with the lighter. As he brought the burning paper close to the twigs, they caught fire immediately.

"It worked!"

Within the next few minutes, the logs cracked loudly and the fire was almost four feet high.

"Let's get you closer." Alex spread something that looked like Mr. Walrus's parka on the snow next to the fire. Then he lifted Cammie again and carefully lowered her onto the parka.

She smiled at the pleasant warmth and took off her gloves.

"Let's remove your skates and look at your feet," Alex said.

Cammie pulled off her boots and her socks and grimaced. Her feet looked white under the thin tights, and she still couldn't move her toes.

"Oh!" Alex appeared to be thinking hard. "You know what? You can't keep them too close to the fire yet. Let me rub them first. It'll let the blood flow back to your toes."

He took her left foot in both hands and rubbed hard. First, Cammie didn't feel anything, but about a minute later, there was a pricking sensation in her toes, and then her whole foot responded in burning pain.

"Ouch! It hurts!"

"Good! That's exactly what we need. Let me do the right foot now."

When Cammie could finally move her toes, Alex covered her feet with a side of Mr. Walrus's parka. "You're nuts. How can you skate outside with only cotton socks on?"

"Well, I wasn't exactly planning on going to the mountains, was I? Although I do have a pair of thick wool socks in Kanga bag, but..." Cammie sighed. "I must have left Kanga in Mr. Walrus's house. Stupid me!"

Alex slapped himself on the forehead. "How could I forget? Okay, Cammie. You're in for a big surprise. Tada!"

He dived into the Zamboni and took out Cammie's Kanga bag.

"Kanga! Oh my God!" Cammie rubbed the brown fur lovingly, feeling as though a long-lost friend had come back to her. "Where did you find it? Oh wait! I have a few Skating Animal Crackers here and two JOBBs."

Alex grinned. "I haven't come empty handed either."

Cammie clapped her hands at the sight of a big box of mitten cookies and a huge thermos.

"It's crossover cocktail, remember?" Alex asked as he poured the steaming liquid into two plastic cups.

Cammie took a sip of her cocktail and squinted as she savored the wonderful feeling of being warm on the inside. She took a bite of her raspberry mitten cookie, thinking that she had never eaten anything better in her life. On the negative side, the moment Cammie finally felt warm and relaxed, she remembered why they were on the snowy road leading to the mountains.

"Alex, I'm going to Mavet's cave. Coach Elliot is in danger. Do you think you could give me a ride? See, my skates are of no use in the snow."

Cammie saw Alex's eyebrows go up, so she began speaking faster.

"I know, I know. It's not safe, and once Mavet finds out he's been exposed, he will definitely want to kill me too. Well, I was lucky before with the witches, wasn't I? But as for you, well, you won't have to take any risks. I promise. The monster won't even see you."

"Cammie!"

"No, wait!" Cammie raised her hand. "You'll drop me off next to Mavet's cave and drive away. And if he asks me how I got there, well…" Cammie took a deep breath, thinking of a good excuse. She surely didn't want to put Alex's life in jeopardy.

"Are you done now?" Alex's voice sounded unnaturally calm.

Cammie looked at his furrowed eyebrows, wondering what he was going to say.

"First of all, Mavet won't try to kill Coach Elliot until midnight. That's what Mr. Walrus told me. And—"

"Alex!" Cammie jumped to her feet, tripped over a loose limb, and fell back into the snow. "You can't trust Mr. Walrus. He's Mavet."

Her voice echoed against the mountain range and came back to her magnified. "Mavet, Mavet, Mavet."

Alex stepped back. "What?"

Skipping words, jumping from one idea to another, Cammie briefly told him about her suspicions.

"Cammie, listen to me! Mr. Walrus isn't Mavet."

"Of course he is. He has all those music instruments and—"

"Mr. Walrus is a righteous man and a talented skater."

"Sure, he poses as one."

"Cammie, Wilhelmina personally asked him to finish off Mavet."

"So? Wilhelmina doesn't know who Mr. Walrus really is. Do you know how many CDs he has in his living room?"

"I'm sure there's a good reason," Alex said, though his voice shook a little. "Perhaps music is his hobby. After all, he writes songs. He calls them Zamboni songs. So—"

"It's not just a hobby, okay? He has every music instrument imaginable, and he can play them. He told me himself."

"Well, I don't know about that. Anyway, Mr. Walrus and Mr. Reed are coming to Mavet's cabin. They're going to perform the dance of life at Mavet's rink."

Cammie sat up straight. "The dance of life?"

"Sure. They'll be skating to a piece written by Mr. Dulcimer. Wilhelmina says the music of life will surely work as an antidote to Mavet's music of death. The monster won't be able to kill Coach Elliot. In fact, chances are that the music of life will destroy Mavet's powers and set free the person he possesses."

"Mavet possesses Mr. Walrus," Cammie said stubbornly.

"Cammie—"

"All right, all right. By the way, I have music of life on a CD too."

Alex appeared startled. "You do?"

"Sure. It's in my skating bag. I won it as a prize." Cammie told Alex about her stellar performance at Mr. Dulcimer's lesson.

Alex grinned. "Cammie, you're really something. First, you win Kanga and then the music of life. You can really skate well when you're motivated."

Cammie pouted. "I always skate well."

They both laughed, looking at the snowflakes dancing around them.

Alex spoke up first. "Anyway, it's great that you have that CD, Cammie. Why didn't you tell Wilhelmina about it?"

Cammie threw a limb in the fire. "She never asked me. All she wanted me to do is get out of her office and stop pestering her."

"Well, it's a shame. Because the only reason Mr. Reed and Mr. Walrus were still there when I left was because they were waiting for Mr. Dulcimer to make them a CD with the music of life. But Mr. Dulcimer was in the hospital, and he had to be examined by the doctor before he was released."

Cammie stretched her hands toward the fire. "See? I hope Wilhelmina will regret not listening to me. And Mr. Reed! He wouldn't even let me say anything; he just kicked me out. It's pathetic, you know. I—"

Alex looked amused. "Whoa. Lighten up. Don't you realize that you're preaching to the choir here?"

"Hmm. I guess."

They spent a few moments in silence, letting the fire warm their hands and feet.

"What else did Wilhelmina tell you?" Cammie asked.

"Well, pretty much the same as what she told you. I went to her office to share my suspicions, and she told me to stay put. Mr. Reed and Mr. Walrus would take care of it. So I went to your dorm."

Cammie looked up at the reflections of fire sparkling in his green eyes. "You did?"

He shrugged. "I knew you wouldn't wait for the adults to take care of the situation. But you weren't there. And Sonia didn't know where you were. And Rita and Angela hadn't seen you at the Green Rink. That's when I realized you had left for Mavet's cave."

He knew her so well. And so did she. Suddenly, Cammie felt calm and joyful. It was amazing how the presence of a friend could transform a cold, scary trip into an exciting adventure.

"So I went to Mr. Walrus's place, and he was really upset that you had taken everything upon yourself. He let me borrow his Zamboni. He said Mr. Reed and he were still waiting for Mr. Dulcimer's music."

Cammie smirked. "See how fake Mr. Walrus is? He told me to go back to the dorm. Yet when you came, he was all smiles and he wanted you to go after me. It's a trap."

"Cammie!" Alex sucked in the air through his teeth. "First of all, Mr. Walrus wasn't all smiles. He looked extremely worried about you. And second, he sent me after you because he realized what danger you'd put yourself into. Yes, that's right. Don't roll your eyes."

Cammie stood up and brushed the snow off her clothes. "So are you rested? Let's go."

"Go where?"

"To a skating practice," Cammie said, feeling anger rise within her. "Are you nuts, Alex, or are you kidding me? I'm going to Mavet's cabin."

"Hmm. Actually"—Alex twirled a twig in his gloved hands—"Mr. Walrus told me to keep you as far away from Mavet's cave as possible."

Cammie hopped in place. "See? That's a proof. He wants to kill Coach Elliot. Anyway, if you aren't taking me, I'll go there on my own."

"Cammie, Mavet isn't going to strike 'til midnight. And by that time Mr. Walrus and Mr. Reed will be there. Don't you get it? You are no match for Mavet."

"How very convenient!" Cammie was almost shouting now. "To get me out of the way and to finish off Prince Elliot easily."

"Cammie, it's not Mr. Walrus!" Alex shook his head. "Come on. We've known him for years. He's always been so nice to us."

Cammie jerked her chin. "So what's your theory? Who's Mavet?"

"My money is on Bob Turner," Alex said.

Cammie sniggered. "He isn't smart enough. Besides, he was still a little kid back in nineteen ninety-two, when Felicia was murdered."

"He must have had an accomplice, then. But I saw him lurking around your dorm and following you everywhere."

"So what? I'm not the target."

"Turner sent you a valentine during the show, and then you got hurt."

Cammie gasped. "It was him?"

"Well, I watched him. He only sent one card, and it was for you."

And she had thought it was Coach Elliot!

Cammie felt her cheeks getting hot. She had to say something and fast. "But…but I've never heard Turner play an instrument or sing."

Alex added a few logs into the fire. "It's a shame we still haven't figured out who the attacker is. The more I think about it, the more I realize that it could be anyone."

"Even Celine," Cammie said.

Alex dropped the log he was carrying.

"Okay. I know you disagree!" Cammie said. "Actually, I don't think it's her anymore."

Alex turned on his side staring at the fire. "Do you really think Celine could be a murderer?"

"Especially the girl you're in love with," Cammie said immediately, wishing she had never said that.

Alex's face became maroon. He turned away.

What if he goes away and leaves me alone? Cammie thought, feeling panicky. *How come I always speak without thinking? So what if Alex has a crush on Celine? He has every right to. We live in a free country after all.*

Alex looked at his right hand and then slowly unclenched his fingers. "I'm not in love with Celine."

"Alex, please—"

"Wait. Let me say it." He took a deep breath. "I mean, yes, I liked her a lot because she's funky, and cute, and a good skater—"

"And good-looking," Cammie added nastily.

Alex pretended he didn't hear her. "I thought Celine was my friend. But lately, it became clear to me that she had been using all of us guys to get to Kyle. Apparently, Kyle is the one she's interested in because he's the junior world champion." Alex's jaw hardened. "She didn't care about any of us, see? And now that Kyle finally noticed her, she won't even acknowledge me, or Jeff, or Michael."

Cammie smiled, her face still turned away so she knew Alex couldn't see her reaction.

"See, I busted myself trying to land that triple axel because she dropped a hint that she would go steady with a man who had a consistent triple axel."

Cammie wondered what would have happened if Alex had really managed to land the tricky jump.

"I almost got myself killed at the show. My legs didn't feel right, yet I went for a triple axel anyway and took a hard fall. It still hurts like crazy!" Alex grimaced as he ran his hand against his right side. "Coach Darrel was really mad. He actually yelled at me. He didn't think I was ready for the triple axel."

"Oh no!" Cammie moved closer to Alex, making sure he could see her angry face. "How could you do that knowing what happened to me last year. What if you had broken a bone? Is a girl worth it?"

Alex stared at the fire biting his lip. "Yes, as crazy as it might sound to you, I thought Celine was worth it."

Cammie gave out a sigh of desperation.

"But then I saw how wrong I was because..." He stirred the logs in the fire, causing a few sparks to shoot up.

Cammie waited for him to go on, but her friend seemed to be deep in thought. She looked up, expecting to see the sky, but it was invisible behind the thick snow.

"Do you remember how I didn't make the nationals last year?" Alex asked.

"Sure."

Last year's Skateland Annual Competition had really turned into quite a humiliating experience for Alex. He had made a few mistakes in the free program and come in fifth, missing the national competition by just one spot.

"Do you remember what you said then?"

She shrugged. "Not really."

"You said you were sorry."

"Of course I was."

"Well, Celine laughed at me," Alex said bitterly. "I fell on that triple axel, and it destroyed my concentration, so the whole program was a mess. And she thought I was a loser."

"I'm sorry," Cammie said again.

"Well, I'm not!" Alex exclaimed. "That show was quite an eye-opener for me. I realized Celine didn't really care about me risking my skating career. She didn't even ask me how I felt. She left with Kyle—"

"Because he landed his triple axel," Cammie said sadly.

"Exactly."

They sat in silence for a while, the fire cracking around them. For some weird reason, Cammie felt as though a huge burden had lifted.

"Alex," she said softly, "you know, it's not really important who Mavet really is. The monster is after Coach Elliot, so we need to do everything we can to rescue him."

"You aren't going anywhere—"

"Alex!"

"Alone," he said firmly. "We're heading for Mavet's cabin together."

"Oh!" Her heart danced in her chest. "It's great! Thank you. Oh, thank you, Alex. I mean, of course, I'm no match for the monster, but together—"

"Together, we'll be able to stop him."

"So why do we have to wait 'til midnight? Let's go now."

Alex looked at his watch. "Actually, it's five of ten already. And you know what? You're right. We'll help

Coach Elliot escape, and then Mr. Walrus and Mr. Reed will deal with Mavet afterward."

If Mr. Walrus doesn't deal with Coach Elliot first, Cammie thought but decided not to press the point.

They threw snow into the fire, waiting for it to die completely. Then they got into the Zamboni.

"Cammie, do you really have a crush on Coach Elliot?" Alex asked as he turned on the engine.

Cammie rubbed her hot cheeks and pretended to be really interested in the pile of sharp rocks on her right.

"Because he's so much older and—"

"And a terrific coach, okay?" Cammie barked.

"Is that so? Hmm. Okay. Let's change the subject. How're your jumps coming along with that terrific coach of yours?"

She straightened up. "Pretty good, actually. Didn't you see my triple salchow at the show?"

The Zamboni swerved to the right.

Alex steadied it. "That was impressive, yes. Unfortunately, you fell at the end, so everybody pretty much only remembered that part."

"I never fall from spins, and you know it. I fell because of Mavet, so it doesn't count. And I assure you it'll never happen again. Because—" Cammie didn't have a chance to finish her sentence. The mountain ahead of them suddenly shook, and a wave of snow started advancing rapidly at them.

"What?" Cammie grabbed the side of the Zamboni.

"An avalanche!" Alex shouted next to her.

"Help!" Cammie tried to shout, but it was too late.

There was snow in her mouth, her eyes, her nose, everywhere. She felt herself lifted up in the air. Everything swirled, and then there was sheer blackness.

MAVET

When Cammie opened her eyes, everything was eerily quiet, as though someone had turned down the volume. Waking up in the dorm, she was used to the steady humming of the radiator, the whistling of the wind outside, and the clanging of dishes in the kitchen. Now there was nothing. She let her eyes graze the dark outline of sharp rocks. Dim light was coming from both sides. She tilted her head and saw rows of shimmering black candles. Where was she? What had happened to her?

She raised her hand and touched her head then patted her belly and her legs. Everything felt all right. She sat up and studied the area. All around her there was nothing but dark gray rocks dotted with patches of snow. She lay on the dirty snow on the edge of a circular pond. The ice was of the same dull color as the rocks. Next to her, Alex lay on his back, his eyes closed.

"Alex!" Cammie called softly.

He stirred slowly, and then his eyelids moved. Alex stared Cammie in the face, his eyes still unfocused. He blinked and rose on his elbows. "Hey, where are we?"

"I wish I knew." Cammie thought hard. "Let's see. We were on our way to Mavet's cave, right? And then—"

"And then there was an avalanche." Alex's eyes lit up. "That's it. We got caught in an avalanche."

"People die in avalanches." Cammie shuddered as she remembered hearing about avalanche victims on the news.

"But we're alive!" Alex stood up and hopped on the hard-pressed snow and then bent over and massaged his calves.

Cammie realized that the snowstorm had stopped. Except for an occasional snowflake, everything was still. Dirty gray fog hung in the air, making the distant sky appear invisible. Alex took a few steps in the direction of the pond.

"Be careful not to touch the ice!" Cammie exclaimed. "It might be cursed."

"Cammie, look at this!" Alex pointed ahead of him.

Cammie rose on her feet, ignoring the pricking sensation in her limbs. She must have been lying in the same position for too long. She followed the direction of Alex's hand and let out a startled *ah!* Directly across from them was a dark hole, probably an opening to a huge cave. Icicles hung from the top, and water was slowly dripping onto the dark ice. The rink narrowed down in front of the cave, and a long ice passage led somewhere into the depth.

"What…what if it's Mavet's cave?" Cammie asked.

378

Alex nodded. "I'm pretty sure it is."

Instinctively, Cammie looked around. They'd better plan their escape ahead of time in case they had to beat feet quickly. Yet except for the cave, there was no other passage or opening. The rocks around them were huge and smooth. They towered around them like silent sentinels.

"Why? What about this water?" Cammie stared at the drops falling onto the gray surface and then turning into little moguls on the ice. "Why isn't it frozen? It's cold here."

Alex stared at the rhythmically falling drops. "I'm afraid there's only one explanation."

"What?"

"You aren't going to like it."

"Come on, tell me!"

"We've been kidnapped by Mavet," Alex said grimly. "And the monster breathes fire, remember? So when he's around, the icicles melt. Mavet's in the cave now. That's for sure."

"How do you know what Mavet looks like?" Cammie asked quickly, trying not to think that the vicious monster could be only a few yards away from them.

"I saw him in the Icy Park."

"What were you doing there?"

Alex shrugged. "I was testing my theory. What else? See, I was almost a hundred percent sure Turner was the monster. So when I saw the guy head for the park one day, I followed. And then I saw him, Mavet." Alex's face contorted. "Man, he seemed to have walked straight out of a horror movie. About a dozen horns and red eyes—"

"There are eight horns. They stand for Skateland's rinks," Cammie said flatly.

"Whatever. And then he opened his mouth and fire shot out of it." Alex cast a surreptitious glance at the cave. "So I got scared and ran for it, and then I saw the police icemobile. Naturally, I thought Turner had transformed into the monster. Wilhelmina had already explained to me how it worked."

"When did Wilhelmina talk to you about Mavet?" Cammie asked quickly.

"She asked me to come to her office after practice once. She told me she was worried about you. She somehow knew you would start digging into those attacks."

Cammie grinned. "Naturally."

"Well, I did my little research too. Sort of." The pink color of Alex's cheeks deepened. "Although my heart wasn't quite in it. I thought too much of Celine."

Of course!

"And Wilhelmina…well, she kind of asked me to keep an eye on you."

So Cammie hadn't been alone all that time.

"Do you still think it's Bob Turner?" Cammie asked.

"Most likely, yes."

Cammie shook her head. "You're wrong. It's Mr. Walrus."

"Well, it looks like we'll find out pretty soon, huh?"

"Oh!" Cammie took a quick step back. She'd better not know. Perhaps if they somehow managed to find

Prince Elliot and escape all together, they wouldn't have to face the monster at all.

Alex rose on his toes. Cammie saw him peering into the blackness of the cave.

"Do you see anything?"

"Not really."

"But Coach Elliot is probably there."

"I'm sure he is." Alex took a deep sigh. "It means we have no choice. We have to get inside."

"Shouldn't we…?" Cammie hugged herself to stop the uncontrolled shivering. "Shouldn't we wait for Mavet to leave?"

Alex looked at his watch. "I'm afraid he's not leaving. It's ten thirty. And Mavet'll attack at midnight. So if we want to get to Coach Elliot before then—"

"Okay," Cammie said in a small voice.

"I only hope this ice is all right." Alex raised his foot.

"Wait. Let's step onto it together."

"No. Let me try it first." Alex gently scraped the gray surface with his toe. "It looks fine to me. Perhaps—"

Before Alex had a chance to finish his sentence, a series of flashes shot from inside the cave. A blast of thunder came, so loud that Cammie's ears began to sting. She screamed and stepped back. Alex grabbed her hand and led her away from the entrance to the farthest side of the pond. Their backs hit the hard rock. There was no place to go.

There was a loud cracking sound, and then two dark silhouettes appeared from the cave.

Cammie blinked. She had expected to see the beast with horns and fiery eyes. Instead, two men were approaching them. One of the guys wore Skateland police uniform. The other man was tall and blond, dressed all in black. He seemed to have skates on, though he moved somewhat clumsily. Yet as little light as the candles provided, Cammie would never mistake the man for anyone else. "Coach Elliot!"

The man turned his head in her direction, and his face twisted in panic. "Cammie, get out of here. Now!"

"We are here to save you!" Cammie felt so happy to see Prince Elliot, she wanted to dance.

Coach Elliot stepped forward but tripped and almost fell.

Cammie wrinkled her forehead. "What's wrong?"

"He has blade brakes on!" Alex exclaimed.

Now Cammie also noticed that Coach Elliot's blades were enclosed in heavy metal guards with rubber patches attached to the bottom. Those were the devices Skateland cops used to immobilize dangerous criminals. What Cammie couldn't understand was why her coach had to wear those cumbersome restrainers.

"Easy, Monroe! Your little student isn't going anywhere," the other man said.

The voice sounded familiar, and as Cammie looked the man in the face, she recognized Captain Greenfield.

"Captain Greenfield! Oh, thank God! You found him. Oh, we were so scared." She felt tremendous relief. Now that the police were involved, everything would be all right.

"Captain Greenfield, we'd better get out of here," Alex said quickly. "Do you see the water dripping?

Mavet is about to show up. He wants to kill Coach Elliot at midnight."

Captain Greenfield chuckled. "Yup. That's exactly what he's going to do."

"We'll all fit into your icemobile, right? So let's get out of here!" Cammie couldn't understand why Captain Greenfield just stood there, leering at Alex and her, when time was running out. They had to get into the police icemobile and leave the horrible place before the evil monster made its appearance.

"Of course I have an icemobile." Captain Greenfield smiled. "And I could probably take you kiddies back to Skateland, except…I'm not going to do it."

"Why?" Cammie and Alex asked at the same time.

"Why?" The man narrowed his hazel eyes, appearing deep in thought. "See, the two of you shouldn't have come here in the first place. You have always annoyed me, Cammie and Alex. You're way too nosy. Hey, if you had just followed our dear president's instructions and stayed behind, you'd be sleeping safely in your dorms now. Yet you chose to disobey the authority again. Sorry for the bad news, but the two of you will never leave this place."

"Now wait a minute!" Alex said loudly.

Cammie pinched herself to make sure she wasn't having a dream.

"You're Mavet!" Alex cried out.

Captain Greenfield's eyes flashed red. "I've always thought of you as a smart guy, Alex Bernard!"

What? Captain Greenfield was Mavet, the vicious monster, the one who had attacked everybody? It couldn't be true. It just couldn't! Black dots swirled in front of Cammie's eyes. Feeling lightheaded, she slowly slumped into the snow.

"But I thought…Lieutenant Turner," Alex said.

Captain Greenfield jerked his head back and laughed. "The rookie? Do you seriously think he has the guts?"

"I, I t-thought it was Mr.….Mr. Walrus," Cammie stuttered, surprised that she could even speak.

Captain Greenfield grabbed his stomach and practically roared. "Is that what you thought? The Zamboni dude! Oh, you've really made my day!"

"But…he has all those music instruments in his house." Cammie didn't even know why she was telling the cop all those things. Nothing was going to change the harsh reality. Alex and she had made a horrible mistake. They would be lucky if they managed to get out of the evil place alive.

"Your Walrus friend is as poor a musician as he's a skater. I, however—" Captain Greenfield stuck his chest forward.

"You are a skater? Hey, you look like someone who was born with blade brakes on your feet," Alex said.

Captain Greenfield's eyes flashed crimson. "Stop being fresh with me! First of all, I'm a policeman, not a murderer. It's my principle not to attack innocent skaters. Under different circumstances, I would let the two of you go. What the heck. Yet now that the two of you know my little secret, I mean my ability to transform, of course, I can't allow you guys to walk away."

"Let them go, Gilbert," Coach Elliot said firmly. "You've got me. Fine. That's what you wanted. But I beg you, don't hurt the children!"

Captain Greenfield shook his head. "Sorry, buddy, but I don't have a choice. Your two little friends would definitely blab my secret to everybody, including Wilhelmina Van Uffeln. And I intend to stay in Skateland and keep my job."

"We won't," Cammie hastened to say. "We won't tell anybody who you are. Just let us go."

"Do you expect me to believe that? Do I look like an idiot to you?'

"No. You look like a murderer!" Alex barked.

The moment he said that, Captain Greenfield's face turned burgundy. A terrible roar came out of his mouth. His chest and hips swelled up to enormous proportions. Thick brown fur appeared on his chest and limbs, and eight horns sprouted out of his head.

"Mavet!" Cammie yelled.

Alex grabbed her hand. She sank her fingernails deep into his palm.

The monster opened his jaws, and fire erupted out of his mouth. Cammie tried to step back, but her body was pressed tight against the hard rock. A wave of heat hit her in the face. *It's all over. He'll burn us all alive.*

Yet the smoke slowly subsided, and Mavet's blood-red eyes moved from Cammie and Alex to Coach Elliot. "So another hour, Elliot, and then we'll start."

"Leave him alone. What has he done to you?" Cammie shouted.

The monster took a deep breath, sending flames of fire to the gray ice. With horror, Cammie watched small puddles appear around the spots where the fire had hit the rink.

"How about that, Elliot?" Mavet asked, sounding exactly like Captain Greenfield. "The ever nice and sweet boy. So are you going to tell the brats what you did, or are you leaving the honor to me?"

"Leave Cammie and Alex alone, Gilbert!" Coach Elliot's voice was soft but strong. "Let them return to their dorms and everything'll be fine. I promise."

"He promises. How about that!" Mavet growled. "Like I'm going to believe a word. Like I'm going to let these punks walk out of here scott free after all you've done to me, after you destroyed my career and everything. No, buddy. It's payback time."

Suddenly, the monster's horns grew back into his head. He started to shrink. The brown fur disappeared, giving way to gray pants and a gray shirt. Now it was Captain Greenfield again, grinning widely.

"I don't know what you're talking about," Coach Elliot said. "Anyway, you can do everything you want to me. Just spare the children."

Only then did Cammie see how gaunt Coach Elliot's face was. Her hands clasped into angry fists as she thought of what the monster was going to do to the man.

"Captain Greenfield, how do you manage to turn into Mavet?" Alex asked.

As Cammie shot him a look of surprise, her friend mouthed, "Keep him talking. Mr. Walrus and Mr. Reed are on their way. Remember?"

"Oh!" Of course, Alex was right. The rescue mission hadn't been cancelled after all. All they needed to do was to stay alive for a few more minutes.

Captain Greenfield folded his arms on his chest, looking smug. "It's a special gift of mine, if you want to know the truth. So you guys liked my dear friend Mavet?"

"Well, it was really very impressive you turning into that...hmm...Mavet!" Alex sounded dead serious, but Cammie didn't miss a quick wink in her direction.

Captain Greenfield smoothed out the invisible creases on his shirt. "Well, you're not that dumb, Alex Bernard. I think it won't hurt you to know how I acquired this wonderful gift. How about you, Cammie Wester? Are you ready to hear the confessions of a brilliant cop?"

Cammie glanced at Alex and saw him nod. "Yes, sure."

"All right. After all, you'll carry my secret to the grave, so why not have a little fun?"

Cammie cringed as she heard the cop talk about the grave. Immediately, Alex's warm hand slid into hers, giving her an encouraging squeeze.

"You see, Elliot and I have known each other since childhood. We were both promising skaters, you know."

"You were a skater?" Cammie couldn't hide her shock.

Captain Greenfield's hazel eyes turned red immediately. "Is that so hard to believe?"

"Uh…no, of course not!" Alex exclaimed, shooting Cammie a warning look.

"Okay. As you might already know, Elliot trained here, in Skateland. I'm from San Francisco. But we often met at different competitions, and I usually won."

"Not always." Coach Elliot smiled for the first time.

"I beat you at the novice level!" Captain Greenfield bellowed. "I came in second while you were only third. You can't deny it, Elliot."

"Like it matters," Coach Elliot muttered.

"Oh, it does!" Captain Greenfield said haughtily. "Actually, it was after that competition that our coaches thought the two of us should try skating pairs. We were both tall for our age and pretty strong already."

Captain Greenfield looked at Coach Elliot, as though waiting for a confirmation. When none came, the cop went on. "Our coaches brought two girls to the audition. The girls were two years younger than us. We were twelve, so the girls were ten. One of them was Felicia."

A dark shadow crossed Coach Elliot's face.

"The other was…hmm…I don't even remember her name anymore."

"It was Inga," Coach Elliot said, his face turned away.

Captain Greenfield cackled. "Look at him! He even remembers my first partner's name." Suddenly, his face contorted. Veins on his forehead bulged. For a second, Cammie feared the man might explode. "If you liked that girl enough to remember her name years later, why didn't you choose her? Ah?"

A lonely snowflake shot up in the air as though frightened by Captain Greenfield's outburst and then slowly descended onto the gray ice.

"It was the coaches' decision, Gilbert," Coach Elliot said softly. "I was supposed to skate with Felicia, and you got Inga. That was it."

"Yes, that was it. Of course. So simple." Captain Greenfield pulled his collar hard as though struggling for air. "You got the petite beauty with excellent jumps while I...well, I was stuck with a fat loser who could barely get off the ice on her double flip. I wanted Felicia. Don't you get it?"

"Why didn't you say anything?"

By that time, the level of Captain Greenfield's voice had reached the sound of blasting thunder. The man's face shone with perspiration. "I spoke to my coach at every practice. Yes, every day. No exceptions. I told her I needed another partner. Yet I was stuck with Inga the Blob for two years, until she became wider than she was taller and lost all of her doubles. She stopped skating altogether."

"Well, it happens all the time, doesn't it?"

It seemed to Cammie that the louder Captain Greenfield got, the calmer Coach Elliot's demeanor became. Her coach didn't appear to be intimidated by the transformed monster in the slightest.

"Well, it didn't happen to Felicia!" Captain Greenfield shouted. "So the two of you were lovey-dovey, winning competitions, and I was nowhere. It was too late to switch back to singles, so my coach engaged in endless search for another partner. Finally, they gave me another girl. Betsy was her name."

The cop stopped to catch his breath, his fingers clasping and unclasping at the chest level.

Alex cleared his throat. "But, Captain Greenfield, there's nothing unusual about your situation. Look, even McKenna and Dayne, who came in first at the Junior Nationals last year, each of them had changed partners three times before they even started winning competitions."

"And why should I care about some stupid kids winning or losing?" Captain Greenfield yelled, his eyes flashing red again. "What does matter is that while I was teaching my sloppy partners side-by-side crossovers, *he* became a junior national champion with Felicia!"

The officer jerked his head in Coach Elliot's direction, spraying the ice with saliva. "If only I had gotten Felicia!"

Cammie glanced at Alex, who shrugged. So far, they hadn't heard anything extraordinary, anything that would justify Captain Greenfield's venomous hatred of Coach Elliot. The man's testimony was a typical story of a young couple trying to make it to the top. Some partners managed to skate together for years. Yet not everybody got that lucky. Very often, skaters would quit for one reason or another. And no one else, to Cammie's knowledge, had managed to transform into Mavet, except for Brenda, Wilhelmina's rival, of course. It was weird, though. Could jealousy be a good enough reason to turn a skater into a murderer?

"Betsy and I still made it to junior nationals," Captain Greenfield said bitterly. "Only we didn't medal. In fact, we came in dead last. But he…they…"

The man seemed to have choked on his own saliva.

"They won!" Cammie exclaimed. Not that she wanted to further annoy Captain Greenfield; the words simply jumped out of her mouth. She didn't miss Coach Elliot's warm smile and a wink.

"For the second time!" Captain Greenfield screeched. "But that's not even the point. They were really much better skaters than us at that time, so I hadn't really expected to beat them. But something happened the night of the closing banquet. And that…"

A coughing fit interrupted the officer's speech. He wrapped his hands around his chest and bent forward as loud barking sounds came out of his mouth. Coach Elliot's face was impassive.

"All the participants were invited to the closing banquet, regardless of the placings," Captain Greenfield said, taking deep breaths almost after each word. "So we were there too. Betsy was whisked away immediately. She had a lot of friends, you see. She never took skating seriously. For her, being at the rink was like a social outing. I didn't really mind her leaving me. I was in a lousy mood, and I wanted to be alone. So I went out to the hotel lobby to cool down. And then I saw her…"

Captain Greenfield's voice softened. Cammie could even discern notes of tenderness.

"She stood by the floor-to-ceiling window, looking at the sunset."

Alex coughed. "Excuse me, sir. Who are you talking about?"

Captain Greenfield turned his head in Alex's direction, and there was almost childlike surprise in his hazel eyes. "Felicia, of course. Didn't I say?"

Coach Elliot appeared puzzled. His darkened eyes were fixed on the cop's face with intense concentration.

"The dark red streaks in the sky matched the color of her hair." Captain Greenfield's face lit up. "You see, her hair had the most amazing shade. Some people called it red. She preferred the word *auburn*. But really, there are no words in English to give Felicia's hair full credit. It had the richest palette I had ever encountered. Every lock appeared different. All the possible shades of red were there, rusty, burgundy, brownish, cognac, you name it. And when she skated, she wore her hair in a bun, and—"

"Now wait a minute!" Coach Elliot straightened up. "Where are you going with all this, Gilbert?"

Captain Greenfield raised his right hand, a glazed look in his eyes. "Wait, Elliot. Let me bask in the glorious memory a little longer, for nothing can bring her back. She's only a memory, a distant image, a ghost, a reflection…"

Cammie gave Alex a questioning look and watched him mouth, *How weird!*

"That night, she had her hair down, and the rich curls fell down her back. And at that moment, I realized that all I wanted in life was to stand by her side and look."

Coach Elliot shifted his feet caught in blade brakes. "Gilbert, you have no right to talk about Felicia like that!"

Captain Greenfield laughed "Oh, I don't, do I? I beg to differ, Elliot. Don't forget, you're my prisoner. So I'll call the shots now. Anyway…where was I? I feel the warmth and the beauty slipping away. The gray ice and the rocks are consuming me…And it's all you!" he roared as he jumped at Coach Elliot. His fist collided with Coach Elliot's face.

Restrained by the blade brakes, Coach Elliot fell hard on his back. Cammie and Alex jumped to their feet. Yet before any of them took a step in Coach Elliot's direction, Captain Greenfield stretched his hand toward them. "You'll stay where you are."

"Leave him alone, you jerk!" Cammie wished her voice weren't so high-pitched.

"You loser!" Alex spat on the snow.

"Manners, kiddies, or I'll kill you first."

Captain Greenfield's eyes were scarlet again, and to her horror, Cammie saw his hat slide off, revealing what looked like burgeoning horns.

"He transforms into Mavet when he gets upset!" Cammie whispered to Alex.

"Looks like it." Alex whispered back, his fists clenched.

"Felicia. Oh, Felicia, why did you do it to me?" Captain Greenfield groaned. "I loved you, I really did!"

He wrapped his hands around his head. The horns seemed to be shrinking slowly.

He had loved Felicia, Coach Elliot's wife? A monster, Mavet, actually being in love?

"I still couldn't open my mouth." Captain Greenfield sighed deeply. His arms fell limply down the sides. "I looked her in the eyes, big and brown, with streaks of gold, and I wanted to say a lot of things, but I just couldn't. And she...she giggled and said, 'Did you bite your tongue off when you fell on that double axel?' Not a nice thing to say to someone who had just lost a competition. What do you think? But I was quiet, staring at her like the biggest loser, and then something rose in me and I asked, 'Will you skate with me?' Because that was what I really wanted. Felicia should have been my partner from the very beginning. We would have been great together. If it hadn't been for that freak Elliot..."

Captain Greenfield moaned loudly. He brought his hands to his throat.

"Well, the coaches chose Coach Elliot to skate with Felicia," Alex said. "So isn't it time to forget about it and move on?"

Captain Greenfield raised his fists and shook them in Alex's direction. "Forget, you say? Oh no. Nothing can bring my luck back. My skating career is ruined. And so is my life. Now—"

"Wait! What did Felicia say when you asked her to skate with you?" Cammie asked quickly. She had been looking around her surreptitiously, waiting, hoping that the next minute, the old black-and-yellow Zamboni would come to their rescue. Even though there was no visible opening in the rocks through which the vehicle could arrive, it didn't matter. Both Mr. Walrus and Mr. Reed had magical powers; they would surely think of something. All Cammie, Alex, and Coach Elliot needed was time. So the best way to distract Mavet from attacking was to keep him talking.

"What do you think she said? She laughed."

Captain Greenfield buried his face in his hands and sat immobile for a few moments.

Coach Elliot spread his arms. "Gilbert, honestly, I had no idea. Surely Felicia couldn't have meant anything bad. She was a jovial girl, you know, so—"

"So you think it's funny, huh?" Captain Greenfield barked. "Huh? Answer me!"

There was pain in Coach Elliot's face.

"The two of you moved up to seniors the next year," Captain Greenfield said bitterly. "We didn't have a chance. It was Betsy who kept us behind, of course. I didn't give up on Felicia, though. I sent her gifts, flowers, little toys—"

"So it was you!" Coach Elliot cried out. "She always wondered—"

"She was almost ready to dump you and accept my proposal!" Captain Greenfield hissed. "I know she was."

"Gilbert"—a pale smile touched Coach Elliot's lips—"I'm sorry, but it's not true. Felicia never wanted—"

"What do you know?" Captain Greenfield advanced toward Coach Elliot. "It was all you. You kept talking her out of switching partners. Of course, all you cared about was your own career. And meanwhile, Betsy decided to go to college. My coach suggested I do the same. 'You are not champion material!'"

"Gilbert, I'm really sorry if I hurt you in some way," Coach Elliot said quietly, "but honestly, I didn't even know—"

"Of course you didn't know!" Captain Greenfield spat out. "And you didn't even care."

"You should have moved on," Cammie said, surprised at her own courage. "Skaters who harbor bitterness against those who have succeeded more in their careers turn into witches."

Captain Greenfield spun on the ice. "Oh, really? Is that what our dear Skateland president told you? Because I can quote her too: 'Once a skater, always a skater.' Ever heard her say that?"

The man waited for Cammie and Alex to say something and then went on.

"I went to the police academy. I tried to forget about skating, Felicia, Elliot, everything. But they were becoming famous. They were on television. They were continuously interviewed. And of course, how could I miss skating competitions? I watched every one of them. And each time I saw Felicia in Elliot's arms, I got sick. I mean it, physically ill. I had high fever and seizures. I felt myself deteriorating. While those two were improving fast, my skills were disappearing at record speed. Even my doubles were already gone. And then…" Captain Greenfield took a deep breath.

"After they won their first senior nationals, the freak asked her to marry him, right at the arena, after they finished their free program. The reporters made a big deal out of it. They never stopped raving about how romantic it had been. But for me, it was the last straw.

Seeing the two of them skate together was bad enough. But the very thought of them living happily thereafter almost ripped me apart. I was thinking of a quick and painless way of ending my life until one day, it dawned on me. Why? Was it my fault? The two of them would enjoy the glory of being national champions, and they would go to the worlds, to the Olympics, while I, Gilbert Greenfield, would rot in the grave. No, that wasn't fair. At that point, it was all about justice for me. I had to make sure the culprits were punished. The two of them had to pay for what they had done to me."

A loud moan came from Coach Elliot's direction. "Wait! So it was you? *You* killed Felicia?"

A horrible grimace of satisfaction settled on the cop's face. "Did you just figure it out? Gosh, Elliot. You're really thick. All those years, you thought I had finally come to grips with being a mediocrity. You probably gloated over the fact that you were better, didn't you?"

Coach Elliot's face was white. "You murdered my wife!" With a horrible shout, Coach Elliot lunged at Captain Greenfield. His blade brakes stuck to the ice. He jerked forward, lost his balance, and fell.

"Ha ha ha!" Captain Greenfield took a few backstrokes and stopped in the middle of the pond, looking amused. "So finally, I got you mad, Elliot. Because you were always sweet, and charming, and kind. What a delight to see you act like a man!"

"You, you…" Coach Elliot rolled on his side and sat up, his face contorted in agony. "You tampered with our music, didn't you?"

"Excellent, Elliot." Captain Greenfield looked like a cat who was about to feast on a delicious fish dinner. "See, planning murder wasn't easy. I didn't want to go to prison. I realized that after I got rid of both of you, my real life would begin."

Coach Elliot got up on his feet slowly and then jumped forward at Captain Greenfield. The heavy blade brakes brought Coach Elliot down again. He fell hard.

Captain Greenfield beamed. "Don't even try!"

"And you think you loved Felicia? You should be ashamed of yourself!" Cammie shouted.

The officer's crimson eyes slid down her face. "Me? Ashamed? What do you know, young lady? Loved her? Not anymore. I hated her as much as I hated Elliot. Do you realize how I suffered because of those two? I had severe seizures each time I saw them. I would throw up and then pass out and wake up drenched in sweat. And afterward, I would be tormented with horrible headaches for days."

Cammie rubbed her forehead. She still couldn't understand. How could a man think of killing another skater only because he and his partner were more successful?

"So one of those nights when I was in deep pain, Mavet visited me," Captain Greenfield said importantly. "See, Mavet is an extremely wise creature. He has tremendous powers. He assured me we would be able to do great things together. Justice would be restored. I allowed him to penetrate me, and the two of us became one. That's when I received the powers I had never even dreamed of. I could cause severe thunderstorms. I used them to punish those who treated me with disrespect. With Mavet's help, I learned to control avalanches. I can send the west wind to blow over a town or village of my choice. At some point, I made myself a home here, in this cave. It might look wild to you, but it's quite comfortable inside and beautifully furnished. I would take you all on a tour, except it's too late. Midnight is coming, and then it will be over for you and a new beginning for me."

Cammie looked up at the dirty gray sky. *Help us!* she prayed silently. *Let Mr. Reed and Mr. Walrus come quickly, please!*

"So what happened next?" Alex asked.

Captain Greenfield smiled. "I never forgot my original goal, of course. I had to punish the Monroes. And Mavet offered me a perfect solution. 'Make it look like an accident,' he said. 'This way, the woman will be dead, and the guy will keep blaming himself for the rest of his life. He might even end up kicking the bucket too.'"

"And…and you weren't even sorry for Felicia?" Alex's voice cracked.

"Nope!"

"You attacked an innocent woman!" Coach Elliot shouted. He made a desperate attempt at getting closer to Captain Greenfield again.

Captain Greenfield chuckled. "What a joy to see you suffer, Elliot! You're getting everything you deserve. Justice has triumphed."

"You…you're a monster!" Cammie cried out.

Captain Greenfield lowered his head in a mocking bow. "That's who I am, young lady, a proud monster. But back to my story. It was important for my retribution to look like a skating accident. I absolutely had to make the two of them fall. And let me tell you something, folks. That wasn't easy. Both Felicia and Elliot were very strong skaters with good technique. What could I do? Tamper with their skates? So what? That would have messed up some of their elements but wouldn't have killed them. And then I had an idea, or actually, it was Mavet who came up with the wonderful plan. You see, in addition to my skating background, I also have music talent. I even took violin and piano lessons when I was younger. My mother always said that a skater who didn't know music was merely a robot, not a true performer. Like him!"

Captain Greenfield giggled as he waved his hand in Coach Elliot's direction.

When neither Cammie nor Alex made a comment, the cop went on.

"And I was actually a good musician. I could even write my own music, and much nicer pieces than your stupid Mr. Walrus, by the way. So Mavet suggested that I write the music of death. It was easy. All I had to do was concentrate on Elliot and Felicia dying when I was composing the piece. Mavet helped me, of course. Together, we created a piece that could be played over the skater's performance music. The music of death changes the basic piece only a little, yet it makes the individual skate faster and faster. Then the skater loses control over his body and starts making mistakes. Or he might simply move around until his heart gives up and he dies. A wonderful death. What do you think?"

Coach Elliot was breathing hard. Cammie felt terribly hollow inside. She still couldn't believe that the man she had known for years, the police officer she had always respected, was capable of such a horrible crime.

"It all worked beautifully," Captain Greenfield went on. "The freak dropped Felicia, and she died instantly. Her loser of a husband retreated from the skating scene. I was finally relieved. That was it; no more torture for me. I got a good job offer from the Skateland president and moved here. Everything went well. Even though Elliot was still alive, it didn't bother me much as long as he didn't skate anymore. And then I got wind of the show *Magic on Ice* coming to Skateland, and, what a surprise, the freak was in it."

Captain Greenfield glared at Coach Elliot's crumpled figure. The man sat with his head buried in his hands.

"The moment I saw him at the show, I knew I wasn't completely healed. I had to get rid of the jerk if I wanted to keep my sanity. But I didn't have my CD with the music of death with me. So Mavet's curse was out. I had to act fast because I was sure that after the show, I might have to look for Elliot overseas. *Magic on Ice* tours a lot, you know. It was easy to intercept a soda bottle. The bottles had to go through security check before being handed to the show participants anyway. It just happened so that I had a full dosage of *Raal* with me."

"The poison," Captain Greenfield explained, apparently noticing Cammie and Alex's startled faces. "Actually, I've been carrying it in a hidden pocket since I first thought of taking my own life. Mavet was the one who helped me to brew it. Perfect poison it is, guys, absolutely outstanding. No side effects. Death is virtually painless."

"That's not what Winja felt!" Alex said through his teeth.

Captain Greenfield chuckled. "The poison was meant for humans, not witches. I was perplexed myself when Winja didn't die. 'What's wrong?' I asked Mavet. I thought *Raal* was perfect. And then Mavet made it clear to me. The poison is only meant for humans, not the witches. How ironic. All the evil Winja had done served as the antidote for this extremely deadly poison. My plan failed."

Captain Greenfield shot a derogatory smile in Coach Elliot's direction.

"And I didn't even manage to poison the witch. For your information, kiddies, I take my duty of keeping Skateland witch-free very seriously. By the way, have you noticed that there have been no witches' attacks here lately? Have you? Hey, talk to me. It's not polite to ignore an officer's question!"

Cammie quickly looked at Alex, who shook his head. She knew what her friend was thinking. The man had the nerve to talk about politeness after he had confessed to killing one person and plotting to kill another.

"Okay. Back to Elliot," Captain Greenfield said. "Right after the show, I found out that the loser was coming to Skateland to teach. I knew once the freak was here, there would be plenty of opportunities to get rid of him. Yet I had to be very careful. Poisoning was out of the question because it would have meant Winja's unfortunate surviving hadn't been accidental. Shooting him? Oh, how I wish I had done it, but unfortunately, the crime would have been easily traced to me. I'm a policeman, after all, and who else but security personnel carry guns here? What do you think?"

Nobody answered him. The only distinct sound was the howling of the wind.

"So I decided what had worked once would definitely be good enough for another murder. I'm talking of the music of death, of course. Tonight, I'll give you all a wonderful opportunity to listen to my masterpiece. In fact, you will be active participants of this performance of death. Okay. It's almost time. Let's start with Elliot."

"Wait!" Cammie yelled. "Did you attack me too during St. Valentine's show?"

Captain Greenfield nodded, smiling brightly. "Guilty as charged."

"How about Dana?" Cammie jumped up.

The officer's smile widened.

"But why?" Alex asked, shaking his fists. "So you hated Coach Elliot. But what was wrong with Dana and Cammie?"

"I'm giving you my last warning, Gilbert," Coach Elliot said. "If you touch the children—"

Captain Greenfield spread his arms. "Then what? What can you do, freak?"

For the first time, Captain Greenfield looked a little sheepish. "Okay. Let me explain to you what happened. Of course, Elliot was my target all along. Unfortunately, no plan is completely devoid of glitches."

"Glitches?" Cammie gasped. He called attacking innocent people *glitches*?

"Sure. Do you know what happened during that audition when Dana was injured? I wasn't even planning on doing anything. I was busy chasing the witches, and I didn't notice the CD with my music falling out of my pocket. Apparently, somebody picked it up and positioned it on top of the other CDs next to the player. Dana put it into the player by mistake. And the rest, as they say, is history." He spread his arms.

Just like that, history, Cammie thought. *The girl gave up skating for good, and he couldn't care less.*

"How about Cammie?" Alex asked.

"Oh, that's obvious," Captain Greenfield groaned. "It was the freak's fault again."

He turned to the ashen-faced Coach Elliot. "Why didn't you make sure your partner's skates were in order before the show? Ah? If you had, you and Christel would have skated when you were supposed to, and Cammie wouldn't have got hurt. By the way, my apology, Cammie."

Cammie turned away from the cop. She felt contaminated even by looking at him.

"Okay. We only have a few seconds left."

As though overhearing Captain Greenfield, a hidden clock struck twelve times from inside the cave.

Cammie shuddered. The next thing she felt was Alex's hand slipping into hers. Captain Greenfield flicked his hand in the direction of the cave. The rock moved, revealing a niche with a CD player. Captain Greenfield pressed an invisible button, and four speakers appeared from hidden niches around the perimeter of the rink.

"See how easy it is with Mavet's help?" Captain Greenfield winked at them. If the guy hadn't just confessed to murder and not promised to kill them all, Cammie might think that he was about to offer them a nice gift. He looked absolutely calm, relaxed. Even the captain's normally pale cheeks were a healthy pink color.

"Enjoy!" Captain Greenfield pressed the *play* button, and the first chords poured from the speakers.

Cammie was sure the music of death would consist entirely of heavy drum beats and wailings. Yet that wasn't the case. She actually recognized a few musical instruments, including trumpets, a saxophone, and a flute. All of them were playing a solemn tune. Several violins joined them, mourning, whining over something precious that had been irreparably destroyed. A cello and a bass echoed in the distance, adding depth to the original melody.

"Okay. That was your prelude, Elliot." With quick, trained moves, Captain Greenfield set Coach Elliot free from blade brakes and pushed him onto the ice.

"Don't!" Cammie shouted. "Coach Elliot, get off this ice now."

Unfortunately, it looked as though Coach Elliot had absolutely no control of his body. The minute his blades touched the ice, he glided forward.

"Coach Elliot, don't skate. Come here!" Alex stood up.

The man spread his arms. "It's just happening. I can't stop." He glided around the perimeter of the rink, looking as polished and graceful as ever.

"Now we'll all sit back and enjoy the show." Captain Greenfield said.

He jumped onto the ice and did a few twizzles in both directions. Fire appeared from nowhere, engulfing the officer's figure, and in another minute, his body started growing. His arms bulged and bent at an unnatural angle. Sharp, yellowish claws replaced the carefully trimmed fingernails. The neatly combed dark brown hair became long and matted. Sharp horns shot from the strangely deformed, squashy head.

"Mavet!" Cammie jerked back instinctively.

Glistening blood-red eyes stared at her from inside the brown, hairy face. "And now let the music tamper with the loser's body rhythm!"

Mavet's front paws moved back and forth as though conducting an invisible orchestra. The music picked up speed. The string instruments screamed as though from pain, and a lonely oboe spat out a warning that something macabre was about to happen. The sound of cymbals blasted, and at the same time, sharp pain shot through Cammie's heart. She cringed as she watched Coach Elliot's left blade slip.

"Ouch!" Next to her, Alex grimaced and pressed his hand against his chest.

On the ice, Coach Elliot did several Arabian cartwheels. He went into a high double axel followed by a triple toe loop.

"I think he's hurting!" Cammie said coarsely as she watched Coach Elliot's chest heaving up and down.

"I wonder how long the freak's going to last." Fire shot out of Mavet's mouth, making Cammie and Alex retreat. Their backs hit the hard rock again.

Nothing bad is going to happen, Cammie told herself as her head brushed the cold stone. *Coach Elliot will finish the program, and then Mr. Walrus and Mr. Reed will come, and we'll all go to Skateland. And tomorrow, this stupid cop will be fired. Surely Wilhelmina won't want him in Skateland after all he has done. Besides, who says he has super powers? He's just a showoff.* Cammie knew that if she believed even for a second that what was happening on the ice was real, she would lose her mind. *Mavet is nothing but a disguise,* she whispered. *It's probably some stupid costume that the cop has been keeping in his closet since Halloween.*

Coach Elliot went into a low sit spin. Textbook perfect, Cammie thought, surprised that she could even think of skating technique at a time like this. Coach Elliot kept spinning, picking up speed as he went around.

"He'd better stop now," Alex said, sounding concerned.

Cammie shook her head. It couldn't be real. Coach Elliot had already done at least a hundred revolutions. "It's enough, Coach Elliot!" Cammie shouted.

The man obviously didn't hear her. He straightened his skating leg, which made him spin even faster.

"He can't stop!" Alex shouted.

"Captain Greenfield, do something!" Cammie screamed.

"Just enjoy it, kiddies!" Mavet did a few power pulls next to the edge of the rink, his brown hair flying in all directions.

"Are you out of your mind?" Cammie yelled. "He'll get sick!"

The monster coughed out a fiery ball. "Correction. He's going to die."

"We've got to stop him." Cammie grabbed Alex's hand.

Alex nodded, his eyes fixed on the tall, spinning figure in the middle of the rink. "I'll block him from the right, and you stand on the left. We'll try to catch him together. Come on!"

Before they could step onto the ice, Mavet took a deep breath and blew in their direction. A huge fiery ball rolled across the rink and stopped right at their feet. "I wouldn't try it, kiddies. Mavet's curse is already operating. This dance is for Elliot alone. Just touch the ice and it'll catch fire."

"No!" The tears in Cammie's eyes made everything appear blurry. She could no longer differentiate between the fiery ball and the gray rocks.

"He's about to fall any minute!" Alex cried out.

Cammie wiped the tears and strained her eyes to see. Coach Elliot's spinning figure was barely discernible;

all she could see was a dark swirl. The music moaned and groaned with another blast of cymbals and drums.

"His heart is about to give out," Alex croaked, and as Cammie glanced at her friend, she saw that his eyes were rounded in horror.

"Alex!" Cammie choked on her tears. She could barely see anything anymore. The rink swam in front of her. Coach Elliot was going to die, and nothing could change it. It was over. Alex shouted something in her ear. She ignored him. She closed her eyes not to see Coach Elliot's spinning figure. If the man was about to die, she'd better not see it. And if Mavet started killing Alex and her too, she would keep her eyes closed until everything was over.

Alex's voice grew louder, as though her friend was trying to block the music of death. It was no use; the morbid melody was too powerful.

"Kanga bag, Cammie! Do you hear me?"

What? Had Alex said, "Kanga bag"? What did her skating bag have to do with anything? Did Alex think Kanga could rescue them? Even if they could escape holding on to Kanga's handle, there was no place to go.

"Cammie, where exactly is Mr. Dulcimer's CD? Where did you put it?"

A CD? What CD? Cammie opened her eyes.

Alex knelt on the snow, rummaging through Kanga bag.

"What?"

"Is this it?" Alex held a silver-and-blue disc.

"What're you...the music of life!" she shouted. Of course, how could she forget? The moment Cammie saw the CD, she remembered her last music interpretation class and Mr. Dulcimer's words.

"The music of life can break the curse of death," the teacher had said.

"Alex, you're a genius! We need to get to the CD player. Now!"

"I told you. Wait here!" Alex picked up the CD and edged his way around to the CD player, making sure his feet didn't touch the ice. Mavet didn't seem to notice Alex's maneuver. His fiery eyes were glued to Coach Elliot's figure.

The music was even more sinister. Cammie could hear the sound of celeste in the background. She knew what it meant. Death was about to swallow Prince Elliot. Cammie clenched her fists. *Hurry, Alex.*

The horrible music stopped suddenly as though tripping over a deep rut on clear ice. Mavet's eight horns turned in the direction of the player. "What the—?"

A soft, tender sound sprang from the player, filling the area, overpowering the stench of death. Cammie recognized a flute, but the tune was bright and uplifting. The whole place seemed to light up immediately, and the heavy load that had been pressing on Cammie's heart lifted. She felt light and airy.

"Wait! What? That's not my music!" Mavet roared. "Stop it now!"

"Cammie, let's skate!"

She looked at Alex, who smiled at her from across the rink.

"But…" She swallowed hard and glanced at the man in the middle of the rink. Coach Elliot wasn't moving anymore. He lay on the ice, his face on top of his hands.

"Coach Elliot!" Cammie jumped onto the ice, expecting something terrible to happen any moment. Yet the hard surface didn't feel any different from what she was used to. She skidded to a stop and knelt by Coach Elliot's side. His eyes were closed, but he was breathing. Yes, he was alive. *He was alive!*

"Cammie, we've got to skate!" Alex called.

"Wait!" She gently touched Coach Elliot's hair. "Coach Elliot, are you all right?"

The man didn't move; he appeared to be asleep.

"Coach Elliot!"

"Cammie, we need to do a program to break the curse of death. Come on!"

What was Alex trying to get her to do, skate? Cammie could barely move. Every limb in her body was numb.

"Cammie, you can do it! Come join me!"

Cammie wondered if sloppy performance would be good enough to break the curse. But the music floated across the rink, and there was lightness to it. Cammie looked at the circular pond. Alex was already gliding across the rink, looking strong and graceful. The music picked up speed. It sang of victory, of the triumph of life over death. At some point, Cammie felt she couldn't take her eyes off Alex. His steps were simple, and he didn't attempt any jumps. Yet Cammie felt she had never seen a more beautiful performance. It was like the dance of snowflakes, like the silvery moon streaks

411

glowing over the dark ice. And suddenly, Cammie realized that she wanted to skate more than anything else in the world.

She didn't even feel tired anymore; her body was strong and light. She took a deep breath, spread her arms, and moved forward in a huge spiral, holding the edge longer than she normally did. The sky swayed over her, and as she turned backward, there was a break in the clouds, and then the moon poured out its silvery light all over her, Alex, and Coach Elliot.

"What? What's going on?" Mavet roared. His claws scraped angrily against the ice.

Cammie skated past him with a bright smile.

"Stop that music! It hurts!" Mavet moaned.

Cammie and Alex ignored him.

In the middle of the rink, Coach Elliot stirred up and then slowly raised his head. "Where am I? What's going on?"

"Coach Elliot!" Cammie skated up to him. "Are you all right?"

"I…I think so." The man looked at his arms and legs and then slowly stood up. "What happened?"

"Argh!" On the edge of the rink, Mavet raised his four paws, apparently trying to get up. His claws buckled, and he sank back, growling wildly.

Before Cammie could say another word, there was a blasting sound, and the big rock on her left cracked in the middle.

"What's that?" Alex skated up to Cammie and Coach Elliot, looking concerned.

The music of life was still playing.

The rock collapsed in front of them like a card structure, and a familiar black-and-yellow Zamboni rolled onto the ice.

"Mr. Walrus!" Cammie shouted.

Help had arrived.

The Zamboni stopped next to the three of them. Mr. Reed sprung off the step, made two revolutions in the air, and landed on his right backward outside edge.

"Just a double, hmm. Well, I'm not wearing my self-spinning boots." Mr. Reed appeared calm, as though they were in the middle of a routine freestyle session.

"You're here!" Alex exclaimed.

"Well, unfortunately, we're a little late." Mr. Walrus joined Mr. Reed on the ice, rubbing his gloved hands. "We got caught in an avalanche, and it took us half an hour to dig out the Zamboni. Thank God you're still alive. I was so worried about you. What's going on?"

Mr. Reed did a quick pivot and then surveyed the scene. His light blue eyes seemed to be taking in everything: Alex frozen in the middle of the rink, his face red with excitement, and Cammie with her arms wrapped around Coach Elliot. Mavet lay in a heap close to the entrance to the cave, his fur steaming.

"What I hear surely doesn't sound like the music of death," Mr. Reed said calmly.

"Excuse me?" Mr. Walrus pressed his red-gloved hand to his ear. His face brightened. "The music of life! The piece is unmistakingly Dulcimer's. But...where did it come from?"

"From Cammie's Kanga bag," Alex said excitedly.

"Please explain." Mr. Walrus's moustache twitched.

"I wasn't aware that you had music of life with you, Cammie!" Mr. Reed's penetrating eyes were fixed on Cammie's face, making her feel uncomfortable.

She smiled nervously. "Uh...Mr. Dulcimer gave it to me as a prize for interpreting music correctly."

"Oh!" Mr. Walrus said.

Mr. Reed's gray eyebrows rose. "If you had only told me—"

For the first time in her life, Cammie felt she had an advantage over the magical skate sharpener. "But you never asked me, sir."

"Well, in that case..." Mr. Reed turned in Mavet's direction.

For some strange reason, the monster no longer looked intimidating but rather grotesque. The once sharp-looking horns hung limply from the creature's head, the eyes were dull, and the brown hair looked matted with sweat and dirt.

"Well, well, Mavet, the spirit of death. It looks like you have just been swallowed up in victory," Mr. Reed said softly.

Mavet's body jerked as though the monster was trying to get up, and then his body shrank again. The beast who had been so intimidating only a few minutes ago now strongly reminded Cammie of a beaten animal, barely alive. Mr. Reed took a few steps forward and moved across the rink in a fast footwork. Cammie recognized several Choctaws, a loop figure, and a few twizzles and counters. The man finished with a mazurka jump and then stopped in the middle of the rink and stretched his slender hand in Mavet's direction. "Mavet, reveal yourself!"

Fire shot out of Mavet's jaws, and the monster was gone. Sitting on the ice, his hands over his face, was Captain Greenfield.

Mr. Walrus grabbed his beard. "On my gosh! Greenfield? I'll be darned!"

"Well, I can't say I'm too surprised," Mr. Reed said.

"Really? No, I had absolutely no idea. I suspected anybody but him. Oh, Gilbert, how could you?"

"I'm not saying I suspected him, but he was at the scene of every attack, wasn't he?" Mr. Reed spoke slowly and distinctly.

"Every attack? You mean…Felicia Monroe too?"

"That's exactly what I said."

"Oh my!"

"Walter, before we continue this discussion, we need to take the felon into custody," Mr. Reed said.

"You have no authority over me!" Captain Greenfield shouted hysterically. "You're not a police officer."

"Sure I'm not. And I'm not giving you any orders; I'm simply asking you to get into the Zamboni." Mr. Reed stretched out his hand. "It's for your own safety, Gilbert. Because if you don't…you know what's going to happen to you, don't you? Come on."

"No!" the cop took a few steps back, a menacing glint in his eyes.

"Gilbert, I've got to warn you—"

"I don't care what you say. Mavet, where are you? Mavet!"

There was a whooshing sound as the cop's body transformed again. The bulky front paws spread, revealing enormous wings. The monster shot in the air, rising high above the gloomy rocks.

"Gilbert!" Mr. Reed called again. "You'd better come back. It's for your own good."

Thunder blasted, or perhaps it was the monster's raucous laughter. For a few seconds, Mavet hung over them like a gigantic bat, and then it glided behind the rocks and disappeared from view.

"He's gone!" Alex slapped himself on the knee. "What a shame. He belongs in prison."

"I wish we could have stopped him!" Mr. Walrus too looked disappointed.

"So do I. But he made his choice," Mr. Reed said calmly, his eyes still fixed on the rock behind which Mavet had just disappeared.

"So tomorrow, he'll attack somebody again," Alex said angrily.

"He might even come back and finish off Coach Elliot," Cammie exclaimed.

Mr. Reed shook his head. "He won't."

Alex cleared his throat. "What makes you so sure, sir?"

"Because he's gone. The music of life destroyed the connection between Captain Greenfield and Mavet. The spirit of death can't reside in the man's body anymore. Yet because Greenfield chose to stay with him, the evil spirit will simply dispose of him."

"Dispose?" Cammie whispered. "What does it mean?"

"He'll kill him, of course," Mr. Reed said, and a dark shadow clouded his pale blue eyes. "Have you ever wondered what happened to Brenda, Wilhelmina's rival?"

"N-no," Cammie stammered. "What?"

"She died shortly after Wilhelmina used the music of life on her." Mr. Walrus came up to Coach Elliot and gently led him to the Zamboni.

"Mrs. Van Uffeln never told me about using the music of life," Cammie said.

"Sure she did," Mr. Reed finally looked her in the face. "Mr. Dulcimer's father wrote it for her when she was rehabilitating from her arthritis. This is the reason she can still skate so well."

So that was it. How wonderful was it that Cammie had taken Wilhelmina's advice about taking her music interpretation class seriously!

"Mrs. Van Uffeln knew exactly what you needed, didn't she?" Mr. Reed asked.

As always, the man could read her thoughts. Before Cammie had a chance to respond, Mr. Walrus called from the Zamboni.

"We'd better go, Mel. We need to take those three to the hospital."

Alex shook his head. "Cammie and I are fine, thank you."

"That's right. It's Coach Elliot who needs help," Cammie said. "He skated to the music of death almost until the end."

"Oh I will live." Coach Elliot waved at them from the Zamboni, where he sat supported by Mr. Walrus.

He was still breathing heavily, and his face was pale, but at least he was alive. Oh how wonderful it was that Prince Elliot was alive!

Mr. Reed put his hand on Cammie's shoulder. "Off we go, then. It's great that you kids are fine, but you surely need to be in bed."

When Cammie and Alex got settled on top of the Zamboni, Cammie remembered one more thing. "Mr. Walrus, how come you had all those musical instruments in your house?"

Mr Walrus turned around. "Oh, yes. You thought I was Mavet, didn't you?"

Cammie felt so embarrassed that she pulled her scarf all the way up to cover her face.

"Well, it's quite understandable. I don't know what I would have thought under the circumstances. Anyway, there was a fire in Mr. Dulcimer's house a few weeks ago."

"What caused it?" Alex asked quickly.

"Not what but who." Mr. Reed grunted. "It was Mavet, of course. He breathed fire on the house to destroy Mr. Dulcimer's instruments. Mavet was well aware of the music of life CD that Mr. Dulcimer had in his possession. The monster didn't want to take any chances."

"Fortunately, Mr. Dulcimer's neighbors saw the smoke and alerted him as quickly as possible," Mr. Walrus said. "By the way, you probably remember that day, Cammie. It was right before your music interpretation class. Mr. Dulcimer had to leave you all for a while to take care of his possessions. And because

I live just around the corner, we decided to keep his instruments and CDs in my living room for a while."

So that was the case. Cammie wished Mr. Dulcimer had told them what had happened.

"You have to trust people more, Cammie," Mr. Reed said gravely.

Cammie sighed. Of course, he was right, but she had thought Captain Greenfield was a good guy too.

"It's all right," Mr. Walrus said as though sensing Cammie's turmoil. "Telling the truth from a lie isn't always easy. But you'll learn in due time."

The ride back to Skateland was shorter than Cammie had anticipated. Gliding through the dark forest in the back of the Zamboni was a nice change from shoveling through deep snow. Covered with Mr. Walrus's old parka, Cammie felt warm and happy. Her friends were by her side, Coach Elliot was alive, and Mavet was gone. Things just couldn't be better. Even the Icy Park no longer appeared intimidating. Moonlight streamed through the gaps between bulky trees on the ice path ahead of them, giving the whole place a silvery glow. The snow coating the fur trees sparkled like Christmas lights. The Zamboni took a sharp turn to the left. They were approaching the Skating Museum. Covered with a thick blanket of snow, Skateland appeared to be asleep.

I could have died and never noticed how beautiful Skateland is at night, Cammie thought.

It was hard to believe that death had been so close. But knowing it made her appreciate being alive even more. And she knew she would never forget it.

EPILOGUE

Cammie and Alex never saw Captain Greenfield again. Three days after their trip to the mountains, news came on the radio that the officer's body had been discovered between two sharp rocks about twenty miles from Skateland. The official version said that the man had been killed by an avalanche. Yet Cammie and Alex knew better. They remembered what Mr. Reed had said about Mavet controlling the officer: "Because Greenfield chose to stay with him, the evil spirit will simply dispose of him."

As Cammie thought about the man she had known for years, she even felt sorry for him. She wished Skateland authorities would let everybody know how envy and jealousy could cause a skater to be possessed by the spirit of death. Unfortunately, the reporters stuck to the official version.

Even though Cammie and Alex had returned from her trip to Mavet's cave unscathed, Wilhelmina insisted on the two of them having a complete physical. Dr. Eislaufer was his funny and friendly self as he assured the Skateland president that both of them were in perfect health.

"But even so, I would recommend that they take a few days off," the doctor said, peering at Cammie through his thick lenses. "After all, witnessing their coach being tortured wasn't exactly a pleasant emotional experience. And to make sure you guys have a really good rest, I will give you something to help you fall asleep."

At the beginning, Cammie didn't think a break from skating would be a good idea. But when she returned to the dorm, she realized how tired she really was. So every morning, when all of the girls went to their skating practice, she stayed in bed, enjoying the wonderful feeling of not having to rush anywhere. With Dr. Eislaufer's blue pills, sleep came easily and naturally.

About a week later, when Cammie was in a deep sleep, in her dorm room, someone coughed by her side.

"Cammie, are you awake?"

"Uh...what?" Cammie raised her head from the pillow, shading her eyes from the bright sun outside.

"Cammie, it's okay if you want to stay in bed longer, but I have good news for you." Mrs. Page folded her hands over her apron. "Mrs. Van Uffeln talked to your parents about your skating career."

"Oh, my gosh, what did they say?" Cammie sat up in bed, wide awake.

"And what do you think? It would be a shame for a fighter like you to give up skating at such a young age."

"Really? So I can skate?"

Mrs. Page's eyes twinkled. "If I were you, I'd go back on the ice as soon as possible. It's not good to get too comfortable."

Cammie got to the rink in time for the afternoon practice. When she stepped onto the green ice, she was concerned that her skating would be too wobbly after a week of complete rest. Surprisingly, her body felt strong and limber. *This is where I belong,* she thought happily.

She tried her double jumps, amazed by how easy they felt. Should I try the triple salchow? Coach Elliot wasn't at the rink; he was probably still in the hospital. Just once!

She bent her left knee and swung her right leg hard. The feeling was wonderful, and she landed securely on her backward outside edge.

"Yes!" She threw her fist in the air.

"There she is!" a very familiar voice said.

She blinked, turned around, and looked up right into Coach Elliot's smiling face.

"Coach Elliot! How're you feeling?"

He grinned. "I'm fine, thank you!"

Coach Elliot might have been just polite, but the truth was Cammie had never seen him happier. Gone was the sadness that had once clouded his eyes. "That was some triple salchow," he said.

"Did you see it? I wasn't sure I would be able to land it because I missed the whole week and—"

"Well, sometimes it pays off to sleep in," a woman's voice said, and Christel approached from behind. Her face was radiant, and as Cammie managed a faint *hello*, Christel slid her hand around Coach Elliot's elbow.

Cammie stared at the two of them, puzzled.

"Cammie, you have improved immensely. I see Elliot has done a good job with you," another familiar voice came.

As Cammie turned her head, she saw Wilhelmina wearing a silvery gray fox coat, leaning against the boards.

"Hello, Mrs. Van Uffeln," Cammie said, wondering what Skateland president was doing at the Green Rink. Wilhelmina and Christel exchanged quick looks. Coach Elliot skated up to Cammie and took her hands in his. "Cammie, working with you has been a wonderful experience. I'm sure you'll be able to master the rest of your triples in no time."

Cammie smiled at his praise, but something didn't feel right.

"Are you? Are you...?" She suddenly forgot every word in the English language.

Christel's eyes sparkled. "Elliot and I received an invitation from *Magic on Ice*."

"No!"

Wilhelmina smiled at her from the boards. "At the beginning, Elliot wasn't so sure he wanted to do it, but I made him understand that was what he needed at the moment."

"But..." Cammie felt horror rising within her. That just couldn't be happening. She was probably hallucinating.

"I know Elliot's an excellent coach, and he seems to be enjoying his position, yet..." Wilhelmina spread her arms. "He'll always be able to go back to teaching

others, but he only has this many years of skating left
for him. And so does Christel. The two of them look so
great together that it would be a crime to let the two of
them bury their talents in the ground."

Christel grinned happily. "If it hadn't been for Elliot,
I wouldn't have even imagined that I could still skate."

"She retired very early, and she never used her true
potential." Wilhelmina winked at her daughter.

"But…" Cammie said again.

It was weird. The three of them were talking as
though she wasn't even there, as though she didn't
even exist. Christel was about to whisk Prince Elliot
away from Skateland, away from Cammie. The two of
them would skate with *Magic on Ice*, doing beautiful
numbers, touring all around the world, gathering big
crowds. For them, there would be stunning numbers,
applause and flowers. Skating fans would be asking for
their autographs. There would be articles about Christel
and Elliot in skating magazines. And in the meantime,
Cammie would be stuck in Skateland alone, without
even a coach. Because every coach in Skateland had
already rejected her. Gosh. Perhaps Cammie wouldn't
even be able to stay in Skateland at all.

Cammie's eyes began to sting. It was a sure sign of
tears approaching. She was even afraid of acknowledging
that for her it wasn't just about losing a coach. Prince
Elliot was leaving her. It meant he had never truly cared
for her. She had made it all up. He liked Christel more.
He had chosen Wilhelmina's daughter over Cammie.

For a few months, those two things had been
connected in Cammie's life, her skating and Coach

Elliot, Coach Elliot and her skating. Now the connection between them was being ripped apart, and it hurt terribly, unbearably.

Cammie didn't really want to cry. She wasn't a ten-year-old anymore, and crying was a sign of weakness. Good athletes didn't cry. And besides, she would never ever want Christel to understand that Cammie loved Prince Elliot even after her coach had preferred an older woman to her. Because the last thing Cammie wanted was for Christel to gloat over the whole thing.

"Cammie?" Coach Elliot's voice was kind.

She wished he wouldn't be so nice to her. She would feel much better if Coach Elliot was actually nasty. Perhaps if he screamed at her and told her she was a lousy skater and that was the reason he was leaving her, at least she would take it as a legitimate excuse to be dumped. But—

"Cammie, you're the best student I've ever taught."

Yeah right. And that's why you're leaving me.

"Cammie, I really wanted to stay, but you know, sometimes we've got to do what's right."

Skating with Christel, of course.

"Cammie, when Felicia got killed, I quit skating. I thought I'd never do it again. That was what Mavet wanted me to do. I let the spirit of death control me. So if I give up and never perform again, it'll mean the monster got his victory after all."

Cammie raised her head. "Oh!"

"That's right, Cammie." Wilhelmina stared at her. "Believe me, it won't be easy for Christel and Elliot to skate in shows now. They haven't done it in years. So even attempting a professional skating career now requires a lot of courage. So I believe the two of them deserve a lot of respect for stepping out of their comfort zone."

Cammie took a deep breath. She looked at Coach Elliot, her lips shaking.

"One day, you might have to make the same decision, Cammie," Wilhelmina said. "And then you'll remember that the most important thing in life is to live up to your true potential so you won't regret later that you could have done something great but because of fear or laziness, you let the opportunity slip away."

As always, Wilhelmina gave Cammie a lot to think about.

"But how about…me?" she stammered. "I won't even have a coach anymore."

Wilhelmina smiled. "Are you kidding me? With all the progress you've recently made? Believe me, Cammie, you might be in for a big surprise. And I want you to remember something. For a serious skater, every change is a promotion."

Hmm. That was surely an interesting idea.

"But how about PRESTO?" Cammie glanced at Coach Elliot. "Will you leave it in Skateland for me to work with?"

Coach Elliot shook his head sadly. "I can't."

"Why not?"

Before he could say something, Wilhelmina raised her finger. "Coach Elliot gets to keep the magical device. You see, not every coach is allowed to work with PRESTO."

"Why not?" Cammie asked again.

The older woman looked serious. "Because using magic properly requires integrity and purity of heart, Cammie. It's probably the most important thing I've said so far. I hope you'll all remember that."

There was a moment's silence.

Christel lowered her head. "We've got to go."

"Cammie, I'm sure we'll see each other again." Coach Elliot hugged Cammie and then gently kissed her on the cheek.

Cammie felt her face burn as she looked into his sky-blue eyes. "Will you come to Skateland with *Magic on Ice?*"

"I'm sure we will," Coach Elliot said, smiling at her for the last time.

And then Wilhelmina spoke up again. "Never forget that all rinks in the world are connected. So if you're a skater, you're a member of one big extended family."

Cammie followed the three of them outside and watched them get into the icemobile. Wilhelmina bent over the dashboard. "Skateland front gate!"

The icemobile shot forward, the ice scraping under its blades. Cammie stood with her hand up in the air until the vehicle disappeared from view. Then she turned around and went back to the rink.